Allure

THE HOODOO APPRENTICE

OTHER BOOKS BY LEA NOLAN

CONJURE

Allure

The Hoodoo Apprentice

Lea Nolan

Entangled Publishing, LLC
2614 South Timberline Road
Suite 109
Fort Collins, CO 80525
Visit our website at www.entangledpublishing.com.

Edited by Liz Pelletier, Robin Haseltine, and Guillian Helm
Cover design by Heather Howland

Print ISBN   978-1-62266-022-3
Ebook ISBN   978-1-62266-023-0

Manufactured in the United States of America

First Edition October 2013

For Riley Finn. May you always be courageous, fair, and noble.

Chapter One

A stiff, hot wind blows across the Beaufort River, carrying the scent of parched sea grass, mucky earth, and belly-up redfish through the car window. Low tide in the South Carolina Lowcountry can be a smelly proposition, especially in the summer when temperatures soar past sweltering. Stinky or not, these salt marshes with their maze of dense green reeds, and downy white egrets are some of the most beautiful places on earth. Definitely paint-worthy.

But before I can grab my canvas and oils, we've got to get Miss Delia home from the hospital in one piece, which shouldn't be a problem with Cooper Beaumont at the wheel. Fixing his eyes on the road ahead, he guides his father's beige station wagon across the Lady's Island bridge heading toward St. Helena Island, my summer home-away-from-home. I on the other hand, prefer to stare at him.

Shooting me a quick sideways glance, he smiles. "What are you looking at?" he asks, just loud enough to hear over the engine's purr.

Caught gawking, my cheeks flush. "You." Because with his square jaw, golden-brown hair, and eyes that appear blue or green to match his clothes, he's just about the most gorgeous guy I've ever seen. And by some miracle, after secretly loving him for more than an entire year, he's officially my boyfriend. It's our very own happily ever after.

Providing we find a way to break the curse that threatens to steal his soul.

Cooper lets his right hand slip from the wheel and inches it across the front seat to clutch mine. Our fingers entwine and he gives me a squeeze. A warm tingle shoots up my arm. Even after a few weeks of being a couple, the excitement of his touch hasn't grown old.

Miss Delia clears her throat. "Best keep both hands on the wheel, boy. I don't want to end up back in Beaufort Memorial. The food's awful."

Though it couldn't possibly be worse than what landed her there in the first place—being attacked by a pack of gigantic, seething, demon dogs with serrated fangs.

Glancing in the rearview mirror, Cooper flashes his devastatingly handsome grin, the one that makes my heart thump a little bit harder. "Don't worry, Miss Delia, I won't let anything happen to you." Still, he heeds her advice and returns his hand to the steering wheel.

Squelching my disappointment at his withdrawal, I twist around to face her in the backseat. The sight still makes me wince. Though most of her stitches have been removed, bright pink scars mar her oniony, brown skin. A few larger abrasions still require bandages, but thankfully most are on her body, hidden behind clothes. Images of the savage attack flash across my mind, making me shudder, but I shake them off because Miss Delia miraculously survived.

"We took care of everything while you were away. I tended the garden and the guys cleaned up the mess from Hurricane Amelia." I work to make my voice sound bright.

Miss Delia smiles. Even her milky-white eye looks a bit clearer. "Thank you, Emma. You're very kind. I knew I picked you for the right reason."

My chest swells. She did pick me. Even though I'm only fourteen, she made me her apprentice. She's the best, most powerful Gullah hoodoo root worker on St. Helena and probably the whole Lowcountry. Though if I'm being honest, she only agreed to pass her mantle to me because I begged. Earlier this summer, my twin brother, and giant pain-in-the-rear, Jack contracted The Creep, an ancient curse that dissolved his flesh, exposed his chalky bones, and made him reek like pond scum. The memory alone churns my stomach. Thanks to Miss Delia, I learned enough hoodoo magic to destroy The Creep and cure Jack, but not enough to protect her from the monsters that nearly ate her for dinner. Which is why she was in the hospital for so long and why the station wagon's rear compartment is crammed with her brand-new wheelchair. The hellhounds weren't content to just slice open her flesh. Their massive paws pounced, bruised her spinal chord, and left her unable to walk.

Cooper hangs a left at the dingy-gray tract house at the corner. The tires crunch as he starts down the unmarked dirt road that leads to Miss Delia's house. Pocked with holes and overgrown vegetation, it's a serious hazard but we've traveled it so often this summer he could probably do it blindfolded. "I hope you don't mind, Miss Delia, but Jack and I made a few changes to your house," he says.

Her snowy-white brow quirks. "What kind of changes?"

"Just a couple accommodations to make it easier to get around. I know you practiced driving that chair in the hospital, but it'll be different in your own house."

She crosses her arms over her teal housedress. "Pshaw." She shakes her head, her lips turned down in disgust. "In all my ninety-seven years, I've never needed an *accommodation*."

"It's not a big deal." I play down the additions, knowing how deep her pride runs and how difficult it must be to accept her new disability. "They just added a ramp to the porch." And widened the front door, rearranged some of her furniture, and hung a few guide rails, but she'll discover all that when she gets there. "Maybe we can come up with some spells to help speed your healing." Though according to her doctors, that's nearly impossible.

She narrows her lids. "Way ahead of you, child."

Rounding the bend, we approach her glistening bottle tree, an enormous live oak that drips with Spanish moss and dwarfs her ramshackle house. On a normal day it's impressive, but today, with the golden, mid-afternoon sun streaming through its thousand multicolored bottles, it's dazzling and almost seems to radiate its own light.

A sleek, silver Mercedes Benz is parked just beyond the tree, in front of Miss Delia's lush garden.

Miss Delia strains forward in her seat. "What do we have here? Your brother hasn't tried to drive again has he?"

I laugh, remembering Jack's last attempt behind the wheel. We all survived, but it's not something I'd recommend him doing any time soon. "No, he's helping our dad with the last of the storm cleanup at High Point Bluff." If it weren't for my father, the plantation's caretaker and sole employee, the place would fall apart.

Cooper pulls up next to the Mercedes and cuts the engine. Scanning the car, he whistles. "Sweet ride."

The garden's perfume floods the open car windows. I inhale the fragrant scent of hundreds of flowers and herbs, some rare, some mere weeds that have been cultivated for centuries by Miss Delia and her ancestors. These plants are the secret ingredients of hoodoo magic. But without her experience and knowledge, it's just an overgrown patch of dirt.

Three designer suitcases covered with gold initials perch on Miss Delia's porch, just steps away from the open front door.

"Were you expecting someone?" I ask.

Just then, a woman in a crisp sea-green linen pantsuit sweeps out of the house and floats across the porch. Her medium-brown skin is flawless and wrinkle-free, making her look somewhere in her midthirties, but something about the regal way she carries herself tells me she's probably a lot older than that. She grasps the railing, her lips curled at the sides, managing a smile that doesn't move past her cheeks.

"Well I'll be." Miss Delia doesn't appear the least bit excited.

A moment later a girl who looks at a couple years older than me follows, flinging the screen door wide and letting it slam behind her. Tall and lithe, she stalks toward the suitcases on the opposite side of the porch, crosses her arms, and then shifts her weight so her right hip pops to the side. Which conveniently provides us the perfect angle to admire her clingy, low-cut halter top, skintight shorts, and fuchsia-streaked bob that perfectly offsets her light brown skin and bright pink lipstick. Though considering the sweltering South Carolina heat, she might want to reconsider the black leather boots.

"That's…interesting," Cooper utters under his breath as I

stifle a laugh.

A pricking sensation works its way around my scalp, a sure sign my spirit guide wants me to take note of what's happening. Though I'm not sure who to be more cautious of—Pink or Mrs. Fancy Pants.

Miss Delia grabs at the door handle with a liver-spotted hand. "Help me out of this car, Cooper." Her voice brims with urgency.

"Sure thing."

In a flash, he's got the rear door open and yanks out the wheelchair. I slip on my flip-flops, then come around to Miss Delia's side, unlatch her seatbelt, and help swing her around so Cooper can lift her out. Through it all, the two on the porch stay put, watching us do all the work. After gently setting Miss Delia in her chair, Cooper pushes her over the uneven earth to the stone path. From there, she takes over, flicking the switch to engage the motor. We follow as she maneuvers her way through the garden and up the new ramp. The wooden structure isn't perfect and doesn't come close to what my dad would have built, but it's safe and sturdy and does the job. When we reach the top, she stops short.

The woman in the pantsuit fans herself. "Lord, I forgot how hot these Carolina summers are. I broke a sweat watching you make your way up here."

Miss Delia nods. "Heaven forbid you strain yourself, Angelica. You must keep those delicate hands safe."

Lifting a set of perfectly manicured fingers, the woman smiles. "Can't argue with you there. These hands change lives." She steps forward and bends to kiss Miss Delia's cheek.

Stiffening, Miss Delia accepts the gesture. "I'm sure they do. Emma, Cooper, say hello to my granddaughter, Dr. Branson.

She's a plastic surgeon in Chicago."

"Hi. Nice to meet you." I wave, feeling way out of place at this little family reunion. Trying not to be rude, I work to keep my eyes trained on Dr. Branson, but can't resist a furtive peek at the girl. She's definitely older than me, maybe even older than Cooper, though not by much. Rather than paying attention to what's happening on the porch, she's staring at the bottle tree, her head tilted as if she's counting the pieces of glass. If so, it's going to take a while.

"Hello, ma'am." Cooper extends his hand toward Dr. Branson. She barely grazes it with her own.

"These *chillun* have been a great help this summer. Especially Emma." Miss Delia clasps my arm with her gnarled hand.

Dr. Branson scans me up and down. "I see. Someone's got to tend the garden." Only she says it like she means something else entirely. And that she totally disapproves.

That's probably my cue to leave. I clear my throat. "Maybe Cooper and I should go so you all can visit."

Cooper nods. "Sure. We can come back tomorrow."

Miss Delia snaps her head toward me. "Nonsense. We've got work to do. Or have you forgotten we're on a deadline?"

Nope. I'm pretty clear on the whole soul-snatching thing.

Three hundred years ago, Cooper's great-great ancestor gave Maggie, an enslaved African girl, to Bloody Bill Ransom and his band of vile pirates in exchange for not sacking High Point Bluff. But things didn't go as planned and they killed her, which enraged her grandmother, Sabina, an African queen with a brutal sense of justice who used her mystical hoodoo powers to seek revenge. She unleashed The Creep on the scurvy pirates, and cursed the Beaumont progeny forever by stealing their souls when they come into their manhood, turning them unspeakably dark and corrupt. If we don't break the Beaumont Curse before Cooper's approaching sixteenth birthday, he'll end up just as gluttonous, selfish, and arrogant as his grotesque father, Beau. With just three weeks to go, time's a-ticking.

Dr. Branson sighs. "See, this is what I feared. At your age you shouldn't be working anymore, even if you do have some sort of…assistant." She flicks her wrist dismissively toward me. "And now this…accident." She scans the scars on Miss Delia's face with an expert eye. "It nearly scared me to death hearing you were in a coma. We flew down just as soon as I cleared my schedule."

"That was very kind, but you ought to know better than to worry after me. You going to introduce me to my great-granddaughter?" Miss Delia nods toward the girl on the other end of the porch.

Now I see the resemblance. Despite the girl's dye job and eye-popping fashion statement, she and Dr. Branson actually have very similar features.

Dr. Branson plasters on a smile. "Of course. Say hello to your great-gran, Taneea." Her voice drips with syrup.

Taneea drags her attention away from the bottle tree, glares at her mother from beneath shaggy bangs, then glances at Miss Delia. "Hi." The diamond chip in the Monroe piercing above her lip glints in the sunlight.

Miss Delia smiles. "Hello to you, too. It's nice to finally meet you in person."

"Uh-huh." Taneea shrugs, then pivots on her thick rubber heels and plops into one of the rocking chairs. It creaks against the cracked porch floor as she rocks back and forth, staring at the tree once again.

An electric shock wave rolls over my scalp. I'm guessing she's the one my spirit guide is warning me about.

Miss Delia turns to Dr. Branson. "I may be old and frailer than you remember, but I wasn't born yesterday. Why are you really here?"

"I know you may not believe it, but I worry about you, Gran. You're getting up there, it's amazing you're able to live alone at ninety-five—"

"Ninety-seven," Miss Delia corrects her.

"Right, ninety-seven. But that's even more to my point. You're vulnerable. Things can happen to you here all by yourself. I mean, look at you, all scraped up from that fall…or whatever you were up to. And now you're stuck in that chair. You need someone to take care of you."

Cooper and I exchange nervous glances. His baby blues reflect the same anxiety that's churning in my gut. The doctors in the hospital already broached this conversation with Miss Delia, offering to find her a nice, quiet assisted-living facility. They didn't get very far. Miss Delia made it clear she's never leaving her house and garden. And now her granddaughter's jumping into the fray, likely spurred on by the hospital doctors. This is liable to turn ugly. Curse deadline or not, maybe Cooper and I should beat it out of here. We can always come back in the morning.

I inch toward the porch steps beside the ramp. Cooper follows my lead.

Miss Delia scoffs. "*You're* going to take care of me, Angelica?"

Dr. Branson smiles. "I wish I could. But I have my practice to consider." She gestures toward her daughter. "I was thinking Taneea might instead. She's missed out not having you in her life. This could be a great opportunity to get to know each other."

Taneea huffs and runs her black-polished nails through her bangs, revealing a silver eyebrow ring. "That's just your excuse for dumping me in butt-crack nowhere."

"Seems your daughter has no interest in caring for her great-gran. Fine by me. Emma's all the help I need."

Dr. Branson chuffs out a laugh. "You can't be serious. Emma isn't family. And she can't keep watch over you twenty-four hours a day. What if you have another fall when you're alone? What if something worse happens? I couldn't live with myself."

Miss Delia stiffens her jaw. "You've managed to live with yourself—and my daughter—for nearly thirty years in Chicago. It didn't bother you to take her away from her home, or her legacy."

Dr. Branson raises her palm. "Please, Gran, I don't want to argue about hoodoo anymore. I know you believe in it, but I've studied science. It's a bunch of bunk. Mama's had a better life with me than if she'd stayed here."

Cooper tugs on the bottom of my T-shirt. It's definitely time to bounce. Walking backward, we climb down one step and then another.

Miss Delia stiffens. "Emma and Cooper, get back here. I thank you for your visit, Angelica, but I think it's time for you and Taneea to leave."

Gulping, I hop back on the porch and stand next to Cooper.

The whites of Dr. Branson's eyes turn misty pink. "I can't." Her voice is suddenly small.

"Sure you can. Climb into that fancy car of yours and drive off my lawn."

A tear spills down Angelica's cheek. "You don't understand. I *can't*. Taneea isn't welcome back at home."

Taneea's expression turns hard. "That's only because you're weak. And your new husband is a giant tool." Pushing herself out of her chair, Taneea strides across the porch, yanks open the screen, and storms into the house, letting the door slam behind her once again.

"It's not my fault. You've left me no other choice," Dr. Branson calls after her, but Taneea doesn't bother to turn around.

A high-pitched squawk echoes across the yard. Turning toward the bottle tree, I search for the sound. It comes again, this time sounding rough and raspy and almost like a strangled cat. The tiny hairs at the nape of my neck rise. A second later a glossy, blue-black crow launches off a high branch and soars across the yard into the woods beyond Miss Delia's house.

Leaning forward in her wheelchair, Miss Delia's stare bores into her granddaughter's eyes. "What is going on?"

Wiping the perspiration from her face, she replies, "Have you ever wanted something so bad you'd be willing to sacrifice everything to have it? No matter what the consequence?"

Chapter Two

$\mathcal{M}$iss Delia closes her eyes and shakes her head. Without looking at us she says, "Cooper, have a seat in the living room and watch one of your sports programs while Emma gets to work in the kitchen. I'll be there shortly."

She doesn't have to ask us twice. Cooper and I dash into the house. As directed, he flicks on the television, spinning the ancient dial to find a station with decent reception. Taneea's nowhere in sight so I'm guessing she's in the back bedroom sulking. Heading into the kitchen, I pop open the swinging door that separates this room from the rest of the house.

It's more than just your average cooking space. This is Miss Delia's sanctum, the place she conjures her magic and stores all her supplies. We've had to move a few things to accommodate her wheelchair, but for the most part it's just as she left it, filled with shelves of apothecary bottles and stone jars teeming with dried herbs, roots, and other curios like graveyard dirt and animal bones.

I grab a bottle of citronella oil and dab a bit on my neck, wrists, and behind my ears. The bright lemony scent swirls around my head, instantly cleansing my spirit in preparation for whatever Miss Delia's got planned. But considering all the weird energy swirling around the house, maybe it needs purifying, too. Slipping Miss Delia's spell book from its hiding place at the back of a cabinet, I flip through and find the entry for PEACE IN THE HOME incense, one of the most basic charms in her ledger. Moments later the crushed rosemary, basil, and sandalwood mixture burns, infusing the air with their sweet and slightly woody fragrance.

The kitchen door swings open. Taneea pops her head in, narrowing her gaze. "What are you doing?"

Startled, I jump back a step. "Lighting some incense." Considering how guarded Miss Delia is, I probably shouldn't have told her that, but it's pretty obvious, so there's no point in lying.

Breathing deep, Taneea waltzes in, leaving the kitchen door propped open. "Why? Does it have to do with the voodoo thing my mom mentioned?" She stalks toward me, her light green eyes gleaming with interest.

Caught in her gaze, I correct her. "Hoodoo."

"What?" She stands close, her ample cleavage at my eye line.

"It's hoodoo." Ignoring her prominent assets, I meet her piercing gaze. "Not voodoo. That's a religion."

"Whatever. What's this?" She points to Miss Delia's spell book.

I flip the old leather-bound book closed. "Nothing, just a list of recipes." Which is kind of true. Though most recipes aren't intended to draw love, money, cast hexes, or break jinxes. But I'm not going to explain all that to her. I'm not even sure she's supposed to be in here. "Listen, your great-grandmother is pretty protective of her kitchen. You should probably hang out in the living room. I think Cooper's probably found something on TV."

"Give me a break. I'm not watching that piece of crap." She crosses the kitchen to read the labels on the stoneware crocks. Her nose crinkles. "Sticklewort? Skunk cabbage? Sounds gross."

Despite the *Peace in the Home* that's swirling through the air, panic bubbles in my gut. This is Miss Delia's sacred space and Taneea feels like an intruder. "Really, I'm serious. She'll get mad if she hasn't invited you in here."

She scoffs. "This is *my* great-grandmother's house. I'll go where I please." She reaches for a jar of *Four Thieves of Vinegar*.

"Is that so?" Miss Delia's voice is deep and stern. Her wheelchair is poised at the kitchen door. I didn't even hear her roll in.

A shiver runs up my spine.

Taneea drops her hand and then spins on her heels. "Well, yeah. What's the big deal? All you've got is a bunch of jars on shelves. Who cares?"

"I do," Miss Delia says. "This is my home and regardless of what's in it, I have rules I expect my guests to follow. If that's too much to ask, I'll put you on the next bus back to Chicago."

Taneea laughs. "A bus? We flew here."

"You sure did. On a one-way ticket."

Taneea pauses for a moment, her brow knit. Setting her hands on her hips, she calls, "Mom?" Her voice is less confident, almost shaky and seems to echo through the house.

"She's gone." Miss Delia's eyes soften.

Holy crap. Dr. Branson pulled a dump and jump. And didn't even bother to say good-bye.

Taneea blinks her heavily mascaraed lashes. "So I'm stuck here? On a frigging island in the middle of nowhere?"

My throat tightens, making it hard to swallow. What kind of a mother does that? Granted, I haven't seen my mom since Jack and I left Washington, DC to visit our dad, but she showered us with affection and special dinners before we left. The only reason we haven't spoken much since we got here is she's on her summer archeological dig in the Jordan desert. Her satellite phone works great in a pinch, but the service is spotty and super-expensive.

Miss Delia rolls into the kitchen keeping her eyes trained on Taneea. "You'll spend the rest of the summer with me. Maybe more, depending on how long it takes to get you straightened out. And for your mother to assess her priorities. Now, if you don't mind, Emma and I have some work to do. I think you've got some fancy bags to unpack."

"Can't I hang out in here? My gran told me a little about your hoodoo stuff even though she knew my mom would have a cow. It sounds pretty cool. I'm supposed to help you right? I could crush up some plants or maybe brew a potion or something."

Miss Delia sucks her teeth as she considers the request. "I'm glad to hear my gal hasn't forgotten her roots, but I don't think it's a good idea."

"Why? Because my mother won't let you? Come on, I'd love to learn some magic to get back at her and her nozzle of a husband."

Miss Delia shakes her head. "Your *maamy*'s got nothing to do with this. Hoodoo isn't something you do lightly, or use to get back at folk. Someday, when you grow up a bit more, you might be ready. When that happens, I'll gladly teach you some hoodoo, but today's not that day."

"Oh, but *she's* grown up?" Taneea flings a hot pink fingernail in my direction.

Miss Delia quirks a brow. "I won't be questioned in my own house."

Stiffening, Taneea mashes her lips and swallows whatever mixture of rage and sadness is playing on her face. "Fine. Whatever. I don't care."

"I know you don't like it, and you might even hate me for it, but I'm making you wait for your own good." Miss Delia's voice is as soft and tender as I've ever heard it. "It won't kill you to learn a little patience and to follow the rules. Until you do, this kitchen is off-limits."

Taneea's lip quivers. "Yes, ma'am." She rushes from the room, swinging the door shut behind her.

Miss Delia breathes deep. "*Peace in the Home*. Nice touch. Though I'm not sure it's enough to douse the fire in her belly."

"What's her deal?" Despite her snootiness toward me, I can't help but feel sorry for her.

Miss Delia shakes her head. "Seems my great-grand-daughter likes to court trouble. Been kicked out of every school Angelica can get her into and the stress has nearly broken up her latest marriage."

"Are you sure it's a good idea for her to stay?" We do have a pretty busy agenda, what with saving Cooper's soul and helping Miss Delia recuperate from her injuries.

She sighs. "It's against my better judgment, but sometimes you've got to do things for family you wouldn't do for anyone else. I expect you understand that better than most."

That's for sure. Cooper and I put our lives on the line to save Jack. Now that Cooper's the one in danger, there's no question

Jack and I will do the same for him. "I do."

"In a way, I suppose I owe this to Angelica. Though not for the reasons she thinks." Miss Delia looks out the back kitchen window into the yard, but it's clear her mind is somewhere else, perhaps reliving the past. A few moments later she shakes her head. "Choosing between a man and your own flesh and blood isn't easy. Though sometimes there's no choice at all."

I'm desperate to ask what she means but I know better than to pry. She rarely speaks about her past. After today's walk down memory lane, I'm sure it's the last thing she wants to discuss. Maybe we should pack it in after all.

"Do you still want to do this today? If it's too much, I can come back tomorrow."

"No, child, that curse isn't going to wait on us." Pushing the joystick on her chair, she drives toward the pedestal that holds the ancestors' mortar. Although she's only had the stone vessel back for a few weeks, aside from her spell book it's probably her most prized possession. As it should be since Cooper, Jack, and I basically risked our lives, or at least prison, to liberate it for her from the King Center, the local Gullah museum.

She strokes its rough granite exterior, her aged fingers tracing the cracks that mar its surface. The worst of them, one deep enough to threaten to split clean through to the inside, was mended by a terrible twist of fate. Buoyed by my success with ending The Creep, I tried to break the Beaumont Curse, too, by throwing Cooper's family heirloom, a ruby necklace, into the fire burning in the mortar. Turns out that was exactly the opposite of what I should have done. The ruby exploded, breaking into three pieces, and the gold melted, bubbling up over the mortar's rim, oozing down the exterior, and filing the fissure. It's probably the world's most costly repair job.

"I've been thinking about your boy's curse," Miss Delia says. "It's going to take some powerful magic to break. Best I can remember from our *Psychic Vision*, Sabina was chewing a *Blue Root* when she worked that curse almost three hundred years ago."

"A what?"

"It's some of the darkest magic there is, especially when used with a black magic potion and a strong incantation. Almost always brings on death of some sort."

A chill races over my arms, raising goose bumps as I recall the harsh curses Sabina wrought to avenge her granddaughter Magnolia's murder. "Wasn't she chewing something when she cast The Creep on the pirate ship, too?"

Miss Delia nods. "She was. Now I've got to figure out what was in that powder she threw when she worked those spells. In the meantime, Cooper needs a powerful protection charm. It won't be potent enough to stop the curse, but it might buy us some extra time."

Pointing to the shelves, she calls out the ingredients we'll need for a super-strong *Protective Shield*. After spending a week in the garden and her kitchen, I've memorized where everything belongs and can finally keep up with her. Within moments, jars filled with agrimony, bay, burdock, black snake root, rue, and verbena are lined up on the counter. Each has the power to turn back a minor jinx, but together, they bind to create a powerful white magic charm. Casting the spell in her ancestor's magic mortar will give it even more power, enhancing its strength, and hopefully shield Cooper from the curse.

I add each ingredient to the ancestors' mortar exactly as she's called them out knowing the order is nearly as important as what is used. Once they're combined, I grind them together with a stone pestle, crushing the dried leaves and tiny chips to release their essential oils. Soon, the agrimony's apricot scent and verbena's lemony notes mix with the balsam flavor of the bay, sweetening the sharp and bitter odor of the black snake root.

A gentle breeze blows around Miss Delia's house. It's a natural consequence of working hoodoo magic, which taps into the natural elements and uses their power. So is the yawn that works its way up my throat. Spells require energy to work, and every charm requires a tribute of sorts from its practitioner. The stronger the magic, the more energy it draws, which is probably why my lids feel like they suddenly weigh about three pounds each. Fighting to keep them open, I rub the pestle against the last remaining chunks in the mortar. My head swoons, begging for sleep, but I power through, knowing I'm nearly finished. Supposedly I'll gain a tolerance for this magic eventually, but that day can't come soon enough.

Finally, the mixture is ready. Miss Delia hands me a small white pouch with an extra long drawstring. It's a gris-gris bag or a mojo, meant to be worn either around the neck or kept in a pocket, as long as it's close to the skin. "Pour the powder in here and cinch it up nice and tight."

I follow her instructions then wipe out the mortar for the next part of the spell, which will kick-start this charm into overdrive. After scattering a few pieces of charcoal in the bottom of the granite mortar, I strike a match and light the coals, then pull back as a wisp of black smoke rises and curls around my face. While it burns, I assemble the last few herbs we'll need. A few minutes later, the briquettes are a dusty gray, a sure sign they're ready. Miss Delia directs me to layer some agrimony first, then the sandalwood, and finally some verbena over the coals. As they heat, the kitchen fills with their creamy, fruity scents.

Bracing myself for the hardest part of the spell, I step to the mortar and hold the gris-gris bag over the smoking fumes.

Rubbing the red and white beads on my *collier*, the necklace that marks me as Miss Delia's apprentice and grants me her protection, I close my eyes and clear all thoughts from my mind. An incantation springs to my lips.

> *"May all the ingredients in this charm*
> *Grant Cooper protection from vengeful harm.*
> *Add in the love that dwells in my heart*
> *So he and his soul will never part."*

The wind picks up, rattling the trees and whipping around the house. A gust of air blows in from the backyard, blasts through the kitchen and past the swinging door, then through the living room and presumably out on to the front porch.

My limbs grow heavy. Blinking hard and fast, I force my eyes open. Just a few more minutes and the charm will be finished. My head bobs, but I give it a good shake to stay awake. I've got to hold on. If the bag drops or I nod off, the spell will fail and we'll have to wait for the mortar to rest before we can work another charm. Which will take three days we don't have.

Finally, the last of the buttery sandalwood burns off and the smoke dissipates. Grasping the gris-gris bag between my fingers, I giggle. It buzzes with brilliant white energy, shooting tingles up my arm.

"Holy cow! Feel this." I hand it off to Miss Delia then dump water into the mortar to drench any remaining embers.

It jiggles in her palm like it's filled with Mexican jumping beans. "Well done, Emma." Miss Delia laughs. "This is a strong mojo. That boy of yours should realize how lucky he is. If you didn't care about him so much, it wouldn't be half as powerful."

Slumping into a stool at the counter, I sink my heavy head against my palm. "I guess that explains why I'm so exhausted. It took a lot out of me." I yawn.

"But you're doing so much better than even a few weeks ago. Back then you'd be asleep by now and couldn't have produced something near as potent. You're learning and your resistance is beginning to build."

Beginning? At this rate, I won't have the strength to get to the end. "Isn't there anything we can do to speed things up? Because I'm not sure how much more of this I can take." Or if I'll make it home before I conk out.

"There's always a way with hoodoo, but I don't like shortcuts."

Easy for her to say. She's not the one who's half-unconscious. But I know better than to argue with her, especially since I can barely concentrate.

"We've done more than enough for today, Emma. Give this bag to Cooper and let's see how it works." She passes it back. It pulses against my palm as images of Cooper and me flash across my mind. Us hand in hand at the beach, in his father's car, on his boat, or just hanging out in his room, they're like little video snippets of some of our happiest times together. And they're literally in my hand.

It's time to show Cooper how powerful my love is.

Chapter Three

A laugh, high-pitched and overly enthusiastic, carries into the kitchen from the living room.

The hair on the back of my neck rises. Something's up.

A surge of reserve energy jolts my system, bolting me upright. Clutching the gris-gris bag, I slip off my stool and push open the swinging door.

Taneea is perched on the couch facing Cooper, her legs tucked beneath her, leaning as close as possible without falling into his lap. At least she's finally taken off those ridiculous boots.

Now I'm awake.

"You're hilarious." She swats his biceps.

"Uh, thanks." Wedged against the end of the couch, his expression is a mixture of panic and pure horror.

"I know. He's a total crack up. He's always leaving me and my brother in stitches." I cross my arms and give her the evil eye to clue her into the fact he's my boyfriend and off-limits.

Cooper leaps off the cushion and bolts to my side. "Emma!

How'd everything go in there?" He slips an arm around my waist and reaches for my hand, which I gladly grasp.

I smile extra-wide. "Great, as usual." Hopefully.

"Ready to go, then?" His light blue eyes plead, letting me know this isn't a request.

"Yeah, sure." I stifle a yawn, a remnant of casting the *Protective Shield*.

"It was great to meet you, Taneea. I'm sure we'll be seeing a lot of each other this summer," he says, ever the southern gentleman.

"I bet we will." Her lips crack into a wicked grin as she twirls a pink curl around her finger. Peeling her eyes away from him she glances at me. "And you too, Emma."

"Sure." I stifle a snicker. As if she's got a chance with Cooper. *My* Cooper. Not likely.

Turning toward the kitchen I pop open the kitchen door. "We're leaving, Miss Delia. See you tomorrow. Call me if you need anything."

She rolls her wheelchair into the living room. "I'll be fine. Besides, I've got my great-granddaughter here now. We've got a lot of catching up to do."

With a grunt, Taneea pushes off the couch and skulks toward one of the back rooms.

• • •

A half hour later, Cooper and I are sitting on the private beach at High Point Bluff, his family's plantation, breathing in the balmy salt air. The late afternoon sun is idyllic as it shimmers off the teal-green water of St. Helena Sound. As usual, I've kicked off my flip-flops and dug my toes into the toasty sand, hunting for the cool, moist grains below the surface.

Cooper leans close and nuzzles my neck. "I couldn't wait to get out of there."

I snort. "Really? Cause it looked like you and Taneea were getting along so well."

"It did?" He pulls back, his eyes fill with alarm.

"I'm kidding."

He laughs; his spicy pine scent fills my nose as he plants a kiss behind my ear, sending a wave of tingles over my body. "Good, because I wouldn't want to give her the wrong idea. I mean, she's hot and all, but she's definitely not my type."

Wait. Did he just say she's hot? As in…attractive?

I lean away. "You think she's good-looking?" My brow knits.

"Well, sort of. In kind of a hot-mess sort of way."

My heart seizes. "For real?"

He gulps. "Uh, yeah?" Only he sounds a whole lot less sure of himself now that he's admitted it out loud. "I mean, her clothes and hair are all about attracting a guy's attention and well, she does."

I look down at my stone-colored twill shorts and scoop neck T-shirt. Boring. Then to my beat-up leather flip-flops. Even more boring. But they're me. The wildest I ever get is a peasant blouse and bohemian skirt. I couldn't pull off short shorts if I tried.

Staring out onto the Sound, I watch an osprey dive-bomb the water feet first, then ascend into the air with a fish clutched between its curved talons. I'm feeling about as optimistic as that trout.

He nudges me in the side with his elbow. "Hey, did you hear *everything* I said? She's not my type." He reaches his strong hand to stroke the side of my face. "You're my girl, Emmaline," he whispers in his sweet Lowcountry drawl.

Ah, there it is, finally. My real name. He's the only one who uses it, except for my parents and that's only when I'm in serious trouble, which is practically never. Brushing a long strand of strawberry-blonde hair off my face, he tucks it behind my ear as his powder-blue eyes search mine. "You always have been."

My heart skips a beat. "Really?" My voice flutters as my knees turn to rubber. It's a good thing I'm already sitting because otherwise, I'd collapse onto the sand.

He nods. "Yes."

His lips graze mine and all my silly, stupid fears slip away. I should know better than to worry about his feelings for me. Especially since we've got a much bigger, and very real, problem to deal with. The Beaumont Curse looms, destined to turn him dark and depraved. Which reminds me about the gris-gris bag that's stuffed in my messenger bag.

Clearing my throat, I dig out the mojo. "Miss Delia and I made this for you." I dangle the necklace with the tiny white pouch before him. "It's a black magic *Protective Shield*."

He drapes it over his head then tucks it under his shirt. "Thanks." He smiles and I swear for a half a nanosecond, he seems to glow. But it must be a trick of the afternoon light because it's gone just as quickly as it appeared. Or maybe I'm still suffering under the effects of working the spell.

"It's probably not enough to break the curse on its own, but it should offer some protection while Miss Delia works on a permanent cure."

He clutches my hand. "If it doesn't work—"

I shake my head. "It'll work. Or the next one will. Or the one after that."

He clasps my hand. "I hope that's true. But if every spell

fails, I want you to know I'm going to fight this thing with all I've got. I don't want to turn out like my father and all the Beaumont men before him." His gorgeous lips grimace as if his mouth is filled with bile. "My choice has to matter for something. I don't want to be greedy and selfish, arrogant and destructive. That's not me." Not to mention his father's gluttonous appetite, ginormous girth, and less-than-stellar hygiene. Those are definitely worth avoiding as well.

Nodding, I meet his gaze. "I know it isn't." I place my palm on his chest and feel his heart pump beneath my hand. "You're a good person. The best I know. That's why I'm going to do everything I can to keep you that way." Including pray for a miracle.

"I swear to you, Emmaline, I won't leave you. I'm going to be around for as long as you can stand me." Gathering me in his arms, he leans forward then dips his head as his mouth meets mine. Shivers race over my flesh. Edging closer to deepen our kiss, I feel the hint of stubble above his firm but tender lips. We could do this all evening.

"Then I'm going to be pretty busy, because I'm planning on having you around for a while." I kiss him again and snuggle close.

Something tugs on the fabric of my shorts. Glancing down, I notice my pocket is stretched toward his. The two pieces of clothing stick together in the most massive case of static cling I've ever seen.

"Huh, that's funny." I pull at my shorts, but it stays put, as if bound to his.

He chuckles. "I don't know, maybe this charm is supposed to do more than protect me from black magic. I bet it's supposed to keep us glued together forever." He winks, then tugs at the cloth, yanking the two pieces apart.

I scowl. "You know I'd never do anything like that." Red magic coercion spells take away a person's free will to love and are just plain wrong.

He nuzzles my neck. "I know. I just like to watch you get all riled up."

"Ha-ha." I yawn. My thigh warms. Digging my hand into my pocket, I finger my third of the broken ruby. Since we couldn't glue the three pieces together after the *Break Jinx* failed to reverse the Beaumont Curse, Cooper, Jack, and I each took one as a sort of souvenir. An insanely expensive and irreplaceable one, but it was better than tossing them into St. Helena Island Sound.

Just thinking about my massive screwup makes me tired, and way too fatigued to think about my clingy pants. Cooper's probably half-right anyway. The spell must have discharged some electromagnetic energy or something. My lids droop and I pull away. "I'm sorry, but I'm exhausted. I should probably head home."

He sighs. "Fine, have it your way." He runs his hand through his loose, golden-brown hair, then flashes me his killer smile. Standing up, he offers me his hand and pulls me to my feet. "Thanks."

"You're welcome." I wink, knowing his gratitude is as much for the kisses as it is for helping to save his soul.

Cooper and I make our way up the bluff and down the path that leads to the Big House. Just as we're about to hop into the golf cart to head to the caretaker's cottage, shouts erupt from Cooper's place and we race toward the sound. It's definitely Cooper's dad, Beau, and someone else. Something smashes. Whatever's going on, it isn't pretty.

Cooper and I wind around the front of the house toward the back patio and veranda.

"Stop!" a hushed voice calls out.

I grind to a halt as Cooper pulls up next to me.

It's my brother, Jack's, voice but I don't see him anywhere.

"Where are you, bro?" Cooper whispers.

The shouts from the house grow louder.

"Over here."

Jack is hunched behind a giant saw palmetto bush on the edge of the yard. Cooper and I rush over to him.

"What are you doing?" I kneel in the mulch and bat away a long, spindly leaf.

"What does it look like? I'm eavesdropping."

Thank you, Sergeant Obvious.

"Yeah, but why?" Cooper crouches next to me.

Jack lifts a finger to his lips to keep us quiet. "Just listen. They've been going at it for about an hour."

Missy, Cooper's very young and very blonde stepmother, skitters out the back door in her trademark stilettos and cutoff shorts, then scurries across the veranda and out onto the patio. "I swear, I'm not lying."

"Then answer my question." Beau's voice booms from inside the house. His thick southern accent is more sluggish than usual. Almost groggy. Another crash booms.

"I did, sugar. About a thousand times."

"No you haven't. I want answers, Missy, and I want them now." Beau's voice bellows as he lumbers to the French doors that open out to the veranda, leaning hard against his cane and staggering with each step.

Cooper's father is humongous, the inevitable result of his extraordinary appetite for all things deep fried and decadent.

He wasn't always like this. I've seen pictures of him and my dad when they were kids. Thirty years ago they were both lean and athletic, but somewhere along the line, probably when the Beaumont Curse snatched his soul, he changed.

Hauling his excessive girth across the threshold of the veranda, Beau heaves for breath. "Where is it?" He sways and reaches for a glass table for support but it tips and crashes to the ground, its top splintering into a thousand pieces. Somehow he manages not to spill on the floor with it. "I want my ruby. Now."

My stomach plummets. Now I understand why Jack's been spying on them. The necklace. A third of which is currently in my pocket. We are so screwed.

"Crud," Cooper whispers as he grips his temple. His heart is beating so hard I can actually hear it in his chest.

"Uh-huh." Jack nods.

My pulse rages as adrenaline surges through my veins. Depending on how Missy answers her husband, things could go very badly for us, especially Cooper. Until last week Missy wore the eighty-carat ruby everywhere the grocery store, the mall, even the gym and spa. But we needed it to break the Beaumont Curse, so we borrowed it—sort of—by working a *Mind Confusion* spell in the middle of her Fourth of July hurricane party. In our defense, I only expected to use it for a couple hours until after the storm passed and the Beaumont Curse was broken. How was I supposed to know everything would go horribly wrong and the necklace would be destroyed?

Gnawing my lip, I stare at Missy, who's gripping the back of a patio chair. "Beau, baby. My jewelry is locked up tight in my treasure box. You know that." She forces a smile and a nervous giggle trickles from her throat.

"Do I?" Though his voice quiets, it's laced with barely

contained fury.

"S-sure you do. Why would you think otherwise?"

"You know. It's funny. You've been saying the same thing all week." His jowls ungulate with each syllable. With a grunt, he steps forward, advancing across the veranda. "I want to believe you. Especially since you know how important that stone is to this family. And how much I value it. Surely you wouldn't dream of losing something that's been handed down to every plantation mistress for nearly three hundred years." He sucks for air, his chest gurgling with each breath as he lurches onto the patio. Even in the twilight, his skin is pastier than normal. This workout is liable to give him a heart attack.

She shakes her platinum head and takes a step back. "No, of course not, baby. I'd never dream of doing anything like that."

Wheezing, he advances toward her. "And after all I've given you, you wouldn't possibly think about stealing from me."

"Never. I'm the luckiest girl in the world. If it wasn't for you I'd still be the checker at the Route 21 convenience mart." Her voice quakes.

He stops right in front of her. "Then why are you lying to me?"

"I'm not."

His pungent, rotten-bologna scent carries on the breeze, burning my throat. He's always reeked, but even from this distance, it's stronger than normal.

Beau nods. "Yes, you are. I looked in that box of yours. The necklace isn't there."

She swallows hard. "I'm sure it's in a safe place."

Jack and Cooper turn to me, their jaws agape. We don't need words to know we're all thinking the same thing: Is she as clueless as she seems, or is she actually covering for us? And if so, why?

Fast as lightning, Beau's arm shoots out and he clutches her tiny jaw in his enormous hand. "You're sure?"

I gasp, surprised by his ability to move so quickly especially after all the huffing and puffing.

His head snaps in our direction.

Cooper, Jack, and I freeze, holding our breath.

For one long minute Beau searches the yard with his gaze, looking for the source of the sound. My lungs burn for fresh air and my muscles ache from being locked in place.

Finally, Beau turns away, apparently satisfied that he and Missy are alone. Releasing her jaw, he strokes the side of her sleek hair with his puffy hand. "Where is the ruby?"

"I'm not sure." Her voice is small.

"What?" he growls.

She whimpers. "I know I wore it to the hurricane party. And I remember talking to Bunny Perkins about the burglaries on the island. We've got so many valuables here, I was worried we'd be robbed next. I'm sure I put it somewhere to keep it safe. I just can't remember where." Her eyes sink like a puppy who knows she's eaten her master's slippers.

Beau grips his cane so tight, I'm sure it'll snap in two. "How is that possible?"

"I had a lot of tequila."

Actually, I'm certain it was the dirt dauber powder, made from ground-up wasp nests. Adding it to the mustard seed and pepper mixture gave the *Mind Confusion* charm an extra-strong kick. And with any luck, long-lasting power because there's no telling what Beau will do if Missy suddenly remembers handing the necklace to us.

Stumbling backward, Beau shakes his fist. "You imbecile!

Do you have any idea what you've done?"

She rushes to him and pats his colossal chest. "Baby, it'll be okay. I didn't leave the Big House that night so it's got to be here somewhere. It'll turn up. I'm sure of it."

His brow furrows. "You might not have left, but how do you know one of your low-life, gold-digging friends didn't take it?"

"That's ridiculous," she snaps. "None of my friends would steal my necklace."

"*My* necklace." He glares with disdain.

She cowers. "Of course. But if it was stolen—which I'm not saying it was—but if it was, doesn't it make sense that the burglars would take it? Our house is full of valuables."

Beau mashes his thin, blue lips. "We'll know soon enough. I've convinced the rest of the King Center board to hire a real investigator to look into the break in. No one steals from my museum and gets away with it. And if these punks looted my home, too, I'll hunt them down and make them pay." He turns and hobbles a few steps toward the veranda. Pausing, he calls over his shoulder. "In the meantime, don't even think of running back to your momma's double-wide. You're staying put so I can keep an eye on you, just in case you're lying to me." Grunting, he plows across the veranda and back into the house.

Missy's legs give out beneath her. Slumping into a lounge chair, she drops her head in her hands and weeps.

Chapter Four

I stare at the dry cereal in my bowl, debating whether to pour some milk and try to eat. After last night, my stomach has been twisted in knots, burning and queasy. I don't know how I didn't puke right there behind the palmetto bush after Beau stormed off, or later during my sleepless night as I peered up at the ceiling, but now there's enough bile in my gut to bore a hole clean through to the outside. If I do manage to swallow these sugar-coated corn flakes, they'll either incinerate on contact, or launch straight back up my throat.

My twin brother breezes into the kitchen and heads to the cabinet for a bowl and spoon, then plops down at the table. "What's the matter?" Jack grabs the cereal box next to me. Judging by his perkiness and the brightness in his voice, he wasn't up all night worrying that Beau will discover we destroyed the ruby necklace *and* stole from the museum.

"Good morning to you, too. Nice to know I'm the only one freaking out about our future."

"Listen, Em, what's done is done. We can't stress about it." He shakes out an extra-large helping for himself.

I drop my spoon. "How can you say that? If Beau finds out, we're dead."

"Maybe, but there's no guarantee he will. Missy seems pretty clueless."

"That's only because it was an extra-strong *Mind Confusion* spell. I have no idea how long it'll last. It could wear off anytime. Or never."

Jack scoffs, pours some milk, and digs in. "Well, it's not as if she was the sharpest needle to begin with. Maybe the extra dose was enough to scramble that pea brain of hers forever."

He's got a point. But that doesn't diminish the danger we'll face if she does regain her memory. "But what if—"

"What if nothing." He crunches with his mouth open, further depleting my appetite. "Listen, I know you don't like it when I say you're emo, but let's face it, you do have a tendency to get worked up about stuff."

My cheeks heat as I prepare to blast him. I so don't need his brotherly crap this morning.

He clasps my wrist, revealing his stumpy middle finger, the sole remnant of his battle with The Creep. We both stare at it, a potent reminder of what we went through together. "Hey, it's cool, I get it. And I'm grateful, too. You're emotional because you care about stuff. And you know, people like me and Coop. If you didn't, I'd be a walking skeleton right now. Or worse." For once, his cool blue eyes are sincere. He offers me a sheepish smile, totally designed to diffuse my anger.

Fine, but that doesn't mean I'm okay with the emo crack. Still, my shoulders relax. "So what's your point?"

"We knew this was coming, Em. Missy isn't like Beau's other

wives who kept the necklace locked in a safe. He was bound to notice it wasn't hanging around her neck." He releases my wrist and goes back to chomping his breakfast.

"Yeah, but I was hoping for a little extra time so we could get past Cooper's birthday. Or maybe after the summer when we were all off the island and back at school."

He laughs. "Nice fantasy but totally unrealistic." He rubs the faint stubble on his chin. "Maybe it's good that Beau thinks the museum burglars took it. It'll throw him off our trail. At least for a little while."

I arch an eyebrow. "Um, do I have to remind you that *we're* the burglars?"

"Technically, you and Cooper are. I'm just the getaway driver." He grins.

"You're guilty by association."

"That's up to a jury to decide. And thanks to Miss Delia's *Semi-Invisibility* Charm, it's not going to come to that." Tipping the bowl to his mouth, he gulps the last of his milk and then scrapes the last remaining flakes with his spoon.

"I hope so. From what Beau said last night, he's taking things personally. Which is kind of weird since he's only a donor. I mean, why would he care if the museum lost the mortar and pirate's dagger? It's not like they're valuable to anyone besides us."

Belching, Jack shrugs. "You know Beau. His family's been here so long he thinks he owns everything. Even a museum about the Gullah. But it doesn't matter what he thinks if he doesn't have any evidence. Pinning the necklace on the burglars is better than him finding out what really happened." Shoving his hand in his pocket, he pulls out his third of the broken ruby and rolls it onto the kitchen table. Even though its cuts are jagged and uneven, the stone fragment is dazzling in the morning sunlight.

My thigh heats, just like last night, except now it's way hotter. Reaching into my pocket, I pull out my own ruby, which strangely feels icy cold to the touch. Once again, I'm totally confused by what my spirit guide is trying to tell me. How the heck am I supposed to interpret hot skin and a cold rock? I've already messed up once. With Cooper's birthday just over three weeks away, I don't have time to screw up again or he'll lose his soul.

My fingers freeze and I drop the stone. It bounces, then rolls across the table as if drawn toward Jack's piece, stopping only when the two pieces click against each other. Like two jigsaw pieces, the fragments are perfectly aligned along the fault line where they split, though the crack is still super obvious.

Jack taps his piece to nudge them apart, but the two fragments remain stuck together. "What the—"

Déjà vu kicks in as I reach over and tug on my piece. It doesn't budge. Pulling a bit harder, I manage to break apart the bond between the two pieces. I think I understand what's happening. It's got nothing to do with the *Protective Shield*. "Cool. It's like a lodestone."

"A what?" Jack asks.

"Lodestone. They're like natural magnets. Miss Delia has a ton of them. She uses them in all kinds of spells. I think they're some kind of iron ore or something."

"But how can a ruby have the same properties as a magnet?"

"I'm not sure but I'm guessing the magic in the ancestors' mortar seeped into the stone when it exploded. There's no telling what kind of power it picked up." And after everything we've seen this summer, I'm not about to question it.

The front door creaks opens. Jack and I scoop up our rubies and slip them into our pockets. Dad's work boots clunk onto the plastic tray by the door and his footsteps pound through the living room.

Moments later, Dad enters the kitchen in his socks. A neat freak, I think he'd rather have a coronary than wear shoes in the house. His face is chiseled with wrinkles and his temples look grayer than normal. I bet he's been working since dawn.

His eyes brighten when he sees us. "Hey, kids. I'm surprised you're still around. Figured you'd be out causing trouble with Cooper by now."

Jack rubs his eyes. "Late night. We'll probably head out soon. Unless…you need me to stay around and help you some more." He looks apprehensive, as if he's only asking to be nice.

Dad laughs, but it's tinged with weariness. He lifts the coffeepot from the machine on the counter and pours a fresh mug. "Nah. I appreciated your help with the storm cleanup, but now that we've repaired the last of the broken shutters, I've just got to run to the hardware store for some paint. I might even get to take the afternoon off."

Jack smiles. "Awesome. 'Cause I didn't want to deal with any more fallen trees."

Dad smirks. "I know. It must be tiring watching me chop all that wood." He takes a swig of coffee. "I'm hungry. You want some pancakes? You haven't touched that cereal of yours, Emma. And I know you can always eat again, Jack."

"Heck yeah." Jack rubs his unfairly flat midsection.

Although my talk with Jack didn't fix our problems, it has calmed my stomach, at least a little bit. Plus Dad's homemade pancakes are about the best in the world. "Yeah, that would be great." I dump the untouched cereal back in the box.

Dad opens the cupboard and pulls a bag of flour, some sugar, and a box of baking powder from the shelf.

The phone rings. Jack jumps to answer, knowing better than to ignore it. No one ever calls on that line except Beau or Missy, and it's usually to demand something ridiculous. Personally, I don't get why my father takes their crap, but it's his job, one he takes very seriously, so we don't give him too much trouble about it.

"Hello?" Jack's eyes stretch wide. "Hang on, this isn't Jed. Let me get my dad." Covering the mouthpiece, Jack shakes his head. "She's totally freaking out. Like more than normal. Says it's an emergency." He hands over the receiver.

No matter what it is, whether it's hanging a drape or changing a lightbulb, in Missy's world, it's always an emergency. Though considering the argument we witnessed between her and Beau last night, maybe there's a reason for it.

Dad takes a deep breath before he lifts the phone to his ear. "Yes, Missy, what can I do for you?" I can't make out her specific words, but from the muffled sounds I can hear, I'm fairly sure she's crying. Dad's brow creases. "Slow down. I don't understand. What's going on? Is it Beau?" He exhales. "All right. Is it the plumbing? Do you smell gas? Then what's the problem?" Moments pass before he pinches the bridge of his nose and asks, "What do you mean broken?" More indiscriminate whelps emerge. He sighs. "Okay. I've got to run to the hardware store first. I promised Beau I'd finish the shutters today." Her shrieks pierce through the speaker, causing Dad to yank the phone from his ear.

"It can't wait." Missy's voice screams from the earpiece, nearly as loud as if she was standing right next to us. "Now get over here and do your job. Unless you want to lose it!" She wails then breaks into uncontrollable sobs.

"Okay. Don't cry. I'll be right there." He cuts off the call then stands frozen as if he doesn't know what to do next.

"What the heck was that about?" Jack brows are quirked.

Dad yanks himself out of his daze and turns to us, a blank look on his face. "I'm going to need to a rain check on that breakfast."

. . .

Cooper, Jack, and I exit the hardware store, our arms laden with supplies for my dad. My stomach grumbles. Again.

"Excuse me." I shift my bags to rub my still-empty and grouchy stomach. After Dad's freaky call from Missy, I forgot all about breakfast. Instead, Jack and I waited for Cooper to pick us up and then drive into Beaufort to get the paint and other stuff Dad called about after he got to the Big House. I'm not sure why he needs drywall tape and joint compound but there's never any rhyme or reason to Missy's demands, so it's not worth contemplating. It might even be related to the Great Burglar Menace, which means there's no worry at all.

Jack's head snaps toward me when my stomach growls again. "Come on, Em. That's the fourth time in an hour. Can we please get you something to eat? You're making me hungry. Let's load this stuff in the car and get a burger or something." He points across the street to Daisy's Diner, one of our favorite spots.

Now that he's mentioned food, the pit in my belly seems to have grown deeper. But we didn't come out for lunch and, unlike Jack, I can hold out if I have to. "What about Dad?"

"We won't be long. Heck, we can even take it to go. But if I have to listen to your stomach again, I might go crazy," Jack says.

"Look, it's Taneea," Cooper says.

"Where?" I twist my head to see where he's pointing.

"Ta *who*?" Jack asks, craning his neck. "Oh. *Dang.*" His eyes look as if they're about to pop from their sockets.

There she is on the sidewalk, in giant black sunglasses, texting on her iPhone. She's wearing yet another statement piece, a curve-hugging, black mini-tank dress and bright pink platform espadrilles that perfectly match her fuchsia streaks. The diamond stud above her lip glints in the sun.

Where's Miss Delia? I scan both sides of the street to see if she's parked her great-grandmother on the sidewalk. But the only things I see are a pair of wrens hopping around the base of a small turkey oak foraging for insects. Out of nowhere, a big, fat crow dives out of the sky, aiming for the tawny little birds, scaring them into flight. The crow squawks in triumph as it flies away, its raspy call so loud it resonates all the way down the block.

"Who is she?" Jack leans over me to get a good look. "And how do you two know her when I don't?"

"We met yesterday," Cooper says. "She's Miss Delia's great-granddaughter. From Chicago."

"What's she doing here?" Jack asks.

"Apparently hard time," I mumble under my breath because I know it's not exactly charitable to be so mean. But given the move she tried to make on Cooper yesterday, she totally deserves it.

"Officially she's here to help Miss Delia for the summer," Cooper says, ever the optimist and proponent of the bright side.

"Unofficially it's because her mom kicked her out," I add.

Jack's eyes brighten with understanding. "That explains a lot." His eyes travel the lengthy distance between her eyebrow ring and hot pink toenails.

Just then, a big, old-looking black car with dark tinted windows pulls up to the curb. Taneea smiles and tosses her cell into her oversize black leather bag. Flipping her shaggy bangs, she prances around to the passenger side, opens the door, and disappears inside. The engine revs then speeds down the street.

Cooper scratches his temple. "After all she said yesterday, I didn't think she knew anyone down here."

"I guess she made a friend," I say. Based on that getup of hers, it probably wasn't hard.

Jack laughs as he shoves the supplies in the trunk. "Wow, I bet she's a ton of fun."

I watch as the car disappears from sight. "Or a bucket of crazy. Doesn't she know not to climb into a car with a stranger?"

"Maybe she's lonely," Cooper says. "What do you think, Jack? She's available. You're available. Maybe you two should hang out. You're a little weird, but you're safer than a random dude with tinted windows."

Jack's smile slips. "No thanks."

"Hey, I didn't mean—"

"No, it's not that. Ever since Maggie, you know, left, I've sworn off chicks."

Maggie didn't leave so much as disappear. Literally. Because she was a ghost, killed nearly three hundred years ago by Bloody Bill and his pirates. And until we broke The Creep, she was his girlfriend.

"Breakups suck, bro," Cooper says. "Maybe a new girlfriend is what you need to get over her."

"Maybe I don't want to get over her." Jack's voice is quiet. "At least not yet."

Chapter Five

Back at the Big House, we haul in Dad's supplies. Something smashes down the hall.

Tensing, Cooper shoots me a look. Without a word, he gently sets down his can of joint compound. Following his lead, Jack and I place our bags on the ground.

Another crash sounds, followed by a yelp.

Jack rakes his fingers through his thick, black hair. "Aw, man. Now what?"

Together we creep through the foyer, past the library. Another bang, followed by a *thunk*. Whatever it is, it's coming from the great room with the picture windows that overlook St. Helena Sound. Picking up our pace, we sprint past Beau's private study and burst through the double French doors at the end of the hall.

We stop short.

"What the—" Jack's jaw drops.

Missy is trashing the place. Standing on a stepladder in

her spiky heels, she yanks books from the wall-length case in a frenzy, tossing them blindly behind her into the middle of the room. Each leather-bound volume lands with a *clunk*, crashing into whatever is in its path. A porcelain lamp sails off a side table, smashing to pieces when it hits the planked floor.

But that's not the only damage. The sofas have been stripped of their cushions, which are scattered around the room, their zippers ripped open and batting yanked out. Window fixtures hang cockeyed as if wrenched from the wall and the drapes lie in heaps on the floor. Every desk and side table drawer has been pulled free, their contents upended.

Cooper rushes to her. "Missy! What are you doing?"

She turns to him, her shiny blue eyes crazed and glossy. "Get out of here!" Her normally silky platinum hair is wild and frayed and looks remarkably like a bird nest. Pink lipstick is smeared across her mouth, the bright color extending beyond her lip line.

"No. This is my house, too."

"I'm the Mistress of the Plantation, and what I say goes!" Her voice is shrill. With a grunt, she reaches for another volume and flings it. It soars across the room, bounces off a disemboweled throw pillow, and plunks against the sideboard along the wall.

"Please get down before you get hurt." Cooper's voice is soft but stern as he reaches up to clasp her arm.

"Don't touch me!" She glares and jerks away, shifting her weight and wobbling the stepladder. Off balance, she overcorrects and tips forward, then topples to the ground. Jack and I sprint forward. She wails. "See what you made me do?"

Cooper's eyes stretch wide. "I tried to *help* you!"

Despite the anger in his gaze, he reaches his hand to lift her up.

And that's why I love Cooper Beaumont. As wretched as Missy has been to him, and as much as I know he detests her, he still manages to be compassionate.

Swatting him away, she scrambles off the floor, then rubs her butt and elbow. "I don't need your help. It's not like y'all can find what I need anyway." Her lips twist into a sneer as she turns her back and rummages through a cabinet beneath the built-in bookcase.

"Could we try?" Though as I survey the wreckage, I'm not sure where to start.

"No thanks, Edith," she says, calling me the wrong name as usual. "I'll handle it myself. Can't trust anybody to do anything right around here." She yanks a stack of folders from the cabinet and tosses them aside.

Jack grinds his teeth as he flashes me a look. We both know who really runs this place and it's definitely not Missy. He's somewhere in this house no doubt fixing another of her messes. But pointing that out would cause Dad more trouble than it's worth.

"Why are you tearing everything apart?" Cooper asks.

Crawling away from the now-empty cabinet, she moves on to the next. "That's none of your business."

"That's where you're wrong. These are my family's things. Some of them antiques that stretch back centuries." He stoops to pick up a jagged piece of an old brown spirits bottle that used to sit on the shelf. "You broke this. And I want to know why." His words are hard and laced with bitterness.

She wheels around and stands, her hands planted on her hips. "Isn't it obvious?"

Cooper's eyes meet mine. I shrug. Jack does the same.

Cooper shakes his head. "No."

"Duh, I'm looking for something. But seeing as it's not here, it must be somewhere else in this house."

I can't help but feel bad. She must be looking for the ruby necklace, a hunk of which is nestled in my pocket. Though not bad enough to tell her what happened. Jack raises one eyebrow and smirks, clueing me into the fact he's thinking the exact same thing.

She wipes her hands and tiptoes over the carnage, making her way to the double French doors.

"Aren't you going to clean this up?" Cooper's brows pinch.

She flicks her gaze at Jack and me. "Isn't that what your little friends are for?"

Jack shakes his head. "Actually, no."

Missy's stilettos freeze in their tracks. Spinning, she paces toward my brother, stopping only when she's right under his nose. Though he's at least eight inches taller, thanks to her supersized platform heels, she's almost able to look him in the eye.

"What did you say?" Her voice is laced with menace.

I bite my tongue, knowing that nothing good can come from getting involved. If anything, it'll only make matters worse.

Jack tilts his gaze to meet hers. "I don't work for you so you can't order me around."

Her lips part, curling up at the side. "But your daddy does. And your daddy's daddy worked for the Beaumonts, just like your great-granddaddy. So really, it's just a matter of time, isn't it, Johnny-boy? So clean up this mess. Now." She pokes an acrylic fingernail into my brother's chest.

Jack's nostrils flare and his clenched jaw ticks.

Cooper lurches forward, wedging himself between Jack and Missy, forcing Jack back a few steps. Looming over his stepmother, both in height and heft, he says, "Let's get something straight. Jack's my best friend, not my employee." He glances over his shoulder and gestures to Jack, whose face is still flushed crimson, to stand down.

Jack draws a deep breath and obeys, stepping back several strides before tripping and collapsing on a cushion-less sofa fame. I scurry over the piles of debris to join him, eager to offer at least some silent support. There, I grab his hand and squeeze tight. It takes several seconds, but he reluctantly grips me back.

Cooper's face softens as he turns back to Missy. "Listen, we didn't come here to give you a hard time."

"Really? You could have fooled me. Now make yourselves useful while I go find that good-for-nothing caretaker." She pushes past Cooper and climbs over the rest of the junk she's strewn over the floor.

Chapter Six

I pull back a cluster of leathery bearberry and snip an extra-fat handful of the bright green stems, dropping them in my sweetgrass gathering basket. After the supreme weirdness with Missy and Beau, Miss Delia's garden is the perfect refuge, a quiet place to breathe in the fresh, raw scent of nature. It would make an ideal subject for an impressionistic painting, with tiny globs of vibrant color standing in for the myriad flowers and plants that fill this little slice of Eden. If only I had the time. For the last several days, rather than breaking out my travel easel and oils, I've been toiling in the dirt, clipping and cataloging the extensive inventory of plants and herbs, then grinding them into powder for Miss Delia to test for our *Break Jinx*. So far, none have had the explosive power we saw in the *Psychic Vision* with Sabina. With two-and-a-half weeks left before Cooper's birthday, I hope we find it soon.

Ordinarily, working the garden would be paradise, but today it's the exact opposite thanks to Taneea. Mercifully, I haven't seen much of her lately since she's either been holed up in her room, or out on one of her "walks" around the island. Though, if the black car we saw the other day has been involved, I doubt she's done much walking. Whatever has kept her busy, she hasn't been here. Until today.

"Could it get any hotter?" Taneea whines for the thousandth time as she fans herself in a rocking chair on the porch.

Miss Delia spins her wheelchair around on the stone path that winds through the garden. "I reckon it will."

Taneea tugs at her clingy low-cut tank. "My clothes are soaked. Haven't you heard of central air?"

"Sure have. But generations of my kin lived without it. I figure I can do the same. A little perspiration never killed anyone."

"Gross." Taneea crosses her arms.

Though I hate to admit it, Taneea's got a point. It is sizzling. But it's South Carolina in the summer, for cripes' sake. If you're not okay with sweating and occasionally stinking, you probably shouldn't get thrown out of your house and forced to live with your great-grandmother on St. Helena's. This island isn't exactly a hot spot, but there's got to be something she can do—go to the library or movies, even volunteer at the hospital—anything but hang around here griping and ruining everyone else's good time.

My patience at its end, I step away from the bearberry, shove my straw hat off my brow, and wipe the trickle of sweat dripping down the side of my face. Hoisting my basket of clippings, I carry it to edge of the porch near Taneea's chair. Her spicy perfume is strong and thick, almost like a guy's cologne, and smells vaguely like Asian spices.

Her lips curl into a self-satisfied grin. "Why don't you get Cooper to come over and drive me to the mall? I'm sure he wouldn't mind hanging out with an older, more experienced girl for awhile."

Oh no she didn't. My fingers ball into a fist, yearning to wipe that smirk off her *older, more experienced,* magenta lips. But instead, I breathe deep, straighten my fingers, and manage to smile back. "Sorry, he's busy with my brother today."

Her brow arches, hoisting her silver eyebrow ring upward. "You've got a brother? Is he hot?"

I choke a little, unaccustomed to thinking about Jack in those terms. "I guess."

She scoffs. "So that's a giant no. But I shouldn't be surprised if he's related to you." Chuckling, she whips out her iPhone. "That's okay. You'd be surprised at how easy it is to meet guys."

Leaning toward her, I keep my voice low so Miss Delia can't hear. "Like the guy in the black car? I bet your great-gran would love to meet him."

She quirks her brow. "How did you—" She cuts herself off, then plasters a big, fat, fake smile on her lips. Leaning toward me, she narrows her gaze. "Don't even think about snitching to the old lady. If I want to hitchhike into town, that's my business, not yours. Or hers. Trust me. You don't know what I'm capable of. And you don't want to find out."

"Hitchhiking? Do you realize how stupid that is?" I snort, completely unimpressed by her tough-girl routine. I've fought demon dogs and broken a flesh-eating curse; Taneea Branson's feeble threats don't even come close.

Her eyes narrow and her nostrils flare. "Listen, you little suck-up. You think that just because you pluck a few weeds in this garden that makes you something special around here. You're *nothing.* Just the hired help."

I square my shoulders, bolstered by the fact that Miss Delia chose me. "I'm not nothing." I almost add that I'm not even hired, that I work for free, but somehow I sense that will only undercut my position.

"Maybe so. But she's *my* great-grandmother. And no matter what she's promised you, blood is thicker than water." She sits back and crosses her arms. Her lips bend as if she's just realized she's held the trump card all along.

Maybe she has. Family is, after all, my bottom line, too. But even though she's struck a chord, I won't give her the satisfaction of backing down.

I set my hands on my hips. "Then you don't know her very well because Miss Delia makes her own decisions, for her own reasons."

"Uh-huh. We'll see. Until then, why don't get back to picking weeds." She snickers as she pushes off her chair and strides into the house, slamming the screen door.

Ignoring her, I walk back down the path to join Miss Delia. She's staring at the trimmed bearberry bush from under the wide brim of her straw hat. "You cut an awful lot of that plant. Too much in my estimation."

Biting my lip, I glance at what's left of the evergreen dotted with tiny pink, pear-shaped flowers that smell like green tea. "You think?"

She levels her gaze at me. "I wouldn't have said anything if I didn't."

"It was overgrown, so I cut it back. Was that okay?"

She narrows her lid over her good eye. "I suppose so. Though I don't generally like taking more than I need at any one time."

Which explains why the garden is so, shall we say, abundant. But she needn't worry, because after I grind some of the bearberry into a powder for her, I'll be using every last leaf for a special tea I'm planning to brew to help boost my energy and make conjuring a lot easier.

I just can't let Miss Delia know. At least not yet.

She hates shortcuts. Knowing her, this tea of mine will definitely qualify as one, but after the simple *Protective Shield* left me as drained as an empty bathtub, I can't imagine what'll happen when I conjure something really big. Say for instance, a spell to save Cooper's soul.

So rather than wait to be sucked dry the next time, I'm taking matters into my own hands, using her spell book and ingredient list to concoct my own formula to build up my reserves. Which, I think is pretty darn brilliant. The magic gets the energy it needs to work, and I get to stay conscious. Win-win.

Miss Delia stiffens in her chair. Her jaw tenses as her eyes search the yard, gazing past the bottle tree to the road beyond. "Something's coming, Emma. Best watch yourself."

A split second later, thick gray clouds roll in, darkening the sky. A cool breeze whips through the clearing, rushing over the bottles dangling from the live oak, creating a low moan. Dread creeps over my skin like a colony of ants. I'm not sure whether to freeze in place or run and hide.

A car engine roars in the distance. The sound grows louder as it nears. Moments later, a shiny black sedan rumbles around the curve in the road. The extra-wide tires chew up the vegetation on the lane leading to Miss Delia's house. Pulling up past the bottle tree, it stops at the foot of the path. I squint hard at the vintage Lincoln. Could it be the same one Taneea climbed into last week? It's similar, but I honestly can't tell because I didn't look at the other one all that closely.

The engine continues to rattle so loud it vibrates my chest.

I'm not the only one affected by the sound. A flock of tiny birds cheep amid the branches of the live oak, then scatter into the wind. Peering into the darkened glass, I try to make out who's driving, but it's impossible to see. After a long few moments, the motor finally cuts off.

The driver's side door opens. One black boot emerges, followed by the other. A second later, a short, rail-thin man with chocolate-brown skin exits the car wearing a pitch-black suit and blue-framed sunglasses. He's not old but he's not young either, though I'd guess he's probably about my dad's age. Grasping a dark leather briefcase, he shuts the door with a *thud*, then smiles, revealing two rows of arctic-white teeth.

My stomach twists. Breathing deep through my nose, I work to compose myself, not knowing what's going on, but somehow realizing I've got to keep my cool.

"Show no fear," Miss Delia mutters under her breath. Clutching the armrests on her chair, she gazes at her visitor.

He nods. "Good day, ma'am. I'm looking for Mrs. Whittaker." His accent is southern, but he's not from South Carolina. Maybe from somewhere in the Deep South, though it's hard to pinpoint where.

"You found her. Though it's *Miss*. Hasn't been Mrs. for a long time." Her voice is low and gravelly.

His narrow chest expands. "I'm Claude Corbeau. Might I come up your walk?" There's a hint of the bayou in his speech, though it's gone almost as quick as I hear it. But there's no mistaking the strained formality of his words, as if he's trying to hide his true roots and come off as something he's not.

"Depends. What are you selling?"

"Oh nothing, I assure you. I'm merely here on a social call." He turns his eyes toward me. "And who might you be?"

My mouth opens to answer but my throat is suddenly as dry as a cotton boll and my tongue as heavy as lead.

"She helps tend my garden. And she's none of your concern." Miss Delia yawns, patting her open mouth with her wrinkled hand. "I'm afraid I'm not up for a visit this afternoon. You know how us old folk need our naps. Perhaps you ought to come back another day."

His smile slips just for a second, but he quickly recovers. "I promise this won't take long."

Taneea opens the screen door and saunters out onto the porch. She's changed into a black corset top and a black miniskirt. "Whew, thank goodness the sun's gone away. Though knowing my luck, it'll probably only last a few minutes." She brushes her bangs off her face. "Well, hello, sir." Her voice is high and flirty.

Miss Delia's face hardens. "Taneea, could you fetch me a glass of sweet tea? I'm mighty thirsty." Her eyes stay trained on Mr. Corbeau. I glance at the table next to her wheelchair. Her glass is still full.

"You've got plenty of tea, Great-gran." Taneea steps off the porch in a pair of black peep-toe sandals.

"I suppose I do," Miss Delia answers without taking her eyes off her visitor.

"You going to introduce me to our guest?" Taneea asks.

Mr. Corbeau beams. "Well hello—Taneea, was it? You can call me Claude. Clearly, you're a young Ms. Whittaker. I can see the obvious resemblance."

Is he blind? They might be related but they look nothing alike.

Claude turns his attention to Miss Delia. "Lord, you must have been a gorgeous woman in your prime." He whistles.

Mrs. Delia crosses her arms. "Sweetmouthing me won't get you very far, Mr. Corbeau. How about you tell me the reason you've come to call?" Her lips mash into a thin line.

He stands on the edge of the garden. "Is that an invitation? It's so much easier to speak face-to-face than shout across your lustrous garden."

"Sure, come on up," Taneea answers before her great-grandmother has a chance to say a word.

Quick as lightning, Claude opens the gate on the picket fence then bounds up the walkway, almost a skip in his step.

Miss Delia's gnarled hands tighten into liver-spotted balls. She shoots me a cautionary glance. This is where I'm supposed to use that strength she warned me about. Against what I'm not sure, but I breathe deep and brace myself just the same.

Approaching the chair, Claude extends his arm toward Miss Delia, a stiff, ivory-colored business card wedged between his first two fingers. "I appreciate you agreeing to my visit on such short notice."

"You mean no notice." Miss Delia doesn't reach for his card.

He pauses, taking her in. "Yes, coming unannounced is unforgivably rude. But given your reputation for generosity, I thought you'd find in your heart to be hospitable." He shoves the card in my direction.

Huh? What the heck is he talking about? I glance at the embossed print on the thick card stock. A surge of electricity zips up my limbs. "You're from the King Center?" The words blurt from my suddenly unfrozen mouth.

He turns his head in my direction. "I just started actually. Are you familiar with the organization?"

I nod. "Y-yes." Only too well.

"What is it?" Taneea twists a fuchsia strand around her

index finger.

"It's the Lowcountry's premier Gullah museum." Claude beams with pride. "We house the most impressive collection of Gullah art and historical artifacts in the country."

"Do you have air-conditioning?" Taneea asks.

He laughs. "Of course. The exhibits require a climate-controlled environment."

"Nice. Is it open to the public? Because when I'm not melting from the heat, I'm losing my mind on this frigging island."

Claude laughs. "Then you must absolutely visit. Our collection is extensive and we're always searching for volunteers. I promise you'll be quite cool. And while you're there, you could see your… grandmother's donation." He scans Miss Delia's face for some confirmation of their relation, but she doesn't twitch.

"Grammy's in Chicago. Delia's my great-gran. She won't buy a new TV or get cable so I seriously doubt she'd donate anything decent to a museum." She laughs as if she's just made some hilarious joke, but instead she's only managed to humiliate the only person willing to take her in.

"That's enough now, child. I think you've got some tidying up to do in the house, don't you?" Miss Delia asks.

Taneea shakes her head. "Nope. I'm done for the day. Your house is so small it doesn't take long to clean." She bats her lashes.

My tongue burns like fire, desperate to utter every nasty insult that's piling up in my brain. If I wasn't trying to make nice in front of a guy who works for the museum I stole from, I'd totally tell her off.

Claude smiles. "Oh, your great-grandmother did indeed make a donation. An impressive one at that. It's the reason for my visit."

"Was there a problem with the paperwork I signed?" Miss Delia asks. "I don't have the best eyesight, as you can tell from my cataract."

"Oh no, everything was in order."

"Then why are you here?" I ask, unable to keep silent. You'd think they'd be happy to get a treasure box filled with pirate gold.

"I just had a few questions. You see, there's an anomaly I just wanted to follow up on."

"Anomaly?" Miss Delia asks.

"Yes, it's means there's something unexpected or unusual."

Miss Delia leans forward, pursing her lips. "I know what it means, young man. What I don't understand is why you've come bothering me about it."

"You gave us a box of pirate doubloons from *The Dagger*, a pirate ship that sank off the tip of Coffin Point in the eighteenth century."

"Yes?"

"It's a remarkable find. Tell me, how did you come to possess such a treasure?"

She leans back in her chair. "I dug it up. In my front garden." She points a gnarled finger toward the catnip bushes in the far corner.

He laughs, gripping his midsection with his spindly hand. "Really? Imagine that."

She smiles. "Yes, indeed."

"Over there?" He puts his briefcase down then steps his wing-tipped feet through a cluster of juniper, past a row of dwarf holly, then leaps over some echinacea to the catnip. Bending down, he scoops up a teeming handful of dark brown earth, then sifts it with his fingers. "It's hard to believe something so valuable was just lying here, waiting to be discovered."

Miss Delia shrugs. "Not really, seeing as it came out of the ground."

He stares at the soil in his hand. "It's rich and moist." He sniffs it. "I believe the term is loamy, isn't? Clumps when you squeeze it."

"And your point is?" Miss Delia is clearly losing her patience with him, his anomaly, and his fascination with the quality of her dirt.

Grinding the last bit of grit between his two forefingers, he seems not to have heard her question. "The secret is plenty of humus. Without it, this would be just another dry patch of ground unable to grow anything."

Miss Delia and I exchange bewildered looks. Did he really come out here to do a soil analysis?

Taneea shifts her hip and crosses her arms. "Um, who cares about her dirt? I thought you were here to talk about her donation."

I'm not sure whether to be happy or insulted that she and I on the same wavelength.

"Oh, I am." He finally pulls his attention away from the dirt and stands. "You see, I can't understand how a wooden box could have stayed so pristine buried in such moist conditions. Surely it would have deteriorated and likely fallen apart after nearly three hundred years."

A wave of relief floods over me. Finally something I can answer. "That's because it was encased in a tabby box. I helped uncover it myself." The words fly from my lips before I can think. Miss Delia's good eye stabs in my direction. She doesn't need words to let me know she thinks I've made a giant mistake.

His smile broadens as his slick brows arch. "Tabby? I didn't think that old concrete was used this far inland. Seems much easier to mix oyster shells and sand along the shore."

My stomach flitters, filled with nerves. Despite Miss Delia's obvious preference to the contrary, I can't clam up now. I've got to answer his questions so he'll hit the road and leave us alone. I shrug. "I don't know about that. All I can say is the box was definitely hidden in a hunk of tabby. But it doesn't matter as much as the fact that Miss Delia gave it to the King Center, right? I mean, it's a piece of St. Helena history. Do you think she should have given it to someone else?"

"How about keeping it for herself and fixing this place up?" Taneea casts a disapproving glance at Miss Delia's house.

"Oh, don't misunderstand me, Miss..." Claude pauses, expecting me to fill in my last name. But judging by the way Miss Delia's brows are knit in a stern and not-so-subtle warning, I keep my mouth shut. An awkward moment later, he continues. "The King Center greatly appreciates Miss Whittaker's bequest. It's an exquisite addition to the collection." He sidesteps some spindly heather, weaves through some lavender bushes, then crosses over the juniper. "Our curator has already planned a seafaring exhibit around it."

"That's nice to know," Miss Delia says. "You be sure to let me know when it's up and running and I'll try to visit sometime. Now, unless you want to trample the rest of my garden, I think we're done."

"It is a lovely plot. Very well stocked. And now that you've explained about the tabby concrete, everything seems so clear." He picks up his briefcase. An ultrawhite smile slides across his face. "Thanks again for your time, Miss Whittaker." He turns around and steps toward the white picket fence. I sigh, glad to finally be rid of his weird energy. But then he pauses and pivots on his heels. "Oh, there's one more thing I forgot to ask." He lifts a slender finger to his chin.

Miss Delia sighs. "What's that?"

"Do you have any idea why the engraving on the box matches an artifact that was recently stolen from the museum?" His voice is as smooth as a polished stone. Spreading his hands about twelve inches apart, he adds, "It was a knife, about yay big. Made from the same type of wood as the box. Our curator thinks they were made around the same time, too. Perhaps even by the same hand."

My stomach plummets as I strain to keep my eyes from popping out of my head.

Sucking her teeth, Miss Delia shakes her head. "Can't say I do."

"Sounds kind of hinky to me," Taneea says.

Claude's eyes flit in Taneea's direction. "Perhaps it's just a coincidence. Though it's funny that one object would show up so soon after the other went missing."

Miss Delia shrugs. "Ain't nothing predicable about the Lowcountry."

His thin lips bend at the ends. "True enough. Well, I've taken enough of your time, ladies. Miss Taneea, I hope you visit the King Center sometime." He bows slightly, then turns his attention back to Miss Delia. "You're not planning on going anywhere, are you? In case I have further questions."

She gestures toward her wheelchair. "Can't go too far." She holds his gaze as their eyes lock in some sort of strategic stare-down, neither one wanting to be the first to look away.

An awkward moment later, he gives in. "Good to know. Have a nice afternoon." He turns on his heels and heads to his car.

Frozen, I watch as he tugs open the door, then slides into the front seat. After he's pulled out of the yard and rounded the bend in the road, I exhale, purging my lungs of stale air. Sucking for breath, the garden's sweet scent does nothing to revive me. Instead, a sense of doom encroaches like the incoming tide.

I made a giant mistake all right. Claude wasn't here for a social call. And he didn't give a rat's tail about Miss Delia's garden. He clearly suspects she was involved in the museum break in, and now, thanks to my blabbering about finding the box in tabby concrete, he knows I'm involved, too.

Chapter Seven

The gray clouds part, revealing the bright sun once again.

Taneea sighs. "He was nice. But now I'm bored. I guess I'll paint my nails again." She stomps back up to the house and slams the screen door.

Swallowing hard, I step close to Miss Delia. "What the heck just happened? Who was that guy?"

She shakes his head. "An investigator. He said so himself."

"Yeah, but he was way weird. And creepy."

"That he was. But I don't want you to worry your head over him. So long as you keep out of his sights, you'll be fine."

Despite the rising heat, a cold sweat breaks out across my forehead, powered by the growing sense of foreboding that's swirling in my gut. "But he obviously suspects you, and probably me now, of being involved in the museum robbery."

She swats her hand. "Shh, never you mind about him. Let me handle him. In the meantime, you've got clippings to prepare for me." She points to the basket I left on the porch.

"Okay. Sure." I pivot on my heels and head up to the house, trying to squelch my worry. But that's almost like telling an ice cube not to melt in this heat, especially since I know something she doesn't: we never got rid of the dagger like we planned.

Inside the safety of Miss Delia's kitchen I fumble with my cell phone, dialing Jack's number.

He answers on the third ring. "Yo, what up?"

"I need you to guys to come get me," I whisper in case Taneea is lurking nearby, listening in.

He laughs. "What, Taneea driving you crazy?"

"No. Well, yeah of course, but she's not the problem. It's something else. Which is why I need you guys. Now."

"Are you serious?" He sounds as if I just canceled his date with the prom queen. "We're about to take off for Hunting Island. I just dropped the dock lines."

"Tie them back up. Send Cooper over to get me and meet us back at the Big House. Oh, and bring the knife with you."

"What knife?"

Is he for real? How many pirate daggers do we have lying around the house? I sigh. "*The* knife. The one we never got around to returning."

After a long moment of silence it finally hits him. "Oh, *that* knife." His voice flattens like a deflated balloon. "Aw man, I really wanted to go sailing."

"Sorry. Maybe another day."

"Yeah, maybe. See you soon." The line goes dead.

Breathing deep, I still my mind to remember all the ingredients for my energy potion. Separating the cuttings I need from those Miss Delia wants for her reserves, I stow mine in a Ziploc bag, then toss them into my messenger bag. There isn't time to do everything I promised, but I can hang most of the fresh cuttings to dry in the heat on her back porch. Just as I finish, I hear the familiar hum of Cooper's station wagon. Finally.

Bolting through the house, I pass Taneea slumped on the couch, her hot-pink toes perched on the coffee table. She's sneering at the thick glass screen on Miss Delia's ancient television. As much as I'd hate to have to watch it myself, I can't help but laugh that she's got no other choice.

Miss Delia has wheeled herself up on the porch and is talking with Cooper. Though his jade-green eyes are filled with concern, they still sparkle when he sees me. "Everything okay, Emmaline?" His gaze shifts between me and Miss Delia.

She waves her hand, dismissing his worry. "Only as much trouble as a horsefly causes a nag. And nothing a swatting tail can't fix." She grins, no doubt to dismiss any lingering concerns.

But it doesn't make me feel any better. Or untwist the knot in my stomach.

• • •

Twenty minutes later, Cooper and I arrive at the Big House. Being with him has helped calmed my nerves, but the jitters aren't entirely gone, because deep in my gut, despite Miss Delia's assurances to the contrary, I know Mr. Claude Corbeau is going to be a problem.

As we step into the foyer, a loud scraping sound echoes down the hall, as if someone's shoving a large piece of furniture across a stone floor.

Cooper grunts as he shakes his head. "Don't tell me Missy's at it again."

Although it's been days since her argument with Beau, she's

still on a rampage, tearing apart nearly every room on the first floor, still searching for the Beaumont ruby. To avoid Beau's rage, Cooper's taken it upon himself to clean up after her and sometimes even help if it means nothing will get broken.

"Ouch! My nail." Missy's voice carries, shrill and angry from the solarium at the end of the east wing.

"Sounds like she's pushing that wrought-iron baker's rack around. I hope she removed the margarita goblets from the top rack first."

Metal grates against flagstone pavers once again. A second later, Missy squeals, followed by a cascade of shattering glass.

Cringing, Cooper and I turn to each other. "Oops."

Beau's voice booms from the library. "Missy! What was that?" His words are slurred.

"Nothing, sugar."

"I don't want any part of that mess." Cooper grabs my hand and sprints up the grand staircase toward his room. I'm not sure if he's talking about the literal mess splattered across the solarium floor, or the inevitable fight that'll erupt when Beau realizes what she's done. Either way, I'm with him.

When we get upstairs, Jack is still not there so I sit at Cooper's desk and open his laptop.

Cooper shuts his door. "You going to tell me what's going on?"

"As soon as Jack gets here, I promise."

He pulls up a chair next to me. "Until then, we could do something other than surf the Web." He grazes the back of my neck with his finger.

A chill, definitely the delicious kind, flits over my skin. Giggling, I inch away. "As much as I'd like that, I need to check something first." I type Claude's name into the search engine hoping to find something. The only result is from last week's *Beaufort Gazette*. Cooper moves closer, nuzzling the flesh behind my ear as I click through and skim a story about the King Center's new security consultant brought in to investigate the recent break-in. Beau was even quoted taking credit for finding the world-class investigator and making the board hire him.

Exhaling, I try to block out the sensations created by Cooper's lips. It's nearly impossible, except for the niggling question that keeps running through my brain: if Claude is so awesome and famous, why aren't there any other references to him or some of the big cases he's solved? I look away from the screen and stare out the window to ponder the possibilities.

Something on the pane draws my attention. Three slimy smudges smear the glass.

"Ew, what's that?"

Cooper pulls away. "What? I thought you liked it when I kiss your neck." He looks insulted. And a little hurt.

I chuckle. "No, I *love* it. I'm talking about *that*." Pointing to the window, I get up to take a closer look.

The clear streaks are thick and goopy, and sort of look like someone's slathered a handful of hair gel across the glass. But that's ridiculous because, for one, who the heck would do that? And two, it's on the exterior side of the pane. Besides, since Cooper doesn't use gel, I doubt there's even a tube of the stuff in the house.

Cooper steps beside me and squints at the splotches on his window. "I don't know. Maybe it's just dirty. I'll ask your dad to zap it with the power washer."

My scalp prickles, but unlike a few moments ago when Cooper's touch made my flesh sizzle, the feeling moves way beyond tickling to almost burning. Though my fingers itch to soothe the fiery sensation, I've done this long enough to know it's got nothing to do with the skin on my head. I'm supposed to take note of this stuff.

"No, I think it's something else." I unhinge the lock and release the side buttons to allow the frame to tilt inside. The humid air gushes in, warming his air-conditioned room and carrying the luscious scent of the pink magnolia beside the house.

Bending down, I peer at the smudge. A whiff of something sharp and bitter slams my nostrils, making me pull away. Nausea swells and my mouth floods with sour saliva. "Ugh, gross!" Covering my mouth with my palm, I gag.

I've smelled something similar once before. Last summer, while Jack and I were down south and my mom was on her dig at the sandstone cliff buildings in Petra, our freezer broke down. When we got back just before school started, the mildewed and rotting food was a biohazard of epic proportions. Even after we got rid of it, the stench lingered in our apartment for almost a week. This smell, the one coming from the residue on Cooper's window, reminds me of the funk that hovered in our kitchen those last few days.

Cooper scoops his head to sniff, then looks up at me, quirking his brow. "It's a little nasty, but it's not that bad."

"Seriously?" I cough, my throat burning. "It's putrid."

"I guess I must be stuffed up or something." Reaching over, he stretches his fingers toward the slime.

A jolt of pain shoots down my arm, zapping my hand. I don't know what it means except Cooper isn't supposed to touch that stuff.

"Don't!" I yank his wrist away.

But it's too late. The gel coats his middle and index fingers. My heart jumps into overdrive, galloping in my chest.

"What's the matter?" His eyes stretch as wide as half-dollars. The skin on my hand radiates heat. "You can't touch it."

"Why?" He laughs, tapping his tacky fingers against his thumb. The glycerin-like substance is wet and stretchy. "It's sap or something. Gross, but nothing dangerous. Really. See?" He pushes his fingers toward my face. The scent stings my eyes.

Tugging my T-shirt over my nose, I take a giant step back and trip onto Cooper's bed. "Get it away from me! I mean it." My voice is laden with desperation.

Jack sweeps open the door to Cooper's bedroom, a rolled paper bag in his hand. "Do you know your stepmonster's going crazy again downstairs?" When he notices me cringing on the bed, he laughs. "What's going on in here?" He's way too amused by my obvious discomfort.

"Emma's afraid of the slime on my window. Seems your sister has inherited your dad's neat-freak gene." He walks to his hamper, flips open the lid, and wipes his hand on a towel at the top of the pile. "As for Missy, there's a reason this was closed." Hooking his toe around the edge of the door, he pushes it shut again.

My mind is still stuck on the neat-freak quip. Is he serious? Hasn't he noticed the charcoal pastels caked under my fingernails, or the oil paint that occasionally frosts my hair? I'm nothing like my disinfectant-obsessed father. Still hypersensitive about being a guest in the caretaker's cottage, Dad takes spotless to a whole new level.

I right myself on the mattress. "It's not that. I just don't want that nasty stuff on me. I don't know how you can stand the stink."

Jack sniffs the air. "What stink?"

"You too?" I inhale through my cotton shirt, dragging the fresh scent of fabric softener up my nose. It's almost enough to eradicate the stench now wafting from the still-open clothes hamper.

Setting the bag on Cooper's desk, he steps toward the pane, then leans over and sniffs. "Marginally foul." Shrugging, he shoots a conspiratorial glance at Cooper. "It's way worse than the neat-freak gene. It's an emo attack." He winks at me, knowing his favorite insult is bound to trip my nerves.

Mission accomplished.

My lids narrow. "Don't be an idiot." I get up and slam the hamper shut.

Tilting his head, he smirks. "Look, I'm not the one spazzing over a few slug trails. Which, by the way you've seen a million times all over this plantation." He tilts the frame upward, clicking the pane in place, then shuts the window and relocks the latch.

Slug trails? My pulse drops to a trot. Okay, maybe I overreacted. A little. I didn't even consider the gooey little shell-less snails could have left behind that glistening, mucous-y film. Though I don't ever remember seeing one suction itself to the second level of the Big House, much less three. But even if I did go a bit overboard, that goop really does reek.

"It's still vile." I shudder, keeping my breath shallow to avoid the dissipating but still lingering odor.

"I just hope Coop and I didn't miss out on sailing for an equally nondisaster disaster." Jack snatches the bag, unrolls the top, and pulls out the dagger we liberated from the museum. The same one I used to slice my palm and then Jack's to bind our blood and break The Creep. The one we were supposed to hide somewhere in the museum to confuse the officials into thinking it was merely misplaced and not, in fact, stolen along with the mortar. "So what's up? And why did I need to get this?" The silver blade shines in the steaming sunlight.

"Trust me, we've got a problem." Sinking into the desk chair, I quickly fill them in on my interaction with Claude at Miss Delia's, telling them everything Claude said and how he linked Miss Delia's donation with the engraving on the knife's wooden handle. And, to ice this particular bad-news cupcake, I add in the part about how I inadvertently implicated myself, at least in finding the treasure.

Midway through my story, Jack and Cooper slump on his bed. By the time I'm done, Cooper's pinching the bridge of his nose and Jack's shaking his head.

"Crap." Jack looks as miserable as someone forced to walk the plank over a shark-infested lagoon. "We could be totally screwed." He grips the knife's handle.

Cooper nods. "Yeah, but what were we supposed to do? Between adding that ramp to Miss Delia's porch and widening her doorways we didn't have time to make another trip to the museum."

"I suppose it's too late to do it now," Jack says.

I sigh. "Now that's Claude's on the case, the museum is off-limits."

Cooper's eyes light up with hopeful possibility. "This Claude guy said he could get Taneea a job there, right? Maybe we could ask her to stick it in some storeroom or something."

Jack and I stare at him, our foreheads etched with identical creases. I love Cooper's optimism, but he's seriously overestimated her trustworthiness.

"Dude, you'd rely on someone who hitchhikes with strangers

and got kicked out of school for something this important? Are you nuts?" Jack asks, conveying my sentiments exactly, albeit way more rudely.

Cooper's shoulder sink. "No, I guess you're right. Besides, if it showed up now, it would raise more suspicions than before."

I nod. "Or seal our fate. Even though we wiped it down, there's no telling what evidence we might leave behind. It was coated in Jack's and my blood, not to mention our fingerprints. What if our DNA is still deep inside that engraving? You know they only need a tiny amount of that stuff to test." I stare at Jack's right hand, which is currently wrapped around the scrolled *BBR*, the initials of Bloody Bill Ransom, the *Dagger's* captain.

Cooper rubs his chin. "You're right. As much as I hoped to return it, we can't."

"But what do we do with it?" Jack asks. "We can't keep it here or at the caretaker's cottage. If someone finds it, they're liable to think Dad or Beau stole it."

I nod. "Definitely. We need to put it somewhere no one's going to find it." I search my mind for the perfect hiding place. An idea pops to mind. "Hey, what about putting it back in the tabby box down at the ruins?" It's where we found it in the first place and where it had been locked up for at least a century.

Before they can answer, Missy's voice travels up the grand staircase, then winds around the second-floor landing and carries down the hall, through the closed door. "Cooper! Where you at? I need you."

Cooper stiffens. "Why can't she leave me alone?"

"Because she's on a mission to destroy your life," Jack answers.

"Maybe if we're quiet she'll go away." Judging from the defeated expression on Cooper's face, he knows that's not likely.

Jack snorts. "Right and maybe I'll sprout wings and fly out

that window."

"I saw that horrible station wagon of yours out front," Missy trills. "I know you're here. Don't make me come up there to get you."

Grinding his teeth, Cooper takes the knife from Jack and slides into the paper bag. "The tabby ruins is the perfect hiding place. But we'll need all day to dig out that box and bury it again so it'll have to wait until tomorrow." Sliding off the bed, he crosses the room to his bookcase and pulls a thick calculus textbook from the bottom shelf. "With my dad and Missy around, we can't risk taking the knife downstairs now. It'll have to keep here until we can hide it for good." Opening the cover, he leafs past the first few pages to reveal a hollowed-out center.

Jack's eyes gleam. "Awesome."

I blink. "Wow." Not that having a secret stash is a huge deal. Heck, Jack's got plenty of them. But Cooper isn't sneaky enough to need one.

Cooper shrugs. "Boarding school. It's the only way to keep anything private from snooping roommates."

"Or smuggle in contraband." Jack waggles his brows.

"It's where I keep my letters from you two. Well, from Emma. You never do more than sign a Christmas card." He scowls at Jack.

Jack rolls his eyes. "Hey, I comment on your Tumblr posts."

Cooper smirks. "Thanks, it's a real comfort during the long, lonely nights."

My heart warms at the thought of him reading my letters, and that they mean enough to hide from his friends.

"Cooper! I'm done waiting on you!" Missy's stilettos clomp up the grand staircase.

"She's coming!" I whisper.

Cooper slams the calculus text closed, shoves it back in its spot on the case, and then covers it with more heavy books.

We sprint to the door and open it just as she reaches the top of the steps.

Cooper smiles, looking as innocent as baby lamb. "Oh hi, Missy. We were just on our way downstairs."

She crosses her arms. "Didn't you hear me calling you? I've been hollering my head off." Her hair is frazzled and her eyes crazed. Her lipstick is off-kilter again and her blush streaks across her cheeks in two wide, rose-colored blocks. She's normally model-perfect, but now she looks like she put on her makeup in the dark.

He nods. "Yes, which is why we're headed downstairs. Did you need something?"

"Why else would I bother chasing after you? And since your little friends are here, they might as well lend a hand, too." She pivots, then stomps back down the stairs.

When we reach the bottom, she points toward the far end of the wing. The lacquered nail on her index finger is jagged and torn. "I, uh…moved some furniture in the solarium that you boys need to put back in place. And, Ella, find a broom. There's a little broken glass on the floor."

Biting my tongue, I pace to the utility closet off the butler's pantry, then grab a sponge mop and dustpan because I can't find a broom. Anger roils in my gut. Hasn't she ever heard the word *please*? Or how about *thank you*? Since when did I become her personal maid? Doesn't she torture her biweekly cleaning-service ladies enough? I don't know what Beau pays them to drive down from Charleston and put up with her crap, but it must be a mint. Slamming the door, I tromp down the hall and join the guys in the solarium.

My eyes pop. A *little* glass? Forget the mop, this destruction is going to require a dump truck. She's not only managed to break the entire twenty-five piece margarita set that used to sit on the baker's rack, but the chandelier that used to hang in the middle of the room is splayed on the floor, every one of its bulbs and dripping crystals smashed to bits on the flagstone. Cooper and Jack stand motionless, equally paralyzed by the wreckage before them. Missy didn't just "move" some furniture. She overturned every piece in the room, including the bar, which was filled with tumblers, snifters, and other glass vessels that likely lie broken beneath it, awaiting cleaning up.

"Dang," Jack finally utters.

"Welcome to my world," Cooper deadpans.

I run my fingers through my long hair, pulling it off my forehead. "This is insane. She can't expect us to clean this up."

Missy's stilettos click behind us. "What are y'all waiting for? Get going." She smacks her gum.

"Missy!" Beau bellows, his voice rough and gravelly. He clambers out of the library, heaving his body forward on unsteady legs and his overburdened cane. He's just as wobbly as he was the night on the veranda, perhaps more so.

"Uh-oh," Jack whispers under his breath.

Cooper shoves an elbow in his side. "Shh."

Missy freezes. "Don't trouble yourself, baby. Go on back to your business pages. Want me to get you another scotch? How about a cigar?" Her voice trembles.

Grunting, he ignores her as he plods toward us, his gelatinous body undulating with each step. He's in such obvious distress, half of me wants to run and help him, but the other half fears he'll trip and crush me.

Just before he reaches the solarium, Missy shuffles forward

on her high heels and clutches his arm. "You need your rest, sugar. Come, let me take you back to the library."

"Don't touch me." Nearly out of breath, he yanks from her grasp. His eyes are bloodshot and sunken in their sockets. The familiar scent of rotten bologna hovers, mixed with a healthy serving of scotch. "I work all day to keep this roof over your head and you can't see fit to give me a moment's peace." With each syllable, he thrusts his gray tongue forward and maneuvers his mouth as if deliberately forming every word. His chest gurgles as he sucks for air through thin blue lips. Then his eyes meet mine. "Ah, Emma, it's wonderful to see you, as always." His tongue hangs slack as his gaze drops and he appears to take me in. Lurching forward, he heads toward me.

Missy scampers after him. "Sweetness, wait—"

But it's too late, he's at the door to the solarium. And he's seen the carnage.

For a second, his skin flushes crimson before returning to its normal pale gray. "Now what have you done?"

Missy swallows hard. "It's all for you, baby." Her voice is high and reedy.

"For me?" Beau's breath quickens. He's breathing so hard, he's likely to keel over. Or inflate like a puffer fish.

Cooper tugs Jack's shirt and motions for him to back up into the hall. Then he slips his hand around mine and leans close to my ear as he guides me quietly away from Beau and Missy. "This is about to get ugly. We're out of here."

Amid their escalating argument, Cooper, Jack, and I pick up our pace down the hall, and then sprint through the foyer and out the front door.

"Where to?" Jack bounds down the front steps.

Cooper tightens his grip on my hand. "Anywhere but here."

Chapter Eight

"Oh man." Cooper stands at the doorway to his bedroom, his face drained of its color.

Last night Cooper slept over at the caretaker's cottage, unable to force himself to face either his father or the destruction in the solarium. He texted both Beau and Missy to say he wouldn't be coming home but got no response. We figured they were too busy arguing to care about where Cooper spent the night and decided it would be best to return this morning after the dust settled, retrieve the dagger, and bury it at tabby ruins. Evidently, we were wrong.

Jack and I stand beside Cooper in stunned silence, taking in the wreckage in his bedroom. The only sound comes from the second hand on his old-school alarm clock as it ticks around the dial. It must be nearby under the rubble.

Finally, Jack breaks the quiet. "Missy," he growls, his fists clenched.

"But why?" She's torn through the rooms on the first floor,

but they're the public areas where her guests hung out during the Fourth of July party. It sort of made sense to look for the Beaumont ruby downstairs. But Cooper's room? She's got no reason to believe the necklace was stashed in here. Yet his bed has been stripped and toppled to the floor, his desk and dresser upended, drawers dumped out, and his clothes and other belongings strewn around. Most importantly, the bookcase has been overturned, its contents tossed and scattered around the room.

"The knife!" Cooper snaps out of his stupor and rushes toward the mound of items that litters his floor. Jack and I join him, rummaging through the clothes, sheets, printer paper, and books. Finally he finds the calculus textbook, nestled beneath his bed frame, its cover closed.

My pulse throbs against my temple as I murmur a silent prayer that the dagger is still hidden inside, gloriously protected from Missy's indiscriminate tossing. But as soon as he cracks it open, those hopes are dashed. The compartment is empty.

Looking around the room, Cooper mutters, "It's got to be here." His voice is gripped with panic and sounds as if he's trying to convince himself it's the truth. "Maybe it fell out of the book and she never saw it." Frenzied, he digs through the piles.

Jack sinks against the flipped over mattress. "Dude, I don't think so. She's got it and God only knows what she's done with it." He chuckles but it's a hollow, futile laugh that lacks a trace of happiness. "I guess it's sort of fair. We did take her necklace. Now she's got our knife."

Cooper shakes his head. "No. She can't have it. She doesn't understand what it means, or what it could do to us." He pushes his belongings around as if that will somehow make it magically appear.

Stretching toward him, I grasp his shoulder. "Cooper, stop. It's no use."

Defeated, he looks at me, his royal-blue eyes wounded. "Why did she do this? And why last night of all nights? I never should have left."

My mouth opens but no words come. Because there is no answer, at least one that makes sense. So instead, I lamely rub his back, hoping it'll do some good.

A moment later, the air-conditioning unit kicks on, humming as cool air blows from the ceiling vent. The alarm clock's second hand keeps on ticking, the sound almost magnified in the leaden silence. Suddenly I'm aware of just how quiet it is. It's not normal for the house to be so still. Especially lately.

My earlobes prick with heat.

"Where's Missy?" I ask, remembering that we passed her car on our way up the driveway. She's home. So why isn't she lurking around, gloating about her conquest and plunder?

Cooper shakes his head. "I don't know. I didn't hear her when we came through the foyer. Maybe she's in the breakfast room?"

Jack shoves his straight, black hair off his forehead. "Or maybe she's sleeping off whatever made her go berserk in here."

Warmth curls around my outer ear, then spreads across my scalp. Despite the blasting AC, the room feels like it's eighty degrees and climbing.

I glance out the open door, toward the empty upstairs hallway and landing. Her bedroom door is closed shut. "But don't you think she'd be waiting for us, ordering us to clean up the solarium and this mess?"

"Don't forget shoving the knife in our faces," Jack adds.

Cooper nods. "You're right. She'd love to find dirt on me." He rises to his feet, yanks the box spring out of his path, and sets it on the frame. "I bet she'd enjoy calling the sheriff to have me arrested."

The searing sensation inches down my neck, then around to the front of my throat. Laying my palm against the spreading heat, my fingers are icy against the sizzling flesh. There's only one reason for this bizarre reaction. My spirit guide is trying hard to tell me something. Just then, my pinkie brushes against the cool beads of my *collier*. Without a thought, my hand slips to grasp the necklace hanging around my neck. Glancing down, I notice my fingers are clasped around the section of green and white beads, the ones that are supposed to convey psychic powers.

A black, amorphous image swirls past my mind's eye, filling my stomach with a sick sense of dread. I'm not sure what I've seen or what it all means, but the feeling is strong. And it's bad. Panic sweeps over my body, blurting the words from my mouth. "What if she's calling them right now? What if they're already on their way?" I swallow hard, willing the swelling anxiety back down into my gut.

"Then there's only one thing we can do." Jack picks himself off the floor and hauls the mattress on top of the box spring.

"What's that?" I ask, still shaken by the ominous sensation gripping my throat.

"Stop her before she gets a chance. And if we're too late, take the dagger so she's got no evidence. Let it be her word against ours." His expression is hard, resolved.

Cooper stiffens. "I'm not sure that's such a great idea. What if something goes wrong?"

Jack's brow pinches. "Come on. After all she's done to

you, you're not going to go all Boy Scout on us, are you? Look around. Do you not see how demented she's become? I'm not going to let her get you or us thrown in jail. She's probably stashed the dagger in her room. We'll be in and out in five minutes flat. And we won't trash the place," he adds sarcastically.

I see where Cooper's coming from, but Jack's got a point. Though I'm not crazy about committing another B&E, I'm certain we need to go into Missy's room. And we can't waste another minute. I jump to my feet. "Jack's right. Come on." I head out of his room and down the hall.

"Wait, Emma!" Cooper calls after me, then catches up and grabs my arm.

I stop short and whirl around. There isn't time to explain my weird, shadowy vision or the menacing sensation that's constraining my breath. At this moment, more than any time before, he's just got to go with me on this. "We have to get in there. Now. You've got to trust me." I pull for air.

He meets my gaze. "I do. But I want to be the one who goes in first. If anyone's going to take it from her, it's going to be me."

I've got to admit, I like this new, forceful Cooper.

He leads the way. Jack and I follow past the landing then down the hall to the master bedroom.

At the door, Cooper draws a deep breath, then raps his knuckles against the solid core panel. "Missy! You in there? We've got to talk." His voice echoes around the ceiling above the foyer.

There's no answer. He knocks again, this time with more force. The door slips the latch, creaking open a sliver.

Missy's strawberry-scented perfume slips past us and dances around our heads.

Cooper pushes on the knob, widening the opening. "This is

your last chance. You can either come talk to us, or we're coming in." After a long pause, he wrenches his neck to look inside.

I peek under his outstretched arm. The vast room is empty. And just like the rest of the house, it's eerily quiet. I've never been inside the master suite, but from what I can tell, nothing looks out of place. The antique cherry bed is made, the matching wooden furniture is upright and unbroken, and nothing is strewn across the floor. In other words, it's the complete opposite of Cooper's room.

But even though all appears to be fine, the nagging sensation at the back of my scalp tells me something isn't right. Though I can't say what.

"She's obviously not here," Jack says. "Let's see if we can find the knife."

Cooper nods as he steps over the threshold and points to the door at the near end of the room. "The safe is in the wall behind the mirror. Let's start there." It's a good thing Beau made him memorize the combination last summer. Otherwise we'd be out of luck.

Shivering, I follow them in, my flip-flops sinking into the plush, stark-white carpet. The soft, natural fibers tickle my feet. It seems crazy, but the air feels denser and colder in here than any other room in the house. It's probably just because the air-conditioning is blaring and the room was closed off.

While Cooper and Jack get to work removing the wall mirror and opening the safe, I look for other good hiding places. Rubbing my goose-bump-covered arms, I peek into the open walk-in closet. Nothing's awry. Then I glance at the vanity table beyond, which is covered with makeup tubes, lipstick barrels, nail polish bottles, and an assortment of creams and lotions. If I was going to stash something really valuable, that's probably where I'd put it. Not in a safe, which is the first place burglars are likely to look. Pulling open the center drawer, I scan its contents. There's nothing more interesting than some foundation bottles, press-on nail kits, and wrinkle creams. Jeez. How many of these does one woman need? Especially someone in their early twenties who doesn't have a line on her face? Shutting it closed, I sift through the side drawers and find more of the same, plus a half-dozen bottles of platinum hair dye.

A couple minutes later, Jack and Cooper set the mirror back in place, scowls on their faces.

"No luck?" Though I can already guess the answer.

Cooper shakes his head. "No, it's filled with her jewelry but there's no knife."

Jack rubs his chin. "Is there anywhere else we could look?"

Cooper shrugs. "Maybe her bathroom?" He thumbs his hand toward a door on the opposite side of the room, past the four-poster bed and sitting area.

I glance in that direction. Something catches my eye. A tiny black drop mars the pristine carpet. The sinking sensation returns full force, repelling me even while it urges me toward the spot.

Forcing my feet forward, I head toward the other side of the room. Another, slightly bigger drop lies just beyond it, closer to the four-poster bed. Drawing near, a few more spots lie off to the side. "Guys..." My voice trails off as a smattering of black spots previously concealed by the bed come into view. I follow the trail that leads toward the sitting area. A biting, bitter scent pierces my nostrils, forcing me to breathe through my mouth. It's like rancid garbage, decaying mulch, and a filthy aquarium all rolled into one. Something deep inside my mind demands that I run from the room, but I can't stop my feet from moving forward. Rounding the corner into the sitting area, I gasp, sucking in a mouthful of the hideous scent. "Cooper, Jack, come quick."

A swath of thick, black goop puddles on the carpet, then trails toward the bathroom door on the far wall. It almost looks like motor oil except it's grainer and looks like it contains a few handfuls of coffee grinds.

Cooper and Jack race toward me.

Cooper stops short. "What the heck is that?"

Jack winces. "Ugh, what is that smell?" He covers his nose and mouth with his palm.

I shake my head. "I don't know. But it leads straight to the bathroom." I point toward the closed door.

Cooper swallows hard. "Maybe we should leave."

"Dude, I'm totally with you. But what if the knife's in there? We have to look."

As much as I want to race out of here, my feet refuse to move. My spirit guide clearly wants me to stay put, for what I'm not sure, but I'm guessing I'm about to find out. Deep inside my gut, confidence surges. Even though I don't want to, I can do this. Drawing a deep breath, I force my right foot forward, careful to avoid the black, sludgy substance.

Cooper's hand grips my shoulder. "Let me do this, Emmaline." His voice is grave and resigned.

Pacing toward the door, he steers clear of the goop. "Missy? Are you in there?" When no answer comes, he knocks and repeats her name. After a moment of silence, he tries the knob. It turns. Swallowing hard, he pushes the door open. His skin turns as gray as a dolphin in St. Helena Sound. Gagging, he covers his mouth and bolts from the room. A moment later I hear him retch in the hall bath, tossing his breakfast.

Jack's eyes are as big as saucers. "What's in there?"

"There's only one way to find out." Grabbing his hand, as much to support him as myself, I lead him toward Missy's bathroom, careful not to step in the tar-like muck. At the threshold, we exchange glances, our twin sense wordlessly guiding us toward what to do next.

"One..." Jack says.

"Two..." I add.

"Three," we say together, then duck our heads inside the door.

Jack's scream bounces off the tile walls, filling my ears, and echoing through my head.

Chapter Nine

Missy is lying on the black-and-white tile floor, rigid and stiff, her skin the exact medium purple shade as a morning glory bloom. Her mouth is stretched wide and her lids are pried open over glossy, cloudy eyeballs.

Racing to her, I kneel at her body and futilely call her name. Jack rushes to my side. "Don't!"

But I reach out anyway, grasping her violet shoulder beneath the skimpy strap of her magenta negligee, but it does no good. She's in full rigor, unresponsive to my touch. And her skin is as dry and unyielding as saddle leather.

There's no mistaking it. She's dead.

"I'm calling an ambulance." Jack leaps to his feet and races from the room before I can tell him not to bother. We need the sheriff. Or an undertaker.

For a moment, it feels as if time stops and the oxygen has been sucked from the room. Her clownish makeup—candy-apple-red lipstick, sky-blue shadow, and shocking pink blush—

contrasts with her navy-blue gums, bright white teeth, and riot of white-blond hair.

Suddenly, the world gushes back and all my senses are on fire. The putrid scent of decay soaks the air, entwined with the lingering fragrance of her strawberry perfume. Water drips from the faucet, slamming into the sink with the force of a missile, then echoes down the drainpipe. A burning, sour taste works its way up my throat. Trembling as my pulse rages, I peel my eyes away from her awful purple skin and scan the room. Aside from her nightie, which is smeared with black sludge, nothing else appears out of place. The knife is nowhere in sight. Out of nowhere, the dark, dank smells of waste, deprivation, and evil shoot straight up my nose and into my brain, jabbing a sharp, wicked pain behind my eyes. Shrieking, I clutch my head, then reel back and stumble out of the bathroom, careful not to touch anything.

Jack's on the phone next to the four-poster bed. He shakes his head. "No, ma'am, I don't think mouth-to-mouth will do any good." He gulps, clearly working to hang on to his pancakes and bacon. "Please, just send someone as fast as you can."

With a shiver he scans his contacts in his phone then selects one of the entries. Tapping on the speaker he glances over at me. "I don't think I can handle this one by myself, Em. You've got to do it for me."

"Do what?" Clutching my head, I rub at the stabbing ache as the phone rings. At least now that I'm out of the bathroom, the ghastly stench has begun to dissipate.

"Beaumont Builder's Development. How may I help you?" The receptionist's voice is bright and bubbly. She sounds like she's barely out of high school.

Oh no. Even if my head wasn't threatening to explode, I

wouldn't want to make this call either. I shoot a pleading glance at Jack, but he shakes his head, his mouth turned down in desperation.

Ugh. Sometimes I *hate* my brother.

"Hello? Anyone there?" Bubbly asks again.

Raging migraine or not, it's got to be done. At the very least, Beau needs the basic details, enough to get him home. I clear my throat. "Yes, um, this is Emma Guthrie at High Point Bluff. Is Beau there? It's really important."

"I'm sorry he's out of the office for the morning. Can I take a message?"

"No, I've got to speak with him. It's an emergency. Please?" I add for good measure, hoping she'll pick up on my misery.

She sighs. "I'll see if I can link you to his cell. Hang on."

While we wait, Jack and I exchange looks and I glare hard enough to let him he owes me big time. Finally Beau gets on the line. "Emma, darling. To what do I owe the pleasure of your unexpected, but very delightful call?" He chuckles the kind of laugh that makes my already queasy stomach twist.

I gulp. "I'm sorry to bother you, but there's been an… accident." My voice trembles.

"Accident? Good Lord, what's Missy up to now?" His voice is a low growl. I can almost see the grimace that's likely plastered across his thin lips. "What'd she do, knock down a wall or something?"

"No, it's nothing like that. But you really need to come home. Now." I could spit it all out, give him the gory details of what lies on his bathroom floor, but I can't bring myself to do that, even to him. Although he and Missy have had their fair share of troubles lately, this kind of news is likely to bring on a heart attack, or make him crash his car on his way home, endangering innocent fellow drivers. Better that he gets here safely first. The sheriff can fill him in on the rest.

"I'm in the middle of a board meeting at The King Center. Can't it wait?" He pauses. "It's not your Daddy, is it?" For the first time ever, I detect a hint of genuine concern for my father.

"No, sir. It's Missy." My throat constricts, making it nearly impossible to utter the words. "An ambulance is on its way. And so is the sheriff."

I can hear his anger simmering through the phone. "I'm about through with my wife's accidents. You tell that ambulance to go on to the hospital without me. I'll join up when I'm finished here. Or when I'm not so angry."

Crud. He's left me no choice. But how do you find the words to express something so horrible? "You don't understand. She's...gone." My voice breaks. I wait for some response but he doesn't say anything. Jeez, he's going to make me explain. I take a deep breath. "As in not alive."

"I'll be right there." The line goes dead.

Jack grasps my wrist. "Come on, we've got to get out of here." He drags me out of the master bedroom.

"To where? We can't leave. We have to wait for the ambulance."

"We're not going anywhere. There's something we've got to take care of before they get here."

My brain spins. "What?"

"Trust me." Pulling me out into the hall he calls, "Cooper? Cooper!" Silence. He calls again. A few seconds later, a low murmur comes from Cooper's room at the end of the hall.

Releasing his grip, Jack charges toward the sound. I follow. Cooper's in his trashed room, huddled in the corner, a look of sheer terror on his face.

Jack kicks his way through the rubble on the floor. "Dude, you've got to pull it together. The ambulance is coming. And so are the sheriff and your dad. We're going to have to talk to them."

Cooper shakes his head. He opens his mouth to say something, but no words come out. Just a jumble of strained sounds.

Jack turns to me. "Emma, we've got to straighten this room. Now."

He wants to *clean*? *Now*? "Why? Who cares what the room looks like? Missy is *dead*." I can't believe I've got to remind him of that gruesome fact.

Cooper makes a wrenching sound.

"Exactly. Which is why we can't let the police see it like this. If they realize Missy tore his room apart, they're going to wonder why. And that will only end up raising their suspicions about Cooper." He snatches an overturned dresser drawer and sets it onto its track, shoving it into place.

The logic clicks in my head, bringing everything into sharp focus. He's right. In a sick way, it makes sense to think Cooper might retaliate for her wrecking the room, or to try and conceal whatever she might have found in here. Thank goodness High Point Bluff is in the boonies. It'll take a few extra minutes for the ambulance and sheriff to arrive.

"Okay, but where do we start?" I will myself to ignore the headache that's causing my left eye to pulse and twitch.

Jack throws his hands into the air. "Anywhere. Just bend down and pick up whatever you can. Hey, Coop, you going to help?" He grabs another drawer and puts it in place.

Cooper doesn't flinch. It's as if he hasn't heard a thing we've said.

A surge of adrenaline hits my system, propelling me forward. There's no time to make the bed properly, so I figure it's best to camouflage things as much as possible. Wadding his bed sheets in a pile, I shove them into the near-full hamper, then drape the stripped mattress with the bedspread and set his pillows in place. It looks as good as new, at least at first glance. Then I scoop up his scattered clothes, cram them into each drawer without any care as to where they should actually go. As Jack rights the desk and replaces the drawers, I do shove the books back on the bookcase. They're not in any discernible order but at least they're all spine-out.

Just as we've finished setting up Cooper's laptop and printer, the ambulance sirens whirr in the distance. The room's not perfect, but at least it doesn't look like a war zone. I don't think I've ever moved so fast, not even when we outran the *plateye* hellhounds at the museum.

Wheezing for air, I kneel beside Cooper and place my hand on his. "They're coming. We're going to have to let them in the door and tell them what happened. Can you get up?"

He looks up at me, his hunter-green eyes rimmed with red and heavy with grief.

The sirens blare up the long oak-lined driveway leading to High Point Bluff.

Jack crouches in front of Cooper. "Dude, just get yourself downstairs, okay? We'll do the talking until your dad shows up. Think you can do that?"

Cooper nods.

"Good. Come on." Standing, Jack extends his hand to Cooper, who takes it and pulls himself up to his feet.

We race through the hall, then down the stairs just as the doorbell rings. Johnson and Briscoe, the two paramedics who helped Miss Delia after she was attacked, are at the door, a stretcher in hand.

"She's in the master bathroom. It's at the back of the master suite at the end of the hall." I point in the general direction.

"Would you like us to come with you?" Jack asks as they push past and mount the stairs.

"No thanks," Briscoe answers. "We'll take it from here. Y'all wait on the sheriff. He ought to be around shortly."

With nowhere else to go, we settle onto the upholstered bench on the side of the grand foyer, waiting for whoever comes next. Cooper grasps my hand, gripping my fingers as if his life depends on it.

"It'll be okay. I promise," I whisper.

He gives me a hard squeeze.

Jack's shoulders slump as if the adrenaline rush has finally worn off and the enormity of everything that's happened has finally hit him. "I can't believe it. Missy is dead." He stares down at the floor, his mouth agape.

A single tear runs down Cooper's cheek. Which is super weird. Of course her death is a horrible shock, but she was pretty awful to him, especially lately. No one would blame him if he didn't exactly mourn her passing.

I search for something to make him feel better. "I'm sorry for your loss. I'm sure you're going to miss her." Lame, but isn't that what you're supposed to say when someone dies?

Both he and Jack turn to me, their brows crinkled in confusion.

"Are you crazy?" Jack asks.

I shrug. "What do you want from me? His stepmother just died and he's obviously upset about it."

Cooper shakes his head. "I'm sorry she's gone. But that's not why I'm upset." He swallows hard.

"Then why?" Jack looks mystified.

Cooper draws a deep breath then exhales, bracing himself. "She looks just like my mom did when she died."

Chapter Ten

"What?" Jack asks, his jaw hanging as slack as mine.

Cooper never talks about his mother. Ever. So to bring her up now—and her death when he was just five years old—amid everything that's happening just makes it all the more jarring.

Cooper opens his mouth but then shuts it again and drops his gaze to the floor.

Sirens wail and speed toward the house. Jack and I spring off the bench and charge to open the front door. Two sheriff cars barrel down the driveway at top speed, kicking up gravel, then skid to a stop behind the ambulance in front of the Big House. The two deputies in the first car barely allow it to come to a stop before jumping out and racing up the front steps.

The first, a thick-necked, muscle-bound specimen of crime-fighting prowess, clasps his hand on the grip of his holstered revolver. "Where's the crime scene?" he asks Jack.

"Upstairs, hang a right, then head to the end of the hall."

Muscles and his partner fly up the stairs. A second later the

Beaufort County sheriff jogs up the porch steps, then wipes the soles of his buffed cowboy boots on the mat before stepping into the house. Moving with less urgency than his deputies, he removes his ten-gallon hat. His close-shorn gray hair sets off his light brown skin. "Morning. I'm Sheriff Walker. Beau home?"

I rise off the bench. "No, but he's on his way. Mrs. Beaumont's upstairs. In the master bathroom. The paramedics are up there, too." Swallowing hard over the lump rising in my throat, I point in the general direction of the growing commotion upstairs. Even from down here, I hear their shocked and almost excited voices. St. Helena's a pretty sleepy island so I'm guessing they don't come across many dead bodies. At least not those belonging to young people.

The sheriff nods. "Sounds like Goodwin and Thomas have it well in hand. But there's likely to be a bunch more folk coming through here and y'all probably don't want to be in the way. Is there some place quiet you can wait for Mr. Beaumont?" His lips curl into a benevolent but unmistakably lethal grin. Though he asked nicely, this isn't a request.

Jack nods. "Uh, sure. I guess we can hang out in the library. Hey, Coop, come on, we're moving out of here."

"Huh?" Cooper's head snaps up. He stares at us for a second. When Jack motions toward the library, Cooper nods. "Oh, yeah. Sure." Pushing off the bench, he heads across the foyer, his expression as flat as an ironing board.

"He's still in shock," I tell the sheriff, as if it's not totally obvious.

"I bet," Sheriff Walker says as he accompanies us to the library door. Ducking his head, he scans the room, then watches as we take our seats. Cooper and I share one of the huge, red-silk sofas while Jack settles into a leather club chair. "It shouldn't be too long. Soon as Beau gets here, we'll have a little talk about how you found her. Until then, I'm going to have a look-see around the house. You don't mind, do you?"

"No, course not." Cooper shakes his head and his eyes drift toward the window to stare out at the rose garden.

When Sheriff Walker steps away, a wave of relief crashes over me. Thank goodness Jack had us straighten Cooper's room. That mess would have definitely raised his suspicions. But then my stomach drops just as fast. The solarium. We didn't think to check it this morning and have no idea whether it's still the shambles it was last night before we left. Knowing Missy, there's no chance she cleaned it up and even less that Beau fixed it. What the heck is the sheriff going to think when he sees it?

Jack shoots me a look, his twin sense undoubtedly on full alert. "What's wrong, Em?"

"The solarium," I whisper, just in case Sheriff Walker's still in the hall, eavesdropping.

A deep grunt rumbles in his chest. "Dang. I didn't even think about that." Sinking back into the club chair, he rubs his chin. "There's nothing we can do about it. If they see it, we'll just say it's under renovation. It already looks like it's been hit by a wrecking ball. Plus, since her fingerprints are all over the place, we're safe. It can't implicate us like the knife."

As if he's just reminded himself of the real danger, Jack lunges forward again. "The knife. Was it in the bathroom?"

"I looked around and didn't see it near her." Then a horrible thought grips me. "Of course it could have been under her."

Jack sinks his forehead against his open palm. "Well, if it's up there, they'll find it."

"What if it's not?" I whisper, my brain spinning with the possible permutations.

Cooper pulls out of his trance. "Then someone else has it."

But who? Before I have a chance to contemplate that, a commotion erupts in the hall. Voices converge and raise, making it impossible to make out any words.

"Enough of this obstruction!" Beau's slurry voice booms above the rest and bounces off the high ceiling in the foyer. "My wife is dead! I demand to see her!" A strange, strangled sound erupts, halfway between a gasp and a stifled wail. If I didn't know he was soulless, I'd swear he sounded heartbroken.

Seconds later, Beau drags himself into the library, grunting as he leans hard against his cane. Huffing for air, he grumbles unintelligible words as he clutches his side with his free hand and hobbles toward the sofa facing Cooper and me. With great effort, he eases into the well-worn depression in the cushions as the wooden frame cracks and squeaks under his weight. As usual, the stench of rancid luncheon meat hovers around him.

"You'll understand that given his obvious distress, Mr. Beaumont won't likely be much help in answering your questions, though we'll be happy to hear what you can tell us about this tragic accident." A familiar voice, heavily accented and slick as oil, carries from the hall. I know I've heard it before but I can't quite place it.

A second later, Claude Corbeau glides into the library with Sheriff Walker. He's wearing the same blue-lensed sunglasses and sharp black suit from yesterday.

My heart seizes. What is he doing here? I shoot a glance at Jack then Cooper, hoping to grab their attention and give him some kind of warning, but neither look my way. Instead, they're both transfixed by the short, wiry man who seems to have the sheriff's rapt attention.

The sheriff smiles. "I understand. Though I do need to get

some basic information, but it should be pretty painless." He sits in a club chair across from Jack.

Claude takes a seat next to Beau. I hunch my shoulders and lean against the arm of the sofa, hoping he won't recognize me. But his eyes catch mine and his brows rise slightly as his lips part in a small smile. He knows exactly who I am.

Beau extends his bloated arm behind him, reaching for the scotch decanter on the far end of the console table behind Claude, but the bottle is just out of reach. Wincing, he recoils, then rolls back on the cushion. His breath is heavy and labored. "What's a man got to do to get a drink around here? I've just learned my wife is dead and I'd like something to calm my nerves." But his voice is so garbled he sounds like he's already drunk.

"It would be my pleasure, Mr. Beaumont." Claude rises to his feet. Without taking his eyes off me, he steps around the sofa, grabs a glass from the mirrored tray, and pours about two inches of the honey-brown liquid. "Here you go, nice and stiff. I know how broken up you are." He places the crystal tumbler in Beau's outstretched hands.

"Thank you, Corbeau. I don't know what I'd do without you." Beau gestures as if to wipe away tears, except there's no trace of liquid, sweat or otherwise, on his pasty face. Then he tosses back his head and downs the scotch in one gulp.

Jack's lids stretch wide as the name registers. We share a silent exchange of looks, confirming this is the same guy who showed up at Miss Delia's yesterday. Cooper must understand, too, because he shoots me a quick side glance and tightens his grip on my hand.

Burping, Beau slams the glass next to the ashtray on the side table and turns his attention to Sheriff Walker. "Let's get down to business, Walker. This here's Claude Corbeau, one of the finest investigators in the country. I brought him to St. Helena as a second set of eyes on the King Center robbery since y'all have done such a crackerjack job finding the robbers yourselves." His sarcasm is thick and, judging by the sheriff's prickly expression, hasn't been lost. Beau continues. "We were in a meeting at the museum when I learned about my beloved Missy. Corbeau's offered to help make sure nothing is overlooked." He lifts a balled fist to his mouth and appears to stifle a sob. But the whites of his eyes are as pale as always and there isn't a tear in sight.

Claude bows his head in some kind of grand show of deference to the sheriff. "I'm merely here to lend my expertise. This is, of course, your jurisdiction, but I'm happy to offer any support as necessary. Might I get you a drink, Sheriff?"

Walker puts up his hand. "No thanks. I'm on duty. And seeing as you're so keen to oversee our work, I wouldn't want to do anything to comprise the integrity of our investigation."

Claude grins. "Of course not! You misunderstand. I wasn't offering a hard beverage. It being July and all, and knowing how long you've been working, I thought you might appreciate a cool, refreshing drink. Surely that can't hurt, can it?" Claude walks to the bar and inspects the minifridge's contents. "I make the absolute best nonalcoholic mint juleps. Believe me, they're so good, you won't miss the bourbon."

The sheriff shakes his head. "Really, that isn't necessary."

But Claude gets to work anyway, filling a shaker with ice, crushing a handful of mint leaves, and pouring a mixture of liquids.

The sheriff takes a notebook from his back pocket and flips open the cover. "Now, Beau, when was the last time you saw

Missy?"

"Last night. Before we went to bed."

The sheriff arches his brow. "Not this morning?"

"No, I left for work just after dawn. We builders work around the sun. Can't afford to waste a minute of daylight. I often sleep downstairs in my study so as not to wake her." He folds his fingers over his wide belly.

"I see. And did she appear well last night?"

"Of course. She was just twenty-two years old. In the height of her prime." Beau sniffs, then leans over to extract a handkerchief from his pocket and rubs his nose. "She was supposed to care for me in my old age. As you can see I'm not exactly the picture of health." His voice breaks. "Forgive me. I can't believe she's gone. She was my angel." His chest shudders.

Jack, Cooper, and I lock eyes. Missy was a lot of things, but an angel wasn't one of them.

Claude carries two tall glasses of light green liquid the long way around the room, passing behind the sofa Cooper and I are sitting on, and offers a glass to the sheriff. "My famous mint julep, minus the alcohol, of course. It's my daddy's recipe." He beams.

"Thank you, but I'm all right." He raises his hand in protest, but Claude shoves the glass in his palm anyway. Reluctantly, Sheriff Walker takes it and rests it on the arm of his club chair.

Turning, Claude walks behind our sofa once again, this time stopping to grip Cooper's shoulder with his spindly hand. He leans close. "I'm sorry for your loss, son. This must be very difficult for you." He pats Cooper's neck and then ruffles the back of his hair.

Cooper twists around, releasing my hand as he does so, to address Claude face-to-face. "Thanks." His voice sounds breathy, vacant.

Claude nods, then glances at me, his eyes twinkling. He looks as if he's about to say something, but must have changed his mind because he goes back to his place next to Beau instead. Glancing over at the sheriff, he raises his glass. "Don't let that go to waste, Sheriff. My daddy would be mighty disappointed if I didn't impress you with his recipe." He takes a sip.

The sheriff tilts his head and stares hard at Claude. "If I didn't know better, I'd think you were a bartender instead of an investigator."

Claude laughs. "Nonsense. Even in this air-conditioning, it's still ungodly hot. I'm just trying to be hospitable. There's enough for your deputies, too, if it meets your approval."

I can't help but notice he didn't make any mock julep for us. Rude. Not that I'd take anything from him, anyway.

"You aren't going to quit, are you?" Sheriff Walker chuckles then lifts the glass and takes a sip. "Hmm, that's mighty tasty. You say this has no bourbon?" He smacks his lips a few times, savoring the flavors.

"Not a drop." Claude sits back and smiles.

The sheriff takes several more swallows. "There's plenty of mint and sugar. But what's your base?"

"It's a family secret, but there's a little of this and a little of that."

"Whatever it is, my compliments to your daddy." The sheriff raises his glass.

"Sadly, he's passed, but he's always with me in spirit." Claude smiles.

Sheriff Walker downs the rest of his drink and squints hard at his notebook, extending his arm from his face to make out the words. "Now, kids, as I understand it, you found Mrs. Beaumont this morning."

Cooper nods. "Yes, sir. I slept over at Emma and Jack's place last night."

Claude leans forward and his lips part in a terrible, snakelike grin. "Emma. That's a beautiful name."

Ugh. I can hear Miss Delia's voice in my head cursing the fact that he's learned my first name. But all's not lost. It's only my nickname, and my last name's still under wraps.

Beau laughs. "It sure is. Though not half as pretty as she is." He winks at me, then nudges Claude's arm with his meaty elbow. "You'd never guess it, but Emma and Jack are twins. Don't look a lick alike."

Claude shakes his head. "Not a lick." He seems positively delighted.

Beau continues, his chest gurgling with every excited word. "Their daddy is my caretaker. He and I used to run wild on this island when we were boys. The Guthries have worked for the Beaumonts for generations. Just as I suspect old Jack here will end up working for my son, eventually." His lips part in a knowing grin.

Jack shakes his head. "No, I won't."

"No, he won't," Cooper says at the same time.

Beau waves his hand. "That's what all the Guthries say. But time has a way of proving them wrong. Just ask your daddy about how he swore he was going north to make his own way. Yet when your momma kicked him out, where'd he go? Straight back here to High Point Bluff." He erupts in laughter, which rattles in his chest and kicks off a coughing fit that causes him to wince and clutch at his side.

White-hot anger boils in my gut. I hate when he belittles my father and detest even more when he speaks of my mother.

He has no idea what happened between them. No one does, actually, since neither one of them has ever told Jack or me why they divorced, but whatever the reason, it's between them. It's none of Beau's business, and it's certainly not Claude's.

Sheriff Walker clears his throat. "So y'all found her this morning?" He hiccups then covers his mouth. "Excuse me."

Cooper nods. "Yes, sir. It was quite a shock."

"I called 9-1-1 as soon as we found her," Jack adds.

"But it was pretty obvious she was…well, you know." I shudder at the memory of her lavender shoulder and blue-black gums. "There wasn't anything we could do."

"I'll bet it was difficult." The sheriff's stomach rumbles. Rubbing his uniform with his palm, he hiccups again, this time with more force. "Goodness, forgive me. I let Thomas talk me into the blue-plate special this morning at Daisy's. Looks like that wasn't the best decision." Chuckling, he looks back at his notebook, stares for a moment, then strokes the black-and-white whiskers in his trimmed beard. He looks a little confused.

Claude tilts his head and peers over his blue glasses. "Did you have any other questions, Sheriff?"

Staring at the paper in his hand, the sheriff bites his bottom lip. Blinking several times, he flicks his wrist, flipping the cover closed. "No, I think that about covers it." Though he doesn't look entirely convinced.

Seriously? I'm no supersleuth, but even I think there's plenty of stuff left to ask. Like for instance, was Missy sick or did she have any health problems? Did she take any weird drugs? Did she have any enemies? Plus a whole list of other questions a kindergartener could probably come up with. Not to mention a query about the solarium. He had to have seen that disaster area. Isn't he at least wondering what the heck happened in there?

Claude peers into the sheriff's eyes. "So what can you tell us? Do you have a cause of death?" His stark-white teeth gleam.

Sheriff Walker hiccups again, this time hard enough to shake his chest. "I probably shouldn't say anything until the coroner completes his examination." He scratches his head and looks around the room. "I suppose it can't hurt to tell you there were no obvious injuries."

Claude narrows his gaze. "So you're thinking natural causes?"

Sheriff Walker nods as he rubs his stomach. "Possibly, though you can never be sure without an autopsy, especially with someone so young." Another hiccup leaps from his mouth, snapping his head back. "Especially when we find an unusual substance near the deceased. It's usually best to wait for the toxicology reports."

Beau wails. "I won't allow my sweet sugar bee to be cut up." His chest shudders and he swallows a sob.

Claude puts his finger up. "What type of substance?" He bores into the sheriff with his stare.

"We're not sure, actually." He blinks a few times, then glances at his notes. "Black, tar-like. None of us has ever seen anything like it before. It could be something, or nothing at all. There's no way to know for sure until we hear back from the lab."

"And if you don't find anything, you'll be right back where you started. With natural causes," Claude says as if it's a predetermined certainty.

The sheriff nods. "Yup. Natural causes. Sounds about right."

Sounds right? Actually, it sounds pretty stupid. And hasty. Not to mention sloppy. Why wouldn't the sheriff want to conduct a full investigation before deciding what happened?

Sheriff Walker hiccups again, but this time, his lids bulge and his cheeks puff outward. "Forgive me, that scrapple is getting the best of me." He jumps from his chair, then scrambles out of the library. His footfalls carry down the hall. A moment later, the powder-room door slams shut.

Claude turns to Beau. "I think I'll check on the deputies' progress upstairs. I'm guessing they might need a little assistance. When I'm through, why don't we meet in your study to finish our discussion about the museum?" He pushes off the sofa, flattens the creases in his black suit pants, and straightens his tie.

Beau beams even though a minute ago he was on the verge of weeping. "Excellent idea, Corbeau."

My body hums with a sick, antsy feeling. What the heck is going on? Claude seems happy to jump into this investigation — maybe too happy. Doesn't he already have his hands full with the museum heist? Does he really need to get so involved in this one? And now that I think of it, the whole natural-causes thing was his idea. How did he get the sheriff to agree so easily? Maybe there was a little something extra in that virgin mint julep after all.

I have no idea why but I'm suddenly feeling as ill as Sheriff Walker. Desperate for fresh air, I could race to the windows and throw them open, but that would only keep me in this musty, old room. I've got to get out of here. Now.

I turn to Cooper. "I'm not feeling too well. I need to get outside and breathe. Maybe sit on the beach for a while."

He nods. "Sure. Whatever." But he doesn't meet my eyes; instead he keeps his gaze trained on his feet.

I pause, surprised he didn't offer to come with me like

usual. Normally he'd grab any chance to get out of here and flee the craziness of this house and his father's cruelty. But this is no ordinary day and it's not fair to expect him to act like it is. Missy's death was a shock, but it's obviously brought up horrible memories of his mother. He needs space to process this. But I need a cool sea breeze and the sun's warm rays to purge the queasiness churning my stomach.

Jack shoots me a look, silently asking if I want his company. I shake my head. Cooper needs him more than I do right now.

"Okay, I'll see you later then." I reach for Cooper's hand, but he pulls it away and waves good-bye instead.

"See you." Again, he doesn't look my way.

"Yeah, see you." Squelching the twinge of worry wiggling at the back of my mind, I rise to my feet and climb over his outstretched legs.

Exiting the library, I head down the hall toward the foyer. Just as I'm rounding the corner, Claude steps into my path.

"So, *Emma Guthrie*." His smile splits his face as he tucks something into his jacket pocket. "Such a lovely name. And a greater pleasure to finally make your acquaintance."

Chapter Eleven

I suck in a breath and blink, transfixed by his slippery, almost serpentlike grin. "Uh, yeah, thanks. Me too," I manage though it's a giant lie. In fact, I could have gone the rest of my life without ever seeing him again and I'd have been happy. But now he knows my relationship to the Beaumonts and my name, a fact that will likely flip Miss Delia's lid.

He looks at me expectantly as if he's waiting for me to elaborate or fill in some mysterious blank. But my head's spinning, propelled by the increasing stuffiness of the foyer and my growing suspicion of him and his motives. All I can think about is getting to the door that leads to the front porch, zipping down the steps, then racing down the beach path. It's so close, just a few long strides away across the wide-planked hardwood floor, except Claude's planted himself between me and that door, blocking my way. Drawing a deep breath, I remember Miss Delia's instructions to stay strong in his presence. Clearing my mind, I mentally block out my fear, then swallow the sick feeling swirling in my stomach, and stare back into his ebony eyes. Confidence swells in my chest, making it feel lighter, and easing the anxiousness that gripped me just moments ago.

Claude's lips part as if he's about to say something, but then Beau grunts, breaking the silence.

"Corbeau!" The tip of his cane strikes the floor as he lumbers out of the library. "You finished upstairs with the deputies? We've got work to do."

Claude pulls his gaze from mine. "Actually sir, I just missed them. They've already taken Mrs. Beaumont to the morgue. Sheriff Walker's on his way there, too."

Twisting slightly, I glance over my shoulder to see Beau chomp his soggy cigar. "Good thing. I couldn't stand to lay eyes on her. Better to wait for the undertaker to clean her up first." Beau's words are so cold and indifferent they sting. I never adored Missy, but natural causes or not, something horrible happened to her. Surely she deserves more care than that, especially from someone who supposedly loved her. Not that I'd expect him to want to see her all stiff and purple, but his words are a far cry from when he first came home.

Claude laughs. "Then you might want to steer clear of the bedroom until you hire a professional cleaning crew. It's a real mess."

My ear lobes prick as images of black sludge spattered against milky white carpet and Missy's pink nightie flash across my mind. How could he possibly think it's funny?

Beau chuckles and his chest gurgles with thick, mucousy fluid. "There isn't anything in there that'll bother me or my man Jed. He'll take care of it. Now quit fussing with Emma and let's get back to business." Shoving the cigar in his mouth, he winks at me, and then propels his body forward, navigating his enormous girth toward his private study.

Claude nods, then turns his sights back to me. "Until we meet again, Emma Guthrie." Brushing past me, he hustles after Beau.

A new, different type of unease bubbles in my gut, replacing the woozy, sick sensation I felt before. Now I'm confused, even angry at Beau's epic emotional flip-flopping. First he's whimpering, then he acts like he couldn't care less, and now he's laughing? What the heck is going on? Granted he's soulless, so maybe I shouldn't be all that surprised, but something isn't right. It's not like he's had a brain-ectomy, too. He's smart enough to rip people off in business while making them believe he gave them a deal. So how is it that he just accepts the sheriff and Claude's assertion that Missy's death was from natural causes? Why doesn't he want her to have an autopsy? And given his preoccupation with the museum robbery and missing Beaumont ruby, why didn't he ask if the house had been broken into? I'd have thought he'd ride that elevator of his to the second floor to make sure his safe hadn't been cracked, and perhaps look at the unusual black stuff they found on the carpet. But no, he doesn't seem to be the least bit bothered by any of these gaps in logic. Which is just plain weird.

A tingling sensation dances at the nape of my neck. There's something I'm supposed to notice. I gnaw my bottom lip and retrace my mental steps, considering the situation. Then it hits me. The black stuff. It might be the only thing that can explain what really happened up there. The sheriff took a sample, but judging by his apparent willingness to say she died from natural causes, I doubt he'll give it the thorough going over it deserves.

But I know one person who will. And with any luck, she'll be able to tell me if there's anything special about that tar-like substance. But I'll need to collect a sample of it first to show Miss Delia.

Glancing down the hall, I check to make sure Claude and Beau aren't still lurking around. They're nowhere in sight. Neither are Cooper and Jack, but I hear the soft murmur of their voices in the library. If I hurry, I can be up there and back without anyone knowing. There's no use in making a big deal about the black gunk, just in case Claude and the sheriff are right about Missy's death.

After racing up the stairs, I sprint around the landing then head to the master suite. The door is shut and draped with yellow police tape, but it only takes five seconds to remove enough to slip under and enter the room. Once inside, I head for the vanity table and grab an empty travel size bottle and the Q-tips I saw earlier, then slip around the bed to the first black spot. It's dry, as are the few scattered drops nearby. I follow the trail to where it's widest, a streak about three inches wide and six inches long. The sludgy substance has thickened, forming a skin on the top like a bowl of pudding left in the refrigerator without a cover.

Crouching down, I dip a Q-tip into the muck, piercing the film to find a bit of the still goopy substance beneath. A rank smell wafts from the sludge, a twisted combination of skunk road-kill and garbage left out under the scorching sun. Holding my breath, I screw off the lid and dip the bottle's lip into the crud, then use the Q-tip to scoop some of the substance into the bottle.

A throat clears, breaking the silence. Surprised, I squeal like a pig in a smokehouse, then look up to find Cooper standing over me, his arms crossed. How did I not hear him come in?

Careful to avoid the black stuff, I roll back on my bottom

and exhale. "You scared the heck out of me."

"Sorry. I thought you were going to the beach."

I nod. "I was. But then I had an idea and needed to stop in here for a second."

"You're taking your own sample." He motions his square jaw toward the bottle in my hand. "Why? The sheriff already took one."

"I know, but something about this stuff bothers me. I've never seen anything like it, and Sheriff Walker didn't seem to know what it was either. Miss Delia might have a few ideas."

He shrugs. "Guess it can't hurt. But I doubt she'll find anything." His gaze travels to the bathroom and back again, and then settles on the four-poster bed. The bedspread and pillows are untouched and don't even have so much as a wrinkle. His lips turn down slightly. He looks lost.

"You okay?" But that's sort of a dumb question because it's clear he isn't.

"I just don't understand." He doesn't look away from the bed. "It all so weird. But at the same time...familiar."

My scalp tingles with heat. I sort of don't want to ask, but now that he's brought it up, I can't help but follow through. "Do you mean your mom?" I push up from the floor and stand next to him at the foot of the bed.

He nods. "Yeah. She died right here in this room." He eyes the right side of the bedspread. "In her sleep. I'd had a nightmare so I came in early one morning and climbed in next to her. She was so cold." He pauses for a long moment as if replaying the scene in his head. "No matter how hard I shook her, she wouldn't move."

A sharp ache pierces my heart. I always assumed she'd been sick or something. I can't imagine how horrible it must have been to be just five years old and find her like that. No wonder he never talks about her. But there's something I don't understand. I inch toward him gently and lay my hand on his back. "But Missy died in the bathroom. What did you mean when you said she looked like your mom? Did they find this black stuff back then, too?"

He shakes his head. "No. Their expressions. They were the same." He shuts his eyes and swallows hard. "Mouths and eyes frozen open. Like their last moments were terrifying." He pulls away, steps over the spree of black spots, and sits on one of the armchairs in the sitting room area. "They said my mom died of natural causes, too." He drags his fingers through his golden-brown waves.

Goose bumps raise on my arms. The coincidences are frightening. And overwhelming. What is it they say about coincidences? That there are none? Missy and his mother's deaths might be separated by almost eleven years, but there's one common link. They were both married to Beau.

Blood pounds in my ears.

I'm almost afraid to ask, but I can't stop myself. "What if it wasn't?" My voice trembles.

Cooper looks up at me, tilting his head. "Wasn't what?"

"Natural causes." I bite my bottom lip. "What if it was something else?"

His brow furrows. "What else could it have been? I was little but I remember the coroner sat me down and explained that sometimes people die even though they aren't injured or sick. I know it's rare in younger people, but it does happen."

"Except now it's happened twice. Missy was acting crazier than normal but she didn't have any diseases. And there's no blood in here so it's clear she wasn't shot or stabbed. There's only this black stuff."

He stiffens. "What are you trying to say, Emmaline? Because I'm not following you." He uses my real name but this time it doesn't ring with his sweet, lilting southern accent. Instead, it's as sharp as barbed wire.

I screwed up once before by not being honest with him. It almost broke us up, and even worse, threatened to destroy our friendship for good. So no matter how hard it might be, I've got to tell him the truth about what I'm thinking. Drawing a deep breath, I square my shoulders. "What if your father had something to do with both their deaths?"

His brow creases, his expression is a mixture of shock, disbelief, and serious concern for my mental welfare. "What are you talking about?"

"Think about it. When someone dies, they always suspect the spouse. Because nine times out of ten, the spouse did it."

"But Sheriff Walker said it's probably natural causes."

"Yeah. Why is that, by the way? Could it have anything to do with the fact that Beau basically funded his campaign? Isn't it possible the sheriff is covering for him? What's to stop him from telling the lab to alter the results on this black slime?" I contemplate adding my suspicion that the sheriff may somehow have been unduly swayed by Beau's new friend, Claude, but realize how crazy it sounds, and decide to keep it to myself until I've got a better idea of what's going on.

Cooper stares at me. I'm not sure if he's considering my reasoning or trying not to erupt. Finally he speaks. "You know, I usually disagree with Jack about you and the emo stuff, but this time I'm not so sure."

My brow knits and my hands fly to my hips. "How can you say that?"

"Because this is my father we're talking about. You've just accused him of killing my mother and stepmother. He's not the most honest business guy in the world, and he's probably a candidate for worst father of the decade, but he's no murderer."

"Have you forgotten the Beaumont Curse? He's got no soul. If he can screw a Gullah family out of their land, and destroy acres of forest to build a useless golf course development, what's to stop him from killing a couple of his wives?"

Cooper's jaw tenses. "Can you stop and listen to yourself for just a second? The two have nothing to do with each other. Besides, what possible motive would my father have for killing them? He divorced his second and third wives after they left him—he could have done the same with my mom and Missy." He stands and paces the carpet.

"But Cooper, set aside for a second that he's your dad. Think about it. Two young wives with similar deaths. Don't you think it's suspicious? Or at the very least coincidental? In any other situation, the cops would be all over him."

"That's the whole point, Emma. I can't forget he's my father. Even for a second. He's disgusting and horrible but he's the only parent I've got. Maybe it's easy for you to write him off because you've got two parents who love you. And you've got Jack who's got your back no matter what. What have I got? Just my dad. If I let myself believe he killed Missy, then I've got to allow for the possibility that he killed my mother, too. And if that's true, and we can prove it…" His voice breaks as his downturned eyes drift toward the bed where his mother perished. "He'll spend the rest of his life in jail or fry in the electric chair. Either way, I'll be an orphan and even more alone than I am now." His expression is so sad it twists my heart.

"You'll never be alone. You'll always have us." My voice is

soft.

He laughs but it's hollow and flat. "Sure. But haven't you heard that blood is thicker than water?"

As a matter of fact, yes I have. From Taneea of all people. Which does nothing to bolster his argument. I cross my arms. "So that means you're willing to turn a blind eye to anything your dad may have done just to keep him out of jail, or worse?"

"That's not what I'm saying."

"Then what do you mean because you've totally confused me."

He sighs. "I'm saying it's not as cut and dry as that. It's easy for you to come in here, collect a bottle of whatever that crap is, and jump to all these conclusions because you have no idea how painful it is to lose one parent, much less two. Unfortunately, I'm not that lucky."

The truth of his words burns. Maybe I've been insensitive. This has been an especially difficult day for him and I probably should have picked my words or timing better. But that doesn't mean I'm wrong. I just have to be a little more delicate about the way I go about it. "Look, I'm sorry. I should have been more considerate. Maybe I'm wrong about your dad and what happened to Missy. But there's only one way to know for sure." I clutch the plastic bottle in my hand. "Are you okay with me taking this to Miss Delia?"

He peers at the bottle. Finally, he nods. "Yeah. Okay."

I smile. "Thanks." Then I hold out my hand. "How about we get out of here and go to the beach? The fresh air will do us both some good."

Ignoring my outstretched fingers, he shakes his head. "I'm going to pass. I want to stay in here a little while longer. Think a bit."

That's the second time he's turned me down today. *Don't push it, Emma.* "Okay, sure. No problem. I'll see you later."

He sits in the armchair and stares at his parents' bed. "Yeah. See you," he says without so much as a glance my way.

Chapter Twelve

Cooper pulls up to Miss Delia's house. He shifts the gear into park but doesn't cut the engine. Instead he stares out the front windshield, his gaze fixed on the enormous canopy of the bottle tree. He's been in a daze all day, nearly silent and unmotivated to do much of anything.

I can't help but wonder if Cooper's attitude has anything to do with what I said about his father yesterday. Under normal circumstances my suggestion that his dad might have killed Missy would be pretty unforgivable, but we are talking about Beau, which makes it almost understandable. Is it possible Cooper's holding a grudge? My mind wonders, but my heart says no. That's just not Cooper.

"Dude, you going to turn off the ignition?" Jack asks as he eyes the steering column. He rode shotgun this morning, stealing the front seat out from under me. I'm not sure what's worse, having to sit in the back, or that Cooper doesn't seem to notice I'm not next to him. "Hello, earth to Coop." Jack snaps his fingers next to Cooper's ear.

Cooper jerks his head toward Jack. "Huh? What?"

"The car's still running. I just wondered if you'd noticed."

"Oh, yeah." Cooper kills the engine.

Jack laughs. "I was worried for a second that you weren't planning on coming with us. Now that The Creep's gone, I'm all for hanging at Miss D's and helping her around the house, but from everything I've heard about that Taneea chick, I'm not psyched to hang with her on my own."

I'd forgotten they've never met in person. Leaning forward between the two front seats, I pat his shoulder. "Don't worry. I'd never sic her on you." Though if we're lucky she's ditched her great-grandmother again to go on one of her mysterious walks.

"What? You're not into crazy train?" Cooper chuffs out a laugh, but it doesn't have its usual lightness. But it's a good sign because at least he's trying.

"No thanks, I've had enough of that this summer. Though she is smoking hot." Jack grins.

I grunt as I shake my head. "Then you deserve whatever happens to you." Picking up my messenger bag, I open the back door and slide out.

"Miss Delia, I'm here," I call as I open the screen door and walk inside. Glancing around, I look for Taneea. She's not in the living room. A quick scan down the hall reveals the two bedroom doors are open and so is the door to the tiny bathroom. Since I'm guessing Miss Delia hasn't allowed her in the kitchen yet, she's not home. Bonus.

Flipping open my messenger bag, I pull out the glass vial that contains the first batch of my special tea, a custom blend intended to boost my energy and make conjuring easier. Miss Delia's spell book didn't have a specific recipe I could follow, so I created one of my own with ginseng for energy and, to strengthen my immune system, a few grains of paradise to ward off unnatural illness, and bearberry to activate my gift to heal.

After unscrewing the bottle, I swig a couple mouthfuls of the muddy-green liquid. The bitter, tangy taste zaps my tongue. Tucking the vial back into my bag, I shut my eyes and wait for a moment to see if anything happens. I'm not sure how fast it's supposed to work, but after thirty seconds, all I've detected is the sound of my own breath. Maybe it wasn't strong enough, or perhaps I should have drunk more, but so far I'm thinking this batch might be a dud.

I push through the swinging door to the kitchen. Miss Delia is rolled up next to the worktable, peering over her spell book. A few hot charcoal briquettes burn in the bottom of the ancestors' mortar. Their smoky aroma fills the air.

"Morning."

She starts, clasping her hand to her chest. "Lord above! You can't sneak up on an old woman like that." Her super-thick lenses magnify and distort her eyes.

"Sorry, I thought you heard me come in." I can't help but chuckle at how adorable she looks in those glasses.

She yanks off her goggle-like specs. "If I had, do you think I'd be gasping for air like a boo hag had been riding my chest?"

Ew, the boo hag, an evil creature that sheds its skin and slips into your house, climbs up on your chest, and rides you while you're sleeping, sucking the life from you. Most times, the boo hag siphons just enough to regenerate itself, but sometimes it goes too far, draining you dead. Occasionally, it jumps into the newly lifeless skin, taking over the body and impersonating its victim. It's sort of the Gullah version of a vampire on steroids. Normally, I'd laugh off the idea, but after the *plateyes* and The

Creep, anything's possible. Though I'm not super-psyched to meet their version of a zombie.

I swallow my laughter. "You're not really scared a boo hag will come in here, are you?"

She shakes her head. "Not in my house. I've worked too many protective charms for one of those foul, slimy creatures to get near. If one is foolish enough to come close, I've got plenty of salt and brooms to take care of them."

"Huh?" She's a master root worker and she's going to rely on *salt* and *brooms*?

"Salt burns their skin and will even kill one if you've got enough of it. Otherwise, you've got to draw the vile monster into the sun without its victim's skin and fry it up like a catfish."

My stomach churns. Up until this second, I loved catfish. Not anymore. "And what do you do with the broom? Sweep up the ashes?"

She smiles. "Believe it or not, it's to distract them. They're cruel, wicked creatures, but put anything with bristles in front of them, and they're putty in your hands. They'll count the straw on a broom until *dayclean*," she says, using the Gullah term for dawn.

I stare hard. "Seriously?"

She smirks. "Yes. They're devilish but easily distracted. That's why I've got a broom in nearly every room in the house."

Now that I think about it, she does. There's one on both the front and back porches, in the kitchen and living room, and even one in her bedroom. I thought she was just really into sweeping, but now I see there's another reason for it.

She waves her hand away. "Enough talk about boo hags. We've got work to do."

She's right. With exactly seventeen days till Cooper's

birthday, we're no closer to breaking the Beaumont Curse.

Without a word, I grab the bottle of citronella oil on the counter and dab it on my pressure points. I cleansed myself earlier this morning, but it never hurts to add a little extra lemon-fresh purification.

Out the rear window, I watch Cooper and Jack make their way into the overgrown backyard, a shovel slung across each of their shoulders. Cooper is also carrying a giant pair of pruning shears. They've decided to clear a path through the garden so Miss Delia can drive her chair around. As usual, Jack is jabbering about something, but unlike normal, Cooper looks preoccupied. It's almost as if he doesn't hear a thing Jack's saying. I'm worried for him. Missy's death has hit him harder than I expected. Though it makes sense, considering how much it's reminded him of his mother.

I pull my attention away from the backyard and switch to another, equally depressing subject. "So, I didn't see Taneea when I came in."

"Pfft." Miss Delia purses her wrinkled lips. "She left hours ago after helping me into my chair. Said she was going for a walk."

"You don't believe her?"

Miss Delia narrows her gaze. "Child, please. My great-granddaughter has about as much interest in exploring this island as you do joining her on a shopping spree at the mall. She's found something to keep her busy all right, but it's got nothing to do with sightseeing."

I don't know why I underestimated Miss Delia. Of course she'd know Taneea was up to something. But that doesn't explain why she's letting her get away with it.

"Do you think it's a good idea to let her be alone for so

long?" Because I thought the idea was to keep her out of trouble, not turn a blind eye.

"It's not my preference, but it's all I can do. Her mother shipped her here to *Sa'leenuh* to keep her off the streets of Chicago. She got her wish."

"Yeah, but as small as St. Helena is, she could still get mixed up in some bad stuff."

Miss Delia smiles. "Sometimes the toughest cases require the softest touch. She's new here and is still testing the boundaries. If I clamp down too hard and make her stay in the house all day, she'll run as soon as she gets the chance. Then she'll find some real trouble. This way, she's home every morning and night to help me get ready. It's more than her mother could get out of her." She pushes on her glasses and turns back to her spell book, a clear sign she's done talking about Taneea and her issues.

My pulse begins to thrum, throbbing gently, but definitely more forcefully in my neck. Maybe my energy tea is working after all.

With a shaky hand, Miss Delia grabs a pinch of powder from one of the crocks beside her and then tosses it onto the smoldering flames. The powder crackles as it bounces off the sizzling coals. A strong, bitter scent wafts up, reminding me of my mother's favorite Thai green-curry dish. And not in a good way.

Wincing, I cover my nose. "Ugh, what is that?"

"Rue. It's an ancient herb with the power to turn back jinxes. I had an idea Sabina could have found a way to reverse its power and used it set the curse." Her lips turn down as she stretches to reach another crock. "But it didn't even catch fire. Not for a second."

"What's this one?" I ask as I push the dish toward her. My hand trembles slightly but the effect is so faint, I doubt she notices.

"Burdock root." Her long, bent fingers dip into the bowl. A second later, the powder splashes on the charcoal. It ignites, but the red flame it creates is quiet as it slowly licks the remains of the pulverized root. The warm, woody smell of sawdust curls up from the mortar. She mutters something in Gullah, probably a cuss word too dirty for me to hear.

"Not enough power, right?" I think back on the explosions Sabina created in the *Psychic Visions*. Small but impactful, they were like pocket-size bundles of dynamite.

She nods. "Uh huh. Not hot enough, either. The flame should burn orange and yellow." Her glasses slip down her nose. She scowls at the mortar and taps a yellowed nail on the arm of her wheelchair. "I've tried nearly everything I can think of. I'm running out of ingredients."

"It has to be something, right? Maybe she used an herb that doesn't grow here anymore."

Shaking her head, she sucks her teeth. "There isn't a plant grown in the Lowcountry that isn't in my pantry." She trains her good eye on the shelf lined with apothecary bottles. "Which makes we wonder if I haven't been fishing in the wrong pond." Her milky eye flicks toward me. "Maybe she didn't use a plant after all. Maybe it's a curio."

"But you've got a ton of those." I point to the shelves devoted to magnetic lodestones, cat's eye shells, badger teeth, pyrite amulets, and hunks of black dog hair, plus a ton of other strange but magical items. "Why don't we just grind those up and see which will burn?"

"Because I don't think the answer is that simple. My curios

are powerful, but I'm guessing whatever Sabina used was filled with dark magic. And hard to come by."

"Oh." I slump into a nearby stool. "I suppose there isn't a neighborhood black magic shop we can visit to stock up on these nefarious items?"

"Not likely. The magic I'm talking about is special. It's homegrown and handmade with the most wicked intentions."

My heart picks up speed at what I think she's implying. I'd blame it on the tea except I'm genuinely afraid so my reaction is just as likely caused by the adrenaline. I'm up for a lot of things but dabbling in black magic isn't one of them. Fighting a curse is one thing. Creating one is another.

Stiffening, I draw back slightly. "You don't mean—"

She cuts me off, anticipating my concern. "Of course not. I've got no interest in working black magic, especially with you. I've only worked one real dark spell in my life, and though it was the right thing to do, I paid for it dearly. But I knew the price going in and it was one I was willing to pay."

I'd love to ask what she's talking about but I know better. If she hasn't told me by now, she's got no intention of spilling the beans.

She points a gnarled finger at me. "You, Emma, will not go down that path if I have anything to do with it. Your hoodoo practice is for good, based in love to save those closest to you. That's the way it's going to stay."

Good to know, because I'm not looking to cross over to the dark side anytime soon.

I scratch my head. "Okay, but what do we do in the meantime? If we need some black magic curios but can't make them, how do we get them?"

She draws a deep breath and stares out the kitchen window,

but doesn't seem to notice Cooper and Jack, who are working so hard they're glistening with sweat. Instead, though her eyes are fixed on something outside, she appears to be lost in thought, reliving an event lodged deep in her memory. A moment later, she shakes her head and turns back to me. "You just leave it to me. These aren't my only supplies."

Peering out the kitchen window, I scan the vast, weed-choked backyard. Did I miss something? The only thing out there besides my brother and boyfriend, and a bunch of plants, is a broken-down shed whose door is nearly hanging off its rusted hinges. Does she have a stash out there?

"Do you need me to get something for you? The guys have only just started clearing the field. I don't think your wheelchair can make it back there."

Her head snaps toward me. "You won't touch a thing. Not yet. Not ever if I had my way. But even I know sometimes you've got to dance with the darkness while you're waiting on the light. That's a fight for another day, when you're strong enough to resist its pull."

The hair on the back of my neck rises. For the first time I'm actually afraid of all this power and its consequences. But I'm sure of one thing: I need to build up my resistance and strength pronto. And brew a stronger tea.

Miss Delia pulls her attention back to the kitchen, and it seems, the present. "I'm tired. Would you mind cleaning up this mess for me?"

"Sure, no problem." Slipping off the stool, my foot nudges my messenger bag. Amid all this talk about darkness and black magic, I've completely forgotten about the sample of sludgy stuff we found on Missy's body. "Before you go, would you mind taking a look at something?" I reach inside and fish out the plastic travel bottle nestled in the interior pocket. Then I bring her up to speed on what happened yesterday.

She shakes her head. "Good Lord, child. How did you not tell me all this when you walked in?"

I shrug. "Because you were in the middle of something. And I suppose there's a chance Claude and the sheriff are right and it really was natural causes. Or something." I twist the top to loosen the seal and hand it to her. "It's just I've never seen this stuff before and thought maybe you'd have a clue what it is."

With a shaky hand, she draws the bottle close and lifts off the cap. The rank smell from yesterday fills the kitchen except the scent of rancid garbage and skunk roadkill has ripened into something truly ghastly. Now, along with those festering odors, there's a hint of fermented decay laced with death. If putrid has a smell, this is it.

She pulls the bottle away and coughs. "This was on her body?"

I blink my stinging eyes and nod, then take the bottle back from her and close the lid. "Yeah. And on the carpet in the bedroom. That's where I took this sample."

She knits her brows. "And the sheriff didn't pay it any mind?"

"Not really. Though they could have been putting on a good show, trying to see if anyone would admit what it was. But to be fair, it didn't stink that bad yesterday. It's…evolved into something truly nasty. Maybe I should have kept it in the refrigerator or something."

She scoffs. "I doubt it would have made much difference. Decomposition is a natural process. No matter how cold you keep something, it'll happen eventually."

I stare at the bottle of dried, chunky gunk. "Is that what this is?"

She nods. "Must be to smell like that."

"Have you seen anything like it before? Do you know what it is?"

She shakes her snowy-white head. "Can't say I have. But it doesn't take much to know it's not something you want to mess with. The stink alone is a warning to stay away."

My pulse picks up. "Do you think it's some sort of curse or something? Maybe it killed Missy."

Miss Delia pats my hand. "Don't let your imagination run ahead of you, Emma. Not everything has a supernatural cause. Sometimes, as strange as it may seem, things are exactly as they appear."

"But—"

"But what?" She shoots me a look that clearly tells me not to question her further.

Dropping my gaze, I flip open the flap on my messenger bag to stow the bottle. I don't understand why she's so calm and disinterested. After all her talk about dark forces, I'd think she'd at least be a little intrigued by this stuff. Instead, she seems as indifferent as Claude and Sheriff Walker. Which is weird, because I'd have bet she'd be as suspicious as I am of Claude's influence over the sheriff.

"Why don't you leave that vial with me? Maybe I can find some kind of spell to test it." Her voice is kind and sweet as she extends an open palm.

"Really?" I fish out the bottle. "Do you want to look now? I could grab your spell book and we could go through it together. I bet there's something in there that will help."

"Maybe later. When I'm feeling more up to it." She slips the bottle into the pocket of her housedress and then places her finger on her wheelchair's joystick and maneuvers out of the kitchen.

I spend the next few minutes cleaning up after her explosion experiments, putting away the crocks of ingredients, and cleaning the ancestors' mortar. Just as I've wiped its smooth stone and gold-filled interior, the front screen door slams. A moment later, raised voices carry into the kitchen. It's Taneea and Miss Delia.

"Tell me where you got that." Miss Delia's voice is firm but heavy with fatigue.

"It's none of your business," Taneea snaps.

That's it. I'm sick of her crap. Tossing my rag on the counter, I race though the swinging kitchen door to the living room. "What's going on?"

The scent of Taneea's spicy perfume smacks me in the face. It's especially strong, as if she just sprayed it on. Today she's wearing a skintight, black and white zebra-striped tank with a chunky belt over black capri leggings. Her neck is dripping with beaded necklaces and her arms are covered with bangles. But she seems especially protective of the quilted, white leather handbag that's slung over her shoulder, its handle gripped in her curled hand. An alligator-foot key chain dangles from one of the gold loops that connects the straps to the bag.

Taneea's upper lip curls as she takes me in, then tucks the key chain into the body of the bag. "Ugh. Why don't you go back into the kitchen where you belong?" Only it's not really a question. From her repulsed expression it's clear she wishes I'd go a lot farther away than the next room. Like maybe Australia. But I'm not going anywhere except to plop on the couch to monitor their confrontation.

"I'll ask you again. Where did you get that?" Miss Delia's

narrowed gaze zeroes in on the bag.

"In Chicago. Before I came here." Taneea's eyes shift down and off to the side.

Miss Delia crosses her arms. "Do I look stupid?"

Taneea's eyes flicker with light and for an instant she looks as if she might answer the rhetorical question, but sanity must take over because she keeps her mouth shut.

"Smart girl," Miss Delia says, and then leans forward in her chair. "Don't think for a second I don't know what comes in and out of this house. Now, this time I'd like the truth. Where did you get that bag?"

"On Hilton Head." Taneea's eyes drop to her patent-leather peep-toe shoes. "In a boutique."

Miss Delia's eyebrows shoot up as she grips the arms of her chair. "How did you pay for it?"

Taneea's jaw juts forward. "With a credit card."

"You don't have one."

"Yes I do. My mother gave me one."

"She gave it to me. For emergencies. And so far we haven't had any."

Taneea shrugs, but her eyes blaze with anger. "Why does it matter whose card I used? It's my bag, and it's not returnable."

"It matters very much. Regardless of who you grow up to be or how rich or poor you are, your character and integrity are all you'll ever have in this world, the only things you truly earn for yourself. Whether you stole your *maamy's* card or got someone else to buy that ugly bag for you, they're shortcuts to getting what you want. You won't appreciate—or deserve—that bag until you can earn it yourself."

Taneea rolls her eyes. "Please, spare me the public service announcement. Not everyone can be Miss-Goody-Two-Shoes like Emma over there." She tosses me a hateful glare, lingering over my cotton shorts and V-neck T-shirt.

Though I know it's dumb, I suddenly feel underdressed. And completely inadequate. Which only propels me to speak before I think. "Hey, don't be mad at me. It's not my fault you bought a hideous bag."

"The fact that you think this bag is hideous proves how little you know about fashion." She forces a condescending laugh as she strokes the gold chains hanging off her new purse.

I want to tell her exactly where she can shove that fugly purse of hers and her equally grotesque key fob. I don't care what she says, she's the one with a hunk of dead alligator dangling from her handbag. If hauling around a piece of a carcass is *fashion*, then I guess that ends my dream of walking the catwalk. Not.

She leans toward me, a smug expression on her lips. "Don't worry. Soon I'll have plenty of money to buy a hundred more just like it."

Miss Delia crosses her arms. "Really? And how are you going to manage that?"

Taneea smirks. "I stopped by the King Center today. That Claude guy gave me a job as his personal assistant."

Chapter Thirteen

Miss Delia's eyes narrow. "Claude Corbeau did what?"

Taneea shifts her weight and pops her hip to the side. "Gave me a job. So I can earn enough money to buy a ticket back to Chicago and get out of this prison."

"What makes you think your *maamy's* going to have you back?" Miss Delia asks.

"If she doesn't, I'll go somewhere else. It's not like I want to live with her lame husband anyway. Maybe I'll go back to Kansas City and try living with my real dad again."

Miss Delia sighs. "Child, no matter where you go, you'll never settle anywhere until you're settled on the inside."

Taneea rolls her eyes. "God, don't you ever get sick of hearing yourself talk? Seriously, who do you think you are? Some kind of Gullah Yoda?"

Miss Delia turns to me, her brow crinkled. "Yo who?"

I shake my head. "Never mind. It's a movie thing." Then I level my evil eye on Taneea. "Nice way to talk to the only person who'd take you in."

"Just because you suck her butt doesn't mean I have to."

Miss Delia throws up her liver-spotted hands. "Enough bickering." She points her crooked finger at Taneea. "You want to get a job, I won't stand in your way. But I don't like the idea of you working for Mr. Corbeau."

"Why not?" Taneea asks.

I'm so sick of her and her crap, I can't stay quiet. "Um, hello? Don't you remember his little visit here? He basically accused your great-grandmother of doing something shady with her donation."

Taneea smirks, causing the diamond stud above her lip to glint in the light. "Accusations don't mean anything unless they're true."

"I didn't do anything I need to explain or justify to you." Miss Delia's voice is deep and stern.

Taneea hoists her bag farther up her shoulder. "Then you shouldn't care if I work for him. By the way, I start tomorrow."

Heavy footsteps clomp up the walkway leading to the front of the house. A second later Jack and Cooper trudge up the porch steps. They must be finished in the backyard. Cooper wipes his work boots on the mat before opening the screen door. Jack follows and does the same.

Whoa. The air fills with the pungent scent of their hard work and sweat. It stinks but at least it's overpowered Taneea's heavy perfume.

Cooper removes his baseball cap, then folds it in half and shoves it into the back pocket of his jeans. "We cleared as much of a path as we could for you, Miss Delia. You should be able to roll your wheelchair back there now, but I still think we ought to lay another stone path for you. I'm afraid you're going to get stuck in the grass."

She waves away his concern. "I'll be fine. Besides, I don't have much need to go back there anyway. Maybe just one or two trips. Emma can handle the bulk of what needs doing out there from now on."

Jack collapses on the couch next to me and drapes his arm around my shoulder, unleashing the full brunt of his armpit stench. I catch my breath and jerk out of his grasp. "Gross!" I push him, unfortunately laying my hands on his soggy shirt. "And get off the sofa, you're going to make the fabric reek too."

"What? You don't like *Eau de Man*?" Jack laughs as he flexes his muscles.

I choke on the odor that's so strong I can almost taste it. "Not really."

Miss Delia levels her gaze at him. "Neither do I. Get up."

Jack springs off the furniture. "Sorry, Miss D." His eyes are filled with contrition.

She shakes her head as her lips strain to hold back a smile.

"Maybe you and Cooper ought to hit the shower before we go home," I say, not looking forward to the ride back in an enclosed car.

Cooper shrugs. "No point. We didn't bring a change of clothes." Turning toward Taneea, he breaks out into a mile-wide grin. "Hey. Nice bag. My stepmom had one just like it."

My earlobes tingle. For real? Since when did he like anything that was Missy's? Or even notice her stuff at all?

She beams. "Hey to you. I haven't seen you around much lately." She slips her hand into the white, puffy tote and retrieves a tube of hand lotion. Flipping the top, she squeezes a dollop into her palm and rubs it in, spreading the yellow cream across her knuckles and between her fingers. The fragrance is thick and musky. What's with this chick and her weird scents?

"Yeah, we've been busy." He lifts the bottom of his shirt to wipe the trickle of sweat from his brow, exposing his ripped abs and the tiny mojo bag I made to protect him from black magic. What the heck is he thinking? Maybe he's dehydrated and delusional from the heat.

Taneea stares at his perfect six pack. "Me too."

Jack nudges Cooper's side with his elbow and clears his throat.

Cooper drops his shirttail and laughs. "This is Jack. He's too shy to introduce himself."

Jack scowls. "Am not."

"Are too." I smirk, trying to keep the mood light. And to keep from yelling at Cooper for flashing Taneea, or at her for gawking at my boyfriend like he's supper.

"I'm Jack." He extends his palm but she leaves him hanging, apparently still fixated on what else lies beneath Cooper's shirt. Jack drops his hand and stares at her, likely waiting for her to notice the lull in the conversation. His gaze travels to her zebra tank. I don't need our twin sense to know he's debating whether to ask if she just broke out of the zoo.

Finally Taneea drags her eyes from Cooper long enough to give Jack a cursory glance. "Hi." Then she quickly steps toward Cooper. "You know we really should hang out more." She grips his biceps and bats her eyes, then giggles and give him a squeeze. "Wow. You're strong."

Fire roars in my stomach as my nails dig into the soft flesh of my palms. Without thinking I leap to my feet and gape at the sight of her skin on his flesh. A thousand words churn in my brain, crashing into each other, and causing a massive traffic jam that keeps them from traveling to my mouth.

To make matters worse, rather than shirking from her touch, he chuckles. "Thanks."

I try to say something but she's still caressing his muscle— and he's not shaking her off—plus my heart's racing a million miles a minute, so only a guttural grunt makes it past my lips.

Cooper's head tilts in my direction. For a second, his blue-gray eyes seem to register my extreme displeasure and distress but then he scratches his temple and the recognition seems to evaporate. He turns his gaze back to Taneea. "Hey, I've got an idea. I know you've been pretty bored around here. Do you want to come to my stepmother's funeral? It's not a party, but there'll be decent food afterward."

Jack head snaps in my direction and he mouths, "What the—" Which is exactly the same thing I'm thinking. I know Cooper is trying to be a nice guy, but this is way over the top. And totally inappropriate.

"Sure. Just tell me when and where and I'll be there." She grins and flashes me a glance.

"It all depends on when the coroner releases her body. I'll let you know."

"Great. Text me." She finally releases him to root through her purse for a piece of paper and pen. Leaning against his broad back for support, she scribbles a number, folds the scrap in half, and tucks it into his other back pocket, the one without the baseball cap.

"Dude, I forgot something in the backyard." Jack charges forward, his normally olive skin magenta, and pushes Cooper backward toward the front door. "I need your help."

Taneea yawns and pats her mouth. "I'm tired. You don't mind if I take nap, do you, Great-gran?"

Miss Delia hitches her brow. "Course not. You need to

rest up for that job of yours." Her voice is laden with so much sarcasm you'd have to be deaf not to hear it.

"Thanks. See you later, Emma. At the funeral party."

My breath quickens as I imagine smearing that smirk from her face but that would only convince her that she's gotten to me. No, she will most definitely not win this war. Cooper is *my* boyfriend. Not hers.

I plaster the fakest smile I can muster. "Right. See you then."

She pivots and saunters down the tiny hall to the second bedroom and slams the door.

I turn to Miss Delia, an inferno blazing in my gut. "Can you believe that? Who does she think she is? Literally trying to steal Cooper right in front of me." I'm so angry I'm surprised I'm not exhaling flames.

Miss Delia's eyes are cold. "You've got to put your boy problems aside. We've got bigger trouble in store."

"What could possibly be bigger than boyfriend stealing?" I sigh, exasperated and so wrapped up in my angst whirlwind that I momentarily forget the curse that threatens Cooper's soul. Which is horrible because as far as problems go, that's a biggie.

Miss Delia claps her twisted hands. "Get a hold of yourself, Emma. I don't give a hoot about who likes who, or who shows up at a party. Claude Corbeau has offered my great-granddaughter a job. Believe me, it wasn't because he thought she'd make a good assistant."

That jerks me back to reality. "Why do you think he did it?"

She sucks her front teeth. "I don't know. But I suspect it was to help him gain information on me. Who knows what she's already told him? Or what she might have said about what we do in that kitchen? In a big stone mortar." She glances toward the closed swinging door.

"But she's never worked a spell with you, right? Or seen you conjure anything?"

She shakes her head. "No." Wringing her hands, she continues. "But I can't be awake all day and night. There's no telling what she might have picked up while I was sleeping."

My pulse thumps in my chest. "So what can we do?"

"I'm not sure. Yet."

Chapter Fourteen

It took almost two weeks for the coroner to release Missy's body, partly because of all the tests that needed to be conducted, but also because Beau didn't seem in a hurry to pick it up. After all the X-rays, toxicology reports, and tissue and body fluid samples, her death was listed as natural causes because there were no discernible injuries and no unusual substances found in her system. Even the stinky, sludgy black stuff was inconclusive. The lab reported it was made of organic matter of unknown origin so their best guess is it was some sort of wacky, dead-plant-and-fertilizer-based skin mask she planned to apply but never got the chance.

Even though I've read the report a hundred times, something still doesn't feel right. I suppose it's technically possible for a healthy twenty-two-year-old to just drop dead, although it's seems pretty unlikely.

But there's no sense in questioning the facts anymore. Jack thinks I'm emo enough and it would definitely rub Cooper wrong. He's already on edge, what with his birthday just four days away and no viable cure for the Beaumont Curse in hand. To keep his mind off his potential tragic destiny, he's been lying low at the Big House helping my dad clean and repair the rooms Missy trashed. In the meantime, Miss Delia and I have been frantically searching for a *Break Jinx*, only taking this morning off so I can attend Missy's funeral.

Dad, Jack, and I take a golf cart to the Beaumont family cemetery at the far northeastern corner of the plantation, along the banks of a salt marsh. Usually, this place is off-limits. During our first summer on the island, Jack and I ventured here once, with Cooper, because he wanted to leave flowers on his mother's grave. But we never found it because I fell down an old dry well and nearly broke my neck in the process. After it took all day to fish me out and seal the hole, Dad banned us from visiting this part of the plantation unsupervised.

Though I remember that day with perfect clarity, I barely recognize this place. It's overgrown and wide swaths are choked with kudzu, the clingy, invasive vine that's the scourge of the South.

Which is totally weird considering how pristine my father keeps the rest of the plantation. As far as the eye can see, every shrub, ornamental tree, and flower, even the blades of grass are pristine and perfectly manicured. High Point Bluff is my father's pride and joy and the perfect outlet for his anal-retentiveness and neat-freakism. So why has the cemetery been allowed to grow so wild and out of control? It looks like it's been forgotten. Or willfully neglected. It would make a pretty awesome, though slightly deranged, painting.

I turn to Dad. "This place is a total mess."

He stiffens. "This is the way Beau wants it."

"But—"

"No buts. Beau's the boss and the boss gets what he wants. Simple as that."

I want to push it, protest that this is not the way to treat your dearly departed ancestors, but it's no use. Dad's not interested in debating the finer point of Beau's management style. My only solace is knowing that, like so many other things, it'll be different when Cooper is in charge. So long as we break the Beaumont Curse in time.

We pass Cooper's parked golf cart and walk deeper into the cemetery, past old, gothic-looking gravestones, to a tent that covers the open gravesite and offers needed shade. Even though it's still morning, the sun is already baking. A hot breeze blows off the marsh, carrying the scent of briny water, mucky earth, and dead fish, which doesn't help matters.

At the front of the tent, the reverend from a local church comforts a heavily made-up blonde woman in a spangly, purple minidress, who can only be Missy's mother. She's weeping and stroking Missy's closed casket that lies waiting to be deposited into the earth. I say a silent prayer of thanks that the lid is shut. I don't know if I could deal with seeing her again, especially since I have to make nice with my other least favorite person, Taneea who's apparently hitched a ride with Cooper. She's dressed for the occasion in a black, see-through crocheted minidress with a neon pink bra and sparkly hot pants beneath. Way to class it up.

"Emma, Jack! Come sit next to us." Taneea grins as she pats an empty folding chair next to her. She and Cooper are perched in the middle of the second row, amid a sea of empty seats. Despite Missy's gaggle of friends, none of them have shown up. Even Beau stayed back at the Big House claiming he couldn't take the pain of watching his beloved laid to rest.

Taneea's crazy if she thinks I'm not sitting next to Cooper. Jack reads my mind. After shooting me a quick glance, he takes the spot next to her and I squeeze past them, climbing over her outstretched legs. She's too busy slathering her skin with her stinky hand cream to tuck them in. Which is rude, but not as rude as polluting the air with that horrible musky scent. I don't know why she likes it so much. It's not exactly feminine.

When I take my seat, Cooper leans over and kisses my cheek. "Hey, Em." He seems stiff, almost robotic. We've barely seen each other over the last ten days. After so much time apart, I'd expect him to be a little happier to see me. I can't help but wonder if he's still mad about what I said about Beau. Or is it just the funeral thing? Or whether something else is up...

He and Taneea did look pretty cozy. An itchy sensation works its way up the back of my neck and a nasty thought worms its way into my brain. Is it possible there's more going on between them than meets the eye?

"Hey." Wary, I search his gaze but his light gray stare is open and unguarded. Which makes me want to kick myself for being so stupid and jealous. This is Cooper Beaumont we're talking about. The sweetest, kindest guy I've ever met, and my best friend for the last eight years. There's no way he'd hurt me like that. I exhale a sigh of relief. "It was nice of you to pick up Taneea."

"He wouldn't let me hitchhike. How cute is that?" She grips, then rubs his biceps.

Jeez, what's with her and all the squeezing? You'd think she'd get enough of that with the other guys she hangs out with.

"Way cute," Jack says, only he doesn't sound the least bit amused.

An acidic, unspoken insult burns my tongue. Ten seconds in

and I'm already sick of her. But I remind myself this is a funeral and try to be positive for Cooper's sake. Better to change the subject. "How's your job at the museum?"

"Great." Her tone is clipped, leaving an awkward silence hanging in the stifling air. Her piercing sparkles, mocking me.

"So what does a personal assistant do anyway?" I might as well collect a little intel of my own for Miss Delia.

"You'd be surprised." She flashes a prissy smile that lets me know that's all I'm getting out of her.

As expected, it's the world's shortest funeral. What is there to say about someone so mean no one besides her mom showed up to pay their respects? Not much it turns out, so after a few compulsory prayers, a short eulogy that proved the reverend had never met Missy, and a few words by us, it's over. We watch the gravediggers slowly lower her casket.

Taneea fans herself. "Can we go? It's so frigging hot out here I'm sweating to death."

If only.

Lost in his thoughts, Cooper doesn't move. He spent most of the service staring out at the Beaumont family tombstones. Some look ancient, their words nearly worn away from the elements and salt in the air from the adjacent salt marsh. Others are broken, slanted, and vine-choked. A few are carved in the shape of a cross, and one looks like a miniature version of the Washington Monument.

"Hello?" Taneea nudges him as she rises to her feet and pushes past Jack to the end of the row.

Jack stands and leans toward me, "I'll take her back to the Big House. That way you and Coop can have a few minutes of peace without her."

My chest swells with joy. For as much as Jack sometimes

hates sharing Cooper with me now that we're boyfriend and girlfriend, he's also ready to help when he can, too.

"Hey, T, you wanna come with me to the Big House to set up for the reception?"

"Uh, I'd rather go with Cooper."

"Actually, he asked me to take you. He said with your sense of style you'd know how to make it look really good." He plasters on his best snake-charmer grin.

"Well, he's right." She shoots me a quick sideways glance, as if debating whether to leave me alone with Cooper, but then a trickle of sweat runs down the side of her face. Annoyed, she wipes it off and turns to Jack. "Do they have air-conditioning up there?"

He grins. "On full blast."

"Why didn't you say so in the first place? Come on. If they want to melt, let them."

She and Jack head down the path to one of the golf carts. Moments later, they zip away to the Big House.

Reaching my hand to stroke Cooper's back, I ask, "You okay?"

"Huh? Yeah." He's quiet for a long moment before he stands and approaches my father who's busy folding chairs under the tent. I follow close behind. "Uncle Jed, where's my mother's grave?"

Dad sets the chair on a rack with the others. He walks up to us, squinting in the bright sunlight, and points to a section just past a cluster of live oaks that is coiled with kudzu. "She's over there."

"Thanks." Cooper pulls his Swiss army knife from his pocket, pries open the large blade, then heads in that direction.

Dad rushes toward him. "What are you doing?"

"I'm going to cut back that crap on her grave."

"No!" Dad grabs his arm, forcing Cooper to stop. "You can't. Beau won't allow it."

"I don't care what my father wants. If he won't take care of her the way she deserves, I will." Cooper wrenches his arm away and then charges toward the headstone.

As if fire ignites inside my father, his chest expands and his eyes fill with steely determination. "I can't let you do that." He races after Cooper and leaps in front of him. "Someday you'll run this plantation but today is not that day." His voice is low-pitched and gravely.

Who the heck is this guy and what did he do with my dad? I've never seen him so bugged-out before, not even when we came here when we were little.

"But she was my mother." The knife falls to Cooper's side.

Dad nods. "She was. And my friend, too. We went back almost as far as Beau and I do. But that doesn't change what Beau wants or my duty to follow his wishes."

"But why? What would it hurt to clean this place up?" Cooper gestures to the graves. "It's our family for cripes' sake."

"When you're in charge you can do things as you see fit. But until then, this site is off-limits unless I'm around." He narrows his gaze at me. "That goes for you too, as well, Emmaline. And your brother. Don't even think of being slippery and saying he wasn't around to hear me say it. Are we clear?"

I nod, stunned by his forcefulness. "Yes, sir."

"Good, now help me finish folding these chairs and we'll go up to the Big House. Maybe some of Missy's friends will show up for the reception."

· · ·

Cooper hardly says a word while we help my dad, or on the way back to the Big House. Though we sit on the rear-facing backseat together, he barely glances my way. When Dad drives up to the plug-in charging station, he cuts the engine and hops out, heading straight for the Big House.

Cooper goes to jump off his seat, but I grab his hand to keep him in place. "What's going on?" I search his pale gray eyes.

"Nothing. Why?" His tone suggests that's anything but the truth.

"You're acting weird."

"No I'm not." His gaze shifts down.

"Yes you are. We've hardly seen each other lately and when we do it's like you couldn't care less to be around me. And I still can't understand why you wanted Taneea here. It's not like she's family."

He pulls his hand from my grasp. "I just did, okay? It's my house. I can invite who I want. And for the record, the Guthries aren't actually family either."

Though true, his words hit like a sucker punch to the gut. A gush of breath whooshes out my lungs. "Yeah, but you don't have to be a jerk about it."

"I'm not. I'm just stating the facts."

I shake my head. "Wow. I know things have been hard with the Beaumont Curse still hanging over your head and Missy's death reminding you of your mom. And it's pretty clear you're still ticked about what I said about your dad and Missy. I'm sorry I hurt you, but I can't sugarcoat what I think. Maybe some couples do, but that's not us. We've always been honest with each other."

"Why do you have to bring my father into this again? The coroner's report said Missy died from natural causes." His eyes are icy.

I level my gaze. "Are you kidding me? After everything we've been through this summer, why are you so willing to take things at face value? Can't you see the weird similarities between your mom's death and Missy's? And don't you think it's strange that your dad doesn't care enough about her memory to at least keep her grave cleared?"

He runs his fingers through this thick, golden-brown curls. "How am I supposed to know? I'm sure he's got his reasons. It doesn't mean he's a murderer."

I search his face. It's rigid, almost fierce. And not my Cooper. I recoil. "Since when did you start defending Beau?"

And then a devastating thought hits me, sending a chill over my body even though it's nearly a hundred degrees. What if the Beaumont Curse is starting to set in early? Cooper's birthday is four days away, but no one ever said there was a precise start date to the curse, only that it would take hold when Cooper came into his manhood. What if that's now?

I yank open the top button of his shirt.

"What are you doing?"

"Checking something." I reach in and grasp the mojo. Clutching the small bag in my palm, I close my eyes and breathe deep, clearing my mind of all negative thoughts. Its electric energy flows through me, dancing up my arm and through my heart. Its power is strong. At least for now. I pull back my hand.

He looks at me like I've lost my mind. "You done?"

I nod. "Yes. You haven't taken that thing off have you?"

"Just to shower. Why?"

I consider sharing my suspicion but given the situation,

it'll likely only add insult to injury. I know I promised to be honest with him at all times—and I fully intend to—when I'm absolutely sure I'm right. "Just make sure you wear it. It's still working so it should protect you from all forms of black magic. But still, we can't be too careful. Your birthday is really close."

"Yeah. I know."

I grab both his hands in mine and peer straight into those cool gray eyes. "Hey, you promised you wouldn't give up without a fight. I need you to stay focused."

He blinks. The creases in his brow relax and his gaze softens. Gently, he grasps my hands, entwining my fingers in his. My shoulders ease. He's my Cooper again. "I will, Emmaline. I don't want to lose you. Or myself." He smiles, and then dips his head to place a kiss on my knuckles.

Warmth spreads over my chest. "Miss Delia and I are going to break the curse. I promise."

I sincerely hope it's the truth.

We hop off the cart and walk hand in hand up the path to the Big House. Cooper's muscular hand feels warm and strong against mine. I've missed this. After we've figured out this curse thing, we're definitely going to have to spend more time together.

As we make our way up the driveway we pass a string of fancy luxury cars. Some of Missy's friends have decided to show up for the reception after all. Figures. Why bother with the sad funeral when you can party instead? Then I notice the shiny, vintage Lincoln. A pit forms in my stomach. Claude's here. What a way to make the day go from bad to worse.

I point to the car. "Why do you think Claude's here today?"

He shrugs. "Who knows? My dad's probably mixing business with personal stuff. As usual."

"I don't like him."

"My dad? Who does?"

I chuckle. "No, Claude. There's something not right about him. And I think it goes beyond his museum investigation." I'd say more, but I'm not sure Cooper's ready to hear the full depth of my suspicions. Plus I don't have any real proof.

"You're just being protective of Miss Delia. But that's what I love about you. You're always thinking of everyone else." He stops and cups my face in his palms, then plants a kiss on my lips. It's nothing like that pathetic, robotic kiss he offered earlier at the gravesite. This time his soft lips yield to mine and send waves of tingles over my flesh. I reach my arms around his back and caress his broad muscles.

I suddenly realize we're in the middle of the walkway that leads to the Big House, in full view of anyone who might look out one of the many front windows. Even though we're dating, it's probably not what a bunch of mourners are interested in seeing. I pull away slightly, just enough to break the kiss.

"Listen, we better save this for later. Someone might see us."

He wipes my bottom lip with his thumb and smiles. "Who cares?" His half-veiled eyes are so gorgeous I can barely stand it.

"I don't. But what about your dad or his guests?" I catch my breath.

"What about them? You're my girl, Emmaline. If I want to kiss you in front of the whole state of South Carolina, I will." He steps close and plants an even deeper, hotter kiss, causing my head to swoon and legs to wobble. His scent, a mix of fresh, piney deodorant and salty sea air envelops me, nearly dragging me under. I reach my arms around his neck and give in as his tongue grazes mine. Turning his head, he trails a line of kisses along my jaw, making his way to the soft spot just behind my ear.

My skin sizzles with energy.

But then another strange sensation makes its way up from the nape of my neck, pricking my scalp as it makes its way to the crown. A deep sense of foreboding constricts my chest. Suddenly the pricks intensify until it feels as if a thousand needles are jabbing at my head. My eyes fly open.

Taneea's standing in the window, staring at us, her arms crossed, and a scowl on her pink lips.

Talk about a buzzkill.

Feeling like I've been caught with a forbidden box of chocolates, I gasp, then unlock my hands from around his neck and step back. Which is totally ridiculous because he's my boyfriend for cripes' sake. We weren't doing anything wrong. In fact, people in a relationship are *supposed* to kiss. Still I can't shake the creeping sense that I've broken some sort of rule.

"What's wrong?" Cooper gazes into my eyes.

"Nothing. Except Taneea's watching us like some kind of perv." I gesture to the window behind him.

"For real?" He turns his head to look at the window.

But Taneea must either be able to read his mind or know what's coming because she loses the scowl and replaces it with a big, juicy, fake grin and waves like an idiot.

He holds his hand up and returns the gesture. "Can you two be nice?" he asks, under his breath and barely moves his lips. "Just for a little while?"

"Sure, so long as she stays out of my way." I laugh.

Squeezing my hand, he pulls me toward the front porch steps. We climb them together, our legs in perfect tandem, then push open the double doors.

Once inside, I set all those mushy-gushy feelings aside and start scoping out for Claude. And, while I'm at it, for Taneea, too, if only to avoid whichever room she's in. She's not in the front parlor and the foyer is empty. The sounds of chatter and tinkling glass carry from the end of the hall. Everyone must be in the Great Room. Cooper and I follow the sound, our hands entwined, ready to get the last part of this day over with.

Beau's reclined in the crook of a sofa, doing his best imitation of a grieving husband for the assembled guests who have formed a circle around him. His face is paler than normal and smattered with blotchy red spots. And his eyes are puffy, no doubt from the tears that are streaming down his cheeks. Reaching his plump hands to his eyes, he dabs at the fluid with an already soggy handkerchief. Under the pressure of his heavy fingers, his face sags, his flesh almost drooping and then snaps back when he withdraws his hand. Then he throws his head back and emits a mournful sob, his chest trembling as he sucks in a few breaths of air. But something catches in his throat and he starts to cough. Clutching his side, he rolls forward, spewing phlegm into his handkerchief.

One of Missy's friends, a redhead in a green sundress and spindly heels, scampers to his aid. "Oh, Beau. I know this is hard on you." She snatches a handful of tissues from the box on the coffee table and thrusts them at him.

"Thanks, Darla. I just can't believe my angel is gone."

Darla wiggles around the table and plants herself next to him on the sofa. "There, there." She reaches her ringless hand to pat his enormous arm.

Jack sides up to Cooper and me. "What the heck took you so long?" he says through clenched teeth, his lips fixed in a sugary smile. "Do you realize how long you've left me alone with Taneea? And Beau? Between the two of them, I was about to lose my mind."

I lean toward him. "Sorry, but we had a couple things to work out."

"Everything okay?" he asks me and Cooper.

Cooper smiles and smacks his arm with one of those quasi-guy hugs. "Yeah, bro. Everything's great." He glances at his supposedly grieving father. "How long has my dad been like this?"

Jack rolls his eyes. "Since the guests arrived. Just after Taneea and I helped set up the buffet and drinks." He thumbs his fist toward the bar where my father stands ready to mix cocktails. Taneea's talking to him, coiling a pink strand around her finger. She points to a few bottles on the bar behind him then giggles, no doubt asking if she can try some. Dad shakes his head. Based on the stone-cold expression on his face, he's figured out her game. She won't be getting any samples out of him. Awesome.

I scan the crowd, but aside from the Missy clones and their antique husbands, I only see Beau. "Where's Claude?" I ask Jack.

He shakes his head. "I haven't seen him. Why?"

"Because I thought I saw his car outside."

He shakes his head. "Doubt it. I bet one of these geezers has an old town car or something that looks similar."

Taneea saunters up to us with a pink drink in her hand. "So I know it's a funeral and all, but this party's lame." She takes a sip from the martini glass.

"What are you drinking?" I ask.

"A cosmo."

I snort. "With alcohol?" I'd bet my pinkie toe my father didn't pour her a drop.

She sighs. "The loser bartender doesn't have the right vodka or Cointreau, so he left them out." She draws another sip.

I nod. "Really? So then you're saying *my dad* mixed you a cranberry juice with lime?" I'm surprised I even remember what goes into that drink, but I've helped my father at enough of Beau's parties to have learned by osmosis.

She glares at me. "Yeah, I guess." Glancing at Dad, she smirks. "So your father's a gravesite helper and a bartender, too. How versatile."

Jack's head whirls around so fast, I'm afraid it'll snap. "And he's the caretaker, too. Got anything clever to say about that?"

She snorts. "I guess not." Her attention drifts to the buffet. "I'm hungry. Want something, Cooper?"

"No thanks. I don't have much of an appetite," he says.

"Your loss." Her lips part in a wicked grin as she turns toward the buffet and takes a step, but her espadrille catches on the rug and she wobbles, flailing her arms to keep her balance. Her cranberry juice mocktail splashes the front of my new sundress, its bright pink instantly staining the pale blue cotton. She squeals as she teeters toward the Oriental rug, but Cooper lunges forward, scooping her up before she face plants, then sets her straight.

I gape at the huge, clingy, pink stain that covers my abdomen and trickles down the skirt.

"Oh my gosh! Thanks, Cooper. Those muscles really do come in handy," she gushes.

"Look what you did!" I gesture to the juice that somehow managed to land only on me. There isn't even a drop on the carpet.

"Oh no!" Cooper races to the bar to grab some napkins. Jack follows.

Taneea clamps her hand across her mouth. "Wow. That

sucks. At least it wasn't a good dress." She snickers.

"What did you say?"

She smirks. "Come on, it's not like it's from a collection. I bet you can get something like it down at the Picky. Though I've never been inside, so that's just a guess."

We did buy it at the cramped local department store that's filled with stuff left over from two years ago, which only makes her comment sting more.

Rage surges from my toenails, straight through my body, and up to my brain. "Right. Because you buy all your clothes from tacky-and-inappropriate-dot-com."

Cooper and Jack come back, each with a wad of napkins. Jack holds out his hand, hovering over my midsection. He looks as if he'd like to blot the liquid but isn't sure which parts might be safe to touch.

With a grunt, I grab the napkins and peel the soaked and clingy fabric off my stomach. Dabbing a few times, the thin paper absorbs a bit of the liquid but not enough to make a real dent. This isn't going to work. "I need to rinse this out for real before it sets. I'll be back."

Pushing through the great room, I stomp down the hall, and head to Cooper's room. There, I can strip off the dress and borrow some of his clothes while I rinse it out with soap. As Taneea so kindly pointed out, this is an off-the-rack dress made of cotton so thin it should only take a few minutes to dry in the dryer.

Nearing the foyer, I hear a door creak and stop short as the hair rises on my arms. I'm sure the sound came from around the corner, in the hall that leads to the west wing. The only door nearby is the one to Beau's private study. Which no one's allowed to enter without him. It's so private, he keeps the key on a chain attached to his pocket. After eight summers in the Lowcountry, Jack and I have never been inside that room. Come to think of it, I doubt Cooper has either. And since Beau's still in the great room earning his Oscar, I know it can't be him.

Tiptoeing toward the corner, I peek my head out. Claude steps from the study and pulls the door shut behind him, then twists the knob to make sure it's locked. He looks first to his right, then turns left. I jerk back, and listen to my heart pulse, praying I moved fast enough for him to miss me.

"Miss Emma Guthrie," Claude calls out.

Dang. Not quick enough.

He sings my name again. "I know you're there. Come out."

Gulping, I force myself to walk around the corner. He's standing in front of the study, his black suit perfectly creased, and wearing his blue-lensed sunglasses even though he's inside. My legs tremble as Miss Delia's words echo in my head reminding me to be strong. Drawing a deep breath, I reach under my collar to rub the blue and pink beads on my *collier*, which are supposed to help me connect with my spirit guide. With her at my side, I'm not technically alone with Claude. A calm rushes over me, starting at my hair follicles, tumbling down to my toenails. Forcing my shoulders back, I quicken my pace. "That's Beau's study." I point to the door.

His lips slip open over his ultra-bright smile. "You're correct."

"His *private* space. No one's allowed in there without him."

"I was just meeting with him."

"Really? Because I just left him in the great room. He's been in there awhile crying about Missy."

His gaze drops to my dress. "Pity, you've had some sort of accident."

As if that's going to deflect my attention from his trespass. Fat chance. Still, my hand clutches the moist spot on my midsection. "Yeah, your assistant tripped and spilled her drink."

He shakes his head as he clucks his tongue. "Clumsy girl. You really ought to stay out of her way. There's no telling what kind of trouble she could cause."

I nod. "Thanks. I'll keep that in mind."

Claude's brow arches above his lenses. "I wonder, Miss Emma, if you find it as interesting as I do that you are acquainted with the Beaumonts and Miss Whittaker?"

"I can't really say, since I don't know how interesting you think it is. This is a small island. Just about everyone knows everyone. And it doesn't explain why you were in Beau's study without him."

Claude rubs his chin with his long, spindly fingers. "It is a small island. Tell me, how does someone like you come to know someone like Miss Delia?"

What he's really asking is how a little white girl like me— or as the Gullah say, a *buckruh* would come in contact with an old Gullah woman. But I'm not going to honor that kind of a stupid question with an answer. "I don't know. I've spent the last eight summers on St. Helena. Who can remember how they met everyone they know?"

"Oh, I suspect you could if you tried."

I shake my head. "Nope, nothing comes to mind."

He leans close, way past the boundary of my personal space and whispers in my ear. "Let me offer you a bit of advice. You may want to steer clear of your dear old friend. My investigation of the museum robbery is far from over and I've developed some promising leads that all seem to end at her rickety doorstep. When I'm through, she may be looking at hard time."

He chuckles. "Though of course, given her advanced age she isn't likely to have much of that left. I'd hate for you to get caught up in this nasty business."

I take a step back. "Do you seriously think a feeble, old lady in a wheelchair broke into the museum?" I work to sound extra snarky and indignant, but the tiny tremor in my voice reveals how scared I am of his power.

"Perhaps. And maybe she had some coconspirators. You never know who an investigation like this may implicate. It's one of the great joys of this job. The mystery." He nudges closer. "The hunt. The capture." His cologne hangs in the air, a nauseating mixture of patchouli, burned smoke, and a hint of something that reminds me of a Jolly Rancher candy.

Realizing I can turn the tables on him, I cross my arms and stand my ground. "You only have this job because of Beau. What do you think he'd say if he knew you were in his study? I'm betting he'd wonder how you got in, seeing as he's got the key literally chained to his body at all times."

Claude's reptilian smile slips for just a second. "How do you know my visit isn't part of my job? Perhaps my investigation has led me to look at the most unusual of suspects. Perhaps even the victims themselves."

"Huh? How's that supposed to work?"

"Can you imagine the real culprit might hire me to redirect the investigation and throw suspicion off themselves? Mr. Beaumont is one of the chief donors to the King Center, which stands to earn a substantial insurance settlement as a result of the robbery. As for his private concerns about a burglary here at High Point Bluff, well, the payout for a stolen ruby of that caliber would be substantial."

I snort. "You'd really turn on your boss like that? Beau got you this job. Without him, you wouldn't even be here."

"Oh, I suspect I would have found a way to St. Helena eventually. Mr. Beaumont may have brought me to this island, but my only allegiance is to righting wrong. A heinous crime was committed on this island, and I'll stop at nothing to make the culprit pay."

Whoa, and I'm the emo one? Okay, so we stole a couple of artifacts—one of which had been stolen from its rightful owner—what we did wasn't totally right, but it wasn't exactly what I'd call heinous, either.

"Trust me, Beau Beaumont didn't rob the museum or steal his own family's ruby necklace."

"No, but perhaps your father, Jed did. He is Beau's sole employee, is he not? Ever loyal. Perhaps to a fault."

My heart seizes. In a matter of moments, he's gone from threatening to prosecute Miss Delia to dragging Beau and my father into this. I remember how he nudged Sheriff Walker into thinking Missy's death was from natural causes. I'm not sure how he accomplished that little trick, but there's nothing stopping him from unleashing his power to mess with my dad. And since the sheriff seems inclined to do whatever Claude wants, my dad will be in the slammer faster than he can spell turpentine.

"That's impossible. My father would never do anything like that. Ever."

He shrugs. "I only go where the evidence leads me. Now, you can either tell Beau you saw me in his study and risk where I might take my investigation, or we can forget this entire conversation ever took place and I can get back to my job."

I don't have a choice, do I? If I say anything about Claude being in the study, there's no telling what accusations he'll lodge against Beau and my dad. I almost couldn't care less about what happens to Beau, though he shouldn't be arrested for something he didn't do. It's my dad I worry about. He's just the caretaker who's got nothing to do with Beau's shady dealings or what Cooper, Jack, and I did this summer.

My shoulders droop as I step aside. "I guess we're done here."

"Nice necklace, by the way. I haven't seen anything like that since I was in Louisiana." He brushes past me and slithers down the hall toward the great room.

I grind my teeth. He may have won this round, but there's no way he'll win the next. I've got hoodoo magic and the element of surprise on my side. And I fully intend to use them.

But first, I've got to warn Miss Delia.

Chapter Fifteen

Except I can't do anything until I take care of my soaked and still-clinging dress. I charge up the stairs to Cooper's room, tear it off, and blot the remaining cranberry juice on my skin with a towel he left tossed on his bed. Then I throw open his dresser and root for some clothes that might fit me. The best I can find is a pair of running shorts with an elastic waistband and a too-big T-shirt that hangs off my shoulders like a sack.

There's no time to rinse this chintzy sundress. Instead, I ball it up and tuck it under my arm, then race back to the great room. Taneea is nestled in the corner of the sofa next to Cooper, and Jack's perched on the arm, tracking her every move. Claude and Beau are deep in conversation on the opposite sofa. Though Claude's still wearing those god-awful blue sunglasses, I feel the weight of his stare as I cross the room to where Cooper and Jack are.

I sit on the coffee table and lean close, keeping my voice low to prevent Claude from overhearing. "Hey, guys, listen. There's something we've got to do."

Taneea snorts. "Nice outfit."

I glare at her.

"Hey, those are mine," Cooper says.

I furrow my brow. "And?" Since when is it a problem that I borrow some of his clothes? He always lets me wear his shirt as a cover-up at the beach.

"Am I going to get them back? That's one of my favorite shirts."

Is he for real? "Uh, yeah, as soon as I wash it. But right now I *need* to go. Like now."

He gestures toward the door. "Okay. So go."

"But I need you to take me."

His face falls flat and his eyes—now the soft gray hue of a pussy-willow catkin—look hollow. "I'm exhausted. Can't we go tomorrow?"

Taneea strokes his arm. "Of course you are. You've been through a lot."

He turns to her and smiles. "Thanks. It's been harder than I thought."

Jack scoffs. "Really, dude?"

Cooper turns to him, his face drawn. "Yeah. It would be nice if you showed a little sympathy."

Jack throws his hands up. "Sorry."

"Hey, I've got an idea. Why don't you give me that tour you promised? I want to see the whole plantation." Taneea pushes off the sofa and hitches her ugly bag over her shoulder, then threads between the sofa and the coffee table, maneuvering around my legs.

"Sure. That sounds good." Cooper stands and follows her, then glances back at me and Jack. "I'll see you guys later."

Jack and I exchange looks.

"Yo, I thought you were tired." My brother rises to his feet.

Cooper spins around. "I am."

"So you're too wiped to drive but not to walk around High Point Bluff? In the heat?" Jack pushes further.

He nods. "Exactly. Later."

Cooper's definitely not himself. My stomach clenches. If I'm right about The Beaumont curse, it must be closer than I thought. Miss Delia had better figure out that last ingredient soon.

"Did that just happen?" Jack asks.

My throat constricts. "Yeah."

"And you're just going to let them go? Why aren't we following them? I could get between them again if you want."

I shake my head. "It won't matter. Besides, we've got other things to worry about." I push off the coffee table and clutch my likely ruined dress close to my chest.

Jack follows. "I'm totally lost. What's going on?"

I fill him in on the walk home, about my suspicions that the Beaumont Curse is edging closer, gnawing on Cooper's soul, and causing his distance and distemper, and on my unintended meeting with Claude, my suspicions about his power to influence, and his not-so-veiled threats against me, Miss Delia, Beau, and our dad.

"This Claude guy's cold. We can't let him turn on Dad. No matter what," Jack says as we climb the steps to the covered porch on the caretaker's house.

"And we can't let him go after Miss Delia either." Crossing the porch, we head into the house.

"No way. If it wasn't for her, I'd be dead right now. Or mostly a skeleton. We've got to warn her. I could borrow Dad's truck to drive you over."

I pretreat my dress, toss it into the washer, then spin the dial to the correct setting. "Are you nuts? You can barely drive a stick shift. You'll crash before we even get to the highway. Not to mention you don't have a driver's license, so it's massively illegal." I push the start button and the tub starts to fill.

"True. How about we take the golf cart?" He rubs the scruff on his chin.

"Also illegal. And superslow. I'll just have to ride that old bike of mine that's still in Dad's workshop." I race up the stairs to change into clothes that won't fall off my body. Then freeze midway up the flight, slapping my palm against my forehead.

With everything that's been going on, I completely forgot to brew another batch of energy tea. My latest version gave me a little jolt, jogged my heart, and bolstered my mood, but it was only marginally stronger than the first and didn't do much to curb my fatigue. Judging by my most recent encounter with Claude, I'm going to need to all the strength I can muster to counteract his plans for Miss Delia and my father. Which means I've got to take the concoction to the next level, adding a few new ingredients and letting it steep overnight.

"What's wrong?" Jack asks.

"I just realized there's something I need to do before I can go over there."

"Like what?"

I contemplate explaining, but seeing as I'm keeping my energy booster from Miss Delia, I can't exactly spill the beans to him. "Nothing much. It's a hoodoo thing. You wouldn't understand."

• • •

In the morning, I squint as I pour an extra-large dose of my new-and-improved super-energy tea into a vial, and then slip it into my messenger bag. Among other things, I added some kola nut to this batch, which is supposed to restore vitality and combat fatigue. Here's hoping it gives me that extra punch I'm looking for.

I've called Cooper about a dozen times this morning, but his cell goes straight to voice mail, and no one's picking up at the Big House either. So I'm guessing he's too tired to answer, much less drive me over to Miss Delia's. But with only three days till his birthday, time's running out.

Desperate, I yank my old ten-speed out of my dad's workshop and sling my messenger bag over my back. I haven't ridden a bike in years but Miss Delia's isn't far so it should be a snap.

A half hour later, I chug my way up the long, uneven drive that leads to her house. Although it's only ten o'clock, the sun is already scorching and sweat has drenched my hair and shirt and dripped down my backside into my shorts. I'd cry if I had any more fluid to spare.

Peddling up to the bottle tree, I lay the bike on the ground and jog up to the hose that feeds the garden. Dumping my messenger bag on the ground, I twist on the spigot and let the cool water flow over my hand, then drink my fill before I douse my hair and clothes anew, washing the sweaty grime from my skin.

Miss Delia wheels out onto the porch. "Lord, child, what are you doing?"

I swallow a few extra mouthfuls before I turn off the spigot.

"Cooling off. I rode my bike, but I almost had a heart attack in the heat." I wring out my hair and T-shirt, splattering the flagstone walkway with water. "Cooper was supposed to drive me, but I couldn't reach him." Leaning over, I scoop up my bag and sling it over my shoulder.

"I suspect not." Her brow is creased and her mouth is turned down.

An eerie sensation creeps up my spine. "What do you mean?" I walk up the path to the porch.

She looks like she's debating whether or not to say something, but then swats her hand. "Aw, heck. There's no sense in sugarcoating it. He was here bright and early this morning to pick up Taneea. Barely said a word before they let out of here."

My stomach drops. "He was?" My voice trembles. I step toward the porch and grip the railing to steady myself.

She nods. "Yes. I'm sorry."

"It's the Beaumont Curse. I'm sure of it." I explain my suspicions about his recent behavior, the proximity of his birthday, and the unusual strength and impatience of the curse.

She sucks her teeth. "It's an interesting theory, but I'm not sure it's right."

My heart stops. "Why?"

"You said he's wearing the mojo bag you made and that it's working?"

I nod. "Checked it myself. It popped in my hand."

"Then he's protected from black magic, at least until he turns sixteen. Once his birthday hits, well, now that's another story."

"But the Beaumont Curse is different, isn't? Couldn't it grab him early?"

"I doubt it. These things follow their own set of rules. If it's supposed to take hold when he comes into his manhood, well, that's when it'll happen."

I run my fingers through my damp hair. "But it's not like that has an exact date either. How does the curse know when to attack?"

"I suppose it just knows. Come inside and towel yourself off. Then you can tell me why you rode over." She wheels her chair back into the house, a definite sign she's done debating this point.

Fine. But she hasn't answered one thing: if the Beaumont Curse isn't causing him to be aloof and spend time with Taneea, then what's up? Potential answers pop into my mind, most having to do with Taneea's see-through clothes and plentiful cleavage, but I force them from my brain. That's not Cooper. But still, he's acting strange. I've heard Miss Delia's side, but this time I can't agree. She's got to be wrong about the Beaumont Curse.

Hopefully Cooper's weirdness can wait a couple days. Claude Corbeau may not.

Wringing out the last drops of fluid from my shirt on the cracked porch, I follow her into the house and head straight to the bathroom to towel myself off. Taking advantage of the privacy, I flip open my bag and pull out my vial of tea, uncork the bottle, then throw my head back and hope for the best.

The muddy liquid is tangy and bitter, like a crushed aspirin tablet that dissolves on your tongue, only a thousand times more potent. I gag, then force down the entire bottle of putrid liquid that could probably peel the paint off Miss Delia's front porch.

My pulse thrums as my blood charges through my veins. The pads of my fingers prickle as they awaken to sensation, registering every single cotton loop on the towel still in my grasp. Glancing down at the sea-green fabric, each thread is magnified and distinct, a separate entity apart from the whole. Dragging my eyes from the wondrous detail of this simple cloth, I peer into the mirror hanging on the wall. My pupils are dilated like saucers, leaving only a tiny sliver of space for my irises. Drawing a quick breath, the flowery scent of the hand soap on the counter fills my nostrils.

Holy cow. I feel strong. Invincible. Like I could get back on that bike and ride to High Point Bluff without so much as breaking a sweat. This tea is amazing.

Miss Delia's in the kitchen, clanging pots she shouldn't be moving in the first place. A few short strides later, I'm down the hall, through the living room, then burst through the swinging door, accidentally slamming the door against the kitchen wall.

Miss Delia startles and clutches her chest. "Lord, Emma, you nearly scared the life from me. I told you before not to sneak up on me."

"Sorry." Clamping my hand over my mouth, I gasp, shocked by my own strength. I'd only thought I'd tapped the door. Better reel it in. Otherwise she'll know something's up. "I'm just really anxious to tell you the latest with Claude. Yesterday, after the funeral—"

She lifts her hand. "Whoa. Slow down, girl. You're moving faster than a hummingbird at a bee balm plant. Sit down. Take a breath." She gestures to the stool next to the worktable.

Oops. I guess I'm not hiding it as well as I thought. Sucking a huge breath, I pace across the kitchen as slowly as I can, but my heart's beating a conga in my chest, propelling me forward. Concentrating on each deliberate step, I finally reach the stool and ease myself down on its well-worn top.

Miss Delia leans toward me, squinting through her good eye.

"You okay?"

I nod. "Yes. Just at little antsy." My pulse throbs in my ears.

"Squirrelly is more like it." Crossing her arms, she takes me in for a long moment. "Well, go on, what's got you so excited?"

Taking my time, I tell her about my encounter with Claude outside Beau's office and his not-so-veiled threats against her and basically everyone else I know.

She sucks her teeth. "That man's got some mighty strong convictions, doesn't he? Not to mention a strong dislike of me."

"Yeah. Why do you think that is? He's new around here. He can't possibly know your history with hoodoo, can he? For all he knows you're just some old lady in a wheelchair. No offense."

She smiles. "None taken. I've been thinking about our Mr. Corbeau. There's always a chance someone has shared my background, but I doubt any *binyah*s would tell such things to a *comeyah*," she says, using the Gullah words for natives and newcomers to the island. "And he is most certainly not from *Sa'leenuh*. But he is quite slick and persuasive, manipulative, even. I suspect he thinks you kids know more than you're telling, and figures if he threatens me, it'll tug on your heart strings enough to get you to roll over."

"There's no way we're going to do that. Ever."

She cackles. "I know you won't. But you won't need to. 'Cause we're going to cast the strongest *Keep off the Law* charm that's ever been created and nip this business in the bud." She points to her shelf. "Fetch me my spell book."

Forgetting myself, I bolt across the kitchen, snap up the ledger, and set it on the table in front of her in about two seconds flat.

Setting her glasses on her nose, she peers over the frames. "Emma, if you don't stop ricocheting around here like a jackrabbit, you're going to give me a coronary."

I bite my lip. "Sorry."

"Okay, now, get me some devil's dung and…" She leafs through her spell book, then stops, lingering over a page. Tilting her head, she asks, "Have you been using my spell book without my knowledge?"

"No. The last time I used it was when we made Cooper's projection mojo. Why?"

She hitches a brow. "You sure? Maybe you decided to cast a few charms on the side?"

My heart throbs even harder. Does she know about my tea? I can't see how that's possible since it's not listed in her book, and besides, it's not technically a spell, just a drink made from ingredients that should increase my strength and energy. Really, when you think about it, aside from a lack of sweeteners and a handful of rare ingredients, it's not all that different from those high-performance energy drinks sold in every convenience store in the country. "Um, no. Why?"

"Because I don't recall mixing anything with Dyer's Bugloss lately, but this page is smudged and there's a dusting of powder in the crease."

My stomach twists. I'd never, ever let anything get on her spell book. It's too valuable and represents too much history. I charge across the room to the table, spin the book around, and scan the entry. Dyer's bugloss, also known as alkanet, or anchusa, is a root bark used to make dye and is considered lucky in bringing good fortune in business and money matters. The page is marred with a bright red stain, as if someone wiped their thumb against the paper. I drag my index finger through the dark green powder that's caked between the pages and then lift the dust to my nostrils. The scent of sweet, wild strawberries fills my nose. "I've never used this before." I turn the book back in her direction.

"You know anybody who's been gambling lately?"

"I don't think so."

"This is a green magic charm used to bring in all kinds of money. Legal and otherwise." She lifts a nearby dishrag and brushes the remaining powder from the spine. "Normally I might be inclined to wonder if your brother had gotten in here trying to make himself a quick buck, but Jack's taken a nice turn since he's been cured, and I doubt he'd disrespect me that way. Besides, he couldn't pull off this kind of spell on his own. It takes advanced knowledge of scripture and knowing how to smoke ingredients without burning them. The only two people in this house with that kind of expertise are you and me."

I shake my head. "I swear. I haven't broken my promise. I'd never share your secrets with anyone. Even Jack and Cooper."

She pats my hand. "I know that." Rubbing her chin she looks out the window into the backyard, slipping into her thoughts once again. Her brow furrows. "I don't see how it's possible," she murmurs, barley above a whisper. Ordinarily I doubt I'd be able to make out her words, but my tea's working overtime allowing me to hear every syllable. She sits in silence, mulling over something in her head.

"Miss Delia?"

She turns toward me. "Yes?"

"Everything okay?"

She smiles, though it doesn't reach her eyes. "Of course, Emma. We've got some *Keep off the Law* spells to cast, don't we? And while we're at it, I'm going to work a few protection charms of my own to make sure we cover all our bases. Let's get to it."

Like I've done a hundred times before, I follow Miss Delia's directions and gather an armful of crocks and apothecary bottles from the shelves and deposit them on the worktable. As we work, the usual breeze kicks up, circling the house and rustling the surrounding trees. An occasional blast of wind blows through the house, rattling the doors and windows and bringing only temporary relief from the summer heat. What we need is a nice, big, fat thunderstorm to douse the parched garden and drop the temperature. But these spells aren't strong enough to draw that kind of elemental energy.

A couple hours later, our supercharged, full-frontal offense is almost complete. Along with a couple new mojo bags for her, we've cast a few protective spells around the house and property. There's just one last charm, and I'm grateful my energy tea is still in full effect. Perched on a stepladder, I hammer a line of eight nails into the threshold above her doorframe.

"Don't bang them all the way," she reminds me for the tenth time.

"I know." I grunt as I pound the last nail, making sure it doesn't go in too far.

"Now, set the penny between the first two nails and bend them," she instructs, craning her neck to make sure I don't do it wrong.

I set the first Indian Head penny, dated 1889, in the first open space. Keeping my finger on the copper coin, I carefully tap the head toward the left to fold it diagonally over the penny, then do the same with the nail on the right. When I'm done, the nails form a perfect "X" over the figure in the feather headdress. Three coins later, the task is complete, and if the spell works, we'll have "X'd-out the Law" from Miss Delia's house.

I lean back. "What do you think?"

She peers at the row of Indian Head pennies. "That's good.

The best we can do. Now we wait to see what Mr. Corbeau tries to do."

An engine roars in the distance. An instant later, wheels screech and brakes wail. Glancing toward the road that leads to Miss Delia's, I squint and listen as the engine revs again and a horn blares, heralding its arrival.

My jaw hangs wide. "Holy crap."

Chapter Sixteen

Janeea is at the wheel of a hot-pink pickup truck with giant monster tires and matching pinwheel spinners that rotate counterclockwise. The truck chews up the road, spitting dirt, gravel, and rocks in all directions until she slams on the brakes a couple feet from Miss Delia's white picket fence. She cuts the motor, then beeps the horn again as if we didn't hear it the first time.

I climb down from my stepladder and gape at the cotton-candy monstrosity on the lawn, then steal a glance at Miss Delia. Her expression is hard and angry. And frankly, terrifying.

"What in the world is going on here?" Her voice resonates with fury.

I shake my head. "No clue."

Another engine, this one familiar, rumbles nearby. A second later, Cooper's beige station wagon glides around the bend in the road, driving considerably slower and more safely than the pickup did a few moments ago. He pulls up to the gate beside the truck. He's not alone. Jack's in the front passenger seat, his arms crossed and brows pinched. They exchange a few words before Jack climbs out, slams the door, and mutters to himself as he makes his way up the garden path. Cooper heads straight to the truck's driver's side and extends his hand to help Taneea clamber down from the giant vehicle.

Is she kidding? It's not *that* high. If she can't get out, she's got no business driving it in the first place.

Stomping up the porch steps, Jack stands between me and Miss Delia. "I'm sorry, Em. He called me early this morning to go out on the boat. On our way there, she called wanting to go car shopping. The next thing I knew she was in the front seat and we were driving her to every dealer in Charleston."

"Don't worry. I get it."

He shakes his head. "No, I don't think you do." His voice wavers with apprehension.

Taneea opens the door and extends her bare legs from the cab, setting her matching hot-pink espadrilles on the running board. Standing straight up, she slings her ugly purse over her shoulder and loses her balance, squealing as she totters into Cooper's awaiting arms. Nestled securely in his sturdy biceps, she throws her head back and erupts in peals of laughter. The sound is like the tinkling of a thousand tiny shards of glass.

Supersonic rage ignites in my gut and then explodes through my body. My fists clench, toes curl, and cheeks burn as my vision literally flashes red. I tremble, straining to contain the deep scream that's working its way up my throat. Jack doesn't need his twin sense to know I'm about to blow.

He grabs hold of my arms, boring into my eyes. "Don't give her the satisfaction."

Somehow the cool blue of his eyes penetrates the lava

swirling through my mind. I take a breath and realize it's the first I've drawn since she fell out of the cab. Jack's right. I can't go crazy in front of her. Later, when I'm alone with Cooper, most definitely. But not now. It will only make her feel like she's won. Dragging a few deep breaths into my aching lungs, I work to screw my lips into a smile and watch as Cooper sets her on the ground, steadying her once again because evidently she can't take a step without falling. Which of course is another load of crap designed to make her look weak and defenseless and in need of Cooper's aid. Pathetic.

Giggling, she adjusts her black corset top and miniskirt, then waves. "Hey, did you see my new truck?"

"How could we miss it?" The astronauts can probably see it from the space station.

Miss Delia's nostrils flare. She's rounded the bend past irate, and is now at full-on seething.

Cooper and Taneea finally make their way up the porch.

"So what do you think?" Taneea asks.

"I think you're going to call whoever let you borrow that eyesore and tell them to get it off my property."

She scoffs. "I didn't borrow it, Great-gran. It's mine."

"Really? And how'd you manage that?" Miss Delia asks.

"I just picked it up at the dealer. Cooper helped me choose the color. I couldn't decide between this or a black one with pink running stripes."

He smiles. "I figure if you're going to get a truck like that, you might as well go all out."

"Is that so?" I plant my hands on my hips.

He nods. "Yeah." His eyes are nearly colorless, a frosty gray that reminds me of ice. And from the oblivious grin on his face, he doesn't seem to have the faintest clue of why I might be upset.

My jaw drops as I stare at him, transfixed by the strange hue of his irises. His eyes have always appeared to change shades, but I've never seen this one, ever. It's cold. Lifeless. Perhaps even soulless. A chill ripples through me. Is this proof that the Beaumont Curse has begun to set in?

Cooper turns his attention back to Taneea, as if I'm not even here.

I glance at Jack who looks equally perplexed. He leans over and whispers, "I don't know what to tell you. He's been like this all day."

Miss Delia tilts her head. "How'd you buy the truck, Taneea?"

Jutting her jaw, she meets her great-grandmother's gaze. "With money."

Narrowing her lid over her good eye, she points her gnarled index finger at Taneea. "Where did you get the money?"

A stiff breeze whips around the front yard, shaking the bottle tree. The branches bend and sway, causing the bottles to swing farther then I've ever seen. A few slam together, smashing on contact, their broken pieces crash to the ground. A fat crow squawks, then zooms off one of the low-lying branches, nearly grazing the porch roof on its escape.

Taneea's shoulders tense as she spins to look at the front yard. "What just happened?"

"The beginning of something far worse if you don't start talking," Miss Delia answers.

I gulp. I didn't know Miss Delia could control the elements with her mind. I thought the weather stuff was just a side effect of doing magic, not a part of it. Jeez, every time I think I understand hoodoo, I realize I don't know the half of it.

Taneea shakes her head as a nervous laugh escapes her lips. "You're bluffing. You can't make the wind blow."

"Oh no?" Miss Delia looks out onto the lawn and turns her eyes skyward. Thunder booms above the bottle tree.

My heart jolts. I clutch my chest but stay rooted in place while Cooper steps back and grabs the porch railing.

"I'm out of here." Jack throws open the porch door and races into the living room.

Taneea cowers, inching backward.

"You going to answer me?" Miss Delia levels her gaze at her great-granddaughter.

"I don't have to tell you. All that matters is it's mine." Taneea tugs her purse straps over her shoulder. The alligator-foot key fob dangles from the chain connected to the purse.

Miss Delia's eyes bulge. "An alligator foot! You've been gambling. And you dipped into my spell book to do it."

So that explains the powder caked in the spine.

Taneea lifts her chin. "So?"

Miss Delia flicks the joystick on her wheelchair and zooms close. "So? Do you think I don't know where you've been playing cards and dice? Backroom clubs and other secret places filled with shady characters. Not to mention, tricking hard-working folk out of their money."

"Please, most of the dupes are rich tourists who come down from Hilton Head looking for some action."

"You don't know what you're playing with, girl. Forces you couldn't possibly understand."

Taneea stands her ground. "And whose fault is that? You won't teach me."

"This is my house. I alone choose to whom I'll pass my mantle."

"But you haven't given me a chance. How do you know I couldn't be great at it?" Taneea's voice breaks.

"Hoodoo isn't for everyone. It's not enough to want it. You've got to be ready for it, mind, body, and soul. You're not there, yet, child. You may never be."

Taneea lets loose a humorless laugh. "Oh but she is? She's not even family." She thrusts an accusing finger at me.

Why the heck is she dragging me into this? I'm not the one who broke the rules and worked magic on the sly. Technically.

Miss Delia leans forward. "She doesn't need to be. Her heart is pure."

Taneea recoils as if she's been slapped across the face. "You don't think mine is?"

Miss Delia shakes her head. "No."

Taneea's eyes flood with fluid. Though she deserves all the trouble that's coming her way, my heart can't help but crack a little for her pain. Miss Delia's words are harsh, and though true, still sting. But Taneea's not about to give in. Throwing her shoulders back, she looks indignant. "How can you say that? You don't know the first thing about me." Her lip trembles.

"That's where you're wrong. I've seen enough in my ninety-seven years to know where you've been and where you're headed. You broke my rules to get your hands on a spell book. And what did you do with that power? Cheated people out of money to buy yourself a bag and truck. That there is selfishness, through and through. And not anything I want in my kitchen."

Taneea's eyes turn dark and cold. "Well, then I'll save you the trouble. I don't need you to teach me anyway. As you said, I learned on my own. And with a little extra help from a friend of mine, I won what I needed for that truck and then some."

"Trust me. Anyone who'd teach you that kind of magic is no

friend of yours. You're messing with fire you can't put out." Miss Delia's voice softens.

Taneea rolls her eyes. "Ooh, I'm so scared. You just want to control me just like my mother and her loser husband. Well guess what? It won't work because you're not the only magic expert around here. So you and Emma can have all the fun you want. I don't need you anyway." She shoots me a sideways glare.

Miss Delia leans her forearms against her chair rests. "Did Claude tell you that?"

Her lips part in a sly grin. "Wouldn't you love to know? Too bad you won't find out." She races down the porch steps, through the garden and gate, then jumps up on the running board, throws open the truck door, and jumps into the cab.

Looks like she's pretty agile on those shoes, after all.

The engine revs. A second later, the wheels squeal as they spin in reverse, chewing up grass and clumps of dirt as the truck backs up. The gears crunch as she shifts into first, then slams on the accelerator, causing puffs of smoke to rise from the wheel wells. When the transmission shrieks, begging for more power, she shifts into second, then third as she speeds down the road.

Jack steps back onto the porch from the relative safety of the living room. "What is her problem?"

Miss Delia sucks her teeth. "She's lost. Lord knows, I've tried to reach her, but sometimes the damage is too great and some folk don't want to be found. Excuse me, I've got to rest before I figure out how to explain this mess to her *maamy*."

Cooper whips around. "Don't do that. Give her another chance. She's just upset because no one understands her and she hasn't felt very welcomed around here."

Miss Delia shakes her head. "I'll have to think on it. I'm a tired, old woman. I'm not sure I can handle any more of her funny business. Please get the door for me."

I want to ask her how she did that nature-element-control thing but realize it can wait. She needs a nap and it's not like I need to mess with the weather any time soon.

Cooper pulls open the screen door and she drives her wheelchair through.

When she's safety inside and out of earshot, Jack steps to Cooper, "What's your deal, bro?"

Cooper squares his chest. "What do you mean?"

"No one understands her? She hasn't felt welcomed?" Jack mocks Cooper's words. "Are you kidding? I just spent the whole day with her. Believe me, I get her. She's one of the most obnoxious people I've ever met."

"And she's been horrible to Miss Delia. She deserves to get sent back to Chicago for breaking the rules," I add, but Cooper doesn't seem to hear me.

Instead he takes a step toward Jack. "You're just like everyone else. She's awesome. I'm sorry you can't see that."

"Dude, you need some serious help if you can't see through her whining, fake flirting, and snotty attitude. Today was the worst day of the summer and that includes every time a chunk of my arm fell off. I only went to the dealerships because you wouldn't let me out of the car. Now that it's over, I'm done. I'm never hanging out with her again."

Cooper's eyes flicker with white-hot light and his chest expands to twice the width of Jack's. "She'll come with us whenever I want. It's not up to you."

My heart skips. And not in a good way. The niggling fear from yesterday rears its ugly head again. Is there a bigger reason he wants her around? Like, maybe he's interested in her as more than a friend? Or, given his father's wandering and soulless eye, is this another reason to think the Beaumont Curse might be making an early move?

Jack's jaw opens and then shuts. "Congratulations, jerkwad, you just sounded exactly like Beau. But guess what? I'm not my father so you don't get to order me around like your servant."

Cooper's fist clenches and his breath comes in short, quick puffs like a bull about to charge. "How dare you?"

Jack takes a long stride forward. "Easy, bro. I just open my mouth and say it."

"Whoa!" Without thinking, I race to wedge my body between them. Planting my palms on their chests, I push hard in both directions, forcing them apart. Caught in the crossfire of their laser-like glares, I suddenly realize how stupid I am to have put myself in this dangerous position. If they come to blows, I'm liable to get a black eye or worse. A low growl rumbles in Cooper's throat. "Knock it off, you idiots!" I grunt and lean hard against Cooper's tight abs. But like elk with locked horns, they don't budge. "Stop it. Please!" My voice breaks.

Jack backs down first, crossing the porch and clomping down the steps and through the garden on his way to cool off under the bottle tree.

I search Cooper's faint gray gaze. "What is wrong with you? Since when do you talk to Jack like that? Or let Taneea come between us?" I'm almost afraid to hear his answer.

He trains his frozen stare on me. His lips are mashed in a hard, unforgiving line, as if he's holding back a string of insults so withering they'd slay me on contact. But then his eyes flicker a bright blue and his brow softens, relaxing the rest of the muscles on his face. My Cooper is back. Then, just as quickly, an expression of sheer desperation grips him. Grabbing my arms, he pulls me close. "Help me, Emmaline. I'm not myself.

Something's wrong…don't let me slip away." His breath comes in quick pants.

My fears and anger ease. Whatever's going on, a sliver of my Cooper is still there, somewhere deep inside. "I won't." I pat his shirt to make sure his mojo is still slung around his neck. It's there, and hopefully, so is his love for me.

A split second later, the color in Cooper's eyes fades again. His hands drop and his expression hardens. Taking a huge step back, he bounds down the porch steps.

"Where are you going?" I call, but he keeps running down the garden path and out to his car.

Jack rises off the bench under the bottle tree. "What's up?"

Cooper jumps into the driver's seat and starts the engine. "I need to look for Taneea. I'm worried she's driving angry. She could crash or something."

My heart cracks. I rub my throbbing temples and try to make sense of his weird flip-flopping. Cooper is sympathetic and caring, but his support of Taneea is too much, even for him. How could he defend her antics and disrespect of Miss Delia? Maybe I'm wrong and he does care for her more for her that I thought. Taneea is more experienced and exciting than I and obviously attractive to guys. But he swore she wasn't his type—unless she's dabbled in more than just green magic spells and found some way to brainwash him—but that kind of spell requires so much advanced hoodoo knowledge, it's practically impossible for her to have pulled off in such a short amount of time. More likely it's the encroaching Beaumont Curse, eager to steal his soul.

Whatever the reason, I promised to help him fight this and I'm not going to back down now.

Chapter Seventeen

Drawing a deep breath, I stare at the intercom panel installed next to the glossy, black double door to High Point Bluff, preparing myself for the inevitable encounter to come. An hour ago, when Jack and I hatched this plan as he walked back home from Miss Delia's, and I rode alongside, it sounded brilliant, but now, not so much.

"Are you going to buzz or not?" Jack nudges my side.

"I will. In a second." Gnawing my lip, I adjust my messenger bag across my back, then turn to him. "Maybe we should just forget the whole thing. It's probably pointless anyway."

He narrows his eyes. "Buzz, or I will."

I nod, knowing he's right. We're here on a mission and can't turn chicken now. Taneea's slip about a "friend" teaching her magic raised too many questions. But one thing's for sure. Someone taught her some pretty advanced hoodoo, enough to afford her awesome toys and the freedom she's so desperately desired. If Miss Delia's right and Claude is the one pulling the strings, then he's no ordinary investigator—he's a conjurer with a dark agenda. Is he really dedicated to uncovering the truth about the robbery at the museum, or does he have some other motive for pursuing Miss Delia like a hound on a fox? And why did he push so hard for Sheriff Walker to agree that Missy's death was from natural causes? Could it have anything to do with why he'd sneak into Beau's private study, then threaten me and everyone I know to keep my discovery secret? We can't explain everything to Beau—how does one describe a three-hundred-year-old, soul-snatching curse?—but we can warn him not to trust Claude.

I mash the doorbell button on the panel. It's one of the new security features Dad put in for Missy after she freaked out about the museum burglars being on the loose.

"Yeah?" Beau's voice crackles from the intercom speaker near the door.

Depressing another button, I lean toward the speaker. "Hey Beau. It's us. Emma and Jack."

"My sweet, darling Emma!" His voice is even more slurred than usual. "Cooper isn't home. And why are you calling on this contraption anyway? Y'all should just walk in."

Jack steps close. "We're actually here to talk to you if that's okay. We didn't want to assume you were free."

A moment passes before he answers. "Come on in, then. And make it quick. I'm busy." The front door buzzes and the latch clicks, allowing us entry.

The light in the library is on, casting a glow on the buffed hall floor. Heading toward it, we run smack into the scent of rancid meat that hangs thick in the air, proof positive of Beau's presence. My eyes sting as I peek through the doorway. As expected, Beau is sprawled on the sofa, sunk into his favorite spot, the cushions slung low and nearly touching the floor.

He toasts us with his drink, a pint-size tumbler nearly filled to the brim with a dark brown liquid. "Set a while."

Veering as far away as possible, I hold my breath as I steer toward the sofa opposite of him and ease into the red silk fabric, laying my bag on the Oriental carpet. Averting my gaze, I try not to stare at his chalky, gray skin that hangs slack and extra rubbery. Jack plops next to me.

"I barely recognize you without that son of mine in tow." Beau drags in slow, heavy breaths. His chest gurgles like it's filled with chunky globs of mucus. He takes a long gulp of his drink, downing half the glass.

"Cooper's busy tonight," Jack says.

Beau's thin eyebrow arches. "Really? Without his sweetheart?" His rheumy eyes search mine as if he suspects there's trouble in paradise. "If my boy isn't treating you right, you best tell me. I'll set him straight."

Creepy unease works its way up my spine. "Thanks. But that isn't necessary."

"I mean it." He swats his right hand, but the movement throws him off-balance and causes him to tip onto his left side.

Jack clears his throat. "If this isn't a good time, we could always come back."

I nod. "Yeah, like tomorrow."

"Nonsense!" he bellows. The phlegmy sound bubbles up in his throat, causing him to cough. Pulling a soiled handkerchief from his pocket, he hacks up something dark and chunky, but quickly crumples the cloth in his fist and stuffs it back into his pocket.

Jack shoots me a look. From his pinched expression, I'm not sure whether he's trying not to laugh or puke. I'm right there with him.

"Maybe you've had enough to drink," I suggest.

"On the contrary," Beau says. "This is my elixir of life, the only thing keeping the blood flowing through my veins. Did you know scotch is a vasodilator? My circulation isn't what it used to be."

Judging by the pasty pallor of his skin, I'd say it's barely pumping at all.

Beau chugs another mouthful of the deep amber liquid. With great effort, he lurches forward and points to Jack. "Now listen here, there's something I want you to remember. I may not be around forever, so you've got to make sure my boy doesn't squander his youthful energy and vigor. He's got to live every day to the fullest and take advantage of all that being a Beaumont affords him. Lord knows I did." A smile edges across his wine-red lips as he rubs his gelatinous midsection. "And despite appearances, I don't regret one day being Beau Beaumont. It's been a fulfilling life."

"Oh-kay," Jack says. "Though hopefully you've got plenty more years ahead." His mouth cracks into an uncomfortable smile.

"I certainly hope so. But life can be so unpredictable. Who'd have guessed I would have ended up with four wives? Though none of those delectable plums can hold a candle to our dear Emma." Chuckling, he gives me the once over. "I've got to hand it to that son of mine. He does have good taste in women." He winks.

My stomach churns. Where's Miss Delia's *Semi-Invisibility* powder when you need it?

"Oh, now darling, don't be shy." His eyes swim in their sockets. "I know you care for the boy. And that's a good thing.

Because I've got my legacy to think of. I'm counting on you two having a long and fruitful relationship. Together, you'll combine forces to build an immense empire. He can't squander his chances with you."

"Uh, sure. But you know sometimes stuff doesn't work out." I hug my arms, uncomfortable with the whole empire-building thing.

He coughs out a laugh and wobbles back against the cushion. "Whatever that boy's busy doing now, it'll end the moment he comes into his manhood."

My gut clenches and my mouth turns dry. That phrase. It's exactly what Sabina said when she worked the Beaumont Curse. Does Beau know that, or is he just repeating an old island expression?

Beau laughs. "Your daddy and me? We got into our share of messes back in the day. But once we turned sixteen, everything changed. The same will happen to Cooper, no doubt. You'll be amazed at the change in him." He guzzles the rest of his drink, then smacks his lips. "Now, I doubt you came here to get relationship advice from a broken, old man. To what do I owe the pleasure of your clandestine visit?"

Sitting up straight, I remind myself of our task. Though considering how impaired Beau is, he probably won't remember a thing we say. This is a waste of time.

Beau's brow furrows. "Spit it out, girl!"

I gulp. "Jack and I wanted to talk to you about Claude Corbeau."

"Ah, good man!" He raises his empty glass in salute.

"Actually we're thinking maybe he isn't."

"What? He's the best investigator either side of the Mississippi."

Jack leans forward. "There are some things you ought to know—"

Beau raises his hand in protest. "Believe me, boy. I did my homework." He digs his finger into his chest. "Examined his credentials myself. Corbeau's the man for the job." A thunderous belch works its way up Beau's throat and a puff of something truly foul floats out of his mouth and across the room. It's like rotten eggs mixed with day-old roadkill topped with liver-fried onions. Oblivious, Beau yammers on, pinching his fat forefinger and thumb together, then squints at his hand. "Besides, Claude is this close to uncovering the burglary ring that stole from the King Center. Would you believe it was one of our donors? A little old Gullah lady in a wheelchair, no less. Can you imagine that?" he whispers as his eyes goggle.

I lean forward slightly. "That sounds pretty impossible if you ask me."

He nods, slow and lazy like his head weighs a hundred pounds. "She's just the mastermind. But after we're done putting the screws to her, she'll roll on her coconspirators, lickety-split. Then we'll find out what they did with my Beaumont ruby." His words are slurred and peppered with a whole lot of sh's that aren't normally there. His eyes close and his head bobs forward, lifeless. The empty glass slips from his grip and clanks against the bottle on the floor.

The room is silent except for the ticking of the clock on the mantle below Lady Rose's portrait. The first mistress of High Point Bluff stares down at us, her crazy bug-eyes appear trained on her unconscious, soulless descendent.

"Is he dead?" Jack asks.

My pulse races, jumping in my neck as I stare at Beau's motionless body. "I don't know."

"We should check." He nudges my side with his elbow.

"*We*?"

"Well, you." Shrugging, he attempts a pathetic smile.

I narrow my gaze and toss him my best reproachful look. "Baby." Gathering my strength, I stand and gingerly step around the coffee table between the two sofas, then clamp a hand over my mouth and nose. His smell is even more putrid up close. I doubt he's showered in the last week. Maybe two. Holding my breath, I lean toward his mammoth arm and give it a shake.

He doesn't move.

My heart gallops against my rib cage. I shove him again, this time a little harder. "Beau?" My voice quivers.

His lids pop open as he starts and gasps for air.

I squeal, the sound so high and piercing, it nearly ruptures my eardrums.

He clutches my hand. "I need my ruby," he rasps. Then his eyes roll back into his head as he slumps onto his side and snores.

My pulse sputters to a trot. He's only passed out, unconscious from his copious consumption of alcohol. Surveying Beau's vast, ashy-gray body, I listen to his labored breathing and can't help but agree that he's probably on his way out. He's abused his body for too long, indulging in every vice known to man, the likely consequence of losing his soul. I almost feel sorry for him.

An image of Cooper, distorted and corrupt zooms across my mind. Shaking my head, I force it from my brain. I can't let him turn into his father.

Glancing at Beau again, I notice the chain that's affixed to his belt loop. The other end is tucked into his pocket, attached to the key to his private study. An idea forms.

"Hey, Jack. What if we found proof that Claude is a liar? That would be enough to get Beau to turn on him, right?"

"Sure but how are we going to do that? It's not like he's going to admit being a conjurer."

"Beau said he checked Claude's credentials himself. That they're the best in the business."

"Uh-huh?"

"What if they're fake? I Googled him but couldn't find anything before he was hired at The King Center. I'm guessing the résumé he gave Beau is full of lies. If we can prove it, Beau will toss him out on his butt."

"Yeah, but where are we going to find it?"

I point the chain. "In the study. Where else?" I turn and maneuver around Beau's splayed legs to scoop up my bag, then head toward the door.

He pushes off the couch. "Hey, you forgot the key."

I spin around. "No I didn't. You're up." I waggle my eyes and thumb my hand toward Beau's expansive waistline.

Jack's eyes goggle. "You want *me* to take it from his pocket?" His voice trembles.

I shrug. "You made me check if he was dead. I'd say it'll make us about even."

He shoots me the evil eye. "Fine." He grumbles to himself as he tiptoes around the couch and sidles up to Beau. Swallowing hard, he extends his long, skinny fingers and skillfully detaches the chain from the belt loop. Beau doesn't stir. With the free end in his grasp, Jack draws a deep breath and tugs on the other, pulling it ever so slowly from Beau's pocket. Finally, it's free. Jack thrusts a victorious fist in the air.

"Congratulations. Now let's go," I whisper and point to the hall. "We have no idea how long he'll be out."

We race from the room and head to the study. The key turns loose and easy. We slip inside and shut the door behind us, pocketing the key in case we might need it again. My pulse thrums as I take a moment to absorb the room. This is Beau's private sanctuary, off-limits to us and Cooper for as long as we can remember. It almost feels like we're in someplace sacred. Which is kind of weird because from the looks of it, it's nothing special. Just an average office, furnished with a desk, leather wing chairs and a sofa, filing cabinets, and a wall of built-in shelves. No big whoop.

"So what are we looking for?" Jack heads toward the desk.

"Files, I guess. Anything he might have used to hire Claude. There's got to be a résumé or a list of references or something." I sling my messenger bag over my shoulder and spin it around my back.

Jack gets to work, opening the desk drawers and leafing through whatever papers he finds, while I head for a file cabinet across the room, situated beneath the window. As I grab the handle on the top drawer, the nearby glass-enclosed shelf catches my eye. A squat, antique bottle twinkles in the sunlight. It's just like the one we found on the beach at the beginning of the summer except this one is green. So much has happened since I stumbled on that first bottle, both good and bad, though lately, it seems like there's been more bad.

Stepping toward the shelf to get a better look, I notice the other objects arranged with the bottle. There's a yellowed beeswax candle, a jeweled hair comb, a cracked silver spoon, and a pewter mug, along with a broken piece of faded china, and a slew of other unrelated historical items that appear to date back to the 1700s. It's kind of like a museum exhibit without a unifying theme. The shelf below has more of the same, though the artifacts look slightly less old, maybe from the nineteenth century. Among the nearly hundred objects is a lacy linen handkerchief next to a pocket watch, a fan with ivory handles, and a hand-painted picture of a landscape, some brass buttons, and a toy soldier figure. There's also a long sword that looks like it was used in the civil war. On and on the shelves go, like densely packed time capsules of every decade of High Point Bluff's history.

"Hey, are you going to get to work?" Jack asks, poised above a stack of files on Beau's desk.

"In a second. Come look at this stuff. It's amazing. It's like a private museum."

Jack scoffs. "I think we've had enough museums this summer, don't you think?"

I chuckle. "Maybe. But this stuff is so cool." Bending down to the look at the last shelf, I squint at a button from the last South Carolina governor's election and a very modern iPhone in a bedazzled case.

My stomach seizes and the air rushes from my lungs in a gush.

"Jack," I try to call but my mouth is suddenly so dry I barely produce a sound. Swallowing hard, I force the words from my throat. "Come here. Now."

Perhaps it's his twin sense, or the fact that I'm trembling and fighting for breath, but he charges across the room.

I point to the last item in the case: the pirate's dagger, encrusted with a dried, black substance.

The color drains from his olive skin. "*Dang.*"

I nod, in total agreement.

"What's it doing there?" His voice is tinged with panic.

"I don't know." My mind races about a thousand miles

a minute, calculating the knowns and unknowns. After considerable mental acrobatics, I come up with a whole lot of nothing. But one thing is for sure—the knife is here, among Beau's private belongings, smattered with strange dark stuff, just like Missy.

A jolt of electricity shoots straight from my feet to my brain. I'm on to something, though exactly, what I'm not sure.

I open the glass case, lean close and take a whiff. The odor is faint, but the lingering scent is familiar. "See this black stuff? I think it's the same gunk that was on Missy's body."

He peers at the knife. "But she didn't have any injuries. So it couldn't have been used to hurt her."

"No, but it means it was with her in the bathroom when she died."

Jack gawks. "Do you think Beau killed her?"

I'd be lying if I said I hadn't wondered the same thing. Heck, I even told Cooper as much. Finding the knife here in Beau's study certainly does seem to implicate him. But still, one thing doesn't make sense. "Why would Beau put it here with that stuff on it? Wouldn't he have wiped it off first?"

Jack nods. "Good point." His eyes light up. "Hey, I know it sounds crazy but what if someone planted it to frame Beau?"

"Who would do that?" Then I recall the morning of Missy's funeral and a chill tap-dances up my spine. "Claude was here, all by himself. He totally could have done it. But that would mean he killed Missy."

Jack rubs the scruff on his chin. "If only there was a way to know for sure."

I smile. "Oh there is." Reaching into the case, I carefully lift the dagger, then wrap it in a blank piece of paper from the desk and tuck it into my messenger bag.

Chapter Eighteen

"You want to go *back* to Miss Delia's? *Now*?" Jack brow is creased with disbelief, but I think he's more upset that I made him return the study key to Beau's pocket.

"We have to. I can't work a *Psychic Vision* charm without the ancestors' mortar."

"But we don't have a car."

"We've got a golf cart."

He flashes me his best you're-a-gigantic-hypocrite look. I can't blame him. I've reminded him it's illegal to drive the main roads a million times, not to mention how terminally slow those carts drive. But that was before, when we could rely on Cooper for transportation. Now, he's nowhere to be found, his cell clicking straight to voice mail. And we can't exactly ask Dad to drive us since that'll raise more questions than we can possibly answer. Desperate times require even more desperate, and occasionally stupid, measures. The golf cart is our only option.

An hour later, after taking as many back roads as possible,

we finally arrive at Miss Delia's. The fluorescent headlights cast a ghostly glow on the bottles hanging from the live oak in front of her house. The electric engine is silent so the only sound is the ground crumbling beneath the cart's small, fat tires.

The front light is on and Miss Delia's out on the porch, her chair midway down the ramp. She stops short. "Who's there?" Her voice is firm, but I could swear there's a there's a hint of fear there, too. "That you, Taneea?"

"It's me, Emma. And Jack," I call back, realizing this is the first time I've ever been here at night. We probably scared the crap out of her.

"Lord, child, if I didn't know better, I'd say you were trying to end me. I thought I'd be alone this evening." She flicks the chair into reverse and rolls backward up the ramp.

"Sorry," I say as we climb the porch steps to meet her. "We didn't interrupt anything did we?"

"Never you mind what an old lady does at night. Now, what's brought you over this evening?"

"We found something important that couldn't wait. I need to do a *Psychic Vision* charm. Like now." I flip open my messenger bag and pull out the pirate's dagger, then point to the dried black substance that's embedded in the engraving on the handle and blade.

Her lips turn down. "I thought we were through with that thing."

"Me too." I reach for the screen door and hold it open for her.

Once inside, Jack plops on the couch. "Emma thinks that black gunk on the blade proves it was with Missy when she died."

I nod. "I'm guessing it was either Beau or Claude, heck

maybe even both of them. Someone put it in Beau's study. A *Psychic Vision* might clear everything up."

Miss Delia's eyes turn hard. "I'd love to know what Claude is really up to. I got a bad feeling the moment I laid eyes on him. At first I though he was just interested in the missing artifacts, but now I'm sure he's the one teaching Taneea hoodoo. Ain't no way she conjured that gambling charm herself."

"But why would he do that? And what's his connection to Beau and Missy?"

She shrugs. "I don't know. Money? Power? Isn't that what most crime usually boils down to? Beau's got both of those in spades. If Claude is a conjurer, there's no end to what he could squeeze out of Beau if he framed him for Missy's death." She nods toward the kitchen. "You've got work to do while Jack and I have a little chat. Call me when you're ready."

Under the bright light of the kitchen's overhead fixture, I purify myself with the citronella oil and then assemble the ingredients necessary for the spell and set the kettle on to boil. Laying out the ingredients, I yawn, deep and cavernous, as fatigue-laced tears spring to my eyes.

It's been the longest day ever between my sweaty bike ride here this morning, casting the *Law Keep Away* spells, the altercation with Taneea and being abandoned by Cooper, then the excruciatingly slow walk home with Jack. Not to mention our strange meeting with Beau. Even if I wasn't practicing hoodoo, I'd be exhausted, but astonishingly, thanks to my energy tea, I'm only slightly tired. *Gold star for Emma!*

Speaking of which, I need some more if I'm going to pull off this *Psychic Vision*. Glancing around to make sure I'm still alone, I slip my hand into my bag and retrieve the flask of tea that I refilled before we left. Flipping the top, I hold my breath and guzzle the vile, bitter concoction.

Yellow pulsing energy swells in my chest, then surges through my body, shivering down through my fingers and toes. My pulse rages and breath speeds as every centimeter of my skin comes alive. I feel my pores open, the pads of my fingers prickle as they clutch the smooth bottle, even the eyelash that's about to tumble from its follicle. I'm literally bursting with energy.

A couple minutes later, hopping like the Energizer Bunny, I lunge through the swinging door. Miss Delia starts. "We're ready," I say and then zoom back into the kitchen. Sitting on my stool next to the mortar, my fingers rap the counter as I wait for her to wheel in. I stare, captivated by the sound and sensation of my nails clicking against the butcher block. My heart keeps pace with my tapping.

Miss Delia rolls in and dabs some citronella on her wrists and behind her ears. Her eyebrow hitches. "Are you sure you're up to this? It's been a long day. We can always do this tomorrow."

My head snaps in her direction. "No, I'm fine." The veins in my neck throb, stretching my skin with each beat.

"You sure? 'Cause messing up the spell will cost us three days, which is all we've got left till that boy's birthday. The mortar will need to rest before it can be used again."

I scoff and wave away her concern. "I know. That's why I want to get this over with now. The sooner we figure this out, the sooner we can get back to the Beaumont Curse."

"Okay." Despite the wary expression on her face, she scoots the chair up to the mortar and pulls her *collier* out from beneath her housedress.

I pull the spent teabags from the mugs and get to work

on the rest of the spell, layering the herbs and roots until the kitchen smells like a musty old church perfumed with ancient incense. Through it all, my blood's tap-dancing through my veins. Gone are the usual magic-induced yawns, drooping eyelids, and crushing fatigue that made my arms and legs feel like lead weights. I've got more than enough zip to complete this charm. Heck, I could probably conjure all night if I had to.

Leaning over the ancestors' mortar, Miss Delia and I each grab an end of the pirate's dagger and hold it above the smoke. Then, with our free hands, we raise our mugs of steaming *Psychic Vision* tea, the ingredient to kick this spell into action.

"Bottoms up!" I laugh a little too loud and then tip the reddish-brown liquid down my throat as she does the same. Compared to my energy brew, the sour-cherry and burned-spinach flavor tastes great. Gulping it down, I smack my lips.

Miss Delia purses her lips in disgust. "You like that nasty stuff?"

I shrug. "It's kind of good."

I close my eyes and breath deep, waiting for my mind to clear and an incantation to spring from my lips.

Nothing comes.

Nada.

Not one single, solitary word.

I peek at the smoke above the mortar. There's no flickering lights, no mini-movie screen on which to watch the vision. Come to think of it, the wind hasn't blown, the rain hasn't fallen, and there's no clap of thunder, either.

Something's wrong.

My heart skips a couple beats, then trips into overdrive, propelling my panic. I clutch at my *collier* and rub the red and white beads, which are supposed to promote spoken word and prayer. Still, no words leap from my mouth.

Adrenaline dumps into my system, increasing both my heart and respiration rate. Sucking in lungfuls of mortar smoke, I beg my mind to quiet, to find a moment of stillness to allow the spell's words to come. But the more I try, the faster it races, and the more errant thoughts crowd in. Why am I thinking about the duck-billed platypus, the Pythagorean Theorem, and my grandfather's scuffed wing-tip shoes, all at the same time? Forcing those images from my brain, they're quickly replaced by even more random ideas.

"What's happening?" Miss Delia's voice is stern.

I lift my eyes to hers. "Nothing."

"I can see that. But why?" She points a bony finger at me. "You've done something to thwart this spell."

I shake my head. "No. Everything's here." I scan the worktable, making sure I haven't screwed something up. "The ingredients are right and I know I layered them in the correct order."

Her lips mash into a hard line. "Then why isn't the charm working?"

I tremble. "I don't know." My fingers shake as I lift them to my silent, treacherous mouth. "No matter how hard I try, the incantation won't come. I swear. I don't understand what's happening."

"I think you do." She drops the knife, causing the blade to dip down into the coals. I scoop it out and set it on the table.

I shake my head, as dumbfounded as before. "I don't. I promise. What could possibly cause this?"

"Some kind of shortcut." The words fly like a vicious accusation.

I recoil as they land like a jab to the chin. Guilty and caught, my shoulders sink and my chest caves. I wish I could crawl under the table and never come out. I glance up at her. "I was only trying to—"

"Outsmart hoodoo. Thinking that somehow, after only a couple months of training you've learned enough to outwit the laws of nature. What did you do? And tell me the truth."

Fighting off tears, I confess everything about the energy tea, including how I created my own recipe using her spell book, the weak first batches and the last, much-more-powerful brew. Though I've bared my soul, I don't feel any better. In fact, now that it's all laid out and the consequences are becoming clear, I feel worse.

She shakes her head. "I should have known. Bouncing around here, talking a mile a minute. You had my head spinning, girl. That energy you're feeling? It's not real."

How is that possible? My muscles are coiled, poised to spring. I could run a Lowcountry marathon in record time.

She must sense my confusion because she leans forward and points to my chest. "Oh, it's got your blood pumping, all right. Your cheeks are about as red as a clown's." My fingers fly to my face. She's right. It's swollen and as hot as a match. "But instead of adding to your power, that drink of yours has sucked it dry. No wonder the *Psychic Vision* wouldn't start. It's like trying to drive a car with a giant hole in the gas tank."

"I was just so tired." My voice trembles. "And my resistance was building so slowly. I was afraid I wouldn't have enough strength to break the Beaumont Curse."

"You kids are all the same. Impatient. Headstrong. Thinking you're so clever you can take the fast, easy route instead of putting in the work and time required for things to happen as they should. Well guess what? You can't shortchange hoodoo."

Her not-so-veiled comparison to Taneea stings worse than a hot poker to the skin. "I'm sorry," I whisper.

"You should be," she snaps, showing me no mercy. "Because of your little stunt, we've lost three good days. And we might run out of time all together."

"I know the ancestors' mortar needs to rest, but we can still do magic with your old mortar can't we?"

Her brow creases. "*I* can. But you're out of commission."

"What?" A tear trickles from my eye. "Are you banning me from doing magic? Please don't. Not with Cooper's birthday so close. Once his soul is safe, I don't care if I never work hoodoo again. But please don't keep me from it now."

She scoffs. "If only it was up to me. I'd punish you longer just to teach you a lesson. But your suspension has nothing to do with me. You've got to wait for that concoction of yours to work its way out of your system. You'll be lucky if it only takes a couple days to restore your natural balance. For all I know, it could take another week."

The room spins as the enormity of my mistake begins to sink in. Gripping the table to keep from fainting, I fight back tears. "I know I screwed up. But I didn't mean to. I really just wanted to do something good. Doesn't that matter for something?"

She cocks her snowy white head. "Sure, if this was a fairy tale. But this is here is real life and no matter how good your intentions, there are consequences to your actions. Those *Law Keep Away* spells we worked this morning? I've got no idea how strong they are because you weren't working at your full strength. And did you even stop to think about what you might do to yourself with that drink? Each of those ingredients is strong on their own, but together, you're lucky you didn't drop dead of a heart attack. And then where would your boy be? Left with only your clueless brother and a paralyzed, old woman to save his soul."

A wave of clammy sickness rolls over me. A moment ago I didn't think I could feel any worse. Now, I wish I could dive into a swamp and bury myself in the muck.

"I'm so, so, sorry." There's nothing else I can possibly say.

"So am I." She looks away and shakes her head. "You best leave before I really get angry."

Chapter Nineteen

Without another word, I slip off my stool and gather my messenger bag and slink out of the kitchen. If this is semi-angry Miss Delia, I don't want to be here when she blows for real.

I duck through the living room. "Come on, Jack." Then push open the screen door and run out onto the porch.

"What's going on?" Within seconds he's followed me outside, down the steps, and through the garden.

I jump into the golf cart. "I don't want to talk about it, okay? Let's just go. Now."

He stands beside the passenger side of the cart. "Huh? I don't understand? Did you see something weird in the vision? Was it Claude? Did he do something to Missy?"

"Will you just shut up and drive?" I snap, sick of hearing his annoying voice and dumb questions.

He throws up his hands. "Whoa. Back off, sis. I'm just trying to find out what happened."

"What happened is I totally screwed something up and now

Miss Delia hates me and Cooper's probably going to lose his soul. Oh, yeah, and Claude is probably a total master hoodoo psychopath but I'll never get to find that out either, all because I. Screwed. Up." Tears stream from my eyes and sear my already scorching cheeks. "There, are you happy? Now will you get in the frigging cart and drive?"

"Uh. Okay." Jack races around to his side and climbs behind the wheel. He turns the key, starting the silent electric engine and clicking the headlights on.

Slipping the gear into reverse, he backs up under the bottle tree, then heads down the long driveway to the main road. A full minute of blessed silence elapses during which I meditate on my colossal transgressions.

Jack clears his throat. "At the risk of getting hit, can I say something?"

Oh my God. I swear, if it's got anything to do with being emo, I'm going to push him out of this moving cart.

"What?"

"I don't exactly understand what happened in there or what the heck you mean by all that stuff, but I'm reasonably sure you're wrong about Miss Delia. She could never hate you. Whatever is going on, it must be some sort of mistake."

"There's no mistake. I did something bad. And now there will be horrible consequences."

"Come on. This is *you* we're talking about, not me. You don't do bad."

A bitter laugh leaps from my lips. "Well, I didn't mean to, but I did." I stare into the dense live oak forest. The Spanish moss casts creepy shadows on the ground but even they don't scare me as much as what might happen thanks to my adventures in brewing energy tea. I force those truly horrific thoughts from my mind.

"Aha! See? I knew it. You couldn't be bad if you tried. Even the museum robbery was for a good cause. Face it, Em, you're just not hardcore enough to do hard time. And Miss Delia knows that, so there's no way she hates you."

"If only that was true."

Jack stops the cart. "Hey, listen to me. Miss Delia loves you. You know that. Whatever it is, she'll get over it."

I'm about sick of his optimism. Maybe he'll change his tune if he knows the truth. Crossing my arms, I cock my head. "I went behind her back and brewed a potion I shouldn't have. Then because I messed up my body's natural balance, I screwed up the *Psychic Vision*, which screwed up the ancestors' mortar so we might miss the deadline to save Cooper's soul. Oh yeah, and I've totally destroyed Miss Delia's trust in me."

He whistles. "Yup, that's pretty bad."

"You're such a jerk." A strangled mixture of crying and laughter blurts from my lips as I swat his shoulder.

He laughs. "Hey, what do you expect? You want me to lie and say you're perfect? Guess what? You're not. But here's a news flash: Miss Delia knows that too. You're a teenager. And an apprentice. You're going to screw up once in a while." He presses the accelerator pedal and continues down the road.

Since when did my brother become such a sage wise man? Still, it doesn't change the outcome.

I sniff my runny nose. "There's screwing up and then there's dooming your boyfriend's soul for eternity."

"Possibly ex-boyfriend," he corrects me.

I gape and fresh tears sprout. "Wow, way to kick a girl when she's down."

He shrugs. "Just for now. I'm sure everything will go back

to normal when the Beaumont Curse is broken and he comes to his senses about Taneea. Which is going to happen because ancestors' mortar or not, you and Miss Delia have mad hoodoo ninja skills."

Though I'm not sure I deserve it, his confidence perks me up.

Near the end of the long road leading from Miss Delia's house, Jack prepares to turn onto the paved side road that will take us to Sea Island Parkway.

A dark, foreboding feeling creeps across my chest. I glance over my shoulder at the forest behind us. My ears fill with the sound of the night—crickets, cicadas, frogs—and something else, not a whisper exactly, but a faint, dissonant chord that echoes deep my head.

I grab his wrist. "Wait. Do you hear that?"

He holds his foot on the break and listens. "No. What is it?"

The chime heightens and intensifies, like an orchestra tuning up. It crescendos, growing until it crowds out all other noises. "That. It's like music, but not," I nearly shout to hear myself over the din.

Jack look at me like I'm crazy. "Why are you yelling at me?"

"Huh?" I ask, shoving my fingers in my ears to block the ringing that's blaring so loud it's vibrating my eardrums.

Suddenly, the sound shatters into a thousand individual tones that cascade and carry on the wind like notes in some weird, harmonic minor scale.

"Are you okay?"

The freaky feeling crawls across my chest and then down my spine. I know the sound. I'd recognize the tones from Miss Delia's bottle tree anywhere. I'm just not sure how I can hear it from this far away. But my spirit guide must think it's important.

"We've got to go back to Miss Delia's. Now."

Jack spins the steering wheel, jerking the cart around.

The scent of burning wood wafts toward us.

No! Miss Delia's house must be on fire! The sound must have been some kind of spiritual fire alarm in my head.

"Hurry!" The eerie sensation crawls down my arms and legs.

"The pedal is on the floor. These things only go so fast you know."

He whizzes the cart back down the dirt road, dodging the pock holes and overgrown lumps of vegetation as best he can in a golf cart with dinky headlights.

Finally, we approach the bend in the road just outside of Miss Delia's house. The smoky aroma hangs thick. A low, ghostly moan resonates through the forest. It's the familiar sound of wind passing through the bottle tree. Through the dense forest and sheets of hanging Spanish moss, I catch a glimpse of fiery red flames.

Jack stops short.

"What are you doing? We've got to get to Miss Delia's. Her house is burning down."

"No it's not. Look." He points toward a space between two trees.

He's right. There's a fire all right. But it's not in her house. Instead, Miss Delia's seated in her wheelchair under the bottle tree, warming herself by a gigantic bonfire.

The eerie sensation evaporates and my heart slows to a trot. "What the heck is she doing?"

"Beats me. You're the root worker."

Remembering her extreme displeasure, I suddenly feel weird being here. "Maybe we should leave."

He turns to me. "You sure?"

The bottle tree's strange music jolts my ears again, this

time sounding like someone blared the volume and then cut it just as suddenly. Nope. My spirit guide wants me here for a reason. I know Miss Delia doesn't appreciate me being clever or headstrong, but this really isn't up to me. My spirit guide's got an agenda. "No. We're supposed to stay and watch whatever's going to happen. Turn off the headlights."

Jack takes a deep breath and kills the lights. "Oh-kay. You do realize hanging out with you is a bizarre experience, right? If you weren't my sister, I'm pretty sure I'd think you're crazy."

I sigh. "Yeah. Sometimes I wonder if I am, too. But honestly, I'm just listening to my spirit guide."

"I'd love to meet her."

"So would I." Actually, maybe not. Frankly, the whole thing is still kind of spooky to me.

Miss Delia starts to speak and wave her arms around, but it's almost impossible to see through the woods.

"Drive up closer so we can get a better look."

Jack steps on the accelerator. The electric engine makes only the faintest noise, allowing us to roll right up to the last tree before her house. We've got a perfect view of the bottle tree and clearing. Miss Delia's seated in front of the fire, a metal lock box in her lap.

With a shaking hand, she unlocks the box, then pries open the lid and pulls out what looks like a mojo bag. Clasping the tiny pocket between her palms as if in prayer, she mumbles to herself, then raises her hands above her head and calls,

"Fire and heat in darkest night,
Join forces to reveal this curio's might
To concoct black magic strange and dark
Sealing one's fate from just a spark."

She tosses the mojo onto the flames. The fire blazes just as before.

Shaking her head, she pulls out another bag and follows the same ritual.

"What is she doing?" Jack whispers.

"Testing something."

"By throwing it into the fire? What the heck is it?"

"Uh, it's a hoodoo thing. I don't think I'm allowed to tell you." It's best not to explain that those bags are likely filled with black magic curios so dark and dangerous Miss Delia's igniting them on her own, because she fears I'm not strong enough to resist their power. And that they're wrapped in those tiny swatches of cotton because she doesn't want their raw materials to touch her skin. No wonder she kicked us out of here. She's been planning this all day. With my energy drained and magical powers out of commission, the stuff in those bags would probably consume me in a second.

For the next few minutes, Miss Delia prays and tosses mojos into the fire. Each time a tiny bag lands in the flickering orange flames, she leans forward as if waiting for something to happen. Seconds pass before she sinks back into her wheelchair looking more disappointed with each failed attempt. I'm not sure what she's waiting for, but it obviously hasn't happened.

A somber expression crosses her face as she withdraws a black packet from the lock box. She crosses herself, then looks to the sky and mouths a prayer.

My scalp pricks. I edge closer on my seat.

Drawing a deep breath, she encases the mojo between her palms and shuts her eyes. Then she raises her hands once again and shouts the incantation. The bag sails from her hands and lands on a flaming log.

A yellow-white flash ignites, shooting sparks up and out of the fire. Tiny embers land in the dry foliage beneath the tree. The ground rumbles, shaking Miss Delia's wheelchair and swaying the low-hanging bottles in the tree.

Jack's eyes pop. "What's going on?"

"Her test worked. It unleashed some powerful magic. Just hold on." I grip the golf cart's dashboard, anticipating the inevitable shockwave that's bound to charge our way.

An explosion blasts in the bonfire, splitting the burning logs and causing them to collapse on themselves. Thick plumes of black smoke billow into the oak's canopy, their sooty tendrils caressing each bottle and causing them to vibrate and glow a sinister red. Within moments, the tree is bathed in crimson light, like a giant burning bush without the flames.

Jack gasps.

The quaking escalates, rattling like a speeding freight train as it stretches across the yard and rocks the golf cart. At the epicenter, Miss Delia tenses and grips the arms on her chair as the quake thrashes her from side to side.

Suddenly her head yanks back as if whiplashed, then snaps forward as she begins to convulse. Her body spasms, flopping around like a fish on a line.

She's having a seizure. This is why I'm here.

"Miss Delia!" I leap from the golf cart and race to her.

"Emma!" Jack's voice echoes behind me.

"Come on! She needs us," I scream over my shoulder. His footsteps follow behind me.

Rushing over the shaking ground, I lose my balance but somehow manage to stay on my feet. Halfway to the bottle tree the earthquake begins to ebb, as the vibrations slow and turn shallower.

Miss Delia's mouth is covered in white foam. My feet kick into overdrive, closing the space between us. Steps away, I reach to console her but she jerks forward and lunges out of the chair, landing face-first in the dirt. Her upper body quivers as her lifeless legs splay on the ground.

The earth finally stills as I kneel at her waist and try to flip her on her side, but she's still flailing around and it's nearly impossible to do by myself.

Jack crouches beside me and pries his hands beneath her side. "On three, okay?" he says, anticipating my request for help.

I nod as he counts. "One."

"Two," I add.

"Three." We say together and push her over.

"We got you, Miss D." Jack clasps her hand.

Her gaze bores into me.

"You're going to be okay. I promise." I hope it's the truth as I wipe the spit from her lips and peer into her mouth to make sure her airway is clear.

The light in the bottles fades, dimming to black. At the same time the fire shrinks, the flames collapsing on themselves as if someone doused the inferno with a bucket of water. Miss Delia stills. A low moan rolls up her throat.

I brush the dirt from her face. "Shh. Don't try to talk. We're going to get you inside, okay?"

She nods, ever so slightly, and her eyes shut.

"Jack, I need you to pick her up and carry her inside. I'll bring up her chair."

"No problem." He slides his arms under her back and knees, then strains to stand with her in his arms. The muscles in his neck pull and his face turns magenta.

He grunts. "For a little old lady, she's heavy."

"You sure you can handle it? Maybe we should carry her together. You can't drop her. She'll break a hip."

"Nah. I got it."

Biting my lip, I push her chair and watch as he struggles to carry her through the yard, past the garden, and up the steps. I can't help but remember how Cooper scooped her up so easily earlier this summer after the *plateyes* first attacked. In his arms, she seemed as light as feather. In Jack's, she looks more like a sack stuffed with of overgrown potatoes.

Inside, we bring her straight to her room and lay her on her bed. Though her eyes are still closed, her pulse is strong. Jack runs to the bathroom for a basin of warm water and a washcloth while I race to the kitchen for a glass of water and a vial of *Four Thieves Vinegar*.

We meet back at the same time and Jack gives us some privacy. As I remove her clothes and cleanse her face and arms, I think about all that has happened tonight. Because of my brainless, wretched mistake, Miss Delia is angry with me. If she dies, I'll have to live with the fact that our last conversation was an argument and that she's lost trust in me. There's only one thing to do—she can't die. Not before I've found a way to make things right between us.

When she's clean, I cover her with a cotton blanket and spoon out a generous helping of vinegar and slide it into her mouth.

She swallows and her eyes fly open. "Emma!"

"I know you're mad that I came back, but please let me explain—"

She clutches my hand. "That's not important now. I know what we need to break the Beaumont Curse. That's all that matters."

Chapter Twenty

Miss Delia pulls me close, her grip surprisingly strong. "The curio Sabina used. It's strong black magic. The worst I've ever known. So powerful. Full of evil." Turning her head, she coughs. "A *Black Cat Bone*."

My mind races, but I don't have any memory of such a curio. "I never read anything about that in your spell book." I lift the glass of water to her lips and help her drink.

She swallows. "Because I don't want anything to do with one. Not in my kitchen, not in my practice. It's evil through and through."

"Then how'd you get one to test?"

Her face turns hard. "I once knew someone who had one, along with a whole slew of other bad magic curios. He hotfooted it out of here in a hurry one day and left his supplies behind. They've been under lock and key ever since, in case I needed them. You never know when you might need to fight fire with fire." She sets her teeth as her gaze drifts out the window, into the backyard. She's slipped into that dark place again.

My heart aches for her. "Who was it?" The words blurt from my mouth before I have a chance to stop them.

Drawing a deep breath, she pats my hand. "A bad man who did bad things and was fixing to do something even worse before I fixed him instead. But that was a long time ago. He's long gone now." Her voice fades. It sounds tired. Old.

Her words sink in and weigh heavy on my chest. Though I don't totally understand what she said, something tells me she's just confided something very serious. And quite possibly grim. It's clear she's finished talking about it and frankly, I'm not sure I want to know more about someone so horrible.

"So the *Black Cat Bone*. Is it what I think it is? Like, literally a bone from a black cat?"

Yeah, definitely a more uplifting subject than bad guys.

She nods. "Harvested after sacrificing the creature alive in a vat of boiling water. When the water cooks off, it's the bone sitting on the top of the pile. Only the most wicked, dark-hearted soul would stoop to create one. Whole, that bone can be used for invisibility spells and to bring back a lost lover. But I got to thinking, what if Sabina ground one into a powder? What would all that all concentrated villainy and terror be capable of?"

"Igniting a revenge curse?" I suggest.

"Like a stick of dynamite."

"So what do we do? How do you combat concentrated villainy and terror?"

"Oldest answer in the book: pure love."

"Okay, but how?" I think back to how I broke The Creep. "Do I have to cut my palm again? Because that hurt like a mother."

"Your blood saved your brother Jack because it represented

your love for him. This hex is something else entirely. You need to find something that's specific to Cooper, the curse it represents, and it's got to hold the power of pure love."

Uh, sure that shouldn't be too hard to find.

My brain starts to pound. "What could that be?" I scratch my head.

"Don't look at me. You're his girlfriend. Besides, you've got the most natural ability I've ever seen. I've no doubt you'll find something in that mansion of theirs that'll work."

Considering tonight's colossal mistake with the energy tea, I'm stunned by her assessment. "You really think so?"

She nods. "I wouldn't say it if I didn't. Though I confess, it is confounding." She reaches for another drink of water.

"Why? Because I'm a *buckruh comeyah*?" I tip the glass to her lips.

Her brow creases as if I've just asked the stupidest thing ever. "No, because you don't come to hoodoo naturally, through your family lineage. It's not often that someone without magic in their blood can be such a strong conjurer. But sometimes hoodoo picks its practitioners and not the other way around."

I think back on her demonstration this morning with Taneea. "Do you think I'll ever learn to do one of those element-control things with my mind?"

Her brow quirks. "What are you talking about?"

"This morning you made the wind blow and thunder boom when you were trying to make a point with Taneea. That was amazing."

She waves her hand. "It wasn't anything more than directing my intention and energy. Under all the herbs, roots, and curios, if the power is within you, and you've got enough focus and determination, you can make anything happen with your mind. Which is why I'm sure you can figure out what to use to counteract the *Black Cat Bone*."

I appreciate her confidence, but since Cooper's not even returning our texts, it might be more difficult than she imagines. At least I've still got a few days to puzzle this out. In the meantime, I'm not leaving her side until I'm sure she's okay. It's the least I can do to make things up to her.

"I don't want to leave you alone tonight."

"You don't have to do that." But judging from the light beaming in her eyes, she doesn't mind one bit.

"I know. But I want to. Besides, I'm betting Tancca's not coming home anytime soon and you need help. I'll call my dad and tell him Jack and I are sleeping over. Of course, he'll think we're up at the Big House, but I don't have to correct him."

She smiles. "Thank you, Emma. You're a good girl."

I can't help but think of our earlier argument. "Not always."

"Enough of the time." Miss Delia's lids sag.

"I'll let you sleep." I pull the sheet up under her chin, turn off the light, and leave her bedroom.

Jack's in the living room, lounging on the couch, squinting at the grainy television picture. "I know Miss D doesn't have the money for a flat screen, but this blows."

"Well, you'd better deal with it. We're staying here tonight."

"I get it. She needs us."

I breathe a sigh of relief that we don't have to fight about this. "Hey, can you give me your cell? I want to call Dad."

"Sure." He fishes in his pocket for his phone, then tosses it to me.

As I'm dialing, Miss Delia shrieks, "Emma! Emma!"

I spin on my heels and race toward her room. Jack's right behind me.

Crashing in her room, I slam on the light switch and dash to her bedside. "What's the matter?"

She's propped up on her elbows, her brown, rheumy eyes filled with panic. "You've got to leave. Right away." Her hand is clutched around the green and white beads of her *collier*.

"What? Why? You can't take care of yourself," I argue.

She shakes her head. "Don't worry about me. I'll be fine. And I won't be alone for long. You've got to go and take my spell book and the ancestors' mortar and dagger with you. Now. You don't have a minute to lose." She's trembling.

"Uh, okay." My heart jackhammers as I spin around and bump into Jack on my way out of her room.

"And gather some agrimony, rue, buchu, and anything else you think you might need while you're at it." Her voice is strained and brimming with alarm.

Charging to the kitchen, I grab the dagger and toss it into the mortar, which still contains the remnants from our failed *Psychic Vision* spell. I'll clean it out later.

"Am I allowed in?" Jack's voice carries through the swinging door. "You're going to need help carrying that thing."

He's right. But he's never been in the kitchen before, though I'm guessing Miss Delia wouldn't give a flying fig plant about her rules right now. "Sure," I answer as I scurry around, grabbing crocks from the shelves and tossing their contents into various Ziploc bags.

Jack sidles up to the granite mortar and tries to lift it. He groans as his muscles tense and bulge, and his face bypasses red and goes straight to purple. Setting it back down he grunts. "That sucker is heavy."

"Yeah, I know." I toss a handful of bags into the vessel and race to fill more. "I'll help you carry it in a second. Why don't you drive the golf cart up to the gate? That way we won't have to drag that thing across the yard."

"Good thinking." He shakes out his arms. "Be right back."

By the time I've gathered the rest of the supplies, Jack's back in the house, my messenger bag in his hands. "Here, I figured you might need this."

"Awesome, thanks." I slip the spell book and pirate's dagger into the bag, then sling it over my shoulder. We're ready to go. Except, I can't leave without saying good-bye to Miss Delia. "I'll be right back." I bolt from the kitchen, then duck my head into her bedroom door. "We're ready. I've got everything you said and a few other things."

"Good girl."

"I guess I'll see you tomorrow?"

She shakes her head, her eyes like glassy pools. "No child. You can't come back. Not for a while. I'll let you know when it's okay. Until then, you must promise you won't come back here."

My heart seizes. "But, what about Cooper's birthday? I still don't know what to do."

"You're smart. You'll figure it out."

"But—"

"But nothing. Go. Now." She points a gnarled finger toward the hall.

"Okay." I run back to the kitchen and stand next to the ancestors' mortar, across from Jack. "You take one side, and I'll take the other."

We lift the mortar slowly, then shuffle across the room in baby steps. Even with his help, I'm reasonably sure my arms might rip from their sockets. This thing was heavy when Cooper and I carried it from the museum, but now I realize how much more of the load he carried. Jack's not a weakling but he's no

Cooper Beaumont.

Finally we make it out of the kitchen, across the living room and porch, down the steps, then out through the yard. There's more grunting and huffing and puffing then a Three Little Pigs story, but somehow we make it to the golf cart without Jack having a hernia. We set the mortar on the back-facing rear seat, then jump in and get out of there as fast as possible. Which isn't saying much considering the cart's top speed is fifteen miles an hour.

Near the end of the long dirt driveway, I hear the rumble of engines nearby. They're idling in place. One is definitely big and loud, a motor as much for show as performance. The other rattles, but doesn't sound quite as impressive.

Jack pulls off the opposite side of the road into a grove of large live oaks and kills the headlights. Slowly, he drives the silent golf cart toward the sound of the engines.

"What are you doing?" I whisper.

"Don't you want to see who it is? This is our chance."

He's right. Though if the panic I saw in Miss Delia's eyes is any indication, we don't want to meet the drivers in person. "Okay, but don't get too close."

Cloaked by the live oaks and their sheets of hanging moss, the cart approaches the end of the dirt road. The cars are pulled over on the side of the street that runs perpendicular to where we are and connects to Sea Island Parkway. Their headlights cast a ghostly glow. Taneea's obnoxious pink truck is in front. Claude's black Lincoln sits behind hers. Taneea and Claude are standing between the two vehicles, locked in serious conversation. Even at night, Claude's wearing his ridiculous glasses.

Jack and I hold our breath in silence and watch as Claude

says something that makes Taneea's face lights up. She jumps up and down and claps her hands. Whatever it is, it's made her happier then I've seen her in weeks. And he looks pretty pleased as well. His ultrabright smile glows in the dark.

A few moments later, Taneea gives him a quick hug and then scampers off to her truck. Once again she doesn't seem to have a problem climbing into the cab. My fist clenches, and I imagine the satisfaction of slamming it into her smirking face.

She revs the engine, then pulls off, spinning her wheels as she turns down the dirt road and races toward Miss Delia's house.

Claude watches, beaming. After she's gone, he looks up at the moon and stares in quiet contemplation. Then he throws back his head and lets loose a wicked cackle. Clutching his side, he bends at the waist and howls in deep, belly-rolling laughter. When he quiets, he climbs into his car, and makes a U-turn, pulling on to Sea Island Parkway, and drives into the night.

Chapter Twenty-one

My eyes fly open, a fully formed plan fresh in my dream-clogged head. It's so obvious I can't believe I didn't think of it last night at Miss Delia's. Cooper's *Protective Shield* mojo, the one I made for him, is all I'll need to break the Beaumont Curse. Crafted especially for him, it's also related to the curse, and it's filled with my love for him.

Easy-peasy lemon-squeezy.

A smile slides across my face as I sink back into my pillow, relieved to have figured it all out with two days to go before his birthday. All it took was a good night's sleep. Now I can get a little more shut-eye before Jack and I figure out what to do with the dagger and the ancestors' mortar.

My eyes spring open again. The dagger and the mortar. It was so dark when we got back, we hid them behind Dad's workshop but they can't stay there, or anywhere Claude is likely to search at High Point Bluff. As much as I'd love to lie under my cozy covers, we've got to find a place to stow them for real.

And fast. After seeing Claude's bizarre moon dance last night, I don't put anything past him.

Kicking off the covers, I throw on some clothes, then rush to Jack's room, but he's already out of bed. I trudge down the stairs and find him at the kitchen table, a giant bowl of cereal in front of him and his cell phone at his side.

"Hey," he mumbles around a mouth full of Crunchy Crumbles.

I slide out a chair and plop down. "We've got to figure out what to do with the mortar and the knife."

"Way ahead of you. The Beaumont cemetery. It's off-limits and so overgrown, no one will notice if we stow them in the crypt."

Occasionally my brother is a genius. This is one of those times.

"Awesome." I breathe a sigh of relief and dive my hand into the cereal box, pulling out a fistful of Crumbles. There's no way Claude would go trudging through that kudzu-infested mess. Though I can't help but feel a wee bit guilty about breaking our promise to our dad. The cemetery is officially off-limits without his supervision, but it's not like we've got any other choice.

He smirks. "I know. You can tell me I'm brilliant now. I won't disagree."

I roll my eyes as I munch the sugar-coated oat clusters, relishing the opportunity to keep the compliment to myself, if only because he's asked for it. "I wouldn't go that far."

He laughs. "You suck."

"Whatever." I shrug and dig in for some more cereal. Something occurs to me. "I don't think we can get the golf cart between those graves. And no offense, but you can't carry that thing through the cemetery. I won't be much help either. My arms are still killing me from last night."

"Got that covered too." He lifts his cell phone. "I've already launched a full-on assault on Coop's voice mail and text messages. That dude's going to call me back one way or another." The phone rings in his hand, flashing Cooper's name on the caller ID. Jack grins. "See? What did I tell you?" Placing the phone on the table, he hits the speaker button. "Yo, where have you been, bro? I've left you about a million messages."

"Yeah. I know. I've been busy." Cooper's voice is more terse than I've ever heard.

"Really? So have we. With a crap-ton of stuff to keep Miss D and us out of jail and break the curse that's hanging over your soul, but that's all right. You keep busy with whatever it is you've been doing. With Taneea, I assume."

I hold my breath, hoping he'll deny it.

Cooper's silent for a few seconds. Then he clears his throat. "What do you want me to say?"

My stomach pings. Not exactly a denial.

"Say you'll meet us at your family's cemetery in a half hour," Jack says.

"Now?" Cooper asks.

"No, next week. Come on, you of all people know how important this is."

"But I've got plans. Can't we do it later?"

"You're joking, right?"

"Fine. I'll be there." The line goes dead.

My jaw hangs open. "He didn't ask about me. Or ask to talk to me. And he's been with her."

Jack's gaze drops to the table. "I'm sorry."

"I don't understand what's happening." Is it possible that she really is his type after all?

"It's got to be the Beaumont Curse. You said so yourself. This is Coop we're talking about. He's not normally such a twonk."

Jack's right. Cooper's behavior has been way off the rails. Even if he has lost his mind and decided to be with Taneea, he's got no reason to ignore me and Jack—his best friends for eight years—especially with all that's hanging over our heads. The Beaumont Curse may not have stolen his soul yet, but it's got to be affecting his thinking.

I slide my chair out from the table and rise to my feet. "The only way to know for sure is to break the curse in time and see if he snaps back to normal. But first we've got to make sure the mortar and dagger are safe."

A half hour later, Jack and I are at the Beaumont family cemetery, sitting in the golf cart waiting for Cooper to show up.

We wait.

Then wait some more.

After three hours, Jack's fuming in the summer heat, hot, hungry, and madder than a rabid raccoon, pacing the kudzu-choked perimeter. If it wasn't for my sketchbook and pastel pencils and the looming live oaks that cast some fairly decent shade, I'd be right there with him. Instead, propped up against this sturdy tree trunk, I'm doing my best to conserve what little energy I've got left and be Zen. It's not too difficult. Despite the fact we're in an old cemetery, the setting is pretty perfect for drawing. Plus, the strange and beautiful birds flying over the adjacent salt marsh make great subjects, too.

"Where is he?" Jack kicks a clump of emerald-green brush. His toe catches the corner of a gravestone hidden beneath the foliage. "Ah!" he howls and cradles his foot in his hand. "This is all Cooper's fault."

"Right. He made you kick a stationary object." I blend the final touches of yellow into the pelican's head then squint at my latest masterpiece.

"Yes, he did," Jack snaps. "Because he broke his word, *again*. And because he made me mad enough to kick it in the first place." He glares.

"You know, we could have rolled the mortar to the crypt in the time we've wasted waiting for him."

"No. I'm not giving him another out. He's going to help us, even if it takes all day." He pulls out his cell and dials Cooper for probably the hundredth time since we've been here.

"Okay." I sigh and flip the page, readying to start another picture. This time I think I'll draw a black skimmer in flight. I love how their white wingspans and underbellies contrast with their black backs and orange beaks.

The plantation's second golf cart hums toward us. Cooper pulls up next to ours and turns off the engine. He steps out of the cart. I do a double take. He's wearing a black leather jacket over what looks like a wife-beater T-shirt, a backward baseball cap, and super-long jean shorts that hang down around his backside, but provide an eye-popping glimpse of the top half of his boxers.

Jack rolls his eyes.

Cooper approaches in neon-orange high tops. "Sorry. I lost track of time." He doesn't look apologetic, but he does look ridiculous. And hot, but not in a good way because that leather definitely doesn't breathe.

"Hey, Cooper." I can't help but gawk at his heinous new clothes.

"Hey." For a split second, he looks embarrassed by this getup, but then recovers his swagger.

Jack sets his foot down and limps toward Cooper. "Dude. How does a half hour turn into three and half? And what's with not answering my calls?"

Cooper shrugs. "I told you I was busy. I can't drop everything just because you want me to. I'm here now so what do you want?"

"For starters, for you not to be such a sphincter and to start helping us because while you've been shopping, we've had to deal with a whole lot of stuff, including hiding evidence."

Cooper's face twists in confusion. "What are you talking about?"

Jack tosses his hands in the air. "I don't even know where to start."

I flip the cover on my sketchbook, then jam it into my messenger bag. Standing up from my comfy spot at the base of the tree, I dust off my shorts and step around a half-dozen graves to get to where they stand. "A lot happened after you left yesterday." I fill him in on all he missed, highlighting our suspicion of Claude.

Cooper scratches his temple. "You could have told me everything back at the Big House. Or on the phone. Why did I have to come here?"

"Dude. Did you miss the part about how Miss Delia made us take the dagger and mortar out of her house and promise to keep it safe? If Claude really is trying to frame your dad, we can't keep that stuff where it can be easily found. We need you to bring the mortar to the crypt. We'll hide the rest of the stuff there too." Jack points to the ancestor's mortar on the backseat of the golf cart.

"You dragged me away from Taneea to *move* something for you? Bulk up and carry it yourself." Cooper's skin flushes a shade of scarlet I've never seen before without a sunburn. He turns and stomps toward his own golf cart.

Jack charges after him. "Hey!"

Cooper pivots on his rubber soles. "What? I've got somewhere to be."

"Do you think we asked you down here for fun? Or that I enjoy harassing you? We need you. When you didn't call us back yesterday, we drove the cart on the road and could have gotten picked up by the sheriff's deputies. Then I almost slipped a disc trying to carry that mortar. We're supposed to be a team but you've gone lone wolf on us and don't seem to give a crap about anything but Taneea, though I can't understand why."

"Listen, I was trying to be nice about it, but I'm with her now, okay? I don't expect you to get our relationship because it's come as a surprise to me as well. But we're good together. Perfect, in fact. There's a good chance I'll lose my soul in two days. Can't I enjoy the time I've got left?"

The blood drains from my head as I work to make sense of his words. But it's impossible because even though we're using the same language, it's as if he's speaking Greek. He and Taneea are perfect together? How is that possible?

Jack's mouth hangs slack. "Well, congratulations. I guess. But I still need you to move the mortar."

"Fine." Cooper strides toward our cart. Whipping off the leather jacket, he takes several deep, preparatory breaths, then hoists the mortar up in his arms. Grunting under the strain of the heavy granite vessel, he begins the slow journey to the crypt. His biceps are ripped and the cords in his throat are pulled taut. Jack follows, his arms filled with other supplies we took from Miss Delia's.

My head spins as I stumble to a nearby grave and collapse

on the low headstone. I know Cooper. He's kind, good, and loving. There's no way in the world he'd magically decide Taneea's his ideal match.

Maybe that's it. Some sort of magic is at work here, blinding him to her flaws, and drawing him close to her. Could it be the Beaumont Curse? If it has begun to take hold, he'll end up as corrupt and depraved as Beau, and Taneea might very well be his ideal match. Or has something equally dark and destructive snared him in its grip? Once I wondered whether Taneea had dabbled in more than gambling spells—what if I was right? With expert help, she could probably force Cooper to do anything. But what possible motive would she have to coerce his affection? She's got her pick of guys. Why bother to force Cooper to love her?

Just as I'm beginning to feel hopeful, another option slams to the front of my mind, seizing my heart. What if his feelings for Taneea are real? She's a virtual boy-magnet so it's not completely far-fetched. And though they seem like a match made in Hades, crazier things have happened. Isn't that why they say opposites attract? Sometimes, no matter what everyone else thinks, two people come together for reasons only they can understand. As painful as this possibility is to contemplate, it might be the truth.

There's only one way to find out—start with what I know and go from there. If I can figure out what kind of *Break Jinx* spell to work on his mojo bag, the Beaumont Curse will be destroyed. With any luck he'll turn back to the Cooper I know and love, and he'll forget this nonsense with Taneea. If not, well, I'll figure out something new then.

Fifteen minutes later, Cooper's back, shaking out his arms, which are likely as limp as cold spaghetti. He stops several feet from me, well out of arm's reach.

"Hey, I'm sorry you had to hear about me and Taneea that way. I'd planned to tell you differently, but I didn't get the chance."

I lift my head to meet his gaze. His eyes are cold and nearly colorless, just the faintest hint of gray swirls in his irises. He doesn't exactly look like a guy in love. He barely even looks like Cooper. An eerie feeling crawls across my scalp. I don't care how much he claims to care for Taneea, something's definitely not right.

I rise to my feet and words fly from my mouth. "Who do you think you are?"

He takes a step forward. The piney fragrance of his deodorant has been replaced with something exotic and spicy that smells a lot like Taneea's perfume mixed with her stinky hand cream. "I know you're hurt and probably furious, but I wish you could be happy for me. I've found real love."

My pulse pounds as I scan his face. "That's not what I mean. Are you even still in there? Or has the Beaumont Curse grabbed you a few days early? Am I wasting my time trying to save your soul?"

He looks wounded. "Of course not. You've got to break the curse. Just as long as you know it's not going to make me take you back. I'm with Taneea now."

Stung, I nod. "Yeah. I got that. Loud and clear." I should probably let it drop, accept this new reality, but my senses nag, not buying his love story. "How do you know she's not working some kind of spell on you? We already caught her working gambling charms. She could be conjuring again. You said yourself you felt like you were slipping away. What if she's causing it?"

He laughs. "That's ridiculous. I know it would make you feel better to think that's what's going on, but when I said that, I was just overreacting to my feelings for her because they're so strong. Trust me, what Taneea and I have is real. That's why I need you to break the Beaumont Curse so she and I can truly be together, without it hanging over our heads. So when do you think you'll be ready to work your magic?"

I don't know what's really behind his epic change of heart, but I doubt it's as neat and simple as he says. If I'm right, I've got no choice but to fight for his soul even though it might break my heart. "Soon. You're still wearing the mojo bag, right?" I scan his tank top, hoping it's tucked neatly underneath.

"No. Taneea didn't like it. She took it off."

My vision flashes white. "She what? You let her? How could you?" The cemetery spins as my brain works to take in all the implications of this seemingly small act.

"It's not really appropriate to keep wearing it."

My brow knits. "It's not like we're talking about a promise ring. That bag isn't about *us*. It's about protecting *you*."

"Emma, come on. Anyone who touches that thing knows better than that. Taneea did and it made her really uncomfortable. She said it's filled with your feelings for me. It's not fair of me to do that to her. Besides, now that things have changed between me and you, it can't possibly have the same power as before."

Faced with this harsh reality, the very significant pieces click into place. First, as he's so coolly pointed out, the mojo can't be the answer to breaking a curse ignited by a *Black Cat Bone*. He's made it clear that we're over. Kaput. Done. So even though the mojo was created for him and was formulated to protect him from a black magic curse, it doesn't represent pure love. Not even close. Pure love is true. Unconditional. Reciprocal.

Our relationship, at least for the time being, is none of the above.

But more important is the fact that the mojo, which has been keeping the Beaumont Curse at bay, is gone. Now he's exposed and vulnerable to an early attack. I don't have the time I thought.

The heat on my neck turns ice cold, and a dreadful feeling crawls across my chest, then inches up my throat, closing it over. I'd thought the mojo was the key, but now I'm back to square one, out of ideas, and out of luck. How am I going to find something that meets all the criteria Miss Delia listed before the curse takes hold?

My breath is shallow. I don't know how, but the effects of my disastrous energy tea seem to be inverting. Instead of feeling pumped up, I'm more like a deflated balloon. Light-headed, I reach out for the only thing that's solid, Cooper's arm, to keep from fainting.

He grabs my hand but only long enough to guide me safely back down to the low headstone, then quickly pulls away. "I told you, I'm with Taneea now."

As if I needed the reminder. But I've got bigger concerns, like trying not to fall on my face in a graveyard. Woozy, I drop my head between my thighs and breathe deep.

"Emma!" Jack calls on his way back from making his own drop-off at the crypt. But he must misinterpret Cooper's body looming over my hunched shoulders because he dashes toward me and kneels at my side. Looking up at Cooper he snaps, "Dude, what is your major damage?"

I lift my head enough to peek at them both.

Ignoring Jack's question, Cooper nods toward me. "Call me

when you've figured out what to do." Then he turns and saunters toward his cart.

"You okay?" Jack searches my gaze.

"I'm fine," I lie. "Go after him. No matter what you do, keep him up at the Big House and don't let him out of your sight until I can figure some stuff out. He's taken off his *Protective Shield* so that curse could take hold whenever it wants."

Chapter Twenty-two

After Jack chases Cooper in our golf cart, I let the tears I've kept locked inside flow. They're as much from my broken heart as from abject frustration and utter cluelessness. Time's running out and I've got no idea what to do next.

Hot liquid stings my cheeks. I've got no working mortar, an ex-boyfriend who's either losing his soul or his mind, and I can't even visit Miss Delia for advice.

I don't think I've ever been so screwed.

Miss Delia's voice echoes in my mind, her last words assuring me I can figure it all out. Which only makes me laugh between garbled sobs. I can't. Every time I think I've come up with something, it comes back to bite me in the rear. Who am I to think I can break a three hundred year old curse by myself? Especially one cast by someone as powerful and vengeful as Sabina? I'm not special. I don't have hoodoo in my blood like Sabina and Miss Delia. I'm just a teenager, a *buckrah comeyah* with a couple month's worth of hoodoo training. In other words,

I'm nothing.

Looks like Taneea was right after all. About everything. Which burns even more.

A fresh set of sobs threatens to well over, but I suck them up. I will not shed them over her or Cooper. Maybe they deserve each other.

Bitter acid coats my tongue. Maybe he deserves everything that's coming to him, including his soulless fate.

I shudder, sickened that I allowed such a hateful thought to pass through my head. I should know better. In his heart, Cooper isn't the canker he's been for the last couple weeks. Maybe Taneea has found a way to magically mess with his feelings. Though I'm inclined to believe the Beaumont Curse has settled in a bit early, snagged him in its claws before he officially comes of age. The only way to bring him back is to break the hex that holds him in its grip.

But that still leaves me clueless about what to do next.

A familiar scent tickles my nose. Lifting my face to get a better whiff, I breathe deep. It's sharp and cloying and almost antiseptic. A charge jolts my body. It's a stargazer lily. Maggie's fragrance. Maggie, Jack's ghostly ex-girlfriend whose evil murder at the hands of Bloody Bill and his pirates kicked off The Creep and the Beaumont Curse in the first place.

But there are no lilies in this cemetery, just rows and rows of faded white headstones and grave markers draped with clinging green vines.

The stargazer perfume swirls around my head, enveloping me.

Which only proves I've officially lost it. Not only am I blathering alone in a cemetery in which I have no dead relatives, but I'm sensing imaginary flowers. I should probably leave before I start hearing voices.

I rise to my feet once again, determined to bolt though I'm not sure to where. The moment my flip-flops touch the ground, my soles tingle. With my luck it's probably an allergic reaction to the kudzu I've been tromping through for the last four-and-a-half hours.

Making a beeline toward the path that leads out of the cemetery, my feet begin to itch. Stooping to scratch them, I don't feel any welts or bug bites, so I pick up my pace. The cloying scent intensifies and seems to follow me as the itching intensifies to a burn. A strange urge implants itself in my brain. If I return to the cemetery to the cool, lush leaves of the kudzu, the stinging will relent. Which is crazy because that's where it started in the first place. I break into a jog, but the urge turns into full-on longing and the burning ratchets so high I can barely stand the feel of my feet at the end of my legs.

Suddenly the King Center comes to mind, along with the sensations I felt when Maggie induced me to pick up the pirate's dagger before we nabbed the ancestors' mortar.

I stop short. The burning quiets, reducing to a low tingling that buzzes on the tender flesh of my feet. The stargazer scent infuses my clothes and hair. I've probably lost it, but it can't hurt to test my theory.

"Maggie?" I call into the air. "Is that you?"

The wind blows past me, toward the cemetery. Maybe that's a sign. Or maybe it's not. I take another step down the path, away from the cemetery to be sure. The burning blasts back, singeing my feet.

I squeal. "Ah! Okay, okay. I get it."

Backtracking toward the cemetery, I stop at the end of the path. "I have no idea where to go," I call to no one, or maybe

Maggie. The sweet perfume wafts under my nose then carries away on the breeze, deeper into the graveyard. Oh-kay. I guess I'll follow it.

Chasing the scent, I make my way through the rows, past Missy's plot and the crypt, to the most kudzu-chocked area of the graveyard. Somewhere in here is Cooper's mother's grave, though thanks to my dad's freak-out, we never saw it. I stand on the cusp of the thick vegetation and look around, not sure where I should put my foot. Who knows what's under the thick emerald carpet? For all I know there could be snakes lurking in there, waiting to bite anyone who passes over them. My flip-flops aren't exactly built for hiking.

An electric shock prods my heels.

Exasperated, I look up into the sky and yell, "I don't know what you want from me. If I climb through here, I'm liable to trip and break my neck."

"Emma Guthrie. You are closer than you know." Maggie's voice, faint, but oh so very clear, carries on the breeze.

Okay. It's official. I'm hearing the voice of a dead girl.

My legs tremble. "If this is some sort of a sick joke, I'm not laughing."

Stargazer scent circles my body. "Emma Guthrie. Have faith. You are closer than you know."

Tears flow and a cool, calm sensation rushes over my body. It is Maggie. And she wants me to trust her. I draw a deep breath. Why not?

Following the scent, I carefully step forward, lifting my flip-flops and placing them on the lush emerald vines as I pass a number of cloaked headstones. Another zap strikes my sole. "What? I'm walking like you wanted me to." I take another step, but this time, the shock is stronger and shoots straight up my leg. I pull up, halting in place. The buzzing stops completely. I'm guessing I'm exactly where I should be. Right in front of a vine-covered headstone so completely cloaked in kudzu it looks like a topiary bush.

The breeze blows, rustling the bright green leaves clinging to the stone.

I'm closer than I know, huh? Stepping nearer, I reach over and claw at the dense vines, yanking them away. The thick strands are stubborn, seeming to cling harder as I pull. There's no way I've come this far to be beaten by a plant. Wedging my foot against the marker for leverage, I lean back, gripping hard on the vine until it finally snaps. Repeating the motion several times, I break enough to make out the name on the marker.

CLARISSA BEAUMONT. BORN: 1973, DIED: 2002.

I do the math. The woman in this grave died when Cooper was just five years old. It's his mother.

I clear the rest of the stone. It's polished and looks practically brand new, as if it hasn't been sitting here, exposed to the elements, for the last eleven years.

And there's something else. Below her name and dates of birth and death, a silver heart-shaped pendant on a chain is embedded in the stone, encased in glass. It's about two inches long and features a mother and child etched on the cover, with tiny ruby hearts embedded in each of their chests. The mother is gazing at the babe in her arms, a smile on her face. Below the glass case, the stone is inscribed, BELOVED WIFE AND MOTHER.

For Cooper's sake, I'm glad I found Clarissa's grave, but I'm not sure what I'm supposed to do with this discovery. Why did Maggie lead me here? Is it too much to hope she'll give up her cryptic messages and just tell me what she means?

"So now what?" I run my hand over the smooth, marble

surface.

The stargazer smell hovers above the stone. I bet Maggie's perched right here, laughing at me. "You know, you could give me a hint."

The sun beams on the glass cover, making the tiny ruby shards sparkle.

My upper thigh heats. The Beaumont ruby shard is acting up again. I shove my hand into my pocket to adjust the stone digging into my flesh. An icy charge shoots up my fingers. Yanking my hand away, I peer at my bright red flesh. The gem is so cold it burned me.

Even I can't ignore the fact that something strange is going on here. It can't be a coincidence that the locket's adorned with rubies and the Beaumont ruby is doing its weird temperature thing again. Maggie and my spirit guide must want me to do something. But exactly what, I'm not sure.

I squint at the locket behind the glass. The only way to see it up close is to break the glass and liberate it.

But I've done that sort of thing a couple times already this summer. And though stealing the ancestor's mortar and pirate's dagger gave us the clues we needed to break The Creep, it also led to trouble with Claude and could possibly end up with Miss Delia or us in jail. Breaking into Beau's study helped us get the dagger back, but it also revealed that someone—though I'm still not sure who—was at the very least present when Missy died. Each larceny has had its consequences, so I'm hoping these bossy spirits will understand that I'm not exactly anxious to rush into another one.

Still, there must be a reason Maggie has brought me here. She is, after all, the one who led us to the treasure in the first place, igniting this whole summer's events.

Running my fingers over the glass, I try to gauge its thickness. It doesn't feel too substantial, though there's really no way to tell from looking at just one side. My palm tingles, then itches. An irresistible urge takes over, willing me to find a rock and smash it against the pane until I free the locket encased within. But I've been through this before. That's Maggie's desire. Not mine. Resisting the compulsion, I try to think for myself. It's one thing to decide to do it on my own; it's another for her to force me.

The ruby chips twinkle in the sunlight, drawing my eye. The expression on the mother's face is tender and filled with so much love, it softens my resolve. And then it hits me. This mother's face is why I'm supposed to get this locket. It must have belonged to Clarissa and very likely dangled close to her heart.

I want the locket. I *need* the locket.

I search for a rock or stick big enough to shatter the glass. But all I see is the endless green carpet of kudzu and the occasional corner of gravestone poking out from under the brush. Shoving my hands down into the leaves, I root around, fumbling for something that will break the compartment. Finally, my hand lands on something cold and hard. It's a round, smooth stone, like one of the rocks that line some of the older graves. It'll do.

Racing back to Clarissa's grave, I hold the stone over my head, ready to strike. Realizing I'm about to desecrate her grave to some extent, I bite my bottom lip and offer a word of apology. "I'm sorry, Mrs. Beaumont, but I'm pretty sure I need to do this."

The rock crashes against the case and cracks the glass. I slam it twice more before it shatters. Carefully, I sift through the shards and lift out my quarry. The silver locket is in perfect condition. I pry it open. Inside are two small photos. One of

Clarissa, the other of Cooper. Snapping it closed, I flip it over. The back is inscribed.

Your heart and mine
Forever entwined
Love everlasting
Till the end of time

My chest swells. The locket is filled with Clarissa's love for her son. A mother's *pure love*. It couldn't be more specific to Cooper. And just like the Beaumont Curse, which was first cast when Lady Rose gave birth to her only child, this too features a mother and son. I'd say that's pretty curse-specific.

This is the key to combating the *Black Cat Bone* and breaking the Beaumont Curse.

But now that I've got it, what am I supposed to do with it? My heart pounds as I gaze at the top of Clarissa's headstone to where I imagine Maggie sitting. "I don't know what to do with this. Cooper's not wearing his mojo anymore, so I'm pretty sure I've got to break the curse as soon as possible. But the ancestors' mortar still needs to rest, and my energy's not back."

"You have everything you need." Maggie's voice carries on the breeze.

"What's that supposed to mean?"

The refrain repeats, this time more faint. "You have everything you need."

Chapter Twenty-three

I set aside Miss Delia's spell book and rub my tired eyes at the table in the caretaker's cottage. I've read it cover to cover three times this afternoon. I think I'm ready. At least I hope I am. Picking up my phone, I dial Jack. He answers on the third ring.

"Hey, can you pick me up at Dad's in about an hour? I've got one more thing to do but then I think we'll be ready to try to break this." Not really. I'm actually only half betting we'll be ready but I'm not going to let him in on that.

"Yeah. Just so you know, you owe me big time. It hasn't been easy to keep him here." His voice is clipped.

"It'll be worth it. I promise. We've got to do this thing tonight. I can feel it." At least that's what I think the green and white psychic power beads on my *collier* have told me.

"You're lucky you've still got feeling. I don't."

Um, I'm not exactly sure what that's supposed to mean, but I'm too busy and overwhelmed to decipher it now. "All right then, see you in an hour. Oh, wait. Before I forget, make sure both you and Cooper have your ruby pieces."

"Sure." He cuts the line.

I glance down at the list I've started on the pad in the middle of the kitchen table. Between the stuff in Dad's workshop, the supplies I brought back from Miss Delia's, and a few plants I can clip from the forest around the cemetery, I should have everything covered.

In the meantime, I've got to take the strongest purifying bath I can whip up and hope the *Planetary Sun* bath crystals I snagged from Miss Delia's will help restore a little bit of my physical vitality. Otherwise, I'm not sure how I'll get through the night.

An hour later, exactly to the minute, Jack pulls up to the caretaker's cottage in the golf cart. Cooper's in the front passenger seat, his arms crossed, and a scowl on his face. Though he's ditched the leather jacket, he's still sporting the rest of his new getup, plus one new accessory: his bottom lip is red and swollen. Jack slides out of the cart and walks around to the screened porch. Though he tries to hide it, there's a hitch in his gait. His left eye is purple and swollen.

I suck in a gasp. "What the heck happened?"

"I kept him at the Big House."

I squint at the shiner. "You okay? Did you ice it?"

"Yeah. I'll be fine. It's nothing compared to losing chunks of my skin. Plus I got in a few good swipes of my own. That felt better than any cold pack." He smiles.

I glance at Cooper who's slumped in the seat, looking about as happy to be there as a kid in the principal's office. "Awesome. I guess. You think he'll help load these in the cart?" I point to the pile of tools I've pulled from Dad's workshop.

Jack smirks. "Doubtful. You're lucky he's here at all. All he wants to do is be with Taneea."

"Great. I'm going to need a little more cooperation when we do this."

"Good luck with that."

Together Jack and I load a few shovels, a pruner, and some other supplies. Luckily Dad's been busy running errands for Beau. Otherwise he'd freak if he saw us taking this stuff.

Twenty minutes later, we're at the cemetery. The sun's just starting to set and the sky's the same orange hue as a ripe cantaloupe. Jack jumps out and gets to work on my instruction to bring back a bunch of tall wildflowers I saw growing along one section of the graveyard. Cooper stays slumped in his seat.

I pause on my way past the cart. "Hey, if you don't want to do this, we can just forget it. The curse can take over and steal your soul."

"I'm here, aren't I? Jack didn't have to hold me prisoner in my own house. I could have spent the day with Taneea and met you guys here."

"Look, I know you think we're working against you, but it's for your own good. Whether you like it or not, taking off the *Protective Shield* mojo made you vulnerable to the curse. And since you keep disappearing and won't take our phone calls, we had to make sure you'd be around when we were ready to try a *Break Jinx*."

"How do I know you're not just using the curse as an excuse to try and get back with me?"

I roll my eyes. "We've been best friends for eight years. If you can't tell when I'm being honest with you or believe that I'm looking out for your best interests, then maybe we're too late. Maybe your soul is already gone."

He steps out of the cart. "No, it's not. I can't know for sure, but I'm guessing if it was, I wouldn't care about the curse. But I want to break it once and for all. What do you need from me?"

My heart skips a beat. Maybe the old Cooper is still in there.

"Your help. With a bunch of things. I ran into a little… trouble with a spell I tried to work for myself so I don't have the strength I normally do. I need to rely on both you and Jack."

"No problem. That kid's a lot stronger than I gave him credit for. Though it was a lucky shot." He rubs his swollen lip.

I smirk. "From the looks of his black eye, I'm betting you had it coming."

"Yeah, I guess so." His mouth pulls up into a half grin.

It's nice to joke with him again, even if it is over Jack and him brawling. The important thing is that he's on board, at least for now. If all goes well, I'll only need his cooperation for a couple more hours. By then, hopefully, he'll be back to the Cooper Beaumont I know. And maybe if I'm lucky, he'll remember how much he used to care for me.

Cooper and I trudge to meet Jack among the wildflowers. He's already cut long spires of mullein, the long, spindly weed that has soft, furry leaves and little yellow flowers. I gather a bunch of stalks and bind them together into six-foot-long bundles with the ball of twine I snagged from Dad's workshop. Cooper and Jack cut as many plants as they can find, then help me create a stack of twelve knotted bunches that we can use as *Magic Candles* when we try to break the curse. When we're finished, Jack and Cooper carry the mullein bundles to the deepest part of the cemetery, not far from the banks of the salt marsh.

While Jack runs to get the rest of our supplies, Cooper and I walk through the section that's blanketed with kudzu. I point to the bright white headstone I uncovered earlier in the afternoon. It's the only object sticking out from the bright green carpet of vegetation.

"See that?"

He nods. "Yeah."

"It's your mom's headstone."

"For real?" His voice is breathy as he drops the pruners and runs right for it. He turns to me. "I can hardly remember the day we buried her. Except that it was cold. Rainy. This stone wasn't here then. There was just a bunch of dirt next to her casket." Kneeling in front of the marker, he rubs his hands on the smooth marble surface and then traces his finger on the edge of the now-empty space that held his mother's locket. His brow creases. "What happened here?"

I bite my bottom lip. "Um, I needed something that was in that compartment for tonight's spell."

He pulls his attention toward me for an explanation but thankfully, Jack walks up with two shovels and distracts him. "What do we do with these?" Jack squints at the gravestone in the dimming light. "Is that…?"

"Yeah. My mom. She's right here." Cooper pats the stone, then rises to his feet. Clearing his throat, he appears to force back the emotions that threaten to overflow and points to the shovels in Jack's hands. "What's next?"

I point to his mother's grave. "You and Cooper need to dig twelve holes in a circle around the headstone and then plant each torch deep enough that it won't fall over, but not so deep that it's shorter than us."

While they dig, I smear the ends of each mullein torch with tallow, rendered beef fat I snagged from Miss Delia's to provide the fuel they'll need to burn, and shake a *Break Jinx* herb mixture on the sticky surface. When the *Magic Candles* are in place, Jack and Cooper prune back the kudzu from around Clarissa's grave and the rest of the circle, creating a little clearing.

As they work, I set up a little altar of sorts on top of Clarissa's headstone with fresh fern leaves from the woods outside the caretaker's cottage, a fat white candle, and a small clay bowl that I fill with a vial of holy water from Miss Delia's shelf. After dipping some acacia leaves in the bowl, I sprinkle the altar with the water, then pull out another small bottle filled with althaea root and place it next to the water. These are the secret ingredients that will hopefully make all the difference to making this spell work.

As Jack and Cooper ignite the mullein torches, I light the candle and close my eyes. Taking a deep breath, I utter a silent prayer that Maggie, my intuition, my spirit guide, and research have all pointed me in the right direction. A recurring fear niggles at the back of my mind, reminding me that I don't have the ancestors' mortar, but I tell myself it shouldn't matter. Miss Delia worked almost eighty years' worth of magic without it after it was stolen from her great-gran. Hopefully I can get through tonight without it, too.

"We're ready." Jack's voice fills the muggy night air.

As the lard and *Break Jinx* sprinkle heat on the torches, the scent of grilled meat peppered with apricots and curry fills the newly cleared space, making it smell more like an Indian restaurant than a Lowcountry cemetery.

I open my eyes. The tallow is on fire, spewing black smoke toward the midnight-blue sky.

It's nearly time to start. I pull out my hunk of ruby from my pocket. It sparkles in the candlelight. "Do you each have yours?"

They dig out their own stones and show them to me. "You really think these will be useful?" Cooper asks.

"They have to be. When we broke The Creep, I knew the Beaumont Curse was in the ruby."

"Yeah, but you threw it into the fire," Jack says, needlessly reminding me of my biggest mistake ever.

"And it broke into three pieces," Cooper adds.

"But the curse wasn't broken. So logically that means it's still in the ruby."

Cooper looks around the clearing. "But Maggie said we needed ice. I don't see any."

"That's because we don't have any. Yet. It'll be here." I sound a lot more confident than I am. Because truthfully, I'm not sure how we'll fill that important void, but I'm putting my faith in Maggie.

"Okay. So what's different this time?" Jack asks.

"Well, for starters, we don't have the mortar so we don't have to worry about me throwing it into another fire. And then there's this." I step toward my messenger bag and pull out a soft piece of paper towel that's folded into fours. Unwrapping it, I hold Clarissa's locket out for them to see. "It was in that little round compartment in her headstone."

Cooper sucks in a breath. "I remember that!" His pale gray eyes turn misty as he reaches to stroke its face with his finger. "I used to open and close it." With a trembling hand, he pries his thumb between the two halves and clicks it open, then stares at the photos. His face softens. It's the first time in more than two weeks that I've recognized him.

"I think it's the key to breaking the curse. If everything goes like I hope, you can have it back later tonight."

He nods. "I'd like that." His voice has a hint of its old softness, which only makes me more anxious to get this over with.

I set the locket on top of the gravestone between the candle and bowl of holy water. "Now, there's one last thing I need. You're not going to like it, but you've got to do it, even if it's the last thing you want to do."

Chapter Twenty-four

I extend my hands toward Cooper and Jack; the ruby fragment twinkles in the center of my left palm.

Cooper's lip twists. "You want to hold hands? Do we have to?"

My heart sinks. I guess his softness only applies to his mom. "Believe me, I wouldn't ask if I didn't have to. I don't have enough of my own energy to work this spell, so I need some of yours."

Cooper's brow creases. "For real?"

Jack clasps his palm over my ruby, then holds out his free hand containing his own stone. "Yeah, she is. And considering this is all for you, I say you do it and be grateful."

"Fine," Cooper grumbles as he takes his place opposite Jack and me. We join our hands, locking us in a circle, though Cooper's grip around my fingers is tentative and less than committed.

Still, their energy courses through me in a circular motion, up through one arm, across my body, then out the other side. I draw a huge breath and fill my lungs. Within seconds, I sense the restoration begin in my muscles as my blood vessels deliver rich, oxygen-filled blood to my tissues. I haven't felt this vibrant in days.

Thick, dark clouds converge over the cemetery, blocking out the stars.

An electric hum vibrates in my chest.

Cooper's eyes pop. "Oh wow."

"Cool." Jack's voice is filled with wonder.

I smile, elated by the tingling sensation that's fortifying and repairing my body's natural balance. "It's an energy circle. It won't drain your strength, just recycle it a bit through all of us. Think of it like a circuit. But no matter what happens in the next few minutes, don't let go. Otherwise, you'll break the connection and the spell will fail." I shoot a pointed glance at Cooper, hoping he gets how serious I am and that I'm not doing this just to cop a feel.

He nods. "Okay." Then grips harder, clutching my hand so tight, his ruby shard digs into my palm.

A jolt of electricity shoots up my forearm, searing the flesh beneath my skin. I gasp and fight the urge to yank my hand from his. Instinctively, I sense this bone-deep pain is due to something more than just the jewel wedged into my hand. I glance into his cool gray eyes. His face is still, as if he's not aware of my discomfort or the intermittent shocks that zap my skin.

Something doesn't want to me keep hold of him. Whatever that something is, it greatly underestimates me. I'm not letting go, no matter what.

The breeze kicks up, shaking the trees, and rattling the kudzu leaves like maracas.

"You okay?" Jack asks.

"I'll be fine." I breathe deep and try to ignore the ache that's jolting my arm. "It's time to start. After I start chanting, you guys can join in."

Closing my eyes, I concentrate on the smooth glass beads of my *collier* that lay against my clammy chest. I'm going to need every section tonight, especially the light blue and pink beads, intended to help hear the voice of spirit. If ever I needed my spirit guide, tonight's the night. Next, I envision the red and white beads that convey the power of spoken word and prayer, hoping they'll help me get this incantation right. Finally, I visualize the most important section, the purple, white, and black beads, the ones intended to make it easier to communicate with the dead. As much as I appreciated Maggie's help this afternoon, there's only one dead person I'm hoping will show up tonight, prodded on by the acacia leaves, althaea root, and holy water.

My mind clears. Lifting my lids, I let the words flow:

"Ancient curse cast at the birth of a son,
Stealing his soul when of age he has come,
Cast in revenge for a hideous crime,
Enduring nearly three centuries of time.
From Lady Rose and her child,
Every Beaumont son reviled,
Through each generation,
Thanks to Sabina's damnation.
But that ends tonight,
As we beckon the light,
And seek the only power,
That can force the curse to cower.
Nothing's as strong as a mother's affection,

It offers pure love and unfailing protection,
So we summon Clarissa to help break this curse,
By calling her spirit and reciting her verse:
'Your heart and mine,
Forever entwined,
Love everlasting,
Till the end of time.'"

The temperature drops at least ten degrees. A crack of thunder booms in the distance.

Cooper's eyes stretch wide. "You're calling my mom?" His voice is breathy and filled with apprehension.

"Shh," I warn, then repeat the verse from the locket two more times. By the time I've completed it, Jack and Cooper have caught on, joining in the recitation.

As we chant, the ground rumbles under our feet. Jack's grip tightens. He's no doubt thinking about the last earthquake we witnessed beneath the bottle tree at Miss Delia's. But that was different. Miss Delia was releasing dark magic from some evil curios. We're doing just the opposite, evoking white magic for protection. I shoot him a reassuring glance and squeeze him back.

A faint yellow light wiggles its way up out of the ground in front of Clarissa's grave.

My chest swells with joy. It's working. I recite the verse from the locket again, this time with more feeling and urgency. Jack and Cooper follow my lead.

The wind kicks up and another blast of thunder crashes, this time closer, somewhere above the salt marsh.

The light brightens as it rises from the rich soil. Finally, it emerges, a wisp of dazzling incandescence that curls up into the air like a fancy cursive *s*. The clearing fills with the sweet scent of jasmine. The light spins slowly toward Cooper, approaching him tentatively, then hovering at his eye level.

"Emma?" His voice quivers.

I complete the last line of the verse, then pause only long enough to answer him. "It's okay, Cooper. She won't hurt you. I promise." I grit my teeth as I swallow the pang trailing up my arm.

Jack and I repeat the poem again, watching as the light encircles Cooper, coils around his arms and torso, then nuzzles his face and hair. It finally comes to rest in the crook of his chest and shoulder.

"It's her," he whispers. In the candlelight, a tear works its way down the side of his face. He gazes at the shimmering light. "I've missed you so much, Mom."

Ignoring the hot sensation that's stinging my eyes, I concentrate on Clarissa's poem, since I'm sure it's the key to breaking the curse.

The shimmering light slides away from Cooper, then hovers above the candle on her gravestone. Though it's just a formless wisp of brilliance, it seems to nod at me, as if it's waiting for me to take the next step.

Except I'm not sure what that is. I've barely gotten us this far, and I don't have a clue what's supposed to happen next.

The light nods at me again.

The ruby fragments in my palms suddenly feel cool. It's a welcome relief for the shock flares that keep racing up my arm from Cooper's touch. Within seconds, the jewels' temperature drop again from a comforting chill to frigid.

I suck in a breath at the sensation that's so cold it's burning. "Do you guys feel that?" I whisper, as they continue to chant.

"Feel what?" Jack whispers back.

"Never mind." It must be the work of my spirit guide though I've got no idea what she's trying to say.

My fingertips sting. A supersized brain-freeze grips my head like a vise. My right hand, the one in Cooper's grasp, spasms from the competing signals that convey hot and cold. I want to let go, but I fight the urge, knowing it'll break the connection and ruin the spell. Competing forces clash. Against my will, my hand flips over, the ruby fragment clutched between my fingers. The back of my hand is still pressed against Cooper's palm, maintaining our link.

I wrench my hand to twist it back over, but it won't move.

Fast as a whip, Clarissa's spirit bounces toward the uncovered ruby and then wraps around our entwined hands. A second later, the radiant light leaps to each of our joined hands, spiraling around our wrists.

She must want to see the rubies.

"Open your hands, but don't break the connection," I whisper, then slip back into the chant. Following my example, they each lift one palm, allowing it to cradle their ruby fragment.

The long, curly light rolls itself into a tight, shimmering ball. The glow intensifies and brightens, then starts to pulse.

Thunder blasts overhead, rattling my chest.

Suddenly the orb shoots three long flares that stretch down to our open palms. The light dances on my hand. It's warm and effervescent and tickles my skin. An instant later, all three beacons grab hold of the ruby pieces like tractor beams and reel them in toward the center of the bright yellow light.

Jack's jaw drops. "Holy crap."

I can't help but laugh because he's expressed my sentiment, and most likely Cooper's, perfectly. Defying gravity is sort of a once-in-a-lifetime thing.

As the rubies grow closer together, their momentum speeds until they finally click together like a three-piece jigsaw. If it weren't for the fissure lines along each break, I'd think the Beaumont ruby had been miraculously repaired. The fiery-red stones gleam in the spirit's light.

Lightning strikes, sending a jagged bolt of white electricity into the cemetery just outside our *Magic Candle* circle.

Jack, Cooper, and I start from the noise. A high-pitched squeal escapes my throat. But rather than slip from each other's grasp, the jolt only causes us to interlace our fingers and clutch harder.

Rain falls, spattering the surrounding kudzu and dotting the newly cleared plot below our feet. I tilt my head toward the shadowy black sky. The cool drops dot my forehead and eyelashes, refreshing my sticky skin.

As my nerves settle, I recite the poem from the locket once again. The words seem to fuel the orb's power. Its yellow hue brightens and flashes like a miniature sun. The ruby cluster spins in midair. Revolving clockwise, the jewels gains momentum. As it whirls in a tight spiral, the rubies' color dims to a dull brick red.

The wind blasts and the sky opens up, dumping a deluge on the clearing. My hair plasters against my head and my clothes are drenched as fat, heavy raindrops pelt the ground so hard, they ricochet and slap my bare legs. Somehow the white altar candle and mullein torches withstand the assault, burning as bright as ever.

A shriek emits from the center of the light, as if the ruby pieces are screaming and begging for their lives. In response, the light appears to rotate faster, whipping the gems around like a centrifuge ride at an amusement park.

The stones' color fades further, first to a murky cayenne, then to a muddied garnet. The shrieking continues through each change, as if the life is literally being squeezed from each mineral.

Thunder crashes, followed by another lash of lightening a millisecond later. The storm is right on top of us. Hail drops from the sky, peppering the clearing, and my head, with tiny, rectangular-shaped ice cubes.

Ice! It's the final ingredient we need to break the Beaumont Curse.

Jack and Cooper seem to make the same connection. Squinting against the onslaught of slashing hail, their chanting picks up speed, driving the rubies' gyration even faster. All color and fire drains from the stones, leaving them as lackluster and muted as a hunk of dried black lava.

Within a few moments, the clearing is blanketed in frozen white crystals. Frost grows on the still spinning jewels.

A flash of light bursts. The stones implode on themselves as an earsplitting crack reverberates through the cemetery. A flurry of pale yellow jasmine petals scatter to the ground and cover the hail.

The sky quiets, turning off the hail and rain like a spigot. The wind stills and the clouds part, revealing the twinkling stars above.

I gasp and blink at the dirt, searching for the rubies. They're gone. Replaced by beautiful, sweet-smelling flowers.

The yellow orb unwinds and zips toward Cooper once again, curling itself around his body from his head to his toes. Unfurling itself, it hovers at his chest, then reaches out to place its energy on his heart. Cooper heaves a huge breath. "I love you, too, Mom. I always will." His bottom lip quivers.

The light retracts and then drifts back to hover above Clarissa's grave. It pauses for a moment and then slips back down into the ground.

The flame on the white altar candle extinguishes.

"What just happened?" Jack asks, breathless.

"I'm pretty sure we just broke the Beaumont Curse." I heave for air as my pulse rages.

A blood-blistering scream echoes in the distance, sending terrified shivers over my body. Vaguely familiar, it seems almost animalistic, though I can't be sure.

Glancing at the guys, it's clear they didn't hear it. So rather than freak them out, I'm going to chalk it up to my utter exhaustion and assume my ears are playing tricks on me.

Jack releases my hand. "Dude, you're free!" He raises his palm for a giant high five, but Cooper doesn't move. Instead, he's frozen in place, probably in major shock.

I glance up at him, afraid of what I'll find. My heart skips a beat.

He's beautiful. His face is filled with joy and gratitude, and most importantly, peace. Pulling me close, he clutches me tight to his chest. A shock of pain jolts through me just as my nose fills with the fragrant scents of jasmine mixed with summer rain and his piney deodorant. Strange, I'd thought the zapping would be over by now. But it's probably just a function of my unbalanced energy and nerve-jangling fatigue.

"Thank you, Emmaline," he gushes in my ear, his warm breath shooting sparks up my neck. "You did more than just break the curse. You gave me back my mom. Even though it only lasted a few minutes, I know she'll always be with me. I'll never forget that as long as I live."

Even though his touch still hurts, my heart soars. My Cooper is back. I was right—the Beaumont Curse was behind his foul attitude and absurd Taneea distraction. This is officially the best day ever.

"You're welcome." Squeezing him tight, I ignore the pangs as I clasp my arms around the thick muscles that line his back. "But I couldn't have done it without you and Jack. We did it together." Pulling back, I meet his gaze. My breath catches. His eyes are still that strange light gray, nearly as colorless as the hail scattered on the ground. Shouldn't they have gone back to normal by now?

"Yeah, I guess we did." He releases me and steps to Clarissa's gravestone, picking up her locket, which doesn't appear to have been impacted by the rain or hail. "Can I have this now?"

I smile. "Yeah, I don't see why not."

He beams. "Great. I can't wait to show it to Taneea."

The air exits my lungs in a whoosh.

Cooper turns to Jack. "You guys don't mind if I take the golf cart, right? I want to get back as fast as I can. She's been waiting on me all day."

My mind reels, trying to make sense of what's happening.

Jack's brow creases. "Sure, why not? We'll just drag all this crap back on our own, trudging through the mud in the dark. No problem." You'd have to be incapacitated to miss his sarcasm.

"Awesome!" Cooper slides the locket into his ridiculous long denim shorts, then takes off in a sprint through the cemetery.

Jack's jaw gapes as he watches Cooper disappear. "What a sphincter."

My stomach twists in a knot as reality sinks in. "He's worse than that. He might actually be in love with her."

Chapter Twenty-five

Could Cooper really be in love with Taneea? The question has looped through my mind a thousand times over the last couple hours as I've tossed and turned, yearning for sleep. The Beaumont Curse was broken, yet he still ran right to her, so I know for sure his feelings weren't caused by the curse.

Taneea's beautiful, more experienced, and is closer to his age. Plus she's got much more cleavage than I do. Most guys would dump a girl like me for someone like her. But Cooper's not most guys. The Cooper I've known wouldn't be interested in someone who disrespects her great-grandmother, gambles, hitchhikes, or gets thrown out of school, no matter how hot she is.

So then why is he fawning all over her? Spending every free second with her and even changing his wardrobe on her command? He doesn't even look like himself anymore in those embarrassing clothes.

The image of his frosty eyes flashes across my mind. They're his, but not his, too. For as long as I've known him, their color shifts between blue and green depending on what he's wearing, but lately, they've only held that strange, colorless hue.

And then it hits me: he's not the Cooper I know. At least not totally. Something is causing him to act this way, and I'm guessing it's got something to do with Taneea and more illicit conjuring.

I need to talk to him, figure out what she's done, and try to snap him out of whatever trance she's got him under. Snatching my cell off my nightstand, I dial his number. Predictably, it goes straight to voice mail.

He's left me with no other choice. Throwing off the covers, I jump out of bed and race to my dresser, then pull out the only thing that's clean: my peasant blouse and bohemian skirt. We had our first date in this outfit, a perfect moonlit night on the beach, complete with lots of kissing under the silver moon. Maybe it's a good omen. With my luck lately, it might be the exact opposite.

Ten minutes later, guided only by the light of the nearly full moon, I burst past the spiny palmetto bush at the end of the path that leads to the Big House. I stop short. Taneea's tacky, hot-pink truck is in the driveway, parked next to Cooper's station wagon. Although it's only a quarter past eleven, the front of the house is pitch-black and quiet.

I've come this far. I'd better suck it up and go the rest of the way. It might even be good to confront them together. Drawing a deep breath, I climb the front steps and ring the bell. After a silent moment, I depress the intercom button on the security system, knowing it'll make every phone in the house ring. Noisy, but it'll get his attention. After a few long minutes and several more rings, I'm still alone on the doorstep.

I stomp down the steps and turn to look at the mansion. I could go home, convince myself I've lost my mind, and give up on this entirely, allowing them to live happily—or not—ever after. Except I can't. Literally. My feet won't pivot and return down the path. The only option is to move forward, skirting along the side of the house toward the back.

The darkness is creepy, heavy almost. Even the crickets, frogs, and other night creatures are hushed. Under the gauzy light of the moon, I make my way toward the backyard and glimpse the only light, which is coming from Cooper's room on the second floor.

Like I've done a thousand times before, I pick up a tiny pebble from the ground and toss it at his window. If I can get his attention, maybe he'll answer the door like a normal person and we can talk.

Though my pebble strikes the sill, he doesn't look out the glass. I toss another and then a third, but still he doesn't answer. This is getting ridiculous.

I slump back against the magnolia's sturdy trunk. Normally these ornamentals are thin and spindly, but under my dad's watchful and very verdant thumb, this tree has flourished.

A crazy idea pops into my head. I can climb up there and ensure I get his attention. It's super-stalkerish, but considering I've given him every opportunity to respond, I don't think it's too outrageous. At least that's what I'm telling myself.

Besides, he can't get too ticked off at me. I did just destroy the Beaumont ruby, end the curse, and help him reconnect with his mom.

Planting my flip-flop on the lowest branch, I grab hold of a bough at my eye level and begin my ascent. The pink magnolia's fragrance is faint but delicious, a combination of cinnamon, rose water, and a hint of hyacinth. As I climb in the dim light, my flip-flop slides off the smooth bark, leaving me dangling. Gasping, I clutch tight and fumble to regain my footing. Note to self: flip-flops are not ideal tree-climbing equipment.

Finally, I scale high enough to peek into his window. But I can only just make out the top of Cooper's golden-brown head across the room. I need to get higher, but the branches are thinner and less sturdy. Biting my bottom lip, I grab hold and yank to test their strength. They're firm and seem steady, so I scramble another couple feet until I'm high enough to see into the room.

A crow flies into the tree, roosting on a skinny branch several feet above me. Which is totally weird because I didn't know crows were nocturnal animals. I stare hard at its glassy black eyes, mentally shooing it away before my attention is drawn back to Cooper's room.

Taneea's standing in front of Cooper as he sits on the edge of his bed. They're talking and he's beaming up at her with those cold, gray-white eyes. He's wearing a fresh wife-beater T-shirt, a clean pair of long denim shorts, and pristine, lime-green high-tops. Yuck. How many pairs of those hideous things did he buy? My eye is drawn to a thick, silver chain around his neck that I've never seen before. It almost looks like one of those metal choke collars for dogs. I guess it's another one of Taneea's fashion statements, though I'm not sure what putting a dog collar on your boyfriend is supposed to symbolize.

The crow flits closer, hopping down to a thicker limb just a foot from me. What the heck is with this thing? Aren't wild birds supposed to be afraid of people? The crow cocks its head as if it's studying me. Evidently I'm not that scary. Well, that's about to change because the last thing I need is a nosy bird. Gripping the trunk with my left hand, I swat at the winged creature with my right. With a whoosh, it leaps away, just in time for me to take in the rest of what's going on in Cooper's room.

Taneea steps forward and runs her long fingers through Cooper's soft curls. She must say something hilarious because he throws his head back and howls in laughter. Then he wraps his arms around her midsection and pulls her close, tilting his face up to her. She leans forward and kisses the spot right next to his lips.

Steamy tears well as my stomach somersaults, churning with bile. I want to puke. And cry. And scream. All at the same time. It's one thing to have wondered what's been going on between them, and even imagined it, but it's another to actually see it with my own eyes. And the worst part is that he looks so… happy. Could he smile that wide if he was under a spell?

From the corner of her eye, Taneea glances toward the window.

I freeze, wondering if somehow I shrieked but didn't hear my own voice. I don't think so, but at this point, anything's possible. Holding my breath, I squelch my tears, and swallow the acidic taste that's working its way up the back of my throat.

Cupping his face in her palms, she leans into his ear and whispers something, then straightens and squares her shoulders. He grabs her hand and smiles, tugging her back toward him. Giggling, she pulls herself free and saunters toward the window, her brow hitched and a wicked grin on her lips. Cooper's mother's locket hangs around her neck.

I tell myself there's a chance she doesn't realize I'm here. Maybe she just interrupted a make-out session to come look at the moon. It could happen.

Except a second later, we come face-to-face, separated only by a thin sheet of glass and the ten feet between the magnolia and the Big House. Staring me down, she winks, then pulls the cord on the blinds, dropping them the full length of the pane. The slats are still open, providing me a view to the room. But a second later, she yanks the other cord and seals them shut.

Oh yeah, she's seen me. Perched in a tree, being a giant, creepy, Peeping Tom stalker.

My brain spins as a thousand thoughts converge at once, imagining what's going on in there behind those blinds. No, I can't go there. Blocking the torturous images, my mind shifts to an even more painful thought: Maybe Cooper isn't under a spell. Maybe he truly does care for her. Maybe I lost him fair and square.

A big, wailing sob works its way up my throat. My bottom lip trembles. Just as I'm about to drop my head and give in to my pity party, the persistent crow flies back into the magnolia. This time, rather than keeping its distance, it aims right for me, alighting on a bough just above my head. I jerk back and shoo it with my right hand again. But rather than taking flight, the crazy bird advances and pecks at my fingers. Ducking away, I swing toward my left to avoid its attack. The crow persists, this time striking my left arm with its beak. Frantic, I release my grip in the trunk and try to scamper down the tree, but descending is harder and slower than the initial climb, especially with a rabid bird on the loose and flip-flops on my feet. Weaving to avoid the bird's sharp bill, I reach for a branch with one hand at the same moment I've released the other, just as my flip-flop slips against the smooth bark.

Untethered, I bow to gravity's command, crashing against hard limbs and fragrant magnolia flowers.

A gust of wind rushes from my lungs as my back slams against the hard ground, followed by the smack of my head.

Everything goes black.

Chapter Twenty-six

My head throbs with pain and my shoulders ache as if they've been whacked by a two-by-four. Swallowing hard, I coax my eyes open, then attempt to focus on the pink dots circling above my head. My vision stops spinning long enough to realize the dancing pink spots are magnolia flowers. Attached to branches. The silver moon hangs in the sky overhead. I reach out my fingers and touch hard, cool soil and fuzzy, green moss.

Why am I on the ground?

Oh my gosh. I fell out of the tree. I extend a shaky hand to explore my screaming head. Inching my fingers around my scalp, I don't sense any cuts or blood. Just a nasty lump on the back of my skull. I'm lucky. I think. Though someone should probably tell my back that.

Squish, suck. Squish, suck. Squish, suck.

The strange sound comes from just outside my peripheral view. It kind of reminds me of the time Jack I and walked home in the pouring rain in our drenched sneakers. Each mushy step sounded like a disgusting bodily function that cracked Jack up.

Craning my neck, I squint toward the wet, pulpy sound.

My heart skips and I draw a quick inhale that burns my smarting ribs.

A long, thin, red-skinned creature with lankly limbs is scaling the exterior wall beneath Cooper's window. It's headed right for him.

I blink to make sure I'm not imagining things. Nope, it's real.

The glistening scarlet creature grips the white paneling with the three suction-cup-like fingers on each of its hands, squelching with each step it takes.

Goose bumps rush over my battered body and a scream leaps from my mouth.

The thing whips its face toward me, glaring its bulbous, crimson eyes—if that's what they are—and hisses. Turning away, it continues its ascent up the brick wall.

I don't know what it is, but I know it shouldn't be there. Adrenaline throws my heart into overdrive, giving me the strength to heave onto my side and try to find a way to stop it. Wincing, I stretch my hand and fumble in the dim light, searching for something to throw. Gripping a handful of hardwood bark, I pull back my throbbing arm and lob.

Most of the hardwood chips miss their target. Only a few pieces graze the creature's feet.

Undeterred, it continues its climb.

Frantic, I suck up the pain and crawl on my hands and knees, searching for something more substantial. Scraping the ground with my nails, I unearth a handful of dirt and tiny rocks. Heaving for breath, I scramble to my knees and launch the dirt bomb. It lands just where I'd hoped, spraying the creature's back.

It swings its slender, hairless head in my direction. Hissing again, this time it spews a mouthful of slimy, viscous spit. I pull back but not quick enough to miss the incoming assault. The monster's slobber splats squarely on my stomach, sliming my peasant shirt. I shriek and instinctively reach for my midsection, planting my hand in the goop. It's hot and sludgy and reeks of rotting garbage and week-old decomposition. Wiping the muck on a tuft of grass, a sudden realization hits me. This is the same stinky stuff I saw on Cooper's window a couple weeks ago. There's a reason it doesn't care about me, my mulch chips, or pebbles. It wants Cooper and will stop at nothing to get him.

"Cooper!" I scream, splitting my headache even further, hoping it'll be enough to warn him.

The creature continues to suction cup its way up the wall making that revolting, sloshy sound. Panicked, I search for anything substantial I can throw at the hideous monster. Finally, I spy a nice round rock. Still on my knees, I clamber toward it, yank it from the earth, and hurl it at the back of the monster's head.

It lands with a satisfying *thunk*.

Which is a giant mistake because the creature launches itself off the wall, landing in front of me in one smooth leap.

I shriek, rattling my eardrums.

"Shut up!" it hisses as it advances toward me. With its long, lanky body and slender rectangular head, it almost looks like a giant stick bug wrapped in inverted human flesh. Its putrid stench, like some kind of trash and manure-propelled tear gas, burns my throat and causes my eyes to water.

I should run, bolt out of here as fast as my pummeled body will take me, but my knees are frozen as if I'm literally planted in the soil. All I can do is stare up at the creature's red, mushy flesh that shines like raw meat.

"Get away!" I force the words from my constricted throat. "Leave us alone."

"Ha, ha, ha!" It laughs, sounding like it's choking on curled cottage cheese. "Silly girl. This is my destiny," it lisps, and then reaches its gangly arms toward me, extending its horrible three-fingered hands. I gawk at the meaty suction cups at their tips.

"Help!" I call, not sure to who since it's clear Cooper is indisposed. And I came here alone without so much as leaving a note in my room. How stupid could I be?

"Emma?" Jack's voice echoes from the somewhere near the front of the Big House.

My heart leaps with joy. I've never been so relieved to hear his voice. "Jack! Help!" I scream just as the creature lunges forward and seizes my throat with its clammy, fetid hands. My voice cuts off as it lifts me off my knees and suspends me in the air.

I stare at my reflection in its bulging, lidless, bloodred gaze. My eyes are stretched wide, my jaw agape, and my skin's pulled taut in a perfect picture of abject horror. Yet the image doesn't come close to conveying the actual terror that has filled my mind and engorged every cell of my body.

"Silence! I don't wish to hurt you, but I will if I must," it says, lingering on each *s* sound. "You see, the smart ones are my least favorite. Not very tasty. Though it's never stopped me in a pinch." Its long, lizard-like tongue shoots from its mouth and licks the length of my jaw, leaving a thick layer of slime.

I gag as an idea forms of what this thing is. *No!* Clawing at its lean arms, I try in vain to make it release me. Its skin is tacky and feels exactly like an uncooked piece of steak that's been left out on the counter for the afternoon.

It laughs again as it tightens its grasp. "So very feisty. Though

I should thank you for breaking the Gullah hag's curse. Now I don't have to wait for the boy's birthday to claim his body. His intact soul will make it harder to separate his life force from his flesh, but it's nothing I haven't done before."

Jack's footfalls pound toward us.

I call to him, but the creature still has my throat in its vise grip so the sound comes out garbled, though loud.

"You asked for it." The creature opens its toothless mouth. Thick white sludge drips over its fine, red lips. It leans in, extending its jaw wide enough to swallow my whole head.

An invisible force flicks on, sucking the life from my body. More than my energy, it feels as if the monster is inhaling both my spirit and soul. My vision blinks white as memories literally unspool from my mind and whoosh toward the monster's throat. Distorted images from when Jack and I were babies, sharing the same crib, and playing on our hobbyhorse yank from my brain. I know they're real and depict actual events, but stolen this way, they're pulled and stretched, a fun house version of my life. Next, my mother and father whiz by as they were one Christmas morning more than a decade ago, in our old house in DC, followed by scenes from preschool and kindergarten and our first trip to St. Helena to see our dad. But rather than reliving the joyous, happy times they were, the pictures are contorted, dark, and frightening. And worst of all, this alternative, warped version of reality feels so real it's enough to make me question my sanity.

"Emma!" Jack's voice, filled with dread, fear, and alarm, is the only thing that breaks through the unfurling events of my fourteen-year-old existence. "Let go of my sister!" he screams.

His arrival must distract the creature because the force field breaks and my early memories snap back into my head like one of those vinyl window shades that retract on a roller. But rather than bouncing back to their former, happy shapes, the images remain buckled and deformed, leaving me terribly unsettled.

The creature glances over its scarlet shoulder. "Go away! This doesn't concern you," it hisses.

"Like hell it doesn't." Jack darts into the woods on the side of the house.

The creature jerks back toward me and tilts its bizarre, thin head. "Now, where were we?" A thin slash of a smile splits its lips. "Oh, yes. Just a tiny nibble more." Its jaw gapes once again and the vacuum-like force switches on.

Just as my brain starts to slip back into that disoriented whirl of disfigured images, I catch a glimpse of Jack running toward the creature, his hands gripped around something long and pointy. He screams just as the creature starts to Hoover my brain again.

White light flashes. Memories flicker. Then everything stops as I'm jostled, then dropped to the ground. Propping myself up on my elbows, I blink up at the red, fleshy creature looming above me. Its hands are wrapped around the end of a tree branch that Jack must have impaled through its midsection.

Cooper's window opens. He pries his face against the screen. "What the—"

The creature stumbles back a few feet. Then, like a magician pulling handkerchiefs from his sleeve, the creature yanks the bough clear through its midsection, leaves and all. When the limb is free, the wound spews a sludgy, black substance, spattering everything within a six-foot radius, including me. It stinks like raw sewage. I shriek as the fetid glop gushes on my legs, stinging my skin, and soiling my clothes.

Slapping its three-fingered hands over its gaping wound, the creature looks up at Cooper. "This isn't over. Your soul may be safe, but your body has always been marked as mine. I won't relinquish my destiny, and you won't escape yours."

The creature vaults over me, clutching its abdomen as it dodges around Jack, then dashes into the woods and fades into the night.

"Emma! Jack!" Cooper yells, then disappears from his window.

I slump to the ground and cough as I heave for air through my crushed throat. Every breath draws in the awful stench that covers my skin and clothes, but I've got bigger problems, starting with the disturbing images that haunt my mind's eye. I tell myself those screwed-up pictures aren't real, that my real memories represent blissful times. But even though I know that to be the truth, fear and anxiety linger in my chest anyway. Maybe if I keep reassuring myself, eventually, I'll believe it. But my still-pounding headache isn't making things any easier. Staring up at the moonlit sky, I attempt to will away the pain.

Jack races for me, diving next to my prone body. "Are you okay?" His searching eyes are filled with shock.

"Ugh." I'm so far past okay, I can barely form words in my mind much less speak them.

He plugs his nose. "Dang. No offense, but you stink."

I nod my head, which only makes it hurt worse. "I know." My voice is rough and raspy as I lift a hand to put pressure on the ache. "How did you know to save me?"

He shrugs. "Twin sense, I guess. I felt you were in trouble, so I went to find you. When you weren't in your room, I figured you must have come out here. Which was beyond moronic by the way, even when a demonic monster isn't trying to kill you."

Cooper flies around the corner from the back of the Big

House. Crouching opposite Jack, he grabs my hand and gazes down at me with his white-gray eyes. "What happened? And what was that…thing?"

I clear my throat. "I'm pretty sure it was a boo hag." I had my suspicions when the creature talked about how tasty people are, but they were confirmed when it claimed Cooper's body. And perhaps most frightening of all, the boo hag is somehow connected to the Beaumont Curse. All that creature's talk about destiny and being marked can only mean one thing: even though we broke the jinx and secured Cooper's soul, Cooper's still in danger.

Cooper gulps. "What does it want?"

Jack turns to him, his brow hitched. "Evidentially, you. Or at least your skin."

My legs move past stinging into full-on burn territory. I suck in a gasp.

"What's wrong?" Cooper asks.

"My legs. They hurt."

Jack gawks. "They're bright red. We've got to get you inside and wash this off, now."

I try to sit up, but my head reels, and I sink back down. "I can't."

"No problem." Cooper stands and then scoops me in his arms in one fluid motion.

A shock jolts my skin where his flesh touches mine, just like it did at the cemetery. Which only confirms my reasons for coming here tonight. Something's definitely up, but between the headache and new twinging sensation, it's impossible to think.

Cooper carries me around the back of the house, through the veranda and main hall, then up the stairs. Jack is right behind him.

Taneea's standing in the second floor hall, her arms crossed over her chest. "What is going on? Why did you run out of here? And why are you with *her*?"

Cooper halts on the top landing. "Uh, Emma's hurt. She needs to wash off. You don't mind, do you?"

She pinches her nose. "Ugh. What is that stink?" Her disapproving gaze travels over my body and the thick black sludge that's spattered across my legs and skirt. "I'm going home. I can't be around something so nasty."

I couldn't agree more. In fact, go away and never, ever come back.

Cooper's brow creases with concern. "Give me a second and I'll walk you out. You shouldn't go out there by yourself."

She shakes her head. "That's okay. I'm fine. Besides, you've got whatever that stuff is on you now, so actually, I'd prefer if you kept your distance."

His face turns down with disappointment. "Okay," He turns to Jack, who's on the stairs below us. "Make sure she makes it to her truck, all right?"

Jack nods. "Sure. Now get Emma into the shower before that stuff burns her any worse, okay?"

Cooper nods and steps toward Taneea, leaning in for a kiss.

Screwing up her face, she throws up her hand and jerks away. "Um. Gross." Then zips past us and dashes down the stairs.

Cooper's cool, gray-white eyes fill with so much sadness, I almost feel sorry for him. But then my compassion slips like water down a drain. If he has chosen Taneea over me, I hope her snotty attitude hurts because it might be the first step to seeing how truly rotten she is.

He glances down at me and seems to remember why I'm in his arms. Sprinting to the hall bathroom, he places me gently in the tub. The shocking jolts mercifully stop as Cooper pulls down the shower wand and turns on the water. It runs frigid at first, but it feels good against my inflamed skin. He sprays the water all over my skirt and legs, rinsing the nasty black gunk off my clothes and down the drain. When the worst of the sludge is gone, he hands me the wand, a bottle of shampoo, and a washcloth.

"You finish up and I'll get you some clean stuff to wear, okay?"

I nod. "Yeah."

He pulls the shower curtain to give me privacy, then darts out of the room. By the time I'm through with the shower, I find a fresh T-shirt and drawstring shorts and two towels on the counter.

It takes longer than normal to dry myself and get dressed. When I flip my hair to wrap it in a towel, my head thumps. I clutch the side of the wall for support as I inch my way out of the bathroom. I should probably ask Jack to take me home to bed but the boo hag's presence has added a bizarre new wrinkle. We've got a lot to figure out first.

I make it to the doorway of Cooper's room. Jack's perched on the desk while Cooper's slouched on his bed, already showered and changed into another of his new fashion statements, an airbrushed T-shirt, black pants, and his fugly orange sneakers. I don't have the energy to look at the Day-Glo footwear, much less comment on them. But I do notice the bizarre dog chain around his neck. And the rumpled covers on his bed. The image of his hands wrapped around her back flashes across my mind, followed by the kiss she planted next to his lips.

"How ya doing?" Jack asks.

I lean against the doorjamb for support. "To be honest, I've been better."

"That black stuff," Jack says, his brow creased with heavy thought. "We've seen it before, right? After Missy died? And on the knife?"

I nod. "By the time we saw it, it was almost dry and much thicker, but yeah, I think it was the same stuff."

"So Missy didn't die of natural causes. The boo hag must have done it." Cooper's voice is somber.

"Right. And now it wants you," I answer.

"But why?"

"I don't know for sure. We'll need to ask Miss Delia about it, if she ever calls. But maybe it makes some strange kind of sense." Gazing at his still-icy eyes and fashion choices, I rub my aching temple and search for a way to explain without provoking him. "I came over tonight because even though we destroyed the Beaumont ruby, there are a couple things that make me worry you're not in the clear. Maybe the boo hag's got something to do with that."

Cooper looks at his window, which is now closed and locked. "I know stuff hasn't been great between us lately, but can you guys sleep over? My dad went to Charleston to get ready for an early morning meeting. I don't want to be alone."

Jack smirks. "Then why did you let Taneea leave? Maybe she could have protected you."

Cooper's nostrils flare. "You can say what you like about me, but I won't let you talk about Taneea like that."

"Oh really? Well, I'm sick of you dumping us when it's convenient but then relying on us when your sorry butt is on the line. And not for nothing, but dude, you had Emma, and you chose Taneea instead. What's that about?"

"Don't talk about my girlfriend!" Cooper launches off

the bed and hurls himself against Jack, who splays against the desktop, scattering the alarm clock, pencil cup, and other items to the floor.

Anxious to steer clear of their tussle, I step away from the door, into the hall. I'd like to avoid another thrashing if I can help it.

Jack and Cooper battle as fists fly and punches land. I've got to admit Cooper's right. Jack is strong, but more important, he's scrappy. And like a honey badger at a beehive, he doesn't give up. Jack manages to squirm out from under him and dash across the room. Cooper gives chase, but just as he's about to make contact, Jack darts to the side. Cooper crashes against his bed, shifting the mattress off the box spring.

Something *thunks* against the wall, then crashes to the floor.

My ears prick, but for all I know that could be another symptom of my epic headache and still-twisted memories. But the stinging intensifies, so I lean into the room. "What was that?"

They stop short.

"It sounded like something just broke." I point toward the wall.

Heaving for breath, Jack launches on top of the displaced mattress and peeks his head between the bed and the wall. "Is there something you want to tell us, Coop? When did you start playing with dolls?"

Cooper frowns. "What are you talking about?"

Jack reaches his hand down. "See for yourself." He retrieves a palm-sized, antique, ceramic kewpie doll that's fractured in two pieces. A tuft of Spanish moss sticks out of the crack that splits its stomach. Jack thrusts it in Cooper's direction.

I gasp as goose bumps rush over my body. "Don't let him touch it! Give it to me right now."

Chapter Twenty-seven

Jack jumps off the bed and runs across the room to hand me the broken kewpie doll. My heart races as I slide down the wall and sit on the floor in the hallway. Though the chubby little doll has a happy, cherubic face, there's definitely something scary, even demonic, about its enormous, offset painted eyes. I've never seen one of these in person before, but I've read about them in Miss Delia's spell book. This one gives me the creeps. Things are beginning to make sense.

Jack plants himself next to me.

Cooper hovers in the doorframe. "That's not mine."

"I'm sure it isn't. But someone created it for you," I answer.

"Huh?" He steps into the hall and kneels across from me and Jack.

"What is it?" Jack asks.

"A doll baby. Some people also call them poppets. Either way, they're used in coercive spells. Depending on what you put in them, you can pretty much make anyone do anything you want."

"You mean like a voodoo doll?" Jack asks.

"That's not what hoodoo root workers call them, but yeah, it's essentially the same idea."

"What's this one used for?" Cooper's voice is filled with apprehension.

"Only one way to find out." Grasping the broken ceramic doll, I pull the two sections apart and lay the bottom half on the floor next to me. Its strange black eyes stare up at me as I tug on the wad of Spanish moss that must have been stuffed into its belly through the little round holes in the bottom of its feet. Placing the doll's top half in my lap, I unfurl the long, green, spongy material on the carpet runner, then pick out the tiny magical herbs and roots that are mixed in.

My thigh warms under the broken kewpie's bulbous head. By now, I've learned to recognize my spirit guide's clues. Glancing down, I pick up what's left of the ceramic doll, turn it over, and peer inside. Just as I suspected, something red is shoved all the way at the top. Poking my fingers inside, I pry out the soft, rolled piece of cloth then spread it out on the floor. It's a two-sided, hand-sewn piece of flannel, cut in the shape of a person and stuffed with fluff. But that's not the most disturbing part. A tiny photograph of Cooper's face is glued to its head.

My mind reels. This explains everything.

"What does it mean?" Cooper asks.

I flick my finger at all the stuff I pulled from the moss. "Each of these are used in standard red magic spells to draw love. They're pretty basic ingredients and generally harmless." But then I point to the little red man adorned with Cooper's smile. "But this is different. It's a poppet that's obviously supposed to be you. You've been allured."

"Dang," Jack says.

"What am I missing?" Cooper shoots me a blank stare.

Why isn't this obvious to him? I lean forward. "Someone put a love charm on you."

He narrows his gaze. "Someone? Are you sure it wasn't *you* trying a little spell to win me back?"

My jaw drops and I recoil. "Don't be an idiot. I'm the one who heard the thing break. Why would I have pointed it out if I had planted in the first place?"

He shrugs. "I don't know. Maybe you figured I'd find it when it broke loose and thought it would be better to act innocent to throw off suspicion."

Jack's brow contorts. "Dude, you're messed up. Emma didn't plant it. I think it's obvious who did."

"Who?" Cooper asks, looking genuinely oblivious.

Jack and I exchange looks before we both turn back to Cooper and say in unison, "Taneea."

Cooper shakes his head. "That's insane. Besides you don't have any proof."

"Hello, what more proof do you need than this?" I pick up the little red poppet and flick it at him but something crackles inside its belly. "Hang on a second." Yanking on the loose, hand-sewn, red thread that binds the two pieces of flannel together, I poke open a hole, then pull it farther apart with my fingers. It's stuffed with a few thin strands of Spanish moss. Pushing them aside, I fish around and retrieve a thin scrap of paper that's folded in fours.

Laying the packet on the floor next to the love-spell ingredients, I carefully fold it open once, anticipating what I'm about to find. This isn't an ordinary piece of pulp. It's naming paper used in advanced hoodoo spells. Whoever did this was no amateur. If Taneea was involved, she had help, which I'm guessing was dressed in a sharp black suit and blue sunglasses.

Swallowing hard, I flip the last fold. There are two handwritten spells scribbled on the scrap of paper and two pieces of hair, one golden-brown, the other pink. The first contains Cooper's name written in script three times in red ink, then crisscrossed with Taneea's three times in black.

It's a common *attraction spell,* or *allurement,* used to draw two people together and then lock them in place. It's bad enough, but the second spell is the one that makes my stomach churn. The words, LOVE ME OR DIE are scrawled seven times down the paper in bold red ink crossed with Cooper's name in black script another seven times.

Relief slides off my shoulders. At least I know for sure he didn't choose Taneea over me. But then my cheeks flush with anger. How could she do this to him?

"Is that for real?" Jack's voice is hushed.

Cooper shakes his head. "No. It can't be."

"It is. And there's more than just her name and handwriting. She combined your *Personal Concerns* together. It's a very powerful allurement." I fold it back up so I don't lose track of the hairs.

His brow crinkles. "I don't believe it. Taneea cares about me. And I care about her."

Jack rolls his eyes. "You only think you do. That's the whole point of the spell."

Cooper glares at him, his icy-gray eyes look as if they could freeze him on contact. "She wouldn't do that to me."

Jack turns to me. "Obviously he's not thinking straight. What do we need to break the charm?"

"Destroy it."

Cooper's chest puffs up. "You're not destroying anything!" He dives for the folded naming paper and red-flannel man, nearly slamming into me.

"Hey!" I yell, but he doesn't seem to notice as he yanks the spell components up off the carpet runner, then scrambles to his feet and charges toward the stairs in those awful fluorescent sneakers.

Without my needing to ask, Jack takes off after him.

What the heck is going on with Cooper? First he didn't believe the charm was real, and now he wants to protect it? This spell is one tough mother. We can't let it do any more damage. It's got to be broken now.

Raising my voice, I call after Jack. "Get those things and bring them back to me. No matter what you do, don't let them get away."

Jack gives me a thumbs-up as he gains ground on Cooper.

I push off the floor, but I move too quickly, causing my brain to spin. Breathing deep, I clutch the wall and force myself to stand, then make my way toward the hall bathroom to wait for Jack.

Leaning toward the railing, I watch as Cooper approaches the bottom of the flight of stairs. If he gets there first, he'll be out the door and in his car in no time, on his way to find Taneea and goodness knows what else.

Jack must do the calculation in his head, too, because he yelps and leaps midflight, landing on top of Cooper, simultaneously executing the single most heroic and stupid maneuver I've ever seen. Clutching to Cooper's broad shoulders like a spider monkey, Jack clings while Cooper yanks the banister in his struggle to stay upright. But the force of the impact is too strong and Cooper's legs give out under him. They tumble down the last few steps, then roll onto the foyer floor.

Jack heaves for air as he picks himself up off the hardwood.

He clutches his forearm, which must have gotten slammed.

Cooper rolls on his side, groaning. "I'm going to kill you!" He growls.

"Fine with me, just so long as I get this first." Jack yanks the little red man and naming paper from Cooper's hands.

"No!" Cooper yells.

But Jack's already sprinting up the stairs toward me. Extending his grip, he thrusts the magical items at me. "Now what?"

"Get me some matches. And keep Cooper out of the bathroom." I turn and amble toward the hall bath, close the door, and depress the lock. Who am I kidding? That's not going to hold him for long. Spinning around, I look for anything that might buy me an extra minute or two. The tall, narrow, wicker hamper in the corner is my best bet. Moving as fast as I can, I slide it across the tile floor, then tilt it toward the door, wedging its top beneath the knob. Just in time, too because Cooper has already started knocking.

"Emma! Let me in!" He twists the knob.

"No. You need to trust me on this. You've been allured. You can't see things for how they really are."

"No! *You* need to trust *me*. You think you know everything and have all the answers but you don't know squat. What Taneea and I have is pure. She's the best thing that's ever happened to me. I won't let you destroy that paper. I can't live without her." His voice is frantic as he pounds on the door.

I lay the flannel poppet in the dry sink faceup and then spread open the naming paper, making sure the two strands of hair lay across the top.

The red and black writing stares up at me, an ugly indictment of how far Taneea will go to get what she wants.

Love me or die. That's it, isn't it? Cooper will literally die if he doesn't love her. I don't know where Taneea found such a sick, monstrous charm or why she thought it would be okay to hex someone like this or if she even realized the danger she put Cooper in. But I'm going to see that she never gets to do it again. I don't care if it's my last act of hoodoo, but I will right this wrong.

"Open this door, or I'll open it for you!" Cooper's voice booms with feral intensity. He crashes against the solid mahogany with what has to be his shoulder.

Where is Jack and what is taking him so long?

"You'd better stop. You're going to split the wood or rip it off its hinges. And then you're dad's going to be pissed because you know it's impossible to replace these antique doors."

"I don't give a crap about my father or his dumb hinges. I'll rip this whole house apart to get what you and Jack stole from me."

Cripes, he really is around the bend. There's no way normal Cooper would ever express this much disrespect for his family's homestead.

Finally I hear Jack's voice. "I'm coming, Em!"

"I'm going to tear your head off," Cooper snarls.

Jack sighs. "Okay, but do it neatly. Otherwise it'll make a huge mess."

Evidentially, Cooper isn't amused because the next thing I hear is the two of them crash to the ground.

On my hands and knees, I peer through the space at the bottom of the door. From my limited vantage point, I can tell Cooper's got Jack splayed on his stomach. But what Cooper doesn't realize is that's exactly what Jack wants. Jack's head swivels toward me, his cheek smushed against the carpet runner. Our eyes meet. He slides his palm toward the door. The matchbook is just below his fingers.

While nudging the matches into the crack between the tile floor and the door, he forces a few words. "This better work. Otherwise I'm toast."

A surge of adrenaline pulses through me, tapping the last of my reserve strength. As the guys wrestle and kick the door, I clamber to the sink. Leaning against the counter, I open the pack, pull off a match, and strike it against the thin dark strip at the back, then toss the kindled match on the hair and naming paper. The enchanted items burst into flame as if doused with kerosene and engulf the poppet. Black smoke rises as the cursed items burn like an inferno.

I flick on the bathroom exhaust fan and watch as the hateful fumes rise to the ceiling and then out of the house.

The guys' shouts quiet. So does the kicking.

The last remnants of the charred paper and poppet crumble in the sink. There's nothing left but sooty, black ashes that have been sucked of their fuel.

An eerie stillness expands on the other side of the door.

Breathing a sigh of relief, I turn on the faucet and rinse the last of the allurement spell down the sink. Then I loosen the hamper, shove it aside, and twist the knob to unlock it.

Gripping the jamb, I open the door to find a seated Cooper propped against the wall, his head collapsed in his hands.

Jack's sitting opposite him, his arms crossed and a wide grin on his face. "Cooper's back. Or at least he will be soon."

Cooper lifts his head. His face is a mixture of agony, confusion, and betrayal. But his eyes are a sight to behold. They're tinged with just the faintest swirl of green. He rubs his forehead. "What happened? I remember...but I also don't.

Things got weird there for a second, didn't they?"

I exhale the breath I've been holding since I opened the door. "For longer than a second. Ever since Missy died." I step out of the doorway and cross to the other side of the hall next to Jack. Though I don't try to sit down because with the way I'm feeling right now, there's a very good chance I won't be able to get back up. Instead I grip the railing overlooking the grand staircase with two hands, praying I won't keel over.

Jack nods. "Taneea made you her pet." When Cooper's brow furrows, Jack points to his chest. "For real. Look at the thing around your neck."

Cooper looks down. His lips curl in disgust. "It's a dog collar. I think we bought it in a shop in Charleston. I remember thinking I didn't want it, but I guess I changed my mind." He glances down at his silk-screened tee with the motorcycle print and then squints at his long jean shorts, and flat-out gawks at the orange high-tops. "What am I wearing?" He kicks off the shoes and pushes them away.

Jack snorts. "Your new wardrobe. She made you *pretty*." He wiggles his fingers and contorts his voice to sound like Igor in a Frankenstein movie. "You've got another pair too. Lime green." He erupts in peals of laughter.

Cooper pinches the bridge of his nose. "Uh. She made me blow my summer allowance on this crap. I don't think I've got any money left," he moans, as his memories appear to be flooding back.

"She made you lose a lot of things." The words fly from my mouth before I can stop them. Harsh, but true. Aside from messing with his memory and stripping him of his dignity, she also drove a wedge between all three of us. And Cooper and me. My mind knows he was allured, but my heart still remembers the pain of being dumped, even if he didn't do it on purpose.

He pushes off the floor and crosses the hall to stand in front of me. His eyes meet mine. They're a pale sea-green foam now, definitely on their way back to normal. His skin is pinker, too, as if he's coming back to life. "But I didn't lose you, did I, Emmaline?" Grasping my hand, he entwines my fingers with his. There's no shocking pain accompanied by his touch. Proof he's been cured. He searches my gaze.

I've longed for this moment. Yet now that it's here, I can't fully embrace it. But it's been a rough night and there's a definite possibility that after falling from the tree and my encounter with the boo hag, I'm not thinking straight. So I try to be as honest and fair as possible when I say, "I'm so glad you're back, Cooper. I really missed you. And while I know none of this was your fault, the truth is, you said some things when you were allured that hurt. I'll get over them, but I just need some time." My fingers slip from his grip. "But we've got bigger problems then whether we're okay. A monster wants to drain your life force and steal your skin."

Chapter Twenty-eight

Sunlight streams through my bedroom window, awakening me to my latest epiphany. We need Miss Delia. Though we're not supposed to go to her house until she says it's safe, we can't wait that long. The boo hag has added a new wrinkle to the situation. Cooper's birthday is tomorrow, and I'm sure the monster is poised to attack at its next opportunity. I need her advice on how to fight it and maybe to figure out how it connects to the now-broken Beaumont Curse. Plus, I've got a new theory about Claude Corbeau that I need to run by her. Since he seems to be at the epicenter of all our recent troubles, I'm wondering how deep his involvement actually goes. If he did plant the pirate's dagger in Beau's study, then he was present when Missy died covered in what now seems to be boo-hag blood. Perhaps Claude Corbeau is even more than he appears to be.

Energized by my new theory, I throw off my covers and pad to the bathroom to wash up. Thankfully, only a sliver of my headache remains. It's nothing a few ibuprofen can't handle.

I yank open the mirrored medicine cabinet door, grab a bottle, and pour out two extra-strength tablets. I switch on the faucet and let it run until it's nice and cold, then fill the plastic cup on the counter and toss back the pills. Swallowing hard, I reach my left hand and swing the cabinet door closed.

Miss Delia's face hovers in the mirror.

I yelp and drop the half-full cup into the sink, splashing the water.

She's not looking at me directly, but her eyes are filled with fright and distress. Her image flickers and fades.

Panicked, I grope at my *collier* and grip the light blue and pink beads, which should help boost my reception if this is a new type of message from my spirit guide. But Miss Delia's face continues to dim, so this must be something different.

An awful thought strikes: *what if Miss Delia's dead?* Maybe this is her spirit saying good-bye.

I spin the necklace and land on the clear and white section, which is supposed to help see spirits. When there's no change in her image, I move to the purple, white, and black beads used for communicating with the dead. Though the vision continues to fade, somehow Miss Delia appears even more terrified with each passing second. Her pupils have dilated and her little brown face is carved with more worry lines then I've ever seen.

Since she's not dead or already a spirit, I've got to find her. But the scene around her is too dark to even guess where she is.

Which leaves me one logical section remaining—the green and white beads for psychic visions. I clutch the glass beads tight. Miss Delia's face zooms into focus and the background brightens, revealing she's in her living room, seated in her wheelchair. I heave a sigh of relief. She's still alive, although whatever's happening, it's not good. In fact, I'm sure it's very,

very bad. And I know one other thing: she needs me.

The vision in the mirror fades. I scrub my face and brush my teeth, then race back to my room to get dressed. Within five minutes I'm downstairs and find Jack and Cooper in the living room watching television. Cooper slept over last night to avoid another encounter with the boo hag.

Cooper rises to his feet. "Morning, Emma! Want to walk to the beach so we can talk?" He looks a little nervous. But there are a couple bright spots—he's back to wearing his faded polo shirt, khaki shorts, and dock shoes. And his eyes are the most gorgeous shade of jade I've ever seen.

"Miss Delia's in trouble. We've got to get over there right away." I dash to the front door and slip on my flip-flops, then snatch my messenger bag off the floor and wince as I drape it over my sore shoulder.

Jack stands and clicks off the TV. "Wait. How do you know? I didn't hear your phone ring."

I open my mouth to explain but realize that's going to take way too long. "Trust me, I'm right. It's a hoodoo thing."

He nods. "Voices?"

I shrug as I reach for the door handle. "Something like that."

. . .

Ten minutes later, we round the bend leading to Miss Delia's house. Cooper drove here in record time, coming as close to speeding as he's done all summer. The bottle tree comes into view. So do two sheriff's cars. Not surprisingly, they're parked right next to Claude's big, shiny Lincoln, and Taneea's pink monster-truck nightmare. A deputy is straining to lift Miss

Delia's motorized wheelchair into the trunk of one of the cars.

We pull up next to him. Miss Delia's in the backseat, her shoulders hunched and her gaze cast down. She looks small and fragile.

My heart races. Throwing off my safety belt, I yank open the back passenger door of Cooper's station wagon and rush to the side of the deputy's car. Jack and Cooper are right behind me.

"What's going on? Are you okay?" I ask, breathless, through the open rear window, then notice she's still wearing slippers. They didn't even let her put on proper shoes. But then my eyes catch the glint of shiny silver around her narrow, bony wrists. They handcuffed her? Seriously?

She lifts her head. "I'll be fine. But you've got to get out of here. This is exactly what I didn't want you messed up in."

"I had a vision you were in trouble. There's no way I could stay away."

Her lip turns up in a faint smile. "That's my Emma. Loyal. Unlike so many others." Her milky eyes drift toward her house.

The deputy grunts and then drops the wheelchair on the ground. He pokes his head around the side of the vehicle. "You shouldn't be talking with her, miss." His cherubic face is red and flushed from straining to lift the cumbersome and nearly two hundred pound motorized monster. It's Deputy Thomas, one of the guys who showed up at the Big House when Missy died.

"She's ninety-seven years old and paralyzed. What do you think we're going to do? Help her run away?" Jack asks.

Thomas shrugs. "You've got a point. Just do me a favor and don't touch her. Or hand her anything." He looks back down at the wheelchair and scratches his head. I wonder how long it's going take him to realize the chair is too big and clunky to fit in the trunk.

"Right, because Miss D's going to shiv someone," Jack mutters under his breath.

"Why have you arrested her?" Cooper asks.

"Good question. You're going to have to take that up with the sheriff." The deputy turns this attention back to the motorized chair.

"We're going to get you out of this," I say.

"Thank you, child. But this may be the one situation I can't get out of. Besides, I'm too old to fight any longer. Perhaps it's best I just give in."

"No! You're not too old. You're still strong and you're as quick as a whip." I bend toward her and keep my voice low. "You were right about the *Black Cat Bone* and how to defeat it. I broke the Beaumont curse last night, all based on what you said."

She smiles and leans back in her seat. "That's wonderful, child. A real relief. That boy deserves a life of his own. So our work is done. I can rest now. That ought to make that Claude fellow happy. He's been like a dog on rawhide."

She wants to give up. Which means she wants to die. I can't let that happen.

Adrenaline kicks into overdrive. "No, you don't understand. I need you even more than ever now. Claude's a very bad man. In fact, he might not actually be a man at all."

Her eyes narrow. "What are you rattling on about?"

I inch even closer. "After we broke the Beaumont curse, we were attacked by a boo hag."

She gasps and her lids stretch wide as her eyes search me, Jack, and Cooper for any injuries.

"Don't worry, Miss Delia. Jack and Emma fought it off," Cooper whispers. He probably thinks he's just reassured her when, in fact, he's just freaked her out that much more.

I shake my head, trying to downplay his story. "There was a little scuffle but we're all fine. Actually, Jack stabbed it."

She peers at Jack. "Have you lost your dang mind?"

I jump in to make sure he doesn't say anything that might scare her even more. "No, he did it to save me. But it was a good thing, because it turns out hags don't bleed red blood. Remember that black gunk we found on Missy's body and the pirate's dagger? It's the same stuff that gushed out of its side. So the boo hag had to be there when she died. And since I'm pretty sure Claude planted the dagger in Beau's study, it looks like he's a lot more than a creepy wanna-be root doctor."

Miss Delia's brow furrows. "Claude a boo hag? Is that why he's been working against me, wedging himself between me and Taneea? If it's true, there's something bigger brewing, and an angle I can't make out. What does he want?"

"I don't know for sure. Except the hag said it didn't matter that the Beaumont Curse had been broken. It had marked Cooper's body and intended to get it. It said it was its destiny." I swallow hard, remembering its vile stench and menacing words.

Claude and Sheriff Walker exit the house and step out onto the porch, accompanied by another deputy who's carrying a box. I glance around for Taneea but she's nowhere in sight. Which is a good thing because I don't think I could be trusted not to plant my fists in her twisted, conniving face.

Claude thrusts his finger at us. "Get those children away from the prisoner!"

The deputy with the box charges down the steps, then over the flagstone path that winds through the garden.

Perking up, Miss Delia leans toward me through the open window. Her rheumy eyes radiate intensity. "Listen close. You're safe during the day, but you've got to be ready near midnight when the boo hag hunts without its skin. I had you take the mortar out of here for a reason. It's hasn't been a full three days, but it might have had enough time to rest, especially since that last spell didn't quite get off the ground. You know what to do. Use the *Psychic Vision* to learn where the hag hides its skin at night and then salt it through and through. And if you get the chance, lure that evil monster into the sunlight and fry it alive, once and for all."

I nod, taking in her instructions. It's a lot to pull off, but at least Miss Delia hasn't given up yet.

Deputy Goodwin pushes through the gate. "I'm going to have to ask you kids to move on. We've got to get her to the station for processing."

Miss Delia calls out the window, "Don't forget the broom! Remember, they love to count."

I smile and give her a thumbs-up. As we step away, I peer into the box in his hands. It's filled with vials of prepared potions, oils, and other mixtures. I breathe a sigh of relief. There's nothing in there I can't replace by using the recipes in Miss Delia's spell book.

My throat tightens as I watch them disappear down the road. Miss Delia's gone and it's all Claude's fault.

I sniff at the wet stuff threatening to drip out my nose. Claude may think he's won, but this isn't over. Miss Delia has given me a plan, and I mean to see it through.

The sheriff and Claude approach the gate.

"Why hello, Emma. Delightful afternoon, isn't?" Claude gazes down at me through round blue lenses. His bracing-white teeth almost seem to cast a light of their own. I don't bother to greet him, but he doesn't seem to notice. Or care.

"You remember Miss Guthrie, and her little friends, don't you, Sheriff?"

Sheriff Walker tips his ten-gallon hat. "Of course. Beau Beaumont's boy, right?"

"Indeed, the sole heir to the Beaumont estate," Claude adds, his lips parting in a serpentlike grin.

Cooper's brow quirks as he eyes Claude warily, then turns toward the sheriff. "Yes, sir. I always wanted a brother or sister, but I guess it wasn't meant to be."

"On the bright side, there's no one to fight over your inheritance with," Claude says.

A tingle shivers up my scalp. Is that what this is all about? Possessing Cooper's body to inherit the Beaumont fortune? Except Beau's still alive so it's not like there's any rush. Though Beau hasn't looked good lately and has been talking a lot about death.

"Why did you arrest Miss Delia?" Cooper asks.

The sheriff opens his mouth, but Claude cuts in. "We've got a strong suspicion Miss Whittaker was the mastermind behind this summer's break-in at The King Center."

Jack laughs. "You're kidding, right?"

"I only wish I was, son," Claude says. Only he doesn't appear the least bit sad. In fact, he looks positively gleeful.

"You need more than suspicion to arrest someone," I blurt as all respect for authority goes out the window. Because Claude will never, ever be an authority figure to me. And it's not just because he cackled at the moon like a lunatic or that he's obviously got a vendetta against Miss Delia or that my gut tells me he's involved in Missy's death and trying to frame Beau and might even be a boo hag. As bad as all that is, I'll never forgive him for what he's taught Taneea about hoodoo. The gambling charms were bad enough, but the allurement spell crossed all bounds.

Claude sneers. "A confidential informant is helping us build a case."

The screened door slams. Taneea stands on the porch glaring at us, her hands planted firmly on her hips. She's wearing yet another corset top, this one black with hot-pink polka dots, black capris, and black pumps. Her fugly bag is hiked over her shoulder and the locket is prominently displayed around her neck.

"I wonder who that informant might be?" I stare her down as my fists clench.

He shrugs. "They're confidential for a reason."

Right. So they can spin their lies in private. "And has your informant helped you find any stolen artifacts? A master plan written out on the back of an envelope? How about blueprints with the layout of the museum?"

Claude chuckles and turns to Sheriff Walker. "The children must watch a lot of television crime shows."

The sheriff laughs. "I'm surprised she didn't ask if we discovered any DNA."

"Did you?" Jack asks, only half-sarcastically.

Sheriff Walker's smile falls. "No, but we didn't need any of those things, because she hasn't been charged with those crimes. Yet."

Cooper, Jack, and I exchange looks.

"Then why did they take her away in handcuffs?" Cooper asks.

"Our informant gave us a tip that Miss Delia's a conjurer who dispenses medicines in the form of potions, oils, and gris-gris bags. It's illegal to practice medicine in South Carolina without a license. She's looking at up to a thousand dollars and two years of jail time for each offense."

"That's ridiculous," Jack says.

"No, it's the law. If y'all really care about her, I suggest you find her a good lawyer. Now if you'll excuse me, I've got to get back down to the station." Sheriff Walker brushes past us to get to his car. Within seconds, he's gone.

Taneea approaches the gate. Claude's smile stretches wider than normal. "Ah, Taneea. Our work here is done. I trust you'll be returning with me to the museum? We've got to update the board on our activities."

Ignoring him, she keeps her eyes trained on Cooper. "I've been calling you all morning." The words snap like the lash of a whip.

"I know," he says.

"Why haven't you picked up? And why aren't you wearing your new clothes? Or your necklace?"

"Because they're heinous." Jack snickers.

"I'll handle this, bro." Cooper steps to the gate, meeting her face-to-face. "It's over." His voice is as deep as a well. Though his face looks perfectly calm, his body radiates anger.

She laughs. "That's not how this works. I'll tell you when it's over."

"That's where you're wrong. We found your doll. I'm done being your robot."

Taneea's jaw drops and her lids stretch wide. "What—"

Claude interjects, clasping Taneea's shoulder. "It's time to go. You two can work out this squabble later."

Jerking out from under Claude's grasp, she plasters a big fake smile across her face. "Doll? I don't know what you're talking about. You're my Cooper Scooper, not my robot." A nervous giggle escapes her lips as she reaches to brush a golden curl off his forehead.

Jack and I exchange looks. *Cooper Scooper?* Seriously?

Cooper steps aside. "Like I said. It's over. Your power is gone."

She gawks at Claude, mystified. "But it was supposed to be unbreakable."

He bores into her with his stare. "I'm sure I don't know what you're talking about. You best learn to still that tongue of yours lest you insult those around you. We're due back at the museum. I expect to see you there shortly." He stomps to the Lincoln without so much as a good-bye, clearly miffed that she tried to drag him into this. But it doesn't matter because we already knew he was involved. After roaring his engine to life, he throws the transmission in reverse, and peels out of Miss Delia's yard.

Straightening her shoulders, Taneea strolls toward us.

Cooper crosses his arms. "Don't ever try it again. If you do, Jack, Emma, and I will crush you in ways you never thought possible."

Defiant, she stares him down. "Sure. Whatever you say."

"And I want my mother's locket back. Now. It was never intended for you." He extends his palm.

Her eyes turn down and her bottom lip quivers ever so slightly as she lifts her arms to unclasp the chain. "Fine. I wouldn't want to keep a piece of junk like this anyway. I was just wearing it out of pity." She slaps it in his hand.

She takes a few steps but then pulls up short. "Oh, Emma, I almost forgot. I've got something for you, too. Obviously I don't need it anymore." She digs her hand into her purse and tosses something small at me.

It's a tube of her stinky hand cream. Gross. "No thanks. I

don't like the smell."

"That's because you're not a guy. Trust me, rub a little of that into your hands and he'll do whatever you want. Worked like a charm for me." She spins on her heels and strides toward her truck.

Of course. Why hadn't I realized it earlier? That lotion of hers was just another coercion charm. I drop the tube on the ground. As far as I'm concerned it's as toxic as poison.

Desperate for understanding, I charge after her. "Why did you do it?"

She climbs on the running board and tosses me a hateful scowl. "You're so perfect, it makes me sick."

Whoa. That's the last thing I expected. Despite how screwed up she is, and how horrible the allurement was, I laugh. "Obviously, you don't know the first thing about me."

"Really? Look at you. Smart. Pretty. You've got my great-gran wrapped around your skinny little finger, your brother's sort of cool, and you've got Cooper. I don't think it's fair that anyone should get everything they want. Plus, it was sort of my duty. Cooper's superhot. Way too hot for you." She opens the door and climbs into the cab.

"That's so warped."

She shrugs. "Maybe. But it was still worth it. He and I had a lot of fun together."

Chapter Twenty-nine

Jack, Cooper, and I race back to High Point Bluff to carry out Miss Delia's instructions. I've got a *Psychic Vision* to pull off. With any luck, the mortar will have rested enough and it'll show us what we need to prove that Claude was involved in Missy's death. And maybe even that he's a boo hag.

After I take a purifying bath and brew a fresh batch of *Psychic Vision* tea, we pull up to the cemetery and then trudge down the now-familiar path through the kudzu-infested landscape, making our way to the crypt where Jack and Cooper stored the supplies to work the spell.

The crypt air is cool and smells kind of musty like my grandmother's old basement. One of the side walls is lined with sealed cement vaults that contain the caskets of several of Cooper's distant relatives. There's a low bench on the opposite side of the room. I wipe it off as best I can, then pull out my supplies and arrange them on top.

Jack hovers in the crypt's doorway, blocking some of the

streaming late-afternoon light. Cooper's right behind him. "Em, is it okay if we watch this time? Coop and I never got to see the visions that helped you figure out The Creep. We think they're really cool."

I have to think about that for a second because I don't want to break any of Miss Delia's rules. After the energy-tea debacle, I'm pretty much done coloring outside her lines. So long as I don't reveal any secrets about how to conduct the spell or its ingredients, I think it'll be okay. There's more than enough *Psychic Vision* tea to share.

"Um, sure. But just so you know, you have to listen to everything I say. Because if we mess up, we're going to have to wait another three days." Which we don't have, considering the boo hag is likely to strike again before Cooper turns sixteen at midnight.

Jack smiles. "Got it. No problem."

But then another thing occurs to me. "You know what, on second thought, you might not want to watch."

"Why?" Cooper asks.

"The spell pulls the last memory of whatever object is being used. Since the dagger was covered in boo-hag blood, I'm guessing it's going to show us the last few minutes of Missy's life. I know we didn't love her, but she was still a person. And if her passing was painful, it'll be difficult to see."

Cooper nods as his shoulders droop. "I see what you mean. Except, if the boo hag was there, shouldn't I see what it's capable of? Since, you know, it's coming after me next."

"He's got a point. Maybe the vision will give us a clue how to fight it, or at least how to stop it from possessing Coop," Jack says.

They're both right. We've got to watch, no matter how bad it is. I nod. "Okay, but no puking in the mortar."

Jack salutes me. "Yes, ma'am."

A few minutes later, we're sitting cross-legged on the crypt floor around the ancestors' mortar. When the charcoal chips are ready, I layer the herbs and roots on the burning coals as I've done so many times before. To my relief, the wind whips up outside, blowing through the leaves on the live oaks. A cool burst of air sweeps through the crypt.

I pull the thermos from my messenger bag and pour enough to fill up the cup and pass it to Cooper. "Now for the hardest part. This stuff tastes nasty, but you've got to drink it down in one gulp. No cheating. Otherwise it won't work. Oh, and another thing. The vision will start as soon as we've all had a drink so keep your eyes open and alert and don't let go of the knife until the vision fades."

He takes a deep breath and chugs. Gagging a couple times, he clamps his lips tight and forces it down.

Jack's face is filled with horror. "Is it really that bad, dude?"

Cooper nods.

I pour a refill and hand Jack the cup. "Drink."

Pinching his nose, he tilts back his head and guzzles. He shudders as the reddish-brown liquid slides down this throat. Then belches a sour-cherry and burned-spinach-flavored burp.

"Gross." The scent is so strong, I nearly taste it myself.

Cooper laughs, but it's high-pitched and kind of woozy so he must be starting to feel the effects of the tea.

It's my turn. As usual, it's terrible, but it's nothing compared to my vile energy tea.

The sky darkens and thunder rumbles in the distance.

I grasp the hilt of the pirate's dagger and direct Jack and Cooper to each grab hold of some part of the metal.

A wave of fatigue hits me as the spell begins to take hold. The sensation feels good. It proves I'm doing hoodoo the right way, allowing the spell to drain my energy, without taking any shortcuts. The knife suddenly feels like it weighs ten pounds.

The spell incantation slips from my lips.

> *"Smoke and mist reveal the past*
> *And how this object was used last.*
> *Reveal the truth about Missy's death,*
> *And whether the boo hag stole her last breath."*

Another clash of thunder booms, this time much closer. Cooper and Jack jump.

"Ignore it. Keep your eyes on the smoke," I whisper.

Rain patters on the roof and ground outside the crypt.

I open my eyes and breathe a sigh of relief. The mortar is working. The incense thickens and condenses, creating the magical movie screen for the vision. A bright light flickers in the middle of the gray haze and images sputter on the illuminated canvas. My head sways. I fix my eyes on the vision as the pictures speed up and come into focus, revealing the master bedroom at High Point Bluff. Missy's wearing her pink nightie and is seated at her vanity table, madly smacking a brush at her rat's nest of frayed blond hair. She's laughing and mumbling to herself as she stares at her mirror.

The vision zooms in on her, as if we're standing next to her shoulder. She cackles as the brush snags on a tangle. "Little brat will finally get his. Everyone thought I was crazy to keep searching, but I showed them. I knew I'd find something if I looked hard enough!" Though the back of her hair is still a matted mess, she slams the brush down and picks up a pot of sky-blue eye shadow. Leaning toward the mirror, she smears it on with the tip of her index finger and then applies some blush with an extra-heavy hand. "You, Missy Tiffany Cartier Beaumont, have bought your ticket to the big time. That nasty old goat can't last too much longer, and with the brat in jail, you'll get everything!" She throws her head back and laughs, then grabs a tube of bright red lipstick and slathers it around her mouth. "Now you just have to convince the goat to call the cops. Which shouldn't be too hard." She squirts perfume on her cleavage and winks at herself.

Beau lumbers into the room, leaning heavily on his cane. "Missy!" he growls.

"Dad?" Cooper says.

"Where's Claude?" Jack asks.

The vision loses focus and begins to flicker.

"Shh, you'll ruin it," I snap.

The guys hunker down and direct their attention to the vision. The movie picks up pace and the images brighten.

Missy rises from her vanity. "Beau, sugar!" Her mouth is twisted in a big, red, garish smile. "I'm surprised to see you upstairs." She baby steps across the carpet in her stilettos. "After our little tiff, I thought you were going to punish me by sleeping in your study again. I was fixing to come down and surprise you with a little midnight snack."

Beau doesn't look amused or grateful. "I thought I made my position on your incessant destruction perfectly clear." His jowls jiggle with each word.

She reaches her hand to stroke his massive chest. "You did, baby, but what's the expression? Nothing searched for, nothing found?" She bats her lashes.

His eyes narrow. "That's not it."

She shrugs. "Oh. Who cares anyway? The point is—"

"The point is, you've wrecked my son's room."

Her shoulders slump and her lips pucker in a cherry-red pout. "How else am I supposed to find that goll-darn ruby necklace?"

His nostrils flare and his pasty gray skin flushes pink. "I fail to see what that has to do with Cooper. Your thieving friends weren't on the second floor the night of the party."

She pats his chest. "Now, sweetie, don't get yourself upset. You know how poorly your circulation is. You're liable to have a coronary. And you know I'd be plum lost without you. Besides, I'm sure my friends didn't take your ruby." A smile crosses her lips.

He totters on his cane. "I must have that necklace. Why hasn't Corbeau identified the thieves yet?" Beau starts to sway. Missy plants her arms against his chest to steady him, but she's far too small to keep him upright. Instead, she uses his momentum to push him toward the sitting room area at the far side of the bed. Heaving for air, Beau plops his massive girth in the love seat. His face turns alabaster and his lips are an almost purply-black hue. Gasping, he points to the small console table by the wall. "Scotch!" His voice ripples with mucus.

She scampers to pour him an extra large tumbler. "Here you go, baby. Drink up!" She tips the crystal glass to his lips and he swills it down.

Within seconds, his skin returns to its normal pasty gray.

She smiles as she saunters to the bureau opposite the bed. "There, there. Now, I don't want to upset you, but there's something you need to see. I was going to bring it to you later, but now's just as good." She slides open the drawer and slips her hand under a cashmere sweater. Spinning around, she thrusts the pirate's dagger at Beau.

He perks up, launching himself forward on the love seat. "That was stolen from the King Center."

"I know. Yet I found it here at High Point Bluff." She walks toward him, but rather than using her normal, cutesy-baby shuffle, she takes several long, determined strides to the love seat.

He quirks his head. "I don't understand."

"Your son stole it."

His wide brow creases. "Impossible."

The blade shines, reflecting the light in the corner of the bedroom.

"It was hidden in his bookshelf. One of those fancy textbooks of his is really a secret compartment, probably uses it to hide drugs or something." Knife in hand, she flicks her wrist and stabs the air with each word. "I thought he'd been acting squirrely, being helpful when he was really trying to see if I found his stash. Well, sonny-boy has met his match. It's just a matter of time before I find that other rock-thing that was stolen... What's it called? A mortal?"

"Mortar." Beau deadpans.

Her lips curl. "What?"

"The other artifact that was stolen. It's a mortar. Not a mortal."

She shrugs. "Whatever, it doesn't matter, because when we get Mr. Corbeau and the sheriff involved they're going to cart Cooper and his freaky little friends off to jail. I wouldn't blame you if you disinherited him tomorrow."

With a grunt, Beau hoists himself off the sofa. "Oh, but it matters a great deal. You see a *mortal* is a living human being who is subject to death. A mortar, on the other hand, is used to grind spices." Leaning hard against his cane, he advances toward her, then lifts the dagger from her hand and sets it down on the console with the scotch decanter.

"Okay, I'll be sure to use the right word when I call the sheriff."

He shakes his head, waggling his jowls. "You won't be doing that."

"Why?"

He steps toward her. "Because I have plans for Cooper and his friends. Crucial, long-range plans that require his utmost freedom and access to his inheritance. He will not be arrested, nor will he serve even a minute's worth of jail time. Nor will Emma and Jack. You see, Emma and Cooper are to be married, and Jack will, as every Guthrie before him, become Cooper's faithful servant."

She inches backward. "But he stole from the museum."

"I don't care."

"He probably took your ruby."

"That, I care about. But if he does in fact have it, my problems will cease to be problems. All will be well and our future will be secure."

"Huh?"

He snickers. "You are pretty, but you are so stupid."

"No I'm not. I'm the one who figured out who the burglars are."

"And I sincerely thank you for that because now I can rest comfortably knowing that I need only to make it to Cooper's birthday and then all my plans will come to fruition, just as they have for nearly three hundred years."

"I-I don't understand." She steps backward, deeper into the room.

"Of course not, sugar. Because as I said earlier, you lack the intellectual capacity to comprehend such things. You have been a mildly amusing distraction these last few months, but I think it's time to go. Don't feel too bad. You were only supposed to be here another couple weeks anyway."

"I'm not leaving. I'm the Mistress of the Plantation!"

"Not for long." He throws his head back and extends his jaw wide. Placing his palms on either side of his face, he tugs on his skin. It pulls, slipping loose from around his eye sockets and nose. His mouth stretches open. A slick, scarlet figure emerges from the gaping pit, shedding Beau's gelatinous skin like a giant rubber suit.

It's the boo hag, glistening with wet, slimy, mucus. Beau's flesh lies hollow and vacant at its feet, pooled on the stark, white carpet.

Missy screams.

"I have waited for this moment." The boo hag advances, flying at her in one fluid leap. It snatches her jaw with its three suction-cup-tipped fingers. Tilting its narrow, rectangular head, it goggles her as if she's a fine piece of art. "I've taken little sips here and there while you slept, especially after the ruby went missing and this body broke down. You have no idea how difficult it's been to restrain myself. The dumb ones are always the most tasty. Do you know why?" Its lispy, sloshy voice is just as terrifying in a vision as in person. It runs its long lizard-like tongue across its slash of a mouth.

Her eyes bulge. "N-n-no."

The red monster leans toward her. "Too much thought toughens the prey. So I'm guessing you'll be especially delicious. It has been a challenge to wait, but I've learned over the years that too much death tends to raise suspicions. As soon as I retrieve the ruby, I won't need quite so many sacrifices to maintain the possession. But these are no longer your concerns.

Since you'll be dead."

"You don't have to kill me. I could run away and never come back just like your second and third wives. I swear, I won't tell anybody. No one would believe me anyway."

"There are a few things you don't understand. They didn't leave me. I enjoyed killing them just as I will enjoy killing you, too." It gleams a toothless grin, then lunges for her, snatching her by the throat with both three-fingered hands. Missy's feet dangle above the cushy white carpet.

Missy's skin flushes as she chokes and gasps for air. She reaches out her right hand, fumbling for the pirate's knife that Beau set on the console table next to the bottle of scotch.

The boo hag extends its massive, square jaw, and turns on its vacuum suction. Missy shudders and her eyes roll up in to her head as the boo hag sucks her life force from her body. A curling white mist floats out of her nose and mouth and inches toward the gaping hole in the boo hag's face.

Missy's fingertips graze the knife's wooden hilt. Stretching another half inch, she grabs the dagger and plunges it into the boo hag's side. A few drops of black sludge spatter the rug.

The boo hag shrieks. It's red eyes flash with eerie, crimson light. Clutching her throat tighter, it launches into the air in a rage, careening through the sitting area and into the master bath, leaving a trickle of blood along its path. It slams her head against a tile wall. She reaches for the knife again, but the boo hag pulls the blade from its side, releasing a gush of chunky, black muck that sprays Missy's nightie and smatters the floor. Opening its mouth once again, the boo hag sucks harder than before, consuming Missy's life force in one smooth gulp. Her face falls slack and her eyes turn empty and blind.

The boo hag drops her lifeless body on the floor then

clutches its side where the knife slit its crimson skin. Hobbling back to the sitting area, it sets the knife down on the carpet and reaches for Beau's skin. It slides its long, thin, legs into Beau's rubbery mouth, and pulls the skin up over its red, meaty body like a flesh-colored wet suit. Yanking Beau's face up over its own, it snaps the elastic skin into place, adjusting Beau's eye sockets and maneuvering his nose into place. Finally, it pumps Beau's jaw, slipping it into place.

With a grunt, the boo hag in the Beau suit bends over and wipes the knife on the carpet. Wincing, it clutches its cut right side, which must be bleeding inside Beau's skin. It rises to its feet, snatches the tumbler from the coffee table and staggers to the console holding the bottle of scotch in one hand, the dagger in the other. After it pours a giant helping, it gulps the amber liquid, then slams the glass down next to the bottle.

"Just a few more weeks, old boy. Then you'll be sixteen and carefree once again. And still very, very rich," it says aloud in Beau's familiar southern accent and then laughs. A wet, mucusy sound rattles in its chest, causing it to cough. It winces again and gropes its side.

When the wave of pain seems to have passed, it grabs the cane with one hand and shambles to the door, holding tight to the knife.

The vision pulls back, clouding over. Sparks shoot up in the ancestors' mortar, and then die out, stifling the incense screen and dispersing the smoke.

I shake my foggy head to focus on Jack and Cooper. They're both as white as marble, revealing the same horror that's gripping my chest.

Cooper's eyes meet mine. They're filled with crushing pain and utter betrayal. "My dad's a boo hag."

Chapter Thirty

Cooper races out of the crypt.

Jack opens his mouth to speak, but no words come. How could they? There are no words to describe the awful brutality we just witnessed, to say nothing about the vision's implications, which are so multilayered and bizarre, my brain's about to break.

How could I have been so wrong? After Missy died, there was a moment I suspected Beau was involved. But then Claude showed up pulling his super-creepy, black magic routine and I got distracted. It looks like Miss Delia was right after all — Claude just wants to wedge himself between Taneea and her, though I don't understand why.

The horrific truth is that Beau is a genuine monster. A serial killer of sorts who not only kills for sustenance but also because it appears to enjoy it. And he's gunning for Cooper next. He never liked his father, but that doesn't make this news any less excruciating.

And then there's the whole marriage-destiny thing the

Beau-boo hag let slip to Missy. Cooper and me? Married? As in forever? Cripes, I'm only fourteen. I've been with him for a little over a month. How the heck am I supposed to process a fated, eternal commitment?

Jack pushes himself off the floor. "I need some air. Hoodoo's cool, but its a good thing I'm not the root worker. I don't think I could handle it." He staggers toward the door, clearly still under the tea's woozy effects.

Knowing I shouldn't leave them alone, I force myself up and drag my groggy body through the crypt. It's pouring and the sky is a sickly chartreuse, that strange yellow-green-gray that only happens during summer storms. Thick fog hugs the ground and envelops their legs. If I didn't know the mist was caused by the cool rain moisturizing the scorching air, I'd be freaked.

Jack's bent over, his hands leaning against his knees. His cheeks are puffed out, and he's dragging deep breaths through his nose.

Water streams down Cooper's face as he stares at the sky. It's probably just precipitation, but it could just as easily be tears. No one could possibly blame him for bawling his eyes out.

Fighting fatigue, I walk to his side. "Are you okay?"

"My father isn't my father. He never really was, was he?" he asks without turning away from the sky.

I shake my head. "I don't think so."

He meets my gaze. "The boo hag must have killed him when he was sixteen. Just like it wants to do to me now."

"That's what it sounds like." There's no use in sugarcoating it. That thing has an ugly agenda that it's not likely to forget.

"And it probably killed my mother, just like it killed Missy. And tried to kill you last night."

My body quakes as I remember how awful the mind suck

was. I've done a good job repressing the sheer terror of my contorted memories, but after seeing what happened to Missy, I realize I was lucky. The boo hag only inhaled me for a few seconds and I retained my sanity. Missy wasn't as fortunate. No wonder she was so demented she couldn't brush her own hair and thought it was okay to destroy her home. The creature literally drove her mad.

Jack straightens and swallows hard. "That thing said it's been at this for almost three hundred years. If that's true, it must have killed every one of the Beaumonts since Sabina cast those first curses."

I gasp as a missing piece finally clicks into place. "That's why it wants the ruby back. Somehow its power is wrapped up with the Beaumont Curse."

"But we destroyed the stone," Jack says.

"The boo hag doesn't know that. It thinks I've got it. We can use that to our advantage," Cooper says, a steely glint in his eyes.

It's the first ray of hope I've felt all day.

Jack's shoulders ease. "That monster's going to be surprised when it finds out Cooper's mom turned it into heap of flower petals."

Cooper's mouth bends into a determined grin. "It'll be more than surprised. That thing stole my parents from me and destroyed my entire family. I'm going to kill it or die trying." His voice is as grim as the expression on his face.

"My vote is that you don't die," Jack says.

Cooper hitches his brow. "Mine too."

Jack turns to me. "So how do we make that happen? Cooper's birthday is tomorrow so it's probably planning a move tonight. We don't have much time to plan."

I draw a deep breath. "Well, for starters, Miss Delia said

we've got to figure out where it hides its skin when it goes out at night, then salt it down so it can't climb back in. What's the most likely place the boo hag would store Beau's skin?"

A lightbulb goes off in my head. Apparently the same thing happens to Jack and Cooper because they both turn to me at the same time. "Beau's study!" we say in unison.

* * *

We spend the rest of the afternoon and evening at the caretaker's cottage waiting for the sun to set and darkness to roll in. When the clock strikes ten, we head out for the Big House, hoping the boo hag has shed Beau's skin and gone out for the night.

The sky's a deep, dusky purple, darkened by thick, opaque clouds that obscure the stars. The only light comes from the full moon that casts an eerie silver-white glow through the haze.

We trek down the path, trying to make as little noise as possible. The Big House comes into view. My heart clenches. Every light in the house is on. Which means Beau has been around. And may even be in there right now. There's only one way to find out.

Cooper opens the front door. My ears prick, on alert for any indication that we're not alone. The foyer is silent. Even the air seems to hang still. We tiptoe toward the main hall, then stop short at the corner and listen for any sound. There's only silence. We crane our necks to peek at the door to Beau's private study.

It's shut. A sliver of light shines through the crack above the floor.

Taking a deep breath, Cooper paces down the hall with me and Jack at his heels. At the door, Cooper holds up his fist to knock. He freezes midair, as if he's afraid to follow though.

I can't blame him. His life, or death, could be waiting for him in there.

"You can do this, Coop. We've got your back," Jack whispers.

Cooper nods, then pounds his fist, hard and fast.

There's no hiding now. If the boo hag's in there, it knows we're out here.

No sound comes from behind the door. Cooper waits another moment before pounding again. "Dad?"

Jack nods at Cooper.

Together, they ram their shoulders into the mahogany door, pounding until they break it in. Finally, it slams against the wall with a *thud*.

If Beau's in here, we're so screwed.

But the room is empty. And except for the window that's wide open and the curtain blowing in the cool evening breeze, it's perfectly still. Just an ordinary office filled with ordinary office furniture.

We race inside, scanning the floor for the rubbery Beau suit. It's nowhere in sight.

"Maybe it's hidden." Jack sprints across the room to the closet. He yanks open the door, but his chest caves at the shelves lined with copier paper and other supplies, and boxes filled with old tax returns.

Cooper tugs open the deep side drawers of the desk. I'm not exactly sure Beau would file his suit away, but I suppose it's worth a try.

Once Jack's satisfied that the closet isn't a Beau suit storage unit, he gets down on his hands and knees to search under the sofa and arm chairs.

I spin my messenger bag around to my back and start on

the file cabinet across the room beneath the open window. My
eyes are drawn to the nearby glass-enclosed shelves that display
the hundreds of artifacts from High Point Bluff. My fingers prick
as I scan the tangible history of the Beaumont family. Before
tonight, I knew this plantation was tainted by its involvement
in slavery and its male progeny cursed for what Edmund
Beaumont and a band of wicked pirates did to an enslaved
African girl. But now, after the *Psychic Vision*, I realize High
Point Bluff's story is much more dismal than I ever imagined.
After the Beaumont men lost their souls, a horrible boo hag
exploited their bodies' vulnerability and possessed their flesh
once they came of age. And, if Clarissa, Missy, and Beau's other
two wives are any indication, the rest of the Beaumont women
weren't spared either.

A queasy feeling grips my stomach. I turn away from the
mini-museum of horrors and direct my attention back to the file
cabinet, clasping the pull. My fingers burn like fire. I yank my
hand away and shake it out to relieve the pain. The collection
glows with a soft yellow light. A deep ache sets into my soles,
urging me toward the display shelves.

Jeez, my spirit guide's working overtime to make a point.

Scanning the items once more, I try to figure out what's
so special about them. It's hard to imagine there's anything
particularly noteworthy about bottles, hair combs, handkerchiefs,
pewter cups, and pocket watches. They look like random items
from lives lived—or more accurately—lost.

Jack pops up on to his knees after rolling back the area rug.
I can only assume he's looking for a trap door of some sort.
"What's up, Em?"

"Um, I'm not sure, but there's something important about
all this stuff." I stroke my chin as I scan the glowing items.

Jack joins me in front of the shelves. "Too bad Mom isn't here. She could probably tell us if any of that stuff is valuable."

Except her specialty is Middle Eastern desert culture, so it's highly doubtful. And there's the whole hoodoo thing, too, which isn't exactly part of her curriculum.

Cooper gives up on the desk drawers and steps to my other side. "It just looks like a bunch of stuff that was handed down through my family."

"I guess. But my spirit guide's kind of making a big deal about it."

Jack's brow arches. "Let me guess, voices?"

I shake my head. "Glowing."

He chuckles. "Dang. How come you get all the fun? I'm your twin, and I don't see squat."

I shake my head. "I don't know. I guess it's my curse."

"Or your gift," Cooper says. "It's let you do some pretty amazing things. And saved me and Jack while you were at it. I wouldn't get too down on those powers of yours." He smiles as his blue-green gaze meets mine.

My chest fills with familiar warmth. "Let's not get ahead of ourselves. I haven't saved you yet. There's still a boo hag hunting for that skin of yours."

He shakes his head. "I haven't forgotten."

"Good, because neither have I." Redoubling my efforts, I drag my eyes from his gorgeous face and turn back to the shelves and squint hard. I gasp. "Holy cow."

"What?" Jack and Cooper ask in unison.

I point to a thick yellow beeswax candle in the corner of the top shelf that's pulsing with bright light. "That!"

"*What*?" They ask again, but this time their words are tinged with annoyance.

Oh, I forgot they can't see what I do. I sigh. "The candle. It's flashing like a beacon."

"If you say so," Jack says.

"I do." I stretch onto my tiptoes, but the candle is just out of reach.

"You sure you should touch it?" Cooper asks.

"Um, pretty much. My spirit guide wouldn't direct me to it otherwise."

"Okay." Reaching over my head, he grabs hold of the candle and tries to snatch it. But rather than lift, it tilts forward. The bottom is connected to some kind of lever that's built into the shelf.

A grinding metal sound churns inside the wall that reminds me of the spinning gears of a clock. With a *click*, the rotating stops and last bookcase pops away from the wall.

"What the…? Ugh!" Jacks words trail off as the brutal aroma of decaying flesh wafts into the room. He groans as he slaps his palm across his nose and mouth.

Cooper coughs then winces as he steps to the opening and pulls on the bookcase. "I think we found what we're looking for."

It swings open to reveal a secret, windowless room. The pent-up, fetid air from inside the compartment gushes out and disperses as it spills into the study, then drifts out the window.

I step inside. The stench is still strong enough to burn my throat. Like the crypt at the cemetery, the sparely furnished room is lined with stone and the air is cool. It's a no-tech refrigerator no doubt intended to help preserve the flesh of the boo hag's latest victim.

Aside from a small table, chair, and a bookcase filled with ancient ledgers, there's a wooden stand in the middle of the room propping up Beau's skin. The flesh husk is posed upright, his lifeless underarms and crotch supported by thick pegs that stick out from a board. Its hollow eyes, nose, and mouth are barren voids of doom.

Cooper swallows hard. "What do we do now?"

"Get it off there and dump salt down its throat," I answer, dreading every moment.

Jack slaps his palms together. "Might as well get to it." He strides to the skin and stares at it for a second, as if sizing up a math problem. Without waiting for me or Cooper, he slips his hand under Beau's meaty left arm and flings it over the peg. The shoulder sags, pulling the skin suit off-kilter. Jack spins around to us, his face gray as he clasps the flaccid skin. "It's not so bad. Kind of feels like a snake. A rotting snake, but if you can get past the stink, it's tolerable." It spills onto the floor in a gelatinous puddle. Splayed on its back, it's vacant face stares up at the ceiling, its mouth a gaping hole.

Cooper kneels beside the pool of flaccid flesh. He stares at what once was his father for a long moment, then lifts his gaze to mine. His eyes are moist and tinged with pink. He extends his hand. "Give me the salt. I want to kill it."

I yank off my messenger bag, flip open the flap, then pull out the three cartons of salt. I pop open the spout on the first and pass it to him. "Pour it into the mouth, then down past the neck, and into the body cavity. That should do the trick."

Cooper takes the container, then leans to where the head lays. "Once I do this, my dad—or what I knew of him—will be gone forever."

I nod. "That's right. The boo hag won't be able to slip back into the skin without being burned."

Jack steps toward Cooper and grips his shoulder. "Your dad's been gone for years. The guy you know was an impersonation. And a pretty bad one at that."

Cooper nods as he peers at the husk. "Look what it did to him. It wasn't enough to destroy his reputation, it desecrated his body, too. Well, that ends tonight. I'm not going to let it do anything more to my dad." He grabs hold of what's left of his father's face. The cheeks jiggle and the neck ripples as he tugs on the mouth to stretch it open. Mashing his lips, Cooper tilts the container to Beau's mouth and pours the white grains in a steady stream.

The pink flesh fizzles and pops.

Jack straddles the center of the skin suit's midsection and strains to lift the chest, allowing Cooper better access to the rest of the cavity. Cooper empties the container, then reaches for the second.

The faint scent of charred meat floats up from the carcass.

Jack gags. "I think we're cooking Beau."

My stomach churns. "Ugh, gross." I peek inside and see the areas that have been salted have already turned a dark gray and hardened like beef jerky. In a sense he's right, but I think this is one of those situations that it's best to downplay the obvious. "No, the salt is just drying out the skin. Try not to breathe."

Jack nods and swallows hard. "Yeah, okay."

When Cooper's finally finished dumping the third container, he and Jack lay the skin back on the floor. It's shriveled and withered and has shrunken in on itself.

Cooper steps back and takes in the desiccated slab of wrinkled flesh. "I'm officially an orphan."

"You always have been. You just didn't know it." Jack's voice is uncharacteristically solemn.

Cooper turns toward me, his eyes misty. "So now what?"

"We destroy the hag before it possesses you or finds another body to snatch before the sun rises," I answer, sounding a whole lot more confident than I actually am. Because as easy as all that sounds, I actually don't have the faintest clue how to pull any of it off.

"Awesome. What's your plan of attack?" Jack asks.

I gnaw my bottom lip, considering whether to be totally honest. "Um, a trap? Ideally, if we could keep it captive until dawn, then the sunlight would fry it alive. We wouldn't have to engage in any hand-to-hand combat."

Jack smiles. "Bonus. I don't want to have to stab that thing again if I can help it."

Cooper hitches his brow. "Traps usually require bait."

"Uh-huh," I answer.

"So what's the lure?" Cooper asks.

After all that's happened, I'm surprised it's not obvious to him by now.

Jack hitches a brow. "Seriously, dude? You."

Chapter Thirty-one

Cooper sucks a chestful of air. "Fine. Where are we setting up my death trap?"

"Um…" I glance up at the shelves. My breath catches. Every single artifact flashes with bright yellow light. It's as if it's a display case of flares rather than discreet historical objects. I walk around the desk and stand before the cabinets, gawking at the show. Bathed in the intense light, each item takes on a different luster and a deeper significance.

These aren't just *things* that were used here at the plantation. They're *possessions* that belonged to the people who once lived here. My ears prickle and heat. The combs, fans, pocket watches, and other knickknacks on these shelves meant something to High Point Bluff's residents. And they were collected by the boo hag, who has possessed every Master of the Plantation since the first, Edmund, died, inhabiting their bodies and hijacking their lives. A stinging sensation inches its way up the back of my scalp as realization dawns. These are trophies.

"What is it?" Jack and Cooper ask.

"Get a couple boxes. We need to bring these with us to the cemetery."

After Jack and Cooper help me load up all the artifacts from the shelves, I grab a pen and clean sheet of paper from the printer on the desk and jot down a note.

So sorry about your skin. :(If you're looking for Cooper you can find him and the Beaumont Ruby down at the cemetery. Happy hunting. :)

I hand it to Jack. "Leave this on top of the carcass. That should make our point."

Jack races into the stone room and delivers the note. We sprint from the study and head toward the kitchen to the side exit. An idea pops in to my head.

I stop short and turn to Cooper. "Do you still have the mojo I made you?" I leave off the part where Taneea made him take it off because it clashed with the hideous new clothes she picked out.

"Yeah, it's in my bedroom. Do you need it?"

I breathe a sigh of relief. "No. You will. Go grab it."

He sets his box on the floor and then races down the hall and upstairs. A few seconds later he's back, his chest heaving for air. "Are you sure it still works?" He extends the little white pouch toward me as his soft green-blue gaze searches mine.

I know what he's really asking: does it still contain my love? I can't help but wonder the same. I clasp the white pouch in my hand. It's soft and worn from lying against Cooper's skin for weeks. White energy warms my fingertips and dances up my arm. My skin tingles as joy and happiness swell in my chest, and my lips bend into a smile. "It's still working. You should put it on now. You can never be too safe."

Fifteen minutes later, after we stop at the caretaker's cottage for a straw broom, Cooper pulls the golf cart up to the cemetery, the one place we aren't supposed to be unsupervised, yet where we've managed to spend an awful lot of time. Instinct or my spirit guide or the green and white psychic beads on my *collier* kick in, drawing me deep into the graveyard. Though I don't expect the boo hag to strike until we near Cooper's birthday at midnight, we stick close, on high alert, squinting through the cloudy night and listening for any indication that our visitor has arrived early.

Jack sets his box on the ground, then props the old wooden doors of the crypt open and dashes inside. A second later he bolts out, the pirate's dagger in his grip. He lifts it for us to see. "For cutting the kudzu." The blade reflects the moon's glow.

We trudge on, wading farther into the cemetery to the section that abuts the salt marsh. The stones are draped with thick, winding vines, and the ground is a lush green carpet that's hard to walk through. And since the sky is covered with thick gray clouds, only sporadic beams of moonlight shine through, bathing the hallowed ground in spooky shadows. The faster we find a safe place to build a fire, the better.

Clarissa's grave is just ahead, near the pile of mullein torches we left stacked on the ground after we broke the Beaumont curse. An awesome idea flashes across my mind. I glance around, but this area is too crowded with graves to set up a boo hag trap.

A short distance away, on the bank above the marsh, we come upon an area with fewer gravestones. My scalp pricks, making me halt. "This is where we need to be. Let's clear the area and find some wood for a fire."

Jack hacks at the vines with the dagger while Cooper uses his pocketknife, a less superior, but adequate tool. I gather up the clippings, and with Cooper and Jack at my side, toss the discarded kudzu into the woods until we collect enough kindling and fallen tree branches for a decent fire. Within minutes, Jack has built a fire big enough to provide plenty of light.

I hold up one of the bundles from Clarissa's grave, then flip the torch over and run my fingers over the spiky, reedy ends. "Miss Delia said boo hags are obsessed with counting things. Especially stuff with bristles. If we shove these into the ground with the tallow ends down, the boo hag will get stuck counting these until dawn. When the sun rises it'll burn alive, and this nightmare will be over."

Cooper scratches his head. "So, you're not planning to do any magic?"

"Um, no? Even if I could use the mortar, the *Psychic Vision* was a drain. I don't trust myself to have enough energy to work a spell."

"But you took a nap," Jack says.

I nod. "I'm not a hundred percent yet. I learned my lesson with trying to cheat hoodoo. Eventually I'll build up enough resistance that it doesn't bother me much, but I'm not there yet. It doesn't matter, because Miss Delia's spell book doesn't contain any charms to kill a boo hag. All she ever told me was to salt the skin and then fry it alive in the sun."

Their faces hang slack. They're not convinced. Not by a long shot.

"Guys, trust me, okay? All we've got to do is keep the boo hag occupied for a few hours in the mullein cage. The sun has to rise. It always does."

"What if it gets out and starts to suck Cooper?" Jack asks.

"It won't. At least it shouldn't. If it does…we'll move to Plan B," I say with all the confidence I can muster.

He snorts. "There is no Plan B. There's barely a Plan A. But we're in this together and we're out of time, so let's build a boo hag coop."

A few minutes later, we've driven the twelve upside-down torches into the soft soil. They're arranged in a circle like fence posts, each about a foot apart to give Cooper room to escape after we've captured the boo hag.

Cooper wiggles into the pen between the torches. "So I'm just supposed to sit in here? And do what?"

"Wait for midnight, I suppose."

"And how do I lure it in here?" Hands on his hips, he turns around in the circle inspecting the torches.

"Trust me, I don't think there'll be any luring," Jack says. "Even before we wrecked Beau's skin, his body was on its last legs. The boo hag needs a fresh victim. It's not going to wait for an invitation."

"Jack's right. You should hold on to this, too. Just in case." I pass Cooper the broom.

He pulls out his cell phone to check the time, then sets his alarm. "Only ten minutes to go. Not too long to wait to die." Gripping the wooden broom handle, he paces around the cage.

I frown. "Hey, you're not going to die."

He stops short and turns to me. "I know." His lips twist into a faint smile that doesn't meet his eyes. His gaze reveals everything he's not saying: he's humoring me by sitting in this cage, but on the inside, he's sure he's toast.

I reach between the mullein bundles and grasp the mojo out from under his T-shirt collar. "I'm serious. You're wearing a powerful *Protective Shield*. It's called that for a reason. As long as you're wearing this you're going to be fine."

He wraps his hand around mine as his gaze searches my face. "Okay." His fingers are warm and strong.

As much as I might like to stand here holding his hand all night, there's work to be done. "I've only got a few minutes to figure out what do to with those artifacts we brought over from the Big House."

He releases his grip. Without looking back, I drag my box near the fire to get a better look.

Jack brings me the other cartons. "So what do you think you're supposed to do with this stuff?"

Surveying the collection, I sigh. "I'm not sure. My spirit guide made a big deal about me hauling it down here, but now she hasn't given me any new clues." I pull out a silver cup and hold it in the flickering light of the flames. Back at the Big House, when this and the other artifacts were glowing, I was sure there had to be something special about them, that they were trophies collected by the boo hag from all its victims. But now, I'm starting to wonder if that's true. There are no flashes of light, no tingles in my fingers. Not even an inscription etched into the silver.

A screech shatters the cloudy night as a shock of red streaks out of the forest, whizzes past me, and lands in the cell with Cooper. A chorus of shrieks and yelps erupts in a mixture of human and otherworldly sounds that curdle my blood.

It's the boo hag, red, slick and shining, trapped in a cage with Cooper. "You're mine!" the boo hag howls.

I scream and nearly jump out of my own skin as I throw up my hands and launch the silver cup skyward. Time seems to slow and my vision tunnels, allowing me to capture every event that happens around me.

The cup somersaults in slow motion as it falls back to earth and then crashes into the fire. Flames engulf the metal, ferociously licking its surface.

A streak of yellow light explodes from a nearby grave and launches into the night sky like a Roman candle. High above the clearing, it bursts like fireworks. But rather than cascading to the ground, the shimmering flecks of yellow iridescence hover in the atmosphere, twinkling with radiant intensity. It's one of the most beautiful things I've ever seen.

The boo hag squeals and flinches at the light, shielding its lidless eyes from its luster.

"The broom!" I shout to Cooper, realizing this is his opportunity to gain the upper hand and distract the boo hag into counting.

Cooper shoves the broom's straw end in the boo hag's face. "Hey, how many strands are there?"

Crouching under the glistening brilliance still floating above, the boo hag's thin, rectangular head tilts toward the broom as its bulging eyes lock onto the bristles. It extends its three-fingered hands toward the broom. "Give it to me!"

Cooper backs away, guiding the boo hag to the center of the cage. He points the broom's end to a mullein bundle. "Only if you promise to count these too."

The boo hag lunges to the post. It clutches its crimson hands around the bundle, becoming mesmerized by the strands and murmuring to itself. Cooper turns sideways and slips between two of the mullein torches. Then he tosses the broom in the center of the cage and races over to us.

"Dude, that was a close one!" Jack slaps Cooper on the shoulder.

Cooper's chest rises and falls as he gasps for breath. "I've got to admit I had my doubts, but man, you were right."

I shake my head. "No. Miss Delia was right."

We watch as the boo hag combs its three-fingered hands through the strands on the post. When it finishes, it hops to the next and begins its count again.

Cooper tilts his head back to look at the light hovering above the clearing. "Is that a spirit? It sparkles like my mom."

"I think so. It shot out when I dropped the cup into the fire. Whatever it is, it scared the crap out of the boo hag." I glance at the silver that's still burning in the flame. Funny. I'd have guessed it might have begun to melt by now.

"What if you tossed in the rest?" Jack asks.

Just as I'm about to tell him that's the dumbest idea ever, that one artifact sacrificed by accident is bad enough, but a hundred on purpose is unforgivable, I reconsider. If the boo hag is frightened, even pained by one stolen Beaumont spirit, what could happen if a hundred are released? The light could be bright enough to rival the sun and we might not have to wait until dawn. If we're lucky, this horror show could be over in a few minutes.

"You're a genius!" A surge of adrenaline shoots through my blood stream as I throw my arms around my brother and give him a hug.

"Of course I am. Why are you so surprised?" he asks.

But rather than answer him and stroke his ego, I dive toward the nearest box and start unloading items into the fire. "Help me!" I cry and point to the other two crates of artifacts.

One by one, the items drop into the fire, feeding the flames like a giant bellows. The graveyard explodes like a bank of fireworks at New Year's Eve as yellow spirits leap from the soil and soar toward the heavens in a stunning pyrotechnics spectacle. The cemetery is bathed in bright, glowing light as spirits dash around and spin with joy as if released from a near-eternal confinement.

With each new burst, the boo hag screams and writhes and shades its eyes, yet continues to obsess over its counting.

Jack lifts the pirate's knife. "What should I do with this? It was on the shelf with the other stuff before we took it from the study."

He's right. If we hadn't found it that day encrusted with dried boo hag blood, we wouldn't have known to try a *Psychic Vision*. "Might as well toss it in, too."

He throws it into the fire with the other objects. The fire blazes, but just like the silver cup, the artifacts appear to remain intact and undisturbed by the flames. When the last of the collection has been added, the boo hag is cringing on the ground, curled around the broom in the center of the mullein cage, relentlessly counting the strands of straw.

My heart sinks. Though the sky is as bright as a ballpark at night, the light has only incapacitated the boo hag and hasn't ended its existence. Is it too much to hope the Beaumont spirits will hang around until the sun rises? At least they'll help keep it cowering and confined in our makeshift jail.

An icy wind blows over the graveyard, sending chills up my spine. A deep, rolling laugh echoes across the clearing.

I've heard that sound before. It's the stuff of my deepest nightmares. Pivoting on my heels, I turn around.

A small but stocky woman with scarified ebony skin is standing atop of one of the gravestones at the far side of the clearing. She's dressed in coarse, dingy-white clothes and her hair is wrapped in a turban. A stubby, dark-colored root juts out from her mouth.

My heart leaps into my throat.

It's Sabina, the African root doctress who created The Creep and the Beaumont Curse nearly three hundred years ago. And she's coming for us.

Chapter Thirty-two

Sabina grinds the root between her crooked teeth. "You've been busy, haven't you, girl?" Her voice is low and gruff, with a jagged edge. The fragrant scent of wisteria floods the clearing, a deceptively sweet but highly poisonous flower. I don't need the olfactory clue to know to stay away. I've seen her work up close and personal and I know how evil she is.

"Emma? Who's that?" Cooper points to Sabina who, despite standing beneath the canopy of luminous light, appears cloaked in shadow.

Not wanting to draw Sabina's attention to the only Beaumont heir, I ignore him. Gathering my courage and wits, I swallow hard. "I-I don't know what you're talking about."

She disappears. A moment later she reappears standing atop a broken stone about halfway across the clearing. "Oh, I'm sure you do. You think I don't keep watch of my spells and who's trying to break them? I've had my eye on you for a while, child."

Jack steps next to me and puffs his skinny chest. "What do

you want?"

She raises a squat finger at him. "You best stay back, boy."

Though I'm more than half a foot shorter, I stand in front of him to act as a shield. "He doesn't mean you any harm, Sabina." I toss in her name hoping to clue Jack and Cooper into how serious this is and prevent them from doing something heroic and stupid.

She chuckles, but it's menacing and full of loathing. "I'm sure of that. Not that he could if he tried."

"He couldn't. He doesn't know hoodoo."

One narrow brow arches. "But you do, don't you? Enough to mess with what I set forth so many moons ago." She hops off the gravestone and levitates off the ground.

I stay put, tapping an unknown source of strength. "I haven't done anything to hurt you. I've only helped my brother and friend."

Her irises vanish and her eyes glow white. "You've destroyed my plans!" She stretches her mouth wide, magnifying her voice until it shakes the ground.

A bitter gust whips through the graveyard, stinging my skin.

"Em?" Jack murmurs.

Sickly sour saliva coats the back of my constricted throat. "Get back, Jack. You too, Cooper." My teeth chatter as I force out the words. Thankfully they listen, moving without any argument.

The spirit lights swarm together, brightening as they coalesce, then vibrate and buzz like a giant swarm of bees.

Sabina glowers at the sky. Raising her fist, she splays her fingers out. "Be gone!" A blast of air shoots straight up, slams into the brilliant orbs, and scatters them across the entire cemetery. The buzzing quiets and they hang still as their light dims.

Laughing, Sabina flies straight for me, stopping just inches from my face. Her eyes are two empty pools of malevolence. The air is icy and smells of bitterness and venom. "You, little girl, have listened to the doctress and that worthless guide of yours. Do you know what that makes you?"

I shake my head. "N-no." My voice is just barely above a whisper.

"A traitor!" she bellows, blowing frigid air over my face and up my nose. Her breath is laced with the corrosive scent of the deadly *Blue Root* clenched between her teeth.

A *traitor*? To who? Not her, that's for sure. I'd never play for Sabina's team. Ever.

She hovers above the ground. "I worked my spells for a reason. It is not for you to decide when the Beaumonts have suffered enough. I won't be satisfied until they are gone forever." The fire flickers, drawing her attention. The pirate's dagger sits atop the pile of burning artifacts. Her nostrils flare as she scowls, her brow creases with thick, dark lines and her eyes blaze with hatred and betrayal. "And now you attempt to purify that knife? Even when you know the evil it has committed?"

"Purify? No, that's not—"

She thrusts her stout palm in my face. "You have overstepped your bounds for the last time. Prophesy or no, your destiny must not be fulfilled." Still floating on air, she zooms backward into the middle of the clearing, then tosses her head back and gazes up into the sky, yelling something in a language I don't recognize. It must be ancient Akan, her native tongue.

High above the stagnant spirits, the black, shadowy clouds part, revealing the moon in its silvery glory. A stiff breeze blows off the salt marsh, through the clearing, rustling leaves and swaying sheets of Spanish moss. Emerald kudzu vines shudder and rattle as they stretch and grow, encroaching toward us from all directions.

I blink to make sure I'm not imagining things. Nope. The kudzu vines are multiplying, rapidly extending their long trailing fingers along the ground.

"Emma!" Jack yells.

"What do we do?" Cooper asks.

Honestly, I don't have the vaguest clue. I've read a lot of nature charms in Miss Delia's spell book, but never one like this. I can't begin to guess at how to make plants grow, much less attack. But even if I had, Miss Delia never got around to teaching me how to blend my energy and intention to do magic with my mind.

After glancing around to find some place to jump or escape the onslaught, I realize it's hopeless. We're at the epicenter of the clearing, the bull's-eye target for Sabina's advancing threat. The nearest tombstone is too far away, and even if I could jump up on it, it's so thin and tilted, it would never hold me, much less Jack and Cooper, too.

Cooper races to my side.

"Stay behind me!" I thrust my palm against his chest and push him back.

He shakes his head. "We're going to face this together."

"Emma, it's coming!" Jack screams, his voice filled with panic.

I twist around to see his eyes are as wide as silver dollars. A thick green vine leaps up from the ground and lashes around Jack's ankle. He screams, and then bends to pull at the snaking greenery, but another strand lurches toward him, binding both his wrists to his already bound ankle. A third, leggy cord whips around his free limb, effectively hog-tying him. He wrenches against the restraints, but another, thicker vine lengthens and encircles his waist. Top heavy and unbalanced, he crashes to the ground.

"Jack!" I shriek and pivot to run to him, but two bright green kudzu ropes lasso both my shins, then coil around the rest of my legs and hips, rooting me where I stand.

Cooper isn't spared either. Vines spiral both his ankles. When he reaches to free me from my ties, two more kudzu lines leap up and corkscrew around his elbows, pinning him in place.

From the corner of my eye, I notice the boo hag's cage is untouched by the creeping vines. Thankfully, the bloodred creature is still writhing on the ground, obsessed with counting the broom straws and completely oblivious to what's going on.

Sabina's laugh roars across the graveyard. "I'll teach you not to mess with what doesn't belong to you! Only after you've experienced loss will you understand the virtue of revenge."

Reflex kicks in and I lunge for Cooper. Just as I pry at the vines fastening his arms, new lines of creeping foliage wrap around my chest and shoulders, then drag me back and away from him. I resist, but the vines grip tighter and pull me down to the ground. My heartbeat pounds in my ears as I frantically yank at the paralyzing vine, but more leggy trails shoot up from the soil to fasten my biceps to my sides. At least my forearms are still free.

Jack whimpers, his voice a muffled grunt. Straining against my binds, I peer over my shoulder. He's also trapped on the ground, completely ensnared by the kudzu, which is even wrapped around his mouth and forehead. Only his pale blue eyes shine through the green leaves.

Fury churns in my gut. With nothing left to lose, I narrow my gaze at Sabina. "Stop this! You worked those spells hundreds of years ago but those charms are broken now. It's over. You need to move on."

She vanishes.

My heart hammers against my ribs as my eyes dart around, wondering if she's actually gone.

Besides the pulse in my ears, the only sound comes from the night creatures beyond the trees and Cooper and Jack's ragged breath.

Maybe all it took was a stern talking to. Could it really have been that easy?

Just as I begin to hope, Sabina reappears, crouched in the kudzu, her face mere inches from mine. "Oh, it's over all right. But not for me," she growls, then chants more foreign words before dropping her jaw wide.

Black mist flows out of her mouth. I hold my breath as it curls around my head, then zips around the clearing. Sabina floats up and away from me, pointing a stocky finger toward the water. The cloud obeys her command and shoots out over the salt marsh. There, I can just make out the black mist spinning, gaining velocity until it creates a tall, thin tornado. Sabina's hand stretches wide and she drags the dark funnel cloud back to the clearing, and aims it directly at the boo-hag cell.

"No!" I scream, anticipating her next move. I strain to sit up.

Sabina laughs. "Foolish little girl, listening to those who have led you astray. So much wasted potential. Despite what the doctress has told you, hate is the most powerful emotion." She shakes her turbaned head. "Love will not save you tonight when you and your friends are slain by an ordinary boo hag." Hitching her brow at the kudzu, the vines tighten and constrict my chest, making it hard to breathe.

She snaps her fingers, unleashing the tornado. It careens toward the mullein posts. Mesmerized by the straw strands in the broom, the boo hag pays no mind to the advancing freak weather phenomenon. Under Sabina's guidance, the tornado skirts around the cell's perimeter, ripping each reedy bundle from the ground, then launching them high into the air and into the surrounding forest. After the last post is knocked out, the funnel cloud dips just far enough inside the cell to snatch the broom from the boo hag's grip and suck it up into its vortex. The tornado whirls back across the clearing, jumps the bank, and dissipates over the marsh, dumping the broom in the water.

Free from its counting fixation, the boo hag springs to its feet and shakes its head as if to clear itself from a trance. It trains is shiny, lidless eyes on me, and then snaps its rectangular head toward Cooper. "You are mine!" It recoils its long, spindly legs, readying to pounce.

Sabina snarls. "No! Take the girl first. After she's gone, you can take your time with the others. I've already wrapped them up for you."

"Yes, Sabina." In one giant leap, the boo hag springs toward me and straddles my bundled body. "Pesky child. Why did you have to be so feisty? It didn't have to end this way. We could have done so much together." It readies to squat on my chest to ride me and suck out my life force.

Cooper jumps in the air, waving his arms. "Hey, meathead! Don't waste your time on her. I'm what you really want. You know you need a new body. Especially after we covered your old one with salt."

The boo hag jerks toward Cooper. Its lizard-like tongue licks its thin lips. Clenching its three-fingered hands, its gaze hops between me and Cooper, as if it can't decide who to feast on next.

"Don't let him distract you. Destroy the girl!" Sabina commands. "Now! While you have the upper hand."

The boo hag snaps its attention back to me. "But you promised I could have her to myself. At least for a little while."

Sabina's eyes fill with rage. "Forget what I said before. I've given you three hundred years of Beaumont men to inhabit, a ruby to help control your possessions, and permitted you to acquire great wealth. You owe me this."

The boo hag nods and sit on my chest, then opens its great jaw.

"Get off her!" Cooper yells, straining at his binds. His face turns cherry red and his biceps flex as he wrenches his arms and pulls against his restraints. With a gutteral shout, he yanks hard and rips the vines from the soil, then jerks up on his legs and tears them free. If his skin was green, I'd swear he was the Hulk. After tugging the kudzu loose from his forearms, Cooper lunges after the boo hag, crashing into the creature with his shoulder and shoving it off me. They land on the ground and wrestle, each trying to get the upper hand on the other.

I scream. Cooper's put himself within the boo hag's grasp, which is exactly what I've been trying to avoid.

The boo hag struggles to pin Cooper down, but each time it manages to get him on his back, Cooper slips out from under its wet, fleshy skin. The boo hag extends its lanky arm, hooks Cooper's chest, and slams him to the ground. But Cooper thrusts his knee and rams it into the boo hag's crotch. The monster howls and swipes its fingers at Cooper's facc, but just as it's about to make contact, Cooper leans back, exposing his chest. The boo hag's suction-cupped middle finger snatches hold of Cooper's mojo bag.

Cooper's eyelids stretch wide.

"What's this?" the boo hag hisses, then laughs. It must realize it's gotten hold of something powerful. It wraps its two remaining fingers around the chord, tugs, and snaps it off Cooper's neck.

My heart and stomach clench at the same time. "*No!*" I try to scream but my lungs are wrapped too tight to generate much sound. Instead I stare helpless as the boo hag cackles while it swings the dangling gris-gris from his fleshy finger. That mojo was the only thing standing between Cooper and black magic. With Jack and I trussed up like Thanksgiving turkeys, he's on his own.

I glance up at the sky and the quiet, but still twinkling, lights. Maybe he's not alone after all.

The boo hag lunges for Cooper and wraps its strange, misshapen hands around his neck. "Finally! You're mine." It extends its jaw, readying to suck Cooper's life force from his body.

Cooper screams as his face forms the perfect picture of horror.

"Clarissa, please help." I whisper, directing my thoughts and what little breath I have toward the shimmering iridescence hanging above the clearing. I'm not sure if my energy is leeching from my body to power my desire, but I'm thinking hard and giving it my all.

The spirit orbs snap back to life, brightening and pulsing with crackling energy.

The boo hag cringes and shades its bulging eyes from the blazing light. Cooper drops to the ground, writhing.

Sabina's face darkens. She thrusts her hand up again, and blasts another wind bomb in the spirits' direction. Just as before, it crashes into them, strewing them around the cemetery.

The boo hag heaves its mucusy lungs for air.

"Resist Sabina. Don't let her win. For Cooper's sake," I say, nearly breathless, hoping Clarissa and the other Beaumont spirits can hear me. I concentrate, sapping my strength to send my intention up to the lights and beyond, into the universe to reach all that's good and powerful.

The disparate spirits merge together and begin to spin, forming a giant pinwheel in the sky. As they rotate, their light brightens and intensifies, and the whirling speeds so fast, they almost look like a brilliant, solid-yellow object.

The boo hag shrieks and crumples to the vine-covered soil.

My palm itches, then burns, as sure a sign from my spirit guide as I've ever received. Responding to her plea, I reach out my forearm as far as the binding vines will allow, then spread open my now-throbbing palm toward the sky.

The center of the spirit pinwheel sinks down and stretches toward me, aiming directly for my flesh. The yellow energy shoots directly into my hand and straight up my arm, into my chest, then pumps through my body. It's invigorating. Effervescent. Revitalizing. My organs thrum with pulsating vibrancy. I haven't felt this good since, well, ever. If I could get free of this clingy kudzu, I could probably run two Lowcountry marathons. In my flip-flops.

The power builds within me, buzzing and vibrating as it recharges my batteries and restocks my reserves. My pulse gallops as the yellow light continues to flow, filling me to the brim and then some, until I feel as if I'm might just explode.

I clench my fist tight, cutting off the energy flow. The energy beam retracts back up to the whirling spirit canopy above us.

Buoyed by my newfound vitality, I wrench against the vines,

prying a few loose enough from the soil to pull myself into a quasi-sitting position. The tightest of the coils breaks loose, allowing me to breathe, though I'm still so ensnared, there's little chance of getting out of this without a hacksaw.

Sabina spies the fallen boo hag. "Get up! You can't quit now." She flicks her fingers and shoots a black cloud toward the crumpled creature. The shadowy mist hovers over the boo hag, giving it cover from the blinding spirits overhead.

The boo hag leaps to its feet and pivots its long, lanky legs toward Cooper, who is crawling, along the ground, attempting to escape its clutches.

"No! End the girl." Sabina's gravely voice booms.

The boo hag hisses. "End her yourself. I must have that body." It pounces after Cooper, who somehow manages to sprint ahead and just slip out of its grasp.

Cooper races toward the bank. "Hey, Emma, the marsh!" He points to the salty body of water beyond as he darts and dodges around, keeping the boo hag at bay.

He's a genius.

Envisioning the red and white beads on my *collier*, I clear my mind and open my mouth, hoping the right words fall out.

> *"Ancient mineral in the water,*
> *Avenge the Beaumont sons and daughters.*
> *End that which stole limb and life*
> *Creating so much pain and strife.*
> *Envelop the evil in your tide*
> *To make things right with all who died."*

Pointing my open palm toward the marsh, I concentrate on the cool, blue-green liquid that's laden with salt, the boo hag's only nemesis aside from the sun. Instantly, I feel a connection to the water and all the life forms in it. It's as if my energy flows into them and theirs into mine. We are one. I sense the throb of their collective pulse as easily as I feel mine ping against my temple.

As I force my hand forward, the water ebbs, receding from the reedy shoreline. As the marsh retreats, its power and strength coils like a spring waiting to be let loose. Even from here, half lying on the ground in the cemetery above the marsh, I can tell the tide has withdrawn at least halfway to where the water normally is. I raise my forearm as far as it will go, lifting the pent-up water in a massive curling wave, then drag it toward the bank.

I can't make the boo hag go into the water, but it looks like I can bring the water to the boo hag.

Sabina's floating form hovers above me, her face drawn and filled with a mixture of surprise and distain. "Your magic is stronger than I realized."

I focus on the tidal wave I'm trying to build and attempt to ignore her. But it's nearly impossible because she looms before me, blocking my view.

"There are others in the Lowcountry with power just as strong who will help me seek my revenge. This is not over. We will meet again. And when we do, any happiness you have, I will crush it, along with those you carry in your heart so that you may know the pain I've endured for nearly three hundred years. Then perhaps, you will understand why I must have my revenge. *If* you manage to escape the boo hag and save your friends," she taunts then floats up into the air, tosses her turbaned head back, and laughs before dematerializing, this time, hopefully for good.

I spy Cooper dashing around the bank, keeping just out of the boo hag's reach. It's so intent on catching him and draining his life force, it doesn't notice the salty death trap looming just over its shoulder.

"Cooper, now!" I yell, hoping he realizes what to do.

"Got it." He calls, then pivots and changes course. Rather than running from the creature, he tucks his shoulder and heads straight for it, barreling into its slimy, crimson gut.

Caught off guard, the boo hag launches off the bank and flies into the waiting wall of water. It shrieks as it crashes into the salt-infused, captured wave. Sparks fly and its gangly limbs flail as the liquid consumes it. Its rectangular head bobs up over the surface, howling as its red flesh melts and oozes with chunky, black sludge. Steam floats off what's left of the dying boo hag as its flesh cooks, turning an ashy gray.

Overwhelmed, I exhale a breath I didn't realize I was holding and blink to make sure I didn't just imagine all this. Nope, there's still a wall of water looming over the bank, pieces of the boo hag are bobbing on the surface, and Cooper's safe. At last.

Cooper throws his arms in the air and shouts in victory. He spins around to face me, his picture perfect smile wide across his face. "We did it, Emma! We did it!" He howls with joy, then curls his hand in a colossal fist pump.

Happiness floods my chest as a sense of security and accomplishment sets in. We did do it. Together. The Beaumonts are finally free. Amazing! Giddy, I clench my own hand into a ball and send him my own fist pump.

Only it's the worst thing possible because I completely forgot that my hand was holding back the wall of water, and that simple gesture is enough to release the flood, releasing its pent-up power on Cooper and the rest of the cemetery.

Cooper must realize what's about to happen because his

face falls slack and his eyes stretch wide. "Emma—" He begins, but the salt marsh crashes down on him and slams the rest of the graveyard.

"Take a breath, Jack!" I manage just as the water gushes over me, lifting me off the ground, but the vines hold tight and keep me in place. The wave finally crests, then recedes after dousing the fire and splashing all the burning artifacts.

The spirit lights dim and slowly shimmer to earth, then wiggle back into their graves.

Gasping, I look for Jack to make sure he's okay.

His pale blue eyes lock on mine. "Mmmm!" His mouth is still covered by vines.

"I'll get you out as soon as I can," I call, then strain my neck to peer over the bank to the salt marsh for Cooper. I don't see anything but a lot of frothy salt water seeking its equilibrium in the normally calm marsh.

With each passing second, my heart races faster. After all we've been through to save him, I might have accidentally drowned Cooper because I foolishly forgot what the heck I was doing.

After a long minute without any sign of him, I'm trembling, and my heart has dropped to somewhere around my knees. I'm sure he's dead and gone thanks to my incompetence. Tears stream down my cheeks as I tear at the kudzu that's wrapped around my body. But since only my forearms are free, it's nearly impossible to break the thick, knotted vines.

A splashing sound cuts the nearly silent night. My heart skips a beat as I peer into the darkness. There are only a handful of spirit lights still hovering in the sky so it's difficult to tell shadows from real objects.

More splashing. A hand slaps against the surface, followed

by the steady beats of kicking feet. It's Cooper's freestyle. I'd know it anywhere.

"He's alive!" I yell to Jack whose eyelids close with relief.

Another long minute later, Cooper hauls himself out of the water, then slogs up the side of the bank.

"Cooper!" I yell, unable to contain myself. I've never been so happy to see him in all my life.

His chest rises and falls as he drags himself across the graveyard. Despite his panting, he grins. "I'm okay. That wave pulled me halfway to St. Helena Island Sound. Wasn't really expecting that."

"I'm so sorry. I didn't mean to drop the water on you."

Staggering toward me, he waves away my concern. "Nah, I needed the exercise." Then he stoops to where the fire was and digs through the artifacts that were scattered by the wave. He picks up the pirate's dagger, then heads straight for me. "Let's cut you loose."

I shake my head. "No, get Jack first. At least I can move a little. Him, not so much."

Cooper glances at Jack and laughs. "You do look pretty funny, bro."

"Mmmm." Jack glowers.

Cooper crosses his arms. "Are you seriously going to back talk me now? After everything I just went through? And before I free you?"

Jack growls.

"Fine." Cooper chuckles then stoops to cut him loose.

"Thanks, dude," Jack says when he's finally liberated and Cooper helps him to his feet. He stretches his arms up over his head. "That was the craziest thing I've ever seen."

Cooper scoffs. "I think I've had my fill of crazy this summer.

What do you think Emma?" He smiles as he crouches next to me and cuts the vines. Amazingly, the knife is pristine, not even scorched. But that's not nearly as amazing as the fact that Cooper is here, next to me, alive and not possessed by a hideous monster. If my biceps weren't still tied to my side, I'd throw my arms around him and weep with joy.

I laugh as my cheeks burn from smiling so wide. "Every time I think it can't possibly get any weirder, somehow it does." Luckily for me, the summer's nearly at its end. Soon I'll be back in DC, safe and sound, and hopefully out of Sabina's vengeful reach.

When the last of the kudzu is cut away, Cooper stands and extends his hand to me. I slip my fingers into his broad palm and he pulls me to my feet.

His strong arms clasp me, tugging me tight to his soaking wet body. He stinks like the marsh, but that hardly matters. I'll take dead fish over boo-hag funk any day.

"Happy birthday, Cooper." I squeeze him tight, grasping the hard muscles in his back as my heart swells with happiness.

"Thank you, Emmaline. For saving my soul. For killing the boo hag and freeing my family. For everything," he whispers, his breath warm against my neck.

"I couldn't have done it without you guys. All I did was say a few words. You're the one who fought off the boo hag and pushed it into the water. I couldn't have done that."

He pulls back just enough to lay his fingers beneath my chin and gently tilt my head to meet his gaze. "No. It was you. It's always been you."

Chapter Thirty-three

We load the last box of artifacts into the golf cart just as the sun rises over the salt marsh. The cemetery is so tranquil it's hard to imagine all that happened here overnight. But it did, and we've got Cooper's freedom to prove it.

The joy I should be feeling is overshadowed by the lingering dread from Sabina's truly demented threat. Why would someone deliberately set out to destroy another person's happiness? To crush not only the love in their heart, but also those responsible for putting it there? If Sabina makes good on her promise, everyone I care about is in danger. That means my father, Jack, Miss Delia, and especially Cooper, will be walking bull's-eyes.

My only hope lies in the fact that Jack and I will be leaving St. Helena in ten days to return to Washington, DC, and Cooper will be back at boarding school, far from my danger zone. Maybe, after we get Miss Delia released from jail, if we lay low and I don't mess with anymore hoodoo, Sabina will realize I'm not a threat and she'll give up on her vendetta.

Ten minutes later, we pull up to the Big House. Dad is sitting on the wide front steps, his arms crossed. He doesn't look happy.

Oops.

As we climb out of the cart, Dad races up to us. "Emmaline Claire, don't take another step!" His face is creased with concern as he heads right for Cooper. I freeze, stunned by his ferocity.

Dad grasps Cooper's arms and stares directly into Cooper's eyes. "Who are you?"

Cooper's eyes stretch wide. "Uh, what's going on, Uncle Jed?"

Jack races up to Dad. "Everything's fine, I promise."

"Stay out of this, Jack. Go stand with your sister." Dad grips Cooper harder. "Forget the Uncle Jed stuff. You're not going to wiggle your way out of it this time by acting dumb. I know something's changed. I can feel it. So tell me, who are you?"

"Cooper. I swear."

My chest sinks. Did the boo hag suck my father and mess with his mind, too?

Dad searches Cooper's eyes, then drops his hands in frustration. He darts toward Jack and snatches his shoulders. "Are you in here this time? Is that how this works? I don't know how, but I'm going to stop you. You won't steal my son."

A chill races over my body. Dad's memories haven't been screwed up. He obviously knows more than we realized.

Cooper, Jack, and I exchange looks. It's time to let him in on our secret.

"There's something you need to see." I take his rough, calloused hand.

A minute later we're at the entrance to Beau's study.

"What the—" Dad asks when I push on the busted mahogany door. Strange, that he doesn't seem to care that it's cracked or that we're venturing into a forbidden room.

"It's a long story. But I promise to tell you everything after you've seen what's behind this door."

I turn the lock and twist the knob. The room is exactly as we left it, except the note we left the boo hag is lying on the floor by the open window. It must have flown out of here in a rage.

The secret bookcase door is wide open.

Dad's jaw drops.

Jack crosses the room. "Come on. It's not half as impressive as what's behind it."

Jack leads the way to the secret stone room. Beau's skin suit is lying in the middle of the floor, more shriveled and desiccated than just a few hours before.

Dad falls to his knees. His head drops into his hands and his shoulders shudder with what can only be silent tears.

Oh no. We didn't prepare him for what he was about to see. He's probably in shock, or maybe even thinks we're murderers.

I stroke his shoulder. "I'm sorry. It isn't what it looks like. We can explain."

Dad lifts his gaze to meet mine, a wide smile across his face. The deep creases are gone and there's a brightness to his eyes I've never seen before. "I don't care how you did it, but I'm glad you did."

That's unexpected.

"Dang." Jack laughs.

"For real?" I ask.

Dad nods. "Where's the creature that was in Beau's skin?"

"Gone. Burned up in the salt marsh forever," Cooper answers.

Dad rises to his feet and squares his shoulders. He looks taller than usual, almost strapping. "From the moment your mother called this morning, waking me up, I knew something had changed. I felt...free. I could speak my mind and do as I chose. I haven't felt this way since I was a teenager. It's been more than a quarter of a century." He glares at the carcass lying on the floor. "Somehow that...*monster* stole my friend when he was just sixteen. And that same day something happened to me that enslaved me to him, stole my free will, and forced me to do his bidding even though I didn't want to. The only thing I could do on my own was keep things clean and orderly to somehow protect them from his filthy reach."

My stomach sinks as his words set in. Somehow, the day the Beaumont Curse took hold of Beau, it also sunk its teeth into my dad. Now I get why he put up with Beau's viciousness and why he's such a huge neat freak. Judging from what I gleaned at the cemetery, Sabina helped the boo hag inhabit Beaumont bodies, so it's reasonable to think she must have had a hand in my father's servitude as well. But what exactly connects a soul-sucking hex like the Beaumont curse with becoming a modern indentured servant? A chill races up my spine as a terrifying thought comes to mind: if the boo hag had possessed Cooper, would Jack have been forced to serve Cooper, too? Is that why Beau kept insisting that despite all the Guthries' attempts to the contrary, they always ended up working for Beaumonts?

Dad turns back to us, a look of utter astonishment on his face. "How did you all know? And how did it not take either of you?" He searches Cooper and Jack, then notices Jack's severed middle finger for the first time. He gawks. "What happened to you?"

Jack runs his hand through his jet-black hair. "It's been a weird summer."

"Emma saved us," Cooper says.

Dad spins toward me, his mouth agape. "*Emma*? My shy,

flower-loving, artist girl? How?"

I sigh. "I haven't had much time to paint lately. But I have gotten into hoodoo magic." I pull my lips into a half grin, knowing that I'm probably shattering his image of me, but that's okay. We'll ease him into the truth slowly.

Jack beams. "She's amazing. You should have seen her call up a bunch of dead Gullah ladies to help kill a pack of *plateyes*, then break a couple of flesh-eating, soul-sucking curses, and crash a tidal wave into the boo hag. She's even got her own archnemesis now, another dead root worker who created the curses almost three hundred years ago. But I'm sure she can handle that psycho after a little more training from Miss D, the hoodoo ninja warrior lady. Of course, we'll have to bust Miss D out of jail first."

Thanks, Jack. Way not to ease him in.

The blood drains from Dad's skin. "I think I need to sit down." He stumbles to the small desk and chair on the side of the small stone room. As he goes to prop his elbow on the surface, he knocks over a stack of papers.

I bend down to scoop up the scattered pages. Most look like accounting sheets for Beaumont Builders, but one is old and yellowed. My fingers tingle as I grasp the thick parchment and squint hard at the tiny, old-time handwriting. It looks like a family tree with two major branches that must go back at least fifteen generations. The names are Beaumont and Guthrie. I can't help wonder if, and how, each one of these people had been impacted by Sabina's curses.

Dad grabs my hand, drawing my attention from the document. "Are you okay? You haven't been injured, have you?"

I grin and place the papers back on the desk. "Yeah, I'm good. It's not as bad as it sounds. Besides, after we help Miss

Delia with her, uh, legal troubles, Jack and I will be back in DC and this will all die down. I'm not planning on working any hoodoo back home so there's no reason for my *archnemesis* to bother us anymore." I frame the words with air quotes as I toss Jack a disapproving glance.

Dad shakes his head. "This is your home now."

"Yeah, for the summer. But we're out of here in ten days," I say.

"That was the plan, but your mother called this morning to say there's been a last-minute shake-up with the staff at the archeological site in Jordan. She's been offered a grant to continue the work and lead the project. It's a once-in-a-lifetime opportunity for her. If she takes a sabbatical this year and makes a couple important discoveries, she could make full professor soon. I told her to take it."

I step back, bracing myself against the cold stone wall. Stay? In the Lowcountry? And face Sabina? My mind spins at this unexpected turn of events.

Jack's brow creases. "But what about soccer? The school paper? My friends? I've got a life I've got to get back to."

"There's a school here that's got plenty of clubs and teams you can join. I'm sure you'll make new friends," Dad says.

"But you're always so busy with the plantation. And with Beau gone, you might not have a job. Unless Cooper wants to keep you here." Jack shoots Cooper a glance.

Dad laughs. "Actually, Beau made me Cooper's guardian, so I'm the one who makes the decisions. At least until Cooper turns eighteen. Then it's all on him."

Cooper crosses his arm. "I don't want to go back to boarding school. I want to stay here. Learn about the plantation."

Dad smiles. "Great idea."

Jack's brow is still furrowed. "Do you really want to handle us full time?"

Dad sits up in his chair. "Are you kidding? This is my chance to finally be the father I always wanted to be but never could. And if what you've told me is half-true, it sounds as if you all might need a little more parental supervision. Or at least help. So what do you say, Emma? You ready to stay here with your old dad? Maybe I can even help you with this archnemesis of yours."

"Ugh, I guess I don't have much of a choice do I?" Despite the air-conditioning, the room is suddenly stifling. I need to get out, now, and breathe some fresh air. "Excuse me, I'm not feeling so well." I sprint from the room and race down the main hall.

My dad might have been forced to serve an evil boo hag and robbed of his free will, but he's obviously clueless about the seriousness of the danger Sabina poses. Until this moment, I didn't think much of her threat because I figured if I skipped town, all of this would blow over.

Now that Jack and I are staying, I'll have to face her and whatever she's got planned. Not to mention Taneea and Claude, who are probably lurking in the background, planning their next move on Cooper, Jack, and anyone else I care about. And Miss Delia, who's frail and paralyzed and looking at spending the rest of her days behind bars. The deputies can't take care of her in there, at least not the way she needs to be cared for. Plus, how can she possibly teach me the rest of what I need to know from a jail cell?

As I charge through the great room, Beau's words from the *Psychic Vision* flood back, sending chills over my scalp. He said Cooper and I were destined to get married. What the heck is that supposed to mean? Sabina threw around the destiny word, too, as well as the word, prophecy. How could anyone possibly know what lies in store for any other person? Don't our own choices account for anything? Sabina was so sure she knew Cooper's destiny, yet we've broken both her curses and now he's free to make the life he wants. I may not know what my own life has in store, but I want to be the one in charge.

I rush out the veranda doors onto the back patio. Staring out over St. Helena Sound, I breathe in the warm, salty air.

A screeching caw shatters the silence. My earlobes heat. After my fall from the magnolia, I'd recognize that sound anywhere.

An iridescent black crow bursts from the nearby forest and soars across the backyard, headed straight for me. Flinging my arms over my head, I scream as I crouch for cover. It squawks as its sharp claws graze my scalp and the back of my hand, then takes flight again.

My heart pounds as I peer up at the sky, sure it's headed for another pass, but it flies off, disappearing into the trees.

Bright red blood oozes from my wound.

I'm no bird expert, but I'm pretty sure that was no accident. And, now that I think about it, neither was my tumble from that tree.

Danger, it seems, is everywhere and it's directed squarely at me. And, by extension, the people I care most about.

Cooper bolts onto the patio. "Are you okay? I heard you scream."

I wipe the blood from the back of my hand and force a smile. "Yeah. I'm good. It was nothing. Just a bird."

"I couldn't stand it if something happened to you." He steps to my side and reaches for my good hand. "I know you said you needed some time, and it's only been two days since we discovered the allurement, but do you think you have it in your heart to forgive me for all the horrible things I said when I was under that spell? Because you know I'd never say them otherwise." He flashes an adorable half grin.

Until a few minutes ago, I assumed everything would go back to normal and we'd spend the last few days of our summer together in bliss. Because honestly, any lingering hurt I felt evaporated when he swam out of that marsh alive and whole.

But now that we're all staying on the island, Sabina's threats echo in my mind and I realize just how treacherous things might get. Especially for him, since he's the source of my greatest joy, and Sabina has vowed to crush whatever happiness I have.

I have to do what I can to protect him. Even if it means breaking my own heart.

"So…are we okay?" His voice is filled with apprehension.

"You've been my best friend since I was six years old. We'll always be okay."

He tugs on my hand. "That's not what I'm asking, Emma. I want to know where we stand. As us. You and me. Together." He lifts my hand and places his mother's silver locket in my open palm. "Because there's no one in the world I'd rather give this to." The ruby shards glint in the bright August sun.

My stomach drops and my mouth turns dry. "Uh, I can't accept this." My voice quivers as pass it back to him, then ball my fists and hold them at my sides. I can't allow myself to touch him. His warm, smooth skin will only break my resolve.

"What? Why?" He looks like I've punched him in the gut.

"My feelings have…changed." I force the words from my lying mouth. They taste like poison.

"Is it because of what happened with Taneea? Because I never cared about her. Not for one single second."

I shake my head. "No, I told you before. I know the allurement wasn't your fault."

"Then why?" His royal-blue eyes search mine.

"Because they just have, okay? When I came here, I thought our relationship was just going to be a summer thing, but now that I'm staying for the year, it's too much for me. I...just can't do it. Why can't you accept that and move on?"

"Because I can't. You and I, we're meant to be. And not because the boo hag said it in that vision. Because I know it here, in my heart." He points at his chest.

I jut my jaw and take a deep breath. "Well, I don't love you." My voice trembles over the worst falsehood I've ever uttered.

He drops my hand, and his gaze bores into me. "I don't believe you."

"Well, I wish you would. Because it would make things a lot easier." I set my hands on my hips for extra emphasis. My knees wobble and threaten to give out under me.

Cooper squares his shoulders. "No matter what you say, I know you love me, Emmaline. Or at least that you did. And now that I've got all the time in the world, I'm going to make you fall in love with me again. Because I'm not going anywhere. And we belong together.

Acknowledgments

As ever, I extend my thanks and gratitude to the Gullah people of the South Carolina and Georgia Sea Islands. I hope this latest installment conveys my enduring respect for your culture and folkways.

Though I've taken some liberties to heighten the dramatic elements and ooey, gooey ick factor of the story, I couldn't write this series without the mini library of Gullah and hoodoo magic books I lug around with me wherever I write and covet with Gollum-like ferocity. These include: *Hoodoo Herb and Root Magic: A Materia Magica of African-American Conjure* by Catherine Yronwode, *Hoodoo Medicine: Gullah Herbal Remedies* by Faith Mitchell, *Lowcountry Voodoo: Beginner's Guide to Tales, Spells and Boo Hags* by Terrance Zepke, *Gullah Fuh Oonuh (Gullah for You): A Guide to the Gullah Language* by Virginia Mixson Geraty, *Hoodoo Mysteries: Folk Magic, Mysticism & Rituals* by Rev. Ray T. Marbrough, *Blue Roots: African-American Folk Magic of the Gullah People* by Roger

Pinckney, and *Encyclopedia of 5,000 Spells* by Judika Illes. The *Lucky Magic Curio Co.* located at www.luckymojo.com has also provided a wealth of information.

Deep and heartfelt thanks go to Christi Barth and Stephanie Dray who sacrificed a winter afternoon to offer unparalleled plot whispering expertise, and to Laura Kaye who, as usual, provided counsel, commiseration, laughter, and was always there to answer the burning question, "Er, does this make sense?" Supreme appreciation goes out to Melissa Landers and Stephanie Dray who read the exceptionally long first draft and offered superior critiques that helped refine the story. Your insights were invaluable. I owe you big time. And to my bestest teen beta reader, Rachel Lefkowtiz, thank you once again for an astute and perceptive review.

Writers are lucky to have one great editor; for this project, I had the pleasure of working with three. Guillian Helm, Robin Haseltine, and Elizabeth Pelletier all had a hand in shaping this book. Thank you for your expert advice and consultation and for accompanying me on this leg of the series' journey.

A special shout out goes to The Apprentices, my street team of enthusiastic readers who loved Conjure and joined on to help promote the Hoodoo Apprentice series. You've inspired me more than you know. Whenever my creaky arthritic hands started to betray me or I hit a writing slump, I'd think of you and plod on, knowing I couldn't let you down.

Exceptional thanks to my most excellent travel companions, Alina Dougherty, Hannah Dougherty, and Gillian Nolan who accompanied my scouting trip to the South Carolina Lowcountry, including Beaufort, and St. Helena Island. Together we partied at the Gullah Festival, toured the Penn Center and its York W. Bailey Museum, discovered ancient ruins, breathtaking marshes, a gorgeous beach, an abandoned cemetery, and even "Cooper's house". Not to mention surviving the Worst. Hotel. Mix-up. Ever. Love to you all, along with a slice of the best key lime pie money can buy after all the restaurants have closed for the night.

Finally, mad props and crazy love to my husband, Patrick who makes so much of this possible. Late nights and writing weekends wouldn't happen without your abiding support and encouragement and late night pep talks. Thank you for helping me live my dream. And to my little pies, Gillian, Riley, and Lila, thanks for putting up with Mommy's "typing". Words strain to convey the depth of my adoration, but here are a few that may come close: *Your hearts and mine, forever entwined. Love everlasting till the end of time.*

And if you loved *Allure*, try Andria Buchanan's

Everlast

the first book in the Chronicles of Nerissette series

Allie Munroe has only ever wanted to belong, maybe even be well liked. But even though she's nice and smart and has a couple of friends, she's still pretty much the invisible girl at school. So when the chance to work with her friends and some of the popular kids on an English project comes up, Allie jumps at the chance to be noticed.

And her plan would have worked out just fine…if they hadn't been sucked into a magical realm through a dusty old book of fairy tales in the middle of the library.

Now, Allie and her classmates are stuck in Nerissette, a world where karma rules and your social status is determined by what you deserve. Which makes a misfit like Allie the Crown Princess, and her archrival the scullery maid. And the only way out is for Allie to rally and lead the people of Nerissette against the evil forces that threaten their very existence.

Available wherever books are sold.